Praise for
A Cowboy Firefighter for Christmas

"With its vividly written firefighting scenes, rich cast of characters, and folksy charm, *A Cowboy Firefighter for Christmas* will keep you warm and toasty and entertained in a big—and I mean Texas big—way."

—*USA Today Happy Ever After*

"A whole new type of holiday read…a little mystery and a lot of heat."

—*Night Owl Reviews*

"The attraction is instant, scorching, and flavored with just a hint of sweet innocence. Add in the distilled essence of a perfect small town, and this tale will melt even the iciest heart."

—*Publishers Weekly* Starred Review

"A fun, sexy read…perfect for the holiday season."

—*RT Book Reviews*

"Highly entertaining… I found myself invested in both of the main characters…and the entire town."

—*Sharon the Librarian*

"This hot and passionate love story has everything: excitement, hot sex, and suspense… I found myself riveted to each page… A very entertaining and emotional tale that is sure to delight the reader."

—*Fresh Fiction*

Also by Kim Redford

Smokin' Hot Cowboys

A Cowboy Firefighter for Christmas
Blazing Hot Cowboy
A Very Cowboy Christmas

A Very
COWBOY
CHRISTMAS

KIM REDFORD

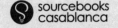

Published by Sourcebooks Casablanca, an imprint of Sourcebooks, Inc.
P.O. Box 4410, Naperville, Illinois 60567-4410
(630) 961-3900
Fax: (630) 961-2168
sourcebooks.com

Printed and bound in the United States of America.
OPM 10 9 8 7 6 5 4 3 2 1

Chapter 1

SYDNEY STEELE STOOD ON THE SIDE OF WILDCAT Road with her hands on her hips in frustration. Christmas was almost upon them, and she had a to-do list to check off that kept getting longer by the day. She didn't need trouble, but it sure had a way of finding her.

She kicked the whitewall front tire of her beauty of a vehicle—a powder-pink 1959 Cadillac convertible. Beauty was one thing. Dead beauty was quite another. She needed that gas-hog of a V8 engine to perk up and do its job so she could get to the Sure-Shot Drive-In and scope out the theater for a possible photo shoot. The Wildcat Bluff cowboy firefighters benefit calendar wasn't going to get done all by its lonesome.

She had about four weeks to get a move on or the season would come and go with no calendar, and they'd lose the much-needed fund-raiser to boost Wildcat Bluff Fire-Rescue's bottom line. But she had a gigantic problem—namely, she'd been unable to round up local cowboy firefighters to complete a photo shoot.

She couldn't prove it, but she had a sneaking suspicion those cowboys would do about anything to avoid filling up a calendar with their photographs. Butter wouldn't melt in their mouths, but so far, they'd been cagey as mountain lions and found a way to sabotage every photo shoot she'd set up. She'd swear Jim Bob had left the county just so she couldn't feature him as

Mr. December. That left a gaping hole for the twelfth month. Much more of their recalcitrant attitude and she just might have to pull out her leather whip to get them in line.

Frustrated, she kicked the flashy whitewall tire again for good measure, but it had little give, and she probably hurt her shoe more than her car. She immediately felt guilty about her disrespect for such a prime vintage vehicle—particularly when it now belonged to her.

At her last visit with dear Mr. Werner, he had insisted on handing over the keys and the title, explaining that he trusted her more than anybody else to give Celeste the proper love and care that she'd had since he'd brought her home new. Maybe he'd had a premonition that he wasn't going to make it to ninety-eight. She sighed aloud, feeling his loss. She missed their poker games every Sunday evening when she'd stop by to check on him. He'd been sharp as a tack and sassy as a teenager. Somehow, she'd thought he'd live forever. Now he was gone, and she had Celeste. As much as she admired the Caddy, it wasn't nearly an even trade.

Still, she had to carry on. Christmas waited for nobody. Mr. Werner had loved the holiday, so she knew he'd want her to use Celeste to help local celebrations. Unfortunately, the Cadillac had sputtered ominously on the road a little earlier, even after she'd had Celeste checked over and pronounced good as new. She'd quickly maneuvered onto the shoulder out of traffic just before the engine completely stopped. She'd looked under the hood, and everything appeared fine, but what did she know? At least she'd found a spare tire in the trunk, if that'd been her problem.

"What a beauty!"

She whipped around to see who'd hollered at her. Of all the people to come along when she needed help, it'd just have to be Dune Barrett. They'd been sparring since the moment they'd met months ago when he'd started work on Cougar Ranch, volunteered as a firefighter, and set her world ablaze. She didn't need a man-size distraction—not then and not now. She had too much to do during the holidays, and she liked her life the way it was, thank you very much. Too bad her body was at war with her mind.

Now here he was as large as life and sizzling with intent. All she could do was sigh out loud as her body perked up as if she'd been presented with a golden trophy engraved with his name.

He gave her a little salute out the open window of his dually with his big, tanned hand before he slowed down, turned around, and headed back.

At least he'd acknowledged her style effort. She'd cleaned up pretty good, getting all gussied up in her new retro outfit to match Celeste. Yet she longed for her comfy jeans, cowgirl boots, and stalwart pickup, even if being called "beauty" fed her ego.

She smoothed down the sides of her long-sleeved forest-green sheath dress that left little room for movement or imagination. She'd like to see herself try to rope a steer in this tight dress with her legs encased in sheer nylons and her feet tottering in black peep-toe high heels. She was still looking for more shoes to add to her vintage collection, but women back then wore smaller sizes, and only open-toes gave her enough room to be comfortable. If she got caught out in a sudden snowstorm, she would simply have to endure cold tootsies.

Bottom line, she didn't do half measures. She was going vintage all the way to plan and promote Christmas at the Sure-Shot Drive-In, a first-time community event to be held at their recently restored small-town drive-in. Plans were for the festival to draw visitors from Wildcat Bluff's popular Christmas in the Country—and vice versa—so folks could celebrate the Saturday before Christmas at the nearby towns with complementing, not competing, events.

She'd volunteered to coordinate the festival at Sure-Shot, but she realized now that she needed help. Unfortunately, most folks were already too busy with Christmas in the Country and their regular lives to carve out time for her.

For now, there was nothing to be done about it, so she thrust that worry from her mind as she kept an eye on Dune. He was unpredictable as wildfire. She preferred order in her life. She'd been spontaneous when she was younger, but not now. She had too many responsibilities. Single moms carried the full load of parenthood, and her daughter, Storm, was wild enough to keep Sydney's heart in her throat much too often. Sydney also helped her mom, granny, and older brother, Slade, run Steele Trap Ranch, their family's big spread on the Texas side of the muddy Red River.

As far as men went, she'd lost her beloved husband, Emery, in the Middle East where he'd fought and died for his country. He'd been special in so many ways. He'd even insisted that she and Storm use her family name, since they'd always work Steele Trap Ranch, and he'd thought it was better to associate their name with their business. Maybe he was right. Maybe not. Some days, she wished she carried his last name simply as a way to keep him close, but other days, she knew her guilt was eating at her because it was getting harder to keep his memory alive as time spiraled outward.

She hated to admit it, but Dune didn't help her guilt one bit. He made her want to consider the possibility of a second chance at love. Two years was a long time to be alone. She knew even Emery would approve of her moving on in life, and her family wanted her to be happy. Still, she felt stuck—unable to go forward or backward.

For now, she wasn't standing on the side of Wildcat Road so she could think about Emery and what might have been if he'd come home to her. She was stranded here because she was determined to help others celebrate Christmas. Emery had always loved this special time of year, just like Mr. Werner, so he'd have supported what she was doing, and he'd have helped her do it. But he wasn't here and wouldn't be again, so she simply needed to continue as she'd been doing for a long time now.

When Dune parked his truck behind her convertible, she wished he was Slade. She'd been about to call her brother for help, but Dune had now stopped that idea in its tracks. She couldn't very well turn down help from another firefighter, particularly one who was always so helpful to others. It'd be insulting besides costing her too much time to get alternate help. She just needed to go with it. If Dune could get her car moving again, she'd be grateful even if the heat between them caused uncomfortable sparks to fly.

She walked, or rather, carefully picked her way

across the loose gravel alongside Celeste so as not to trip and fall at Dune's feet. No telling how he'd take that bit of horseplay, but she suspected he'd view it as Sydney Steele finally succumbing to Dune Barrett's bird-dogging persistence.

She sighed again. She might as well go ahead and acknowledge the fact that there was something about him that resonated with her. Maybe it was the under-standing tinged with kindness in his eyes that he usually kept hidden with his teasing ways. She kept a world of hurt hidden behind her own teasing ways, too.

He was also real fine in another way. He had a cow-boy's eye for good vehicles. He drove a pristine white dually with red and yellow racing stripes that had the front bumper replaced by a large black metal cowcatcher with two tow hooks that protected the shiny chrome grill. The truck's big, growly engine sounded like a one-ton that complemented the extra set of rear tires—plenty of muscle to get most any hauling job done—along with the obvious four-wheel drive, since the vehicle sat high off the ground. She smiled at the sight, knowing how tall cowboys loved their tall pickups. No doubt about it, Dune was as fine a specimen of a man as his dually was of a truck.

He opened his door, stepped out with one long, muscular, jean-clad leg, and planted a cowboy boot the color of rich, aged whisky onto the chrome-edged ranch-hand bumper. When he stepped all the way down, he planted both feet firmly on the ground, adjusted his crimson pearl-snap shirt, tossed his russet felt cowboy hat back inside onto the seat, and stalked toward her Cadillac.

As long as she was admitting things to herself, she might as well say he was one tall drink of water that probably left most gals as thirsty as a Texas summer scorcher. But she'd seen plenty of cowboys with their too-broad shoulders, too-tight butts, and way too-hot swaggers. She ought to be immune. Still, Dune had thick, shaggy dark-blond hair worn a trifle long that simply begged to be mussed by a cowgirl's strong fingers, and he had eyes the color of a lapis pond that must surely make a gal wonder what passions lay hidden in those blue depths. She quickly shook her head as if she were a horse getting rid of an annoying fly. No way was she going to get caught by cowboy honey.

"Even more beautiful up close," Dune said in a deep, reverential tone.

She nodded politely at his words, feeling a righteous sense of accomplishment. She'd worked hard to achieve this elegant look to complement Celeste's beauty. Of course, she'd be modest in her response so as not to let him think he had anything to do with her current ultra-feminine appearance. "Thank you."

And yet Dune didn't give her a single glance as he walked right up to the trunk of her convertible, gave a slight growl deep in his throat as he touched the tip of the round red taillight, then reached up and stroked down the long rocket fin with its top line of bright, shiny chrome.

She felt her jaw drop in surprise, then quickly snapped her teeth together. He hadn't noticed her at all, hot vintage clothes or not. All he had eyes for was her pretty pink Cadillac.

He never broke contact with the lustrous paint that

gleamed like satin in the sunlight as he slowly walked
down the long length—on par with a prize Texas football field—to the chrome door handle. He stopped to
clutch it, looking into the interior of black leather bench
seats, chrome steering wheel, black carpet floors, and an
AM radio display with a round dial.

She took a deep breath, reevaluating the situation as
she caught up to him, almost tripping in the gravel with
her high heels.

When he reached the front end, he whistled in appreciation. "What an absolute beauty! I'd heard Mr. Werner
gave you his prize Caddy, but I never dreamed you'd
actually drive her around the county."

"I'll do anything to help launch Christmas at the
Sure-Shot Drive-In, and that includes using Celeste to
promote the event. She's perfect, isn't she?" Sydney
tried to keep the irritation out of her voice at his lack of
appreciation for her, but doubted if she'd managed it.
Not that Dune would notice, seeing as how he was mired
in the depths of starstruck infatuation.

"You nailed it perfectly. I didn't know this legendary
Cadillac had a name, but I'm not surprised at the news.
I'd heard Mr. Werner doted on her and kept her squirreled
away in a temperature-controlled garage. I never thought
I'd get a chance to see her, much less touch her." Dune
pointed at the front. "Look, she's even got longhorns!"

Sydney cocked her head as she examined her handi-
work. She had to admit the red and green tinsel looked
festive. She'd snaked it around the pale, dark-tipped
horns that spanned the width of the hood in front of the
shiny chrome snarl of a grill with its impressive dual
headlights on each side.

"What year?" He rubbed out a smudge on the hood with the pad of his thumb. "No, wait. Let me guess. Nineteen sixty. Right?"

"Close. Fifty-nine. Series 62 convertible. Eight cylinder. Automatic. I was told this is the most sought after Cadillac."

"I believe it." He stroked down one side of the longhorns, but still didn't toss a single glance her way. "Luxury at its finest—then or now."

She knew she shouldn't feel irritated that he was all about Celeste instead of her, but she couldn't help it. She was stranded on the side of the road, and he was doing nothing but ogling her vehicle. "If you don't mind, you're getting my pristine car dirty."

"Oh no!" He jerked his hand back as if stung. "You're right. Who knows what kind of dirt and oil I've got on my hands." He quickly popped open his pearl-snap shirt, pulled the tail out from under his wide leather belt with the big gold rodeo buckle, and jerked the fabric off his shoulders.

"What are you doing?" She stared at him in shock, because he was giving her a feast of sun-kissed skin stretched tight across thick muscles with a line of dark-blond hair that ran suggestively from his chest down into his tight jeans. She caught his scent, somewhere between sage and leather and testosterone. All of a sudden, the cool December day felt as hot as the Fourth of July. Talk about cowboy honey.

He quickly bunched his shirt in his right fist and got busy putting elbow grease into rubbing his fingerprints off the pink paint.

She no longer felt irritation. She felt steamy and achy

and hungry as she watched the play of his muscles. Arms, shoulders, back were just plain yummy. Soon he added a sheen of sweat to the smooth skin of his rippling muscles. She swallowed hard. When he leaned over farther and gave her a great view of his tight ass, she actually felt weak in the knees—or maybe that was from standing in heels for too long.

"Like what you see?"

Embarrassed, she tore her gaze from his butt to his face. Wouldn't you just know it, *now* he saw her. "I'm only making sure you don't scratch the paint."

"Sure you are." He grinned, revealing bright-white teeth with one front tooth slightly overlapped to mar his perfection. "Just so you know, I'm an appreciative kind of guy with the right kind of gal."

"I suppose my Caddy is the right kind of gal for you."

"I'd never turn down taking Celeste for a spin." He grinned even bigger. "Not too many hot beauties around nowadays. They're a treasure."

Sydney tried to shrug, but her body was no longer responding to her brain. She'd taken a dive into the blue depths of his eyes and felt scorched by the steamy heat. With a start, she realized he was no longer talking about her pink Cadillac. He'd finally turned his attention to her. A bit scary—oh yes, she'd admit it—but oh so tempting in that leap-off-a-cliff, gut-wrenching kind of way that spelled nothing but trouble. If she hadn't actually liked him, despite all her best intentions, it'd be easier to simply take a plunge, get him out of her system, and move on. It'd be much harder to let go if she got in too deep. He wasn't just a hot body. He'd gradually earned her respect as they'd fought fires together over the last several months. She felt her heart speed up in alarm, and she wondered if she had actually come to care for him, despite all her protestations, during that time?

And then she had a second revelation. Dune was teasing her about her new clothes, putting a humorous twist on the situation as a clever Texas male on the prowl would do. She sniffed—actually sniffed as if she were a fifties lady. He had his nerve playing with her when she was in dire straits with a dead vehicle and a needy body. Even worse, he'd lured her in way too close, causing her hormones to wake up and salute him just as he'd earlier saluted her.

"Treasures, right?" He pushed his point as mischievous light danced in his eyes.

"Put on your shirt, you big goof," she said with a grin to match his own exposed pearly whites. She was more than the sum of her hormones. Two could play this game. And she intended to win it.

"Big goof?" He laughed, shaking his shaggy head. "That's how me shirtless affects you?"

"You shirtless affects me not at all."

"You sure?" He stalked toward her, challenging her with his searing blue gaze.

She raised her chin, not about to back down, even if he did resemble a big ole determined bull. "My Cadillac is serious business."

"You're too serious by half."

"Life is serious."

"That's why we need to play now and again."

She held up a hand to stop him coming any closer. She really didn't trust her body not to betray her once she actually felt the heat he was radiating as if he were his own personal sun. Besides, she needed to get her world back on track. She didn't have time for play—or temptation. "At the moment, I just need to get Celeste up and running again."

"Die on you?"

She nodded, trying to focus on his face instead of his washboard abs.

"Bet it's just a little dirt on your carburetor."

"Dirty?"

"Yeah." He flashed another white-toothed grin, reminding her of a predator on the prowl. "Dirty can be good, but in this case, I'd better knock off the dirt and get you going."

"Get me going?" She hated to admit it, but he'd already gotten her going, and he hadn't done a single thing except take off his shirt—well, that and ply her with verbal foreplay.

"I'll just reach under the hood and toy with her a bit, if that's okay by you." He grinned again with eyes alight at his double-meaning tease.

She took a deep breath and actually sighed with the thought of his strong hands doing all sorts of amazing things. And then she got a grip. "If you can fix Celeste, I'll be grateful."

"How grateful?" He shook out his crumpled shirt, gave it a baleful look, and slipped his arms into the sleeves, leaving the front flapping open.

"I'll let you drive her sometime."

"That's the best deal I've heard in a blue moon. How about you let me hand wash her, too?"

"You want to do that?"

"Sure do." He glanced at the Caddy, then back at her.

"I'll rub her all over real soft and slow and tender with a leather chamois. She'll be purring within an inch of her life in no time."

Sydney swallowed hard, trying not to envision that little scene in relation to anything except cars. "Fine. I'll let you fix her up just in time for Christmas."

"You got it."

She cocked her head as a thought struck her. She knew how to win this game and come out ahead. "Even better, I'd like to see Celeste pristine for a cowboy firefighter photo shoot."

"Okay by me."

She stalked toward him, feeling energized with purpose. She could just see Dune sitting on top of the black leather back seat with his legs spread wide and his shirt open exactly as it was now. He'd be hot as a firecracker. Maybe she should even go for a few shots of him washing and polishing her car. He'd be wet all over with nothing but low-slung jeans hugging his hard body. She bet that photo alone would drive sales through the roof. "You never volunteered to be in my calendar, did you?"

He stepped back, shaking his head. "Nope. I'm not the best material for that sort of thing."

"Of course you are. You're a cowboy firefighter, aren't you?"

"Yeah. But I'm no model." He took another step back.

"I want real rough-and-tumble kind of cowboys."

"Ask Kent or Trey or Slade."

"Oh, they're all on my list, but I've got twelve months to fill." She closed the distance between them.

"Lots of cowboys around here can do it."

"But you're prime Grade A material." She grabbed the ends of his shirttail with both hands and tugged him toward her. "In fact, you're the perfect *Mr. December*."

Chapter 2

DUNE BARRETT CLENCHED HIS FISTS TO KEEP FROM crushing Sydney against his chest. There was just something about her that had set him to firing on all cylinders from the first moment he'd met her.

And he sure as hell hadn't been looking for love or even a roll in the hay. He'd arrived in Wildcat Bluff on a "Sunday morning coming down," to quote Kris Kristofferson, one of his favorite singer-songwriters. Dune had eased his way onto Cougar Ranch, grateful that his good ole buddy Kent Duval from his rodeo days had given him a place, no questions asked, where a beat-up guy could work as a no-name cowboy and lick his wounds in private. The only downside had turned out to be extra duty as a volunteer firefighter—and lusting after Sydney Steele.

And now that lust, or to be more accurate, this tall, curvy cowgirl, had him ready to do anything— whenever, wherever, whatever—she might care to put to him. If it'd been an itch he could scratch and get over it, he'd take that easy way out. But the more he was around her, the more he actually liked her. He recognized those fleeting looks of sadness in her eyes, despite her best attempts at putting on a brave face and taking care of others. She was strong, not only physically but mentally and emotionally. A single mom needed those traits, but even so, he understood that core of loneliness because he lived with it every day, too. Still, respecting her, liking her, lusting after her didn't mean he had any intention of posing for her cowboy firefighter calendar. So far, he'd managed to outmaneuver her photo shoots, and he had no intention of giving in now.

"Please, be my Mr. December?" she wheedled in a husky voice as she leaned in closer.

He groaned in response, feeling his blood heat up and head south as he caught her fruity scent. No sweet, cloying aroma for her—just straight up tangy. His kind of cowgirl. She was upping his temperature to the blazing point. Good thing they were out in the open or he'd be setting off automatic sprinklers to put out his fire. If she closed that last inch between them and he felt the hard tips of her breasts against his chest, he'd be a goner.

"Pretty please with sugar on it?"

He groaned louder—unable to form words—because any brain cells he had left with her hands tugging on his shirt had stalled in neutral.

"I'll let you wear a red stocking cap."

That shocked him out of his lethargy. She wanted to photograph him naked as a jaybird? He wouldn't mind one bit shucking down to his birthday suit with her, but not for public consumption. He stared hard into her big hazel eyes that appeared innocent when he damn well knew better. "And nothing else?"

"Oh, no! It's not that kind of calendar."

He felt a surge of male satisfaction to see her turn a pretty pink color to rival Celeste. She'd never be able to hide her emotions, because she was a strawberry blond with the fair skin that'd always give her away. He'd be happy to put that pretty blush all over her luscious body with her long legs that could twine around a guy and hold him tight while he sent them on a rush up a mountaintop. His fingers itched to do it. And if not that, he'd settle for thrusting his fingers into her thick hair and holding her for a kiss that'd curl her toes and steam up her insides. He stopped his thoughts, because they were nothing but his lust-filled fantasies trying to take over just as they did every time he saw her—and riding him hard even when he didn't see her.

"I don't know why you'd even think something like that." She gave his shirttail a hard jerk and stepped back to put space between them. "Or of me."

Now he'd put his foot in it. He couldn't tell her the truth, that he'd been thinking about little else except naked bodies since he'd met her. And if he wasn't careful, he was going to have to admit to himself that he'd come to care for her, and that fact would open up another can of worms in a life that he was trying to keep simple. "You said stocking cap. I didn't."

"But you…oh, never mind. I don't have time to get into who said what when."

"I can apologize if it'll help." Not that he'd mean it, but he didn't want to get on her bad side—if there was one. He tried to cool off by counting the scattering of freckles across her straight nose, but that just made the situation worse, because he took a dive straight down into her bra, wondering if more freckles lurked there just waiting for his discovery. Shape. Size. Color.

"No need. Confusion, that's all." She took a deep breath, full breasts straining against her dress, as if she was preparing to start over.

But his mind had gone into vapor lock again at that

sight. What was she wearing? He'd seen her in nothing but cowgirl clothes before this day. Those were bad enough, but all this exposed leg, tight little dress, and high heels that made him want to see her wearing nothing else had sent him barreling over a high cliff down into the raging rapids of a hungry river. Much more of this sexy vintage stuff and he might as well be put down for the count.

"So, what do you say?" she asked in an irritated tone.

He did his best to slew his mind back to the subject at hand, but he'd totally lost the drift of their conversation. "About what?"

She put her hands on her hips and jutted out her chin as she leaned toward him. "Okay. I've had about enough of your tricks."

"I'm not—"

"You're my Mr. December whether you like it or not." She gave him a hard stare, then stomped over to Celeste, put her hands on the hood, and leaned forward as if she was carrying such a load that she needed the support.

A lightbulb went off in his head. She was getting no help. He knew she was coordinating Christmas at the Sure-Shot Drive-In. He knew she was putting the benefit calendar together. He knew she was raising a daughter, as well as working at Steele Trap Ranch and part time at the Chuckwagon Café. But he'd been so far gone into his own lust, problems, and trying to keep life simple that he hadn't looked beyond his selfish interests. He suddenly felt small—real small.

Reality hit him like a sledgehammer. Wildcat Bluff's community had welcomed him with open arms, given him a quiet place to heal, and asked for nothing in return except cowboy work. He'd given little back except as a volunteer firefighter, and he'd grumbled mightily about that. Not like him. Not like him at all.

He knew the problem. It all went back to that last horrendous refinery fire. Until that day, he'd thought he was about as good as the late Red Adair, who was famous for stopping a thousand international oil well fires. That was then. Now he knew he didn't even come close to Red's gutsy track record, particularly as he was played by John Wayne in *Hellfighters*, the 1968 film about Red's life.

Dune had come out of that final fire alive, but Vonda hadn't been so lucky. He'd never know what had caused her to turn back at the last minute. Had she heard somebody or seen something? He still couldn't fathom it. They'd done all they could do. They'd contained the fire. They'd saved lives. It was cut and dried. Move on. But she didn't.

He hadn't realized she was running back or he'd have grabbed her and hauled her to safety. Instead, all he'd had time to do was realize the situation, look back, and see her disappear under a fiery structure collapse. He'd started after her, feeling his heart beat hard in fear for her. But he'd only taken a few steps before he'd been stopped by another firefighter. He'd fought his friend to go to her, and he'd broken free, but just for a moment. In the end, it'd taken three firefighters to haul him back from where Vonda had disappeared forever.

He'd failed her. He'd failed their future together. He'd failed his firefighter vows. Now he carried emotional scars that haunted him. He'd wake in the middle of the night in a cold sweat, so he worked hard on the ranch every day, hoping to wear himself out so he could manage a few hours of sleep at night. Yet nothing so far helped relieve his guilt.

Maybe Sydney had been put in his path as the perfect torment to punish his charred soul. She'd come along at the wrong time in his life, because he didn't feel as if he had enough to give a woman like her. She deserved a man who'd fall at her feet and hand her everything—love and lust and cuddles and support. Now she wanted him to pose half naked as a heroic firefighter when he was no hero at all. He was embarrassed even to think about it.

Still, there she stood with so many burdens on her shoulders that he was surprised she hadn't crumbled under the weight. And here he stood with not much of anything that gave his life value to anybody, not even himself. He took a step toward her, feeling a slight touch of hope blossom in his chest. Maybe—just maybe—she was more than a constant ache in his belly. Maybe she was the path to his redemption.

He walked over, putting one reluctant foot in front of the other. He knew there'd be no turning back, not when he committed to her. He wasn't sure if it was right or wrong, good or bad, different or indifferent. He just knew he had to do what was in his heart at this moment.

"I'll help," he said as he reached her side, knowing better than to touch her or offer consolation. She carried a fragile type of sadness that she covered well, but he recognized it because he dealt with his own every day. Kindness—even understanding—of any type could tip her over the edge. He knew that for a fact, because it'd have the same effect on him.

She straightened her back as she turned to look at him. "What do you mean?"

"I mean I'll help if Kent okays it. I can't think why he wouldn't want me to take a little time off to help with Christmas and the calendar. Everybody around here is overworked except me, so I guess I'm feeling guilty or—"

"Left out?"

He wanted to say, "Not hardly," but he didn't. Instead, he nodded, as if in agreement. What he felt like was a damn fool who was getting in too deep, knowing it and still doing it, because she needed his help, and he realized now that he'd come to care for her.

"You'll be my Mr. December?"

He nodded again, hoping he could pull his cowboy hat down low and conceal his face. Back in the Hill Country where his family ran the ranch they'd had for generations, his brother would laugh himself silly when he saw Dune posing—half naked—in a firefighter calendar. He'd probably guess a cowgirl had put Dune up to it. Fact of the matter, Dune would be on that ranch right now if he'd ever been able to settle down, but he'd always been drawn to find something he couldn't name and didn't understand. He'd been a rolling stone, letting his brother manage the ranch with their parents. For the first time in Dune's life, he felt glued to a single spot, and he couldn't figure out why.

"Will you help persuade the other firefighters to pose for our calendar?"

He nodded once more, digging his hole deeper with each nod of his head. A little bit more and he'd be too deep to ever dig his way out. For some bronc-busting reason, the idea didn't sit as heavy on him as he'd have thought. It probably had to do with the unrelieved desire he'd been living with for so long till he'd do about anything to make her smile at him.

"Thanks." She gave him a quick grin. "They've been avoiding me, as if that'd get me off their backs. If weather permits, I want to schedule our photo shoot as soon as possible. Hopefully we can make it happen in the next few days."

"Guess you need to get this show on the road."

"Sure do."

He took a deep breath, wanting to sigh out loud, but he caught her tantalizing scent and the hopeful look in her bright eyes. He didn't back out or let himself off easy. "That's doable. You want some help with the drive-in deal, too?"

She reached behind her and put a hand on her convertible's hood as if so surprised by his offer that she needed support. "Are you volunteering to help me?"

"Like I said, everybody's taken on some of the Christmas load except me."

"That'd be—well, it'd be a real blessing."

"I don't know about that, but I'll help if I can. Christmas at the Sure-Shot Drive-In is a big undertaking for one person. You ought to have a whole team instead of just me."

She cocked her head to one side, hazel eyes looking him over as if seeing him for the first time. "Maybe I misjudged you."

"Maybe you didn't." He shrugged, not about to let her think he was a hero just because he was volunteering a bit of time for a deserving community.

She narrowed her eyes, as if still considering him. "Maybe you misjudge yourself."

He gave a snort at that one, shaking his head. "Not damn likely."

"Whatever the case, I appreciate your help, and I gladly accept it." She stuck out her hand for a shake.

He wanted to draw her against his chest and give her a big, hard hug to seal the deal. But he didn't figure he could stop hugging her if he ever started, and he wasn't sure she'd appreciate the gesture. He settled for a quick, gentle shake of her soft, strong hand. It wasn't much on the Richter scale, but it still shook him like a leaf in a wild storm. How the hell was he going to be around her when she kept him on fire every single minute? He'd better buy a pair of loose-fitting jeans. And then he thought of the photo shoot.

All he could say was that, sure as shootin', the ladies buying the cowboy firefighter calendar were going to get their money's worth with Mr. December.

Chapter 3

SYDNEY COULD HARDLY BELIEVE HER GOOD LUCK. Out of the blue, Dune Barrett had simply volunteered his services for the calendar—as well as Christmas at the Sure-Shot Drive-In. If she were the suspicious type, she'd think he had an ulterior motive. But she wouldn't let it matter one way or another, because she could ill afford to look a gift horse in the mouth. Whatever his motives, she desperately needed somebody's help. Now that she had it, she could forge ahead.

First, she had to go to Sure-Shot and get a lay of the land. Bert Holloway owned the drive-in with his son, Bert Two. He'd said they'd upgraded and updated the place while keeping as much of the original structure and fixtures as possible. Wishful thinking or actual reality, she didn't know, but she needed to find out. One thing for sure, she'd seen the trashy, overgrown mess last spring when they'd bought it, so almost anything would be an improvement.

She felt the heat of Dune's gaze and glanced up at him. He'd moved closer. She inched toward Celeste, but if she backed up any farther, she'd be impaled on the longhorns. Drat that gleam in his blue eyes. He had it whenever he was around her, and it had a tendency to strike sparks in her.

"You want me to look under the hood?" He leaned forward with a little quirk of his sensual lips.

So kissable. She squashed that thought and imme-diately was swamped with another one that had him looking under her *skirt* instead of the hood. What was wrong with her? She definitely did not want him looking anywhere but at her convertible. She had to get her mind back on business.

"Are you in a hurry?"

"Yes!" She was in a hurry to get away from him, or she'd be wearing tank tops instead of sweaters this Christmas.

"You want to step away from Celeste?"

How could she when he was right in front of her? If she made a single move, she'd be right up against his body. If she could've, she would've looked into the dis-tance to try to clear her mind of unacceptable thoughts, but she couldn't see over his broad shoulders. He totally filled her world with his presence.

"Guess you've got a lot on your mind."

She rolled her eyes. He didn't know the half of it. She caught her lower lip with her upper teeth in frustration.

He reached out, tugged her lip free with the pad of his thumb, and gently rubbed back and forth as if to soothe a hurt. "No need to worry. I'm here to help you now."

She felt chills run up her spine at his gentleness and concern. She didn't mean to do it—and wouldn't have been so bold if he hadn't short-circuited her brain—but she flicked the tip of her tongue over the edge of his thumb and tasted the essence of him. *All male*.

"Now, why'd you go and do something I can't resist?" He eased his thumb across her lower lip, down her jaw, and captured the back of her neck with his fingers to hold her head in place as he lowered his face toward her.

She knew a kiss was coming—right on the side of Wildcat Road in front of the whole county—and she knew she should say something or do something to stop him, but she wanted his kiss more than anything else she could imagine at that moment. It'd been so long since a man had held her or kissed her that she wasn't sure she even knew how to respond anymore.

When his lips finally touched hers—just a gentle brush really, as if he was gauging her response—she felt swept up in a blazing wildfire.

And yet she sought to keep her wits about her. She should focus on business, not her own sudden need. She put her hands flat against his broad chest to push him back, but she quickly realized she couldn't budge him, because he was so much bigger and stronger. She felt a little shock. She was five ten—although she'd claimed to be six feet tall since her high school basketball days when height was critical—and sported enough muscle to work a ranch, but he made her feel almost petite.

She intended to push him away—absolutely, no doubt about it. Instead, she found her hands slowly sliding up his chest, making her hyperaware of the soft cotton of his shirt as his muscles hardened under her touch. All her senses came shockingly alive. She heard a mockingbird's song, caught the tangy scent of cedar trees, and Dune's taste still lingered on her tongue. He didn't move a millimeter—as if he'd waited a lifetime for her to touch him.

When she reached his shoulders, he gave her another feather-light kiss that promised more than it gave. Not nearly enough, not now that her mind had given way to her body. She sighed against his soft lips and clasped his shoulders to pull him closer. He groaned as if the ragged sound was torn from his gut at her response to him. She returned his kiss, teasing his lips with the tip of her tongue until she tore another groan from him, and he plunged inside while he crushed her against him, holding her head in one hand and her waist in the other as if he'd never let her go.

She moaned as she thrust her fingers into his thick hair, shivering with heat as he plundered her mouth and made her weak in the knees. She quickly realized that she had an answer to her question. No, indeed, she hadn't forgotten how to give or receive a kiss, particularly one of this magnitude.

Finally, when she was putty in his hands, he raised his head and looked at her with eyes the color of midnight. She simply blinked in response, unable to articulate a single word.

"If you let me into your life, I promise not to disappoint you."

She took a deep breath, trying to bring her mind back online. "I doubt you could disappoint me, not after that, that—"

"Hot kiss?"

She nodded, feeling her chill turn to heat as if her body were waking up from a long winter's nap.

He pressed a soft kiss to her lips, then stepped back, reluctantly letting her go. "If you want me to apologize for rushing you, I will, but—"

"No, I'm not sorry."

"Good. I'm not either."

She shook her head to discourage him, trying to think business instead of pleasure, but for the life of her, she couldn't say the words that would support her gesture. Instead, she quickly walked away from him. She stopped and looked back. With distance between them, she felt her brain kick into gear again. "Why don't we forget our momentary lapse in judgment?"

"I won't forget. Can you?"

"Yes." She deliberately looked away so he wouldn't see the untruth in her eyes. She just didn't know if she was ready—if she'd ever be ready—to move on with her life.

"Don't lie to me," he said with a growl, stalking toward her. "We both deserve better."

She held up a hand. "Please, I've got so much to do and—"

"I told you I'd help." He put his hands on his hips as he stared hard at her. "I won't lie to you. I want you, and that's not going to change because we're working together."

"You know I'm a widow." She wished he hadn't come right out and said what'd been between them since the day they'd met, because now she had to deal with it in the open.

"I heard your husband was a hero." He hesitated, as if considering what to say next. "You have my sympathy for your loss."

"Thank you." She usually kept her emotions private, and that meant she wanted to get past this awkward moment as quickly as possible. "What I'm trying to say is that I doubt I'll ever get over my grief, even after two years."

He raised one hand as if to implore her to change her mind, then dropped it to his side. "I understand how you feel. I really do. But if you'll give us a chance—"

She felt her heart beat faster at the thought of finding solace in this man's arms. "Why don't we just focus on work?"

"That's a lot easier said than done."

She nodded in agreement, realizing that she wanted to explore Dune's kisses to see where they'd take her—maybe far, far from her old anguish. But could she so easily set aside her lost love?

"Okay. I'm willing to put us on a slow boil. *For now*."

"It's for the best, surely."

"I'm not so sure, but—"

"For now," she interrupted, determined to get back on track and away from painful emotions. "I need to get to Sure-Shot and check out the drive-in."

"Make that *us* from now on. I'll give Kent a quick call later, but I doubt he'll say no to my request for some time off. If he does, you've got me when I can get away from the ranch."

"Thanks." For some reason, she felt surprisingly happy about that single word "us." She must've been kidding herself for months that she didn't want Dune's attention, because the opposite was obviously true.

"Okay." He turned toward Celeste. "Let's get this beauty back on the road. Did you run over any potholes getting here? Maybe something jarred loose."

"The road out of the ranch has gotten pretty rough this winter. Slade said he'd take care of it, but he hasn't had time. I doubt it'll get any better till after the holidays."

"If Celeste is in good shape like you were told, I'd guess it's probably a loose cable. If so, I can fix it right now."

"That'd be perfect."

"I'll take a look." He opened the hood and bent over the engine. "These babies are built tough."

She walked around so she could watch him. Of course, he was stretched out over the engine and looking as fine as her pretty Caddy. She felt her heart speed up at the sight. If she didn't get over his hot body, working with him would be sheer torture.

"Here we go." He stuck a hand into the car's innards. "Battery cable came loose."

"Is that a big problem?"

"No. Looks like a new battery. I guess somebody didn't tighten the nut on the terminal enough, so the cable came off." He stood up, closed the hood, and turned around. "I tightened it with my fingers. She'll go now and get you away from the side of the road, but I still need to finish the job with a wrench or even pliers later."

"Thanks." She noticed he had grease or dirt or something dark on his fingers. "Let me get you a wet wipe."

He glanced down at his hands. "It's not the first time I got dirty fixing something. And it won't be the last. Rags in my pickup will do the trick."

"You're sure you wouldn't want—"

"Why don't you see if she'll start now?"

Sydney nodded, realizing that wet wipes—so handy with kids around—were probably not nearly macho enough for a cowboy. She smiled at the idea, then opened the car door, sat down inside, and turned the key in the ignition. Celeste's engine immediately roared to life.

Dune walked over, leaned down, and smiled at her. "That's just what I wanted to hear. She's got a well-tuned motor, so all should be fine now."

"What a relief." She returned his smile. "I'd hate to be stranded out on the open road."

"Could be dangerous," he said in a serious tone. "You've got my number in your phone, don't you?"

"Just in case, I have all the volunteer firefighters' cell numbers."

"Good. If you get into any more trouble, call me first."

"But you said—"

"I don't expect any problems from this beauty, but you never know. I want you to be safe."

She felt touched by the concern in his eyes. It'd been a long time since she'd gotten that protective look from a man. But she also felt sadness, because he reminded her of all that was gone from her life.

"Are you headed to the drive-in?"

"That's my plan."

"How about I follow you to make sure you get there without trouble. And I can finish tightening that loose nut there."

"I don't want to put you out."

"Remember, we're in this together now."

She nodded, feeling the warmth he'd generated spread outward to engulf her entire body. "Okay. I'll see you at the drive-in, Mr. December."

He laughed, shaking his head, as he turned and sauntered toward his dually with one hand in the air to wave goodbye.

She watched him a moment, then put Celeste in gear and tore off down Wildcat Road as if she could escape the burning inside her.

Chapter 4

DUNE TRAILED SYDNEY IN HIS PICKUP LIKE AN OLD-timey cowhand on his horse dogging two thousand head of longhorns on a cattle drive that covered six hundred miles or more of rough territory. In those days, he'd be headed north toward Kansas, instead of southwest toward Sure-Shot. Still, direction or timeline made little difference. He was a cowboy with a goal to make life better in Wildcat Bluff County and in particular for a cowgirl named Sydney Steele.

She turned heads just as she always did wherever she went. Vehicles slowed so passersby could get a better look at the powder-pink convertible driven by a hot woman with her blond hair whipped wild by the wind.

He wanted Sydney wild in his arms, but he might have to settle for sedate by his side. At least she'd be in his life, and he'd get a chance to explore his super-charged feelings for her.

As he drove, he glanced at the countryside. It was a study in contrasts. Folks here lived easily with the past existing right alongside the present. Fact of the matter, they took pride in their heritage and encouraged visitors to do the same thing. He'd been around long enough to contract that same bug and get some education on local history.

Wildcat Road had originally been known as Wildcat Trail. Now the old wagon lane had been paved and was the major highway in and out of the small town of Wildcat Bluff, which had started out as a ferry point on the Red River between Texas and Indian Territory.

He was traveling down a section of land called the Cross Timbers that had originally been part of the Comancheria—the Comanche empire that had stretched from central Kansas to Mexico. The unique prairie was densely bordered by interwoven trees, shrubs, and vines—such as post oak, cedar elm, bois d'arc, dogwood, Virginia creeper, and blackberry—and could be as narrow as three miles in some places or spread out to thirty miles in others. In the old days, there'd been a brush fire every year, and the border would grow back too dense to penetrate. Comanche warriors had used the prairie between the two vegetative lines as a secret passage so that enemies couldn't see or attack them.

Now much of the Cross Timbers old growth was gone, but folks in Wildcat Bluff County had saved their section for posterity. He figured that was because many of the residents were descended from the Comanche and still protected their original homeland, where rich grasslands and rolling hills provided grazing for cattle, buffalo, horses, and wild critters such as deer.

He felt an affinity with the Comanche, because his German ancestors had long ago made a treaty with them to settle and farm fertile land in the Comanche territory now known as the Hill Country. Interestingly enough, the German-Comanche treaty was the only one in the United States that had never been broken by settlers. To commemorate their long-standing connection, an annual German-Comanche parade was held in Fredericksburg.

As he thought about cultural events, he was reminded

to call Kent about taking time off to help Sydney. He had his cell on the dash, so he hit speed dial and speaker phone.

"Where'd you disappear to?" Kent asked when he answered his phone.

Dune chuckled, knowing how his response was going to affect his friend. "I had to see a cowgirl about a pink Cadillac."

Kent guffawed on the other end of the line. "Hot?"

"Yeah."

"I mean the Caddy, not the gal."

Dune laughed harder. "Both."

"Vintage?"

"Car, not cowgirl."

"You got some way about you." Kent snorted. "I don't know why I'm even surprised you could be out on a mostly empty road and snag a hot cowgirl—and a vintage Caddy. What year?"

"Nineteen fifty-nine convertible. Prime."

"And you're calling, why? To gloat?"

"Nope. Anyhow, you'd only be interested in the Cadillac since you got hooked up with gorgeous Lauren."

"True enough. So, wait a minute, are you talking about Mr. Werner's famous Celeste?"

"Right."

"That means you're talking about Sydney, aren't you?"

"Yep." Dune was trying to sound casual, but he doubted if he was hitting that tone. "Any problem with me taking some time off till after Christmas?"

"Are you going to the Hill Country?"

"Nope. I'm suddenly civic-minded."

"I've got cows in the pasture making more sense than you."

Dune rubbed the back of his neck, knowing Kent wouldn't make it easy on him once he learned Sydney was the cause of his change in heart. "I'll still feed or whatever needs doing first thing in the mornings, but—"

"Okay," Kent said with a chuckle. "This has got Sydney's name written all over it. You've been bird-dogging her for months with not a chance in hell of getting anywhere. And now—now you want time off. What have you gone and done?"

"If you'll give me a chance, I'll tell you."

Kent laughed harder.

"Okay. With that attitude, you'll get the short version." Dune watched Sydney streak ahead of him, beckoning like pink lemonade on a hot summer day—tart and oh-so-sweet.

"Hey, Dune, you still there?"

"Yeah. Got a little distracted for a moment."

"Bet I know why. Now tell me what's going on."

"I volunteered to help her with Christmas at the Sure-Shot Drive-In and the cowboy firefighter calendar."

Kent didn't say anything for a moment. "You've got it bad, don't you?"

"No idea what you're talking about." Dune wouldn't admit it, not yet anyway, but his old friend just might be right. "Celeste broke down on Wildcat Road."

"And you just happened along?"

"That's the truth of it."

"You've got all the luck. I used to say it at the rodeos, and I'll say it again. Once you're on a winning streak, nothing can stop you."

"Sydney's trying to do everything alone, and she needs help. So I volunteered."

"Civic-minded, sure." Kent chuckled again. "You're right, she does need help, but we're all stretched too thin to give her what she needs."

"I'll give her everything she needs."

"That's what worries me," Kent said in a suddenly serious voice. "I don't want to see her hurt. She's still emotionally fragile, whether she'll admit it or not. And I don't want you hurt either."

"No need to head down that road so fast." Dune tried to sound disinterested in Sydney, but he knew it fell flat. "I'm going to assist her. That's all."

"Okay. Take the time off, but stay available in case something comes up. I'm glad you're going to help her get Christmas at the Sure-Shot Drive-in off to a good start. Nobody else has time. Do whatever needs to be done—except leave me out of that calendar. And I'd better not hear about any broken hearts. You got it?"

"Got it."

"Bye."

Dune glared at his phone, feeling glad the call was over. It'd gone about as well as he'd expected it to go. He'd get the same blowback when Sydney's brother Slade heard about Dune's volunteer work. They were as protective as all get-out about Sydney, and he didn't blame them. He was protective of her, too, but in a different way. He figured he could negotiate that minefield, but how in hell was he going to keep his word to Sydney about corralling cowboy firefighters for the calendar?

When she turned west onto Highway 82, he followed in her wake. He watched as the fence lines that stretched along both sides of the road changed from barbwire to white round pipe or four-slat wooden enclosures, so he knew they'd moved from cattle country to horse country. One ranch after another flashed by, announcing their names—from whimsical to practical—in black sheet metal cutouts or burned into wood arches that towered over entryways.

Thoroughbred horses with rich chestnut coats in a variety of shades grazed in some pastures, while in others, brown-and-white painted ponies sought shelter from the sun under the spreading limbs of green live oaks. Crimson barns and metal corrals, along with houses ranging from redbrick, single-story fifties ranch-style to cream-colored stone, two-story contemporaries, had been built well back from the road for privacy and convenience.

Soon he turned south behind Sydney at a sign with western-style letters that read "Sure as Shootin', You're in Sure-Shot!" under the black-and-white silhouette of a smoking Colt .45 revolver.

He'd never spent much time in Sure-Shot like he had in Wildcat Bluff. Still, he couldn't help but appreciate that the town had been named for Annie Oakley, the famous sharpshooter and exhibition shooter who'd been called "Little Miss Sure Shot" on the Wild West show circuit back in the day.

He headed down the asphalt two-lane road that turned into Sure-Shot's Main Street. The small town still nestled at what had once been the vital intersection of an old cattle drive trail that ran north to south and the railway line that crossed east to west.

Sure-Shot looked similar to the set of an Old West film. Old Town in Wildcat Bluff was built of brick and stone, while Sure-Shot had a classic wooden false-front commercial district. A line of single-story businesses connected by a boardwalk, covered porticos, and tall facade parapets extending above the roofs were individually painted in green, blue, or yellow with white trim. Small clapboard houses with wide front porches and fancy double-wides fanned out around the downtown area.

Once upon a time, Sure-Shot had catered to cowboys on their cattle drives from Texas to Kansas and back again. Lively dance halls and noisy saloons, along with the mercantile, café, blacksmith shop, livery stable, bathhouse, bank, and freight depot had all done a brisk business just like the same type of stores had in Wildcat Bluff.

He felt as if he'd stepped back in time. A few pickups and Jeeps were parked in front of the businesses, but a couple of saddlehorses with their reins wrapped around the hitching post in front of the Bluebonnet Café switched their tails at flies. He had no doubt that riders wore hats, boots, and spurs while they waited for takeout or sat down for an early supper inside the café. Life around here had its own tempo. It might not be fast, but it was steady. At one time he wouldn't have appreciated that pace, but he'd come to realize it was exactly what he needed to help him get back on track.

He drove past an open field that in winter was nothing more than the golden stubble of dry grass. In spring the area would be transformed into a colorful swathe of wildflowers that'd range from orange Indian paintbrush to bright bluebonnets to crimson clover. Maybe he'd still be around the area to see it.

He figured there'd once been a couple of other

buildings that had connected the current downtown with the old Sinclair gas station up ahead that stood by its lonesome, because it had the same tall, flat, wooden false front as the other structures. He'd helped save the station—along with other Wildcat Bluff firefighters— from what could have been a devastating fire last spring.

As he recalled, the station had two sets of faded green, three-hinged doors that opened to make wide automobile bays. The old Sinclair logo had still been readable on the tall false front even if it'd been half worn away by the passage of time and scourge of elements. The corrugated tin roof and outside walls must have been shiny silver at one time, but too much rain had turned the metal a rusty brown. It'd been a sad, forlorn picture of decay.

Ahead of him, Sydney slowed down and pointed toward the structure. He put on his brakes and looked at the old station in shock. It'd been transformed from eyesore to eye candy.

"Sure-Shot Beauty Station" was emblazoned in a Western-style typeface in bright turquoise against a white background where the old Sinclair logo had once reigned supreme. Instead of bay doors, the entire front was now clear glass so passersby could see the goings-on inside and customers could watch the goings-on outside. Mirrors dominated the interior walls with the turquoise chairs filled to capacity.

He just shook his head in amazement and gave a thumbs-up to Sydney, who gunned her engine and tore off down the road.

He followed, appreciating Wildcat Bluff County more all the time. After seeing the gas station's transformation,

he wondered what Bert and Bert Two had done to the
drive-in. Folks around here had the uncanny ability
and get-up-and-go to re-create and renew, no matter
the century or condition or challenge. Maybe he'd get
upgraded and revitalized, too. He chuckled at that idea,
even though he knew it might be just what would jump-
start him.

Sydney surged ahead of him, but he kept right on
her tail. He passed more empty fields that sported short,
golden grass and leafless, gray-limbed trees until he saw
the top of the drive-in screen up ahead. Not a bad location, since it was easily accessible from downtown and
that was undoubtedly the original intent. Out-of-towners
would probably be charmed by the quaint town and its
classic drive-in.

Main Street abruptly ended in front of a huge white
screen that towered over the flat prairie around it.
Sydney wheeled to a stop in front of the closed gate, so
he parked next to her, letting his engine idle as he automatically looked around for fire hazards or other danger.

The drive-in was surrounded by a two-layer, silver-
pipe fence with a wide gate—big enough to allow cars
to enter and exit at the same time on either side of the
wide screen. The gate was closed by a thick, metal chain
wrapped around the end bars and secured with a big
padlock. Wheels on the bottom of each side of the gate
allowed it to be rolled back out of the way when the
drive-in was open for business.

He didn't like what he saw. As far as he could tell, he
was looking at 1950s–60s style, small-town security—
meaning there wasn't much at all. He hoped there were
hidden cameras with a feed into somebody's phone and

laptop, particularly since there'd been a rash of fires involving property owned by the Holloways. At least in case of fire, escape on foot would be easy through the open-rail fence. He wondered if Bert and Bert Two were relying on an occasional drive-by from the sheriff's department. He hoped that wasn't all of their security.

Now he was doubly glad that he'd volunteered to help Sydney and come along to check out the place. He didn't think much of the idea of her being here alone. Help wasn't too far away, but oftentimes, seconds made the difference between life and death. She was strong and capable, so she'd probably be fine on her own, but he never took chances with lives.

When she opened her car door and stepped out, one tantalizing leg after the other, she rocked a little in her high heels, proving she was used to the steady gait afforded by cowgirl boots. He let his gaze travel up her long, long legs. She was wearing shiny hose that gleamed like oiled skin in the sunlight. Was she wearing a garter belt to hold up her nylons? He burned at the thought.

She gave a little wave before she made a grand gesture with an outstretched arm as if she were a classy model showing off the best features of a new car at a county fair or other vehicle exhibit.

No doubt about it, he was buying whatever she was selling. He just hoped it involved lacy underwear with a sexy vintage twist. He chuckled at the idea. Pretty quick, she'd have him in such a frame of mind that he'd be humming Dean Martin tunes while wearing a narrow tie and fedora—while at the mercy of a classy broad named Sydney.

He had to get his mind back on business or forget trying to help. But he had no intention of throwing in the towel, so he turned off his engine, stepped outside, and walked to the back of his truck. He leveraged up, tromped across the black rhino bed liner that kept anything he tossed back there in place, opened the lid to his tool chest, and rummaged around in an assortment of stuff till he found a pair of pliers that'd fix Celeste.

He shut the lid, jumped down, and walked over to Sydney, holding up the pliers. "Let me tighten that bolt."

"Thanks."

He raised the Caddy's hood, glanced around the engine to make sure nothing else wrong caught his attention, then quickly tightened the bolt and called it good. He lowered the long, sleek hood and patted the excellent paint job. "Ought to be fine and dandy now."

"That was quick," she said.

"Nothing to it." He walked back to his pickup, opened the passenger door, and tossed the pliers onto the floorboard. He'd deal with them later when he had time. Right now, he was focused on Sydney, so he quickly joined her by the closed gate.

She grinned as she pulled a set of keys out of her purse and jingled them in the air. "Are you ready for your first view of the new and improved Sure-Shot Drive-In?"

"I'm breathless in anticipation," he teased her.

"Oh!" She put a hand on one hip. "I'm not sure you've got the right attitude to see everything."

He grinned mischievously. "If you'll show me everything, I promise I'll have the right attitude."

She gave him a narrow-eyed look of rebuke while a smile hovered on her lips. "If you're going to be bad—"

He threw up his hands in mock surrender. "I'm yours to command."

"Just remember that when you're Mr. December." She cocked a hip, bent low over the gate, and inserted her key into the lock.

He decided—right then and there—that the folks of Wildcat Bluff needed a cowgirl calendar a whole lot more than they needed a cowboy firefighter calendar. He could see something on the order of the vintage Pangburn's Western Style Chocolates boxes with their delectable cowgirls displayed on the covers.

And he'd make Sydney his year-round cowgirl pinup.

Chapter 5

SYDNEY OPENED THE PADLOCK, PULLED THE CHAIN loose from one side of the gate, and then hooked the open lock onto the chain. She rolled the gate back far enough so they could walk onto the drive-in grounds.

"Do you think that gate is the only security here?" Dune asked as he walked toward her.

"Security?" She hadn't even thought about it. She glanced down at the padlock, then around at the fence that was more decorative than anything. She felt a chill run up her spine.

"Yep. This may be a retro drive-in, but we don't live in such innocent times nowadays."

"We've never had trouble at Christmas in the Country. Why would you think we'd get it at Christmas at the Sure-Shot Drive-In?" She didn't want to think about security, not now when everything was coming together so well. She glanced down and adjusted her long pouch purse by its plastic handle over her arm. She'd found it by sheer luck in a resale shop and fallen in love with the colorful flowers captured forever under clear plastic and accented with a gold-colored metal frame with a top snap lock.

He stopped beside her. "I'm not talking about the events. I'm thinking about how the Holloway buildings have a way of getting torched."

"What?" She dragged her gaze from her handbag to his face.

"I don't want to see this place get burned down."

"But those other structures were abandoned and in bad shape. The drive-in has been refurbished and is in excellent condition."

"I hope that makes a difference."

"We're talking apples and oranges here—no comparison."

"Maybe so, but I'd feel better if we had a few security cameras around at the least."

"Bert and Bert Two may have already considered it." She supposed Dune had a good point, even if she'd prefer not to go there.

"We can check with them."

She nodded in agreement as she rethought the situation. "I suppose cameras at the entrance and exit wouldn't hurt, but I doubt folks sitting in their cars watching movies will want eyes on them."

"Yeah. But if it was me, I'd at least get cameras installed at both those points and the snack shed, too."

"Good point."

He pointed at the fence. "That's not going to stop anybody."

"I doubt it's meant to keep out more than cars."

"Someone on foot could easily get inside and cause a lot of damage. Cameras wouldn't stop them, but at least we might get a face to run down."

"Let's follow up with Bert and Bert Two." She gestured toward the drive-in screen. "For now, why don't we take a look around the place?"

"I'll keep an eye out for security while we're at it."

She nodded, although she hadn't counted on security being an issue. It still wasn't high on her to-do list, because she had so many other vital matters on her mind, even if Dune was stuck in a security groove—like a needle going round and round on a vintage 45 RPM vinyl record. She smiled at that thought, suddenly feeling mischievous. She turned back toward him. "I'm thinking the first thing to do is contact Morning Glory."

"About security?" He cocked his head as he wrinkled his brow in puzzlement.

"I bet she'd be happy to bring sweetgrass and sage to cleanse the snack shed with a good old-fashioned smudge." She knew Dune would know just what she meant, because he'd lived in Wildcat Bluff long enough to be aware that Morning Glory—the perennial, classic sixties love child—watched over the county from Morning's Glory, her herbal, incense, and candle store where she made specialty items such as lotions, creams, and shampoos.

"Good idea," he said dryly as he gave a quick eye roll. "I'm sure sage and sweetgrass will stop arsonists in their tracks."

She chuckled, knowing she'd gotten to him. "We can use all the positive energy we can get out here. I'm desperate for this Christmas event to be a success."

He spread his open-palmed hands wide. "I'm not saying another word. Nobody wants to get in trouble with Morning Glory."

"I'm sure she'd be disappointed if we didn't ask her to smudge."

"Suits me. I'm for covering all the bases."

Sydney wished she'd thought of a traditional smudge earlier, but she'd just had too much else on her mind. Morning Glory would've been hurt if she hadn't been included in the important event. She had the biggest heart in the county, and she could always be counted on to help folks even if not quite in the way they might expect.

And that brought her thoughts full circle to Dune. Maybe he'd latched on to the idea of security because he didn't really want to help her with the calendar or the drive-in. She couldn't blame him for having second thoughts. It'd be a lot of work, but the happiness on folks' faces and the funding for fire-rescue would make it all worthwhile.

He needed to be in or out, because from here on, they were committed to working together—not turning back, not giving up, not giving in. If he was going to reject her, now was the time to do it before they got in deeper. She couldn't afford to be let down later when she had no time to start over. She felt a little stab of panic at the thought of losing his help. If he said he didn't want the trouble or hassle she'd brought him, she'd accept his decision. But she knew she'd feel disappointed, because he'd drawn her in, shown her there could be more in life, and made her want to grasp it with both hands. Still, she steeled herself for reality.

"Maybe this is more than you bargained for, what with the security and all." She heard her voice waver and straightened her spine. She was strong enough to go on alone. That'd been her plan from the get-go. "I mean, if you're too busy—"

"Stop right there. I'm never too busy for you—unless you're trying to get rid of me. Besides, I already talked with Kent, and he's on board with me helping you."

"Oh, okay. I just want to give you a chance to back out now, if you want to before we go on."

He gave her a dangerous-to-your-heart look with his
blue eyes. "I'm all in—for the long haul."

"Thanks." She didn't know if she should feel relieved
or disturbed by his agreement. He was fast becoming
a fierce wind blowing apart her carefully controlled
world. And yet she felt her resistance slipping away, or
maybe she was tossing it away in a bid for freedom.

"You ready to get started with the tour?" he
asked, giving her a grin that was part challenge, part
encouragement.

"Right this way." She smiled back, then turned and
walked up the wide swathe of pale cement with its dark
runners of old cracks.

She couldn't help but wonder how many cars—
and how many styles and colors over the years—had
passed through here on their way to entertainment and
pleasure. She bet Mr. Werner and Celeste had even
spent a few memorable evenings right here. She was
proud to be part of the restoration and renewal of such
a vital part of America's love affair with automobiles
and movies.

When Dune joined her, she pointed up at the screen
that was constructed in three connected sections. In
the middle one, "Sure-Shot Drive-in" was painted on
a white background in large forest-green Western-style
letters accented by neon that would glow brightly
after dark. They'd hung Christmas decorations of blue
stars above Santa in his sleigh pulled by reindeer, with
Rudolph the Red-Nosed Reindeer's neon, crimson nose
leading the way.

A loudspeaker was mounted on top of the screen,
while at the bottom, a red-and-white marquee listed

"Saturday. Christmas at the Sure-Shot Drive-In. Classic Holiday Films."

The other two sections of the big screen were set back from the center and braced with tall, white, metal struts for extra support. A small ticket booth painted white with green trim nestled in front of the right section near the entry lane. A vintage, green metal chair waited for the ticket-taker under a small green awning attached to the booth.

"So we're going to walk into the drive-in?" Dune asked as he caught up with her.

She chuckled as she glanced over at him. "You just want to drive my pretty Caddy, don't you?"

"Never crossed my mind," he teased as he caught her hand, twined their fingers together, then swung their arms back and forth as they walked past the ticket booth. "Do you feel like a teenager again?"

"We keep this up and I just might." She laughed out loud as she enjoyed the feel of his strong, warm fingers clasping her hand. She glanced up at him and was caught by the hot gleam in his eyes. Suddenly she *did* feel young—almost innocent—with an excited knot in the pit of her stomach as if she were on her first date with a cute guy.

She stopped in her tracks, jerked her hand free, and stepped away, rubbing her tummy in comforting circles. How could she be so disloyal to Emery? Twenty-nine wasn't young. And she was certainly no innocent. She needed to remember her priorities. Storm came first in her life, and then her family and ranch. She ought not to be acting giddy as if she were a teenager out to have fun.

"Sydney?" Dune asked. "Did I say something to upset you?"

She took a deep breath, knowing she had to be smart, practical, and business-oriented. "I think we'd better get back on track."

"That's what I was doing." He grinned mischievously. "I was getting us into a drive-in kind of mood."

She couldn't help but laugh at his clever squirming out of holding her hand just because he wanted to do it. "For that, I think we need Celeste."

"She's got a big back seat, doesn't she?"

"Football field size."

"That sounds about right for what I've got in mind."

"And just what do you have in mind?" She was onto his teasing game, and she'd let him dig a deep hole and watch him try to get out of it. But he'd set her heart to beating faster at the thought of being in the back seat with him.

"I figure we could raid the snack shop and spread out our goodies while we watched *The Thing from Another World* or some such classic."

"Is that the film with James Arness as some creature?"

"I see you're a lady of discerning taste. He was totally memorable as the vegetable man from Mars."

She laughed, noticing for the first time that Dune could be funny as well as everything else that upped her interest. "Discerning? I'm not sure that movie even rates a B."

"But it helped start Arness's acting career that led to about a million years on TV starring as Matt Dillon in *Gunsmoke*. I figure they cast him as the vegetable man because of his size. He was six seven."

"I didn't know you were a film buff."

"I've seen a few," Dune said in a voice gone serious. He glanced to the side, as if drawing a curtain over the window of his eyes to shutter his expression or suppress a memory. "Fact of the matter, I've worked as a professional firefighter. Sometimes movies can fill the downtime and help with the stress."

"Really?"

"Yeah." He gave a rueful chuckle. "I've been a firefighter. I've been a cowboy. I guess now I'm a cowboy firefighter."

She chuckled at his attempt to lighten the mood. "I imagine you're good at it all."

"I do my best." He took a deep breath as he pointed past the big screen. "Come one. Let's take a look."

She wanted to push, to ask more, to get to know him better, but she respected personal privacy. In time, he'd tell her what he wanted her to know about him. Until then, she'd already learned a lot. She hadn't meant to do it, but she was starting to see Dune as a three-dimensional man instead of a one-dimensional cowboy.

She felt as if a lightbulb had gone off in her head. Maybe that was just the quality that she needed to give her calendar an extra oomph. She grabbed Dune's hand in excitement.

He looked at her in surprise. "I thought we were through holding hands."

She squeezed his fingers, then let go. "I've just had a great idea."

"What?"

"For the calendar, we'll make each month special by describing what our volunteers do in their regular lives or something that makes them unique. We'll put names and personalities with the photos. What do you think?" She glanced up just in time to see Dune look a little sick.

"No," he said, shaking his head.

"No?"

"I don't want my name and past splashed over a calendar that'll sell everywhere. I doubt anybody else will either."

"I guess we don't have to go there. It was just an idea. I don't want to annoy our cowboy firefighters more than they already seem to be over posing for the calendar. I can't seem to make them understand that it's for a worthy cause." She wasn't ready to give up on her concept yet, but now didn't seem to be a good time to pursue it. She gave Dune a closer look, realizing there was something going on with him that he was keeping from her. A deep, dark secret? She couldn't imagine. He appeared to be such a straight-up guy. But then, she didn't know him very well yet, so maybe she should be less trusting or maybe just more concerned that there was something in his past that bothered him.

"They understand the cause, all right. If you keep after them, they may all leave the county till it's safe to come home again."

She chuckled at his words, tossing her head. "They may as well get used to the idea. With you helping me, we'll get them in line one way or another."

"I wouldn't count that chicken before it's hatched."

"Oh yes, I will. And soon."

"Come on." He clasped her hand again. "Let's see if they've stocked the snack shed."

This time, she let him hold her hand, appreciating the

distraction from her worries, appreciating his help, and simply appreciating him. "If it is, let's pick the most fun food there."

"I'll spring for it."

"Thanks. You're way too good to me." She laughed, teasing him as she felt lighthearted again.

He chuckled with her as he squeezed her hand. "I'll even leave cash in the till for Bert."

"Too bad there won't be fresh popcorn. How about chocolate mints?"

"Not bad. Giant dill pickle."

"Peanut butter cups."

"I think we can do better. Let's go take a look."

"You're on, pardner."

He stopped and fixed her with eyes the color of a deep, dark-blue pond in winter just waiting for an early spring thaw. "Yeah. I like the sound of that. *Partners*."

Chapter 6

SYDNEY TRIED TO CONTROL HER RESPONSE TO DUNE, even as she felt sudden heat singe her. *Partners*. If he hadn't used just that tone of voice or just that emphasis or even just that twist to suggest so much more than a working relationship, she'd be fine. Instead, she was obviously becoming so attuned to him that she got the nuances in his voice.

She wanted to be clueless, but she wasn't. He'd been flirting with her for months. Still, that was vintage Texas guys and gals. They were born—or raised—with the flirt gene in ascendancy. But it could mean almost anything, from lifting sagging spirits to "hey, let's rent a room." In this instance, she was left with no doubt that Dune sincerely meant the latter. Even more, she was moving toward taking him up on his unspoken offer—or at least, her body was headed fast in that direction. Only smarts would keep her from leaping off that dangerous cliff and throwing caution to the wind. She had to remember what was important in life, and that was her commitments, responsibilities, and promises. All those had been made before Dune entered her life, and they'd be with her long after he exited her life.

"Maybe I should've asked if you're hungry," Dune said, cocking his head in inquiry.

She came back to reality at the sound of his voice. "Just wool-gathering."

"There's a lot to think about, but we'll think even better with the inspiration of snack food."

"So true." She breathed a sigh of relief at being drawn away from her thoughts. Maybe she was overthinking the situation. In any case, she needed to focus on the issue at hand.

"I'll tell you one thing for sure." He stopped by the side of the big screen. "Clean-up alone made a huge difference out here. I saw the overgrown weeds, blown-in trash, and general disrepair when the Holloways first bought the property."

"That's Moore Chatham's doing, isn't it?"

"Yep." Dune kicked aside a stray rock with the toe of his boot. "After Moore set the old Sinclair station on fire, I'd never have dreamed he'd turn his life around so fast."

She nodded in agreement. "But Sheriff Calhoun saw frustration instead of meanness in Moore's actions and gave him a second chance."

"I have to admit Moore's willingness to work surprised me," Dune added thoughtfully. "And he turned out to be a right smart handyman. He did a lot of the work turning the gas station into the beauty station, didn't he?"

"Sure did. I knew you'd be impressed, so I slowed down so you could take a gander at it." She stopped beside Dune, following his line of sight upward. "I think Moore was inspired by Serena Simmons, besides being sweet on her."

Dune chuckled as he glanced at Sydney. "Sounds as if she's a chip off the old block. Isn't her mom one of the best horse breeders and trainers around here?"

"Right. I don't know what we'd do without Billye Jo's support for our Sure-Shot Christmas event. She's providing some horses, and Serena is grooming them. You know folks can take their horses to the back of the beauty station to have their manes and tails plaited, don't you?"

"I hadn't heard it. Folks in Sure-Shot definitely have a strong can-do attitude."

Sydney nodded in agreement. "Once Serena got that cosmetology degree in her hot little hands, she didn't let any grass grow under her feet." She smiled mischievously. "Come on. Let's take a look. You've lollygagged long enough."

"Me?" He spread his hands wide in denial, grinning at her. "You're the one giving the tour."

She chuckled, knowing he knew she'd intentionally reversed the situation just to needle him and hear his protest. Any Texas cowgirl worth her salt couldn't let a cowboy get the upper hand for long, particularly when he was sidling in too close for comfort.

She quickly walked around the side of the big screen and then gestured at the entire area for Dune's benefit.

"Wow." He stopped beside her and looked around, clearly impressed with the transformation.

"It's really great, isn't it?"

"I'd hire Moore any time. Pretty quick, he's going to have more work than he can shake a stick at."

"I bet." Sydney pointed toward the big screen. "You know, at the height of their popularity, there were something like four thousand drive-ins across the country."

Dune quirked an eyebrow at her. "I wonder how many working ones are left now."

She sighed, thinking about it. "Do you suppose there are even a hundred still drawing customers?"

"Maybe not that many."

"Seems a shame."

"That's life—and technology. Folks are home watching big screens and controlling what they see."

"Yeah," she agreed. "But it doesn't have the same hometown charm."

"Worse yet," he said with a sly grin and a teasing glint in his eyes, "guys don't get a chance to check out the hot babes in the snack shed."

She shook her head, chuckling. "I bet there was a lot of that going on both sides of the aisle."

He gestured ahead of them. "You know this was called the Passion Pit back in the day, don't you?"

She stopped in her tracks and stared at him in surprise. "Where did you hear such a thing?"

He shrugged, grinning bigger. "Morning Glory. And Bert."

Sydney thought a moment, then nodded in acknowledgment. "I guess if anybody'd know, they'd be the ones. But Hedy'd know, too. I might ask her when I see her at the station later."

"She'll either be there taking care of business or over at her store. She's sure been a firecracker since Lauren got her out of that wheelchair and on the back of a horse again."

"Night and day." Sydney smiled in remembered pleasure. "Who knew horse-assisted therapy could work such wonders?"

"Guess we all do now."

She glanced at a small stand-alone white sign with

black letters on the right side of the entrance lane beside the white fence that read "RADIO SOUND," with the call number of an FM radio station. She knew sound, music, and announcements had once been piped through speakers attached to car windows, but now folks had this new option to listen using their own car stereo.

As she walked with Dune down the single-entry lane, they passed a long, high, board-on-board white fence on either side of the road. One section ran from the edge of the screen inside the drive-in while the other section extended along the outer perimeter to keep folks outside from seeing inside. She doubted if anybody could see much considering the location at the end of the road, but Bert and Bert Two had made a point of retaining the original design of the drive-in.

When she came to the end of the inside fence, the drive-in opened up like a huge asphalt amphitheater. At the end of each curved row, a large, long red arrow on the white background of a rectangular box on top of a white metal pole would light up at night to show drivers where to turn and park. Silver metal poles with dark gray metal speakers on top—one on each side of a pole—that could be hooked to vehicle windows sprang up along each row with just enough room for cars between them. Each row was elevated on one side so that the front ends of vehicles were at a good viewing angle.

She glanced toward the entrance, where the white screen—put together in rectangular sections—rose upward to dominate the deep blue sky. A large, flat platform painted gray held the screen high above the vehicle area. A long row of neatly trimmed green bushes fronted the base along with a wide lawn of dried golden grass in front.

"I'm so excited by the transformation. What do you think?" She turned toward Dune to get his reaction.

"I think we've stepped back in time." He pointed toward the screen. "I wonder why there's that row of bushes and bit of turf?"

"Original stuff. Maybe it was a play area for kids or simply made the drive-in nicer for folks."

"I like it."

"I heard Hedy and Morning Glory say they used to ride their horses here and let them graze on the grass while they watched a movie. But that could be a tall tale."

He chuckled, nodding. "I wouldn't be a bit surprised at their antics."

"Me either." She turned away from the screen and pointed toward the center of the drive-in. "What do you think of the snack shed?"

"If it's got snacks, I like it."

"I mean its design." Maybe the building wasn't too spectacular by current standards, but it was a classic Midcentury Modern design that had an almost flat roof with a wide overhang and white shingles for siding. An inset doorway obviously led to the interior of the snack shed. She loved the fact that folks could lounge in shiny green, blue, red, or yellow vintage metal lawn chairs on a cement patio surrounded by a silver metal pipe fence. Loudspeakers were tucked up under the eaves to broadcast movie soundtracks and announcements, along with silver double-cone bow-tie outdoor lights.

"You really like this place, don't you?" Dune turned to glance down at her with a smile.

"It's adorable. And all digital now. There's not a projection booth or projectionist like there used to be to show films."

"Makes sense. Who's handling the movies?"

"Moore."

"He's a jack of all trades, isn't he?"

"He's turning out to be good for Sure-Shot." She didn't say it—and she hated to even think it—but she still felt a little uneasy about Moore despite all his hard work after starting the fires. She guessed she was just letting her firefighter training get in the way of completely accepting Moore's change in attitude.

"I heard Bert say they were thinking about having a swap meet out here once a month."

"That's a good idea. It'll draw people from all over and help out local businesses."

"Sure-Shot's starting to be an up-and-coming town again." He headed for the back door of the snack shed. "Right now, you know what's on my mind."

She smiled as she followed in his wake, beginning to imagine sitting in Celeste, sharing snacks with Dune during a movie. But that wasn't part of their deal, so she needed to keep her mind on business. The colorful chairs would make good props for her photo shoot, but she'd need more than that to garner interest in the calendar. On the other hand, maybe all she really needed were cowboy firefighters.

"You got a key?" Dune called as he rattled the snack shed's doorknob.

She opened her handbag and extracted a key ring with a metal, white, red-rhinestone-eyed poodle fob.

"Cute poodle," he said with a chuckle.

"Vintage, of course." She laughed as she glanced up and caught the twinkle in his eyes. "I told you. I'm going retro all the way."

"I got it. No point in doing something halfway."

"Right." She stepped in front of him to open the flat, pale, solid wood door with a single diamond-shape, upper window. She quickly stuck her key in the lock of the round doorknob surrounded by a shiny starburst escutcheon. She loved the retro door. Bert and Bert Two had really put wonderful detail into their renovation.

She opened the door, found a light switch on the wall, flipped it, and stepped inside. A brass Sputnik chandelier with its many outstretched arms, each supporting a single small lightbulb, cast soft, golden light over a long glass counter. Along the back wall, a row of brass conical lamps illuminated the long aisle where servers would prepare hot dogs, curly fries, popcorn, and drinks while they also sold pickles, candy, and other goodies. A row of vinyl aqua booths with glitter laminate tabletops nestled invitingly against the opposite wall.

Dune walked across the buffed-to-a-high-sheen turquoise vinyl floor, twisting his head in every direction. "They really did this up right, didn't they?"

"It's absolutely perfect."

He pointed at the ceiling, then at several walls. "Sprinkler system. Fire extinguishers. Unobstructed exits. Looks updated and upgraded to county and state fire codes."

"I never doubted Bert and Bert Two would be on top of things."

"This looks good, but I still want to talk with them about security."

"We'll do it."

He leaned over the glass counter, gave it a long look, and shook his head. "Missed one vital thing."

"What?"

He tapped his fingertip against the countertop. "Candy's not stocked yet."

"That's a shame. I thought maybe the deliveries would be here. Looks like no treats for us."

He turned back around. "All's not lost."

She smiled as she followed his gaze to the restored Seeburg jukebox set against a far wall with a small, square, parquet wood dance floor in front. The jukebox was a beauty with its aqua, yellow, and red innards visible through a clear, rounded top and two plastic translucent pilasters with rotating-color vertical cylinders on each corner of the front.

"Now that jukebox is retro in overdrive," he said.

"Pretty is as pretty does. Bert told me it'll play both sides of fifty 45s. He stocked it with rock 'n' roll, as well as country and western classics, everything from Bill Haley's 'Rock Around the Clock' to Hank Williams's 'Your Cheatin' Heart.'"

"That makes a hundred tunes to get stuck in your head."

She laughed. "I guess that's one way of putting it."

"You know what else I like about this place?" Dune flung his arms wide open. "It's flat-out fun—and it's going to be more fun when it all comes together for Christmas at the Sure-Shot Drive-In."

She took another look around, nodding in agreement. "You're right. I think I got so caught up in all the work that I forgot the most important part of a drive-in. *Fun*."

"We can fix that right now." He gave her a mischievous

grin, then walked over to the jukebox, punched several play buttons, and turned to let his gaze trace over her body as if he was using a Fourth of July hot sparkler to outline her in bright, searing light.

She felt her breath catch in her throat when she heard the snack shed fill with the romantic lyrics and soaring music of "Unchained Melody."

"Oh, my love, my darling... I've hungered for your touch..."

He stepped onto the dance floor and held out his strong, long-fingered hand with palm turned upward in invitation. "Dance with me."

Chapter 7

DUNE HAD CHOSEN THE SONG, BUT HE HADN'T COUNTED on it feeling like a punch to his gut as soaring violins swept Elvis Presley's unmistakably smooth voice into the stratosphere of emotional desire: "...*I need your love, I need your love...*"

Now he had to wonder if he'd been kidding himself all along that what he'd wanted was a quick, simple roll in the hay. What if he needed *love*—two hearts that beat together with enough love to last a lifetime?

He felt as if the floor shifted under his feet, leaving him completely off-kilter as the song got deeper under his skin. If he'd wanted to stay a rolling stone and keep living the way he'd been living, he should've pushed any buttons on the jukebox except the ones that filled the snack shed with the unrelenting, driving force of "Unchained Melody."

And yet he stood there with his hand outstretched to Sydney, wanting her, needing her, maybe even loving her. And just like the song, he felt his emotions soar with trepidation and anticipation. Would she cross the shiny aqua floor—so similar to a wide blue sea that separated them—and take hold of his hand, or would she turn away and keep them an ocean apart forever?

She stood there and looked at him, eyes wide with wonder. Finally, she gave a little shake, as if coming awake, took a step toward him, then stopped and hesitated, as if changing her mind about joining him.

He raised his outstretched hand higher. At least she was of two minds where he was concerned, and that gave him hope that she'd tilt in his favor. Maybe she just needed a little persuasion. "I didn't figure you jitterbugged, so I thought a slow dance was in order."

She gave a little half smile, raising one corner of her pink lips. "Didn't I tell you I don't do anything halfway?"

He groaned under his breath. Couldn't she say or do one blasted thing that didn't turn his burners up to full flame? Nothing was halfway about her, and that was exactly the way he wanted her. Needed her. Maybe even…but he wasn't going there, despite how the song was leading him along the path to red velvet roses and a white picket fence.

She gave him a quick nod, walked over to the booths, set her purse down on top of a table with a snap, and turned toward him. "Do you two-step or, by any chance, do you jitterbug?"

"And here I thought I could get away with a little slow dance."

"Did you really think I'd let you off that easy?"

He gave a negative shake of his head as the song came to an end, and he dropped his hand to his side. So much for getting Sydney into his arms and holding her close for the few tantalizing moments of a tune.

"I've been taking dance lessons. At least, Morning Glory and Hedy have been instructing me in the finer points of the classic jitterbug."

He groaned out loud this time. "Oh no. I've seen those old movies where the guy is tossing his partner over his shoulder, sliding her across the floor, and twirling her around in circles."

"Fred Astaire and Ginger Rogers we are not."

Sydney walked past him, studied the jukebox for a moment, punched several play buttons, and turned back toward him. "But wouldn't it be fun to demonstrate a few jitterbug moves right here during Christmas at the Sure-Shot Drive-In?"

"That sounds about as much up my alley as the photo shoot." First, the calendar. Second, a dance demonstration. He didn't even want to think about what might be waiting for him on third. Maybe, if he played his cards right, he'd hit a home run—with Sydney as his prize.

No matter where it all ended up, he didn't know how he'd gotten in so deep so fast. One thing for sure, she knew exactly how to pull his strings and make him dance like a marionette. If his brother down at the ranch ever found out, he'd laugh himself silly at the idea that Dune had finally met his match.

If nothing else, he'd at least better give a good accounting, or he'd never be able to look himself in the mirror again.

"*Fun*. I thought you wanted the drive-in to be fun." She tossed him a mischievous look as she stepped onto the dance floor and held out her hand to him just as the first guitar riff of Chuck Berry's "Maybellene" tore through the snack shed.

"*Pink in the mirror on top of the hill… First thing I saw that Cadillac grille.*"

Dune couldn't keep from grinning at Sydney's choice of songs. "Are you trying to make me regret I stopped to check out your pink Cadillac?" And then he thought of Bruce Springsteen's classic "Pink Cadillac." Most folks knew what that particular phrase meant by now. He grinned even bigger.

"Nineteen fifty-five. Rockabilly. Top of the charts." Sydney swung her hips to the rhythm of the music, twirled around twice, and held her hands straight out to him. "You'd never pass up the chance to ride in a pink Cadillac."

"Not with you in the driver's seat." He gave up trying to resist her, particularly not with her pink Cadillac on his mind. Anyway, he had a few moves of his own that he'd learned the hard way on the polka dance floors of the old German halls in the Hill Country.

He clasped her hands, thinking that she was soft and warm and a little vulnerable since she was so much smaller and less muscular than him, even if she was a tall woman.

He felt a little tender, knowing he must be gentle not to accidentally hurt her, till she abruptly slung their arms over their heads, still holding hands, and then released him to dramatically trail her fingertips down his shoulder with one hand while still holding his other hand so she could curl her body in next to him. Just when he was enjoying her close touch, she swept out from him again, twirled around, and then sashayed outward, still keeping their hands together.

She threw back her head, laughing with delight as her hazel eyes—a fascinating mixture of brown, green, and gold—twinkled and her white teeth sparkled in the radiant light of the Sputnik chandelier.

He was totally captivated by her. He'd never seen her let go and simply enjoy herself before now. And it was heady stuff. She took him right back in time before life had hit him like a sledgehammer and rocked him to his core. He grasped that feeling and clung to it as he caught her around the waist with one hand and clasped her hand with the other. He executed a modified polka move, a real fancy two-step, swung her out away from him, and twirled her back toward him.

As "Maybellene" drilled down to the last searing note, they were breathing fast and laughing loud until the moment when Sydney completed her twirl and landed against his chest with her breasts pressed tight to him. And then silence descended on the snack shed as they gazed at each other, caught in a moment of joy and abandonment where nothing existed except the two of them.

He'd never know how or why it happened, nor did he care, because the jukebox picked that moment to give him a second chance. The soaring music of "Unchained Melody" suddenly filled the snack shed again.

"Oh my love, my darling… I've hungered for your touch…"

He slowly caught Sydney's wrists and raised her hands to his shoulders, watching her face for dismay or rejection. Instead, she gave him a slight smile, a mere lifting of the corners of her mouth, and ran her palms over his shoulders to clasp him behind his neck. Emboldened, he caught her waist with both hands and pulled her close, so close that their bodies became one as he guided them across the floor in the slowest of slow dances.

When she pressed her cheek against his broad shoulder—and sighed in pleasure and contentment—he knew he'd forever remember this moment as a turning point. He could no longer go on alone or hide from life. It was unworthy of the way he'd been raised, because he'd been trained as a man to always step up to the plate. He didn't know if what he felt was love or powerful lust, but he intended to follow his feelings to the end of the road, where maybe a white picket fence and a trellis of wild roses awaited him...along with Sydney.

He didn't expect a miracle. They both carried baggage from their pasts. Still and all, happiness could go a long way toward healing old wounds and creating new memories. He just wanted a chance for both of them to find their way into the future. Maybe together.

But for now, he simply needed to hold her, be close to her, warm the cold places in his heart with her. He gently pressed a kiss to her soft hair, inhaling the lavender and sage and something-he-couldn't-identify fragrance that could only be a Morning Glory special blend made for Sydney alone. It suited her—and it suited him even more to draw her scent deep into his lungs, feeling as if he were joining them beyond the closeness of their bodies.

When she trembled in his arms, he pressed his lips to her hair again and then trailed a line of kisses to the pulse point of her temple. He lingered there, noticing how her pulse sped up until their hearts beat in time together. He slowly slid one hand upward, acutely aware of the smooth texture of her dress, the outline of her bra, and the strong muscles of her back. He rubbed her neck, massaging in slow circles till she tilted her face up to look at him with heavy-lidded eyes.

He inhaled her tantalizing scent again as he studied her face with its high cheekbones, square jaw, and pointed chin. She had strong features—handsome rather than pretty—that suited her to a tee, because she was a mother, rancher, and cowgirl who took care of business first and herself last.

For now, he wanted to put her first and foremost. Would she let him? Only a kiss would tell. And so he touched his lips to hers, as softly as if he were gentling a horse grown skittish from former negligent riders. He toyed with the fullness of her lower lip, teasing with his tongue, nibbling with his teeth, from one corner of her mouth to the other while he pulled her harder against his body until her heat melded with his own and they set each other on fire.

When she thrust her fingers into his thick hair and opened her lips to draw him into her soft, warm depths, he instantly turned feral, like a stallion put too long out to pasture. He crushed her lips and delved deep in a kiss to possess, claim, ignite until there was nothing else in the world except the two of them—and he felt her hunger for his touch just as he'd long hungered for her.

As the last refrain of the song faded away, he stopped any semblance of pretending to dance. Nothing mattered anymore—not music, not motion, not location—except the fact that they were wrapped in each other's arms, straining for the deepest of connections with heated kisses, entwined bodies, and desperate desire.

She tasted of bliss, as if every good thing in life had been rolled into one searing kiss. She felt of heaven, as if an angel had descended to Earth to clasp him in her arms. And she smelled good enough to eat, so he clasped her face between his palms and kissed her deeper, harder, feeling caught in a powerful undertow that drove them relentlessly through the white-water rapids of a raging river.

Yet none of it was enough. Maybe nothing would ever be enough until he was buried to the hilt in her hot, moist center with her cries of ecstasy ringing in his ears until he drove them both over the edge. And still maybe that wouldn't be enough to sate him. He wanted to *own* her—body and soul—and he wanted her to *own* him.

With that last thought, he felt as if he'd been dumped in cold water. Nobody thought that way nowadays. *Own?* Where the hell had that idea come from? He didn't think that way, and he could be damn sure she didn't either. And yet that desire stayed with him, wanting and needing in a way he never had before, not even with his dearest Vonda. He had to get a grip before he lost all sense of self-control, self-preservation, and self-interest.

Sydney was special. Yes, he'd admit it. But no, he didn't want to own or be owned. It just wasn't in the cards, not for him or her. He wanted what he wanted, but he didn't need to get in too deep to go there. He couldn't fathom that she would want to be corralled any more than him.

Christmas. He blamed his soft-headed and soft-hearted feelings on the time of year that had almost lured him into believing in miracles such as love and happiness and forever. He had to be stronger than the season.

With reluctance that he didn't understand, he raised his head, eased back from her, and gave a rueful smile. "Guess there's a good reason they call this the Passion Pit."

Chapter 8

SYDNEY FELT AS IF SHE'D BEEN DOUSED WITH COLD water by Dune's words. *Passion Pit?* She'd felt something special, while he'd obviously only been looking for a good time. Well, she'd asked for it. He'd said he simply wanted to have fun. She'd agreed—until he'd made her want so much more with that single, slow dance to heartrending, heart-mending music. And now?

She wasn't a basketball player, barrel racer, and rancher for nothing. If the game he played wasn't for keeps, then she knew exactly how to play it. They were both better off that way. She could tease and torment with the best of Texas women to keep her feelings deep in the dark for protection's sake. If fun was the name of the game, she could handle it, because she now realized that she deserved to enjoy herself in a way she hadn't in a long, lonely time.

But for now, she needed to be practical. She'd had a lot of practice at it. She forced a chuckle between her lips, pushed out of his arms, and stepped back. She didn't look into his eyes, afraid of what she might see there—good or bad—because she wanted her fantasy of happily-ever-after to stay true for a moment longer.

But he didn't move either, as if he was clinging to the spell the music had cast around them. Finally, he cleared his throat as he stood facing her, arms hanging loose at his sides.

She was vitally aware of him, as if she were tied to him by an invisible rope, so that he couldn't make a move that she wouldn't follow.

Finally, he balled his hands into fists, turned on the parquet floor, walked over to the jukebox, gripped its sides with both hands, and slowly leaned over to examine the contents.

She watched his every movement until she saw his face appear reflected in the clear plastic cover of the jukebox's top. What she saw made her heart speed up. No matter his words, he was no less affected than she'd been by their dance. Was he being a strong Texas male carrying the burden for two without words, without emotion, without help? She shivered at her insight into his character, but she wished he'd let her help with a decision that affected both of them.

And yet he was right to back off and make light of their dance. She didn't resent or question his action. She understood only too well. They had an important job to do, and they couldn't allow distractions such as personal attraction get in the way of Christmas. Maybe after Sure-Shot's event was all said and done, they could pick up where they'd left off, or maybe by then whatever was between them would have disappeared into the sunset much as an unneeded, unwanted, unfulfilled dream that never reached reality.

She took a deep breath. "Looks like we christened the Passion Pit with our dance."

He glanced over at her, a slight smile tugging at his full lips. "This old music sure knows how to—"

"Yeah. It's all about the music."

"Right."

She smiled back at him, knowing the movement didn't reach her eyes any more than his smile reached his gaze. They were both stretching the truth to the breaking point and knew it, but if it helped them get past this awkward moment, she was all for it. "I guess we ought to make plans for the calendar."

"Guess so."

"And Christmas at the Sure-Shot Drive-In."

He nodded as he turned away from the jukebox. "Other than food, this place looks ready to roll."

"You really like it?"

He smiled, and this time his blue eyes lit up with pleasure. "What's not to like? It ought to be a big hit."

"I hope so." She glanced up at the Sputnik chandelier. "Bert and Bert Two put a lot of time, energy, and money into the place."

"They appear to be upstanding citizens of the county."

She heard the query in his voice, even if he didn't voice it. "I know some folks around here question if they've been torching their own properties for the insurance money, but this proves they're not the arsonists."

"How so?"

She spread her arms wide to encompass the snack shed. "If they were going to burn down this place, they'd have done it before they invested so much in rebuilding it."

"It's worth more now."

She pointed at the chandelier. "They'd never get their money or time back. Bert told me they hunted down all sorts of retro pieces for authenticity. We'd probably miss them at first glance."

He looked around, nodding in agreement. "I'm just

stating what I've heard around town. I've got no opinion one way or another. I'm the new kid on the block, so I don't know history here. But I still think security ought to be high on our list of things to check out."

"Okay. I'm with you on that one."

"Good. Now what comes next?"

"I guess we'd better focus on the calendar first." She walked over to an aqua booth, slid across the vinyl to sit down, and opened her purse.

"You got a list in there or something?" he asked as he sat down across from her.

She pulled out her cell phone and called up notes to start a list. "I'm putting you down for December in the Cadillac."

"It's your call, but isn't this a firefighter calendar?"

She set down her phone and looked at him. "What do you mean?"

"Shouldn't there be some firefighter stuff in the pictures. I don't know, but maybe gear or rigs or stations."

She gave a big sigh, rolling her eyes in exasperation. "I hate to admit it, but you're right. I guess I've been so focused on Christmas at the Sure-Shot Drive-In that I stopped thinking about cowboys as firefighters. Besides, they've given me such a runaround that I'm trying to think out of the box."

"But aren't cowboy firefighters the point of the calendar?"

"Of course they are," she snapped, feeling as if she'd lost ground on the project by not keeping her thinking clear as she tried to come up with a location that might entice the cowboys to show up for a photo shoot.

"Don't take it out on me. I'm just the messenger."

She slumped against the high padded seatback. "It's not you. It's me. I need to be on top of my game."

"Maybe you just needed a sounding board."

"*Maybe?* I'd say that's exactly what I need, so thanks."

"Anytime."

"But I can still see you on top of the back seat of Celeste."

He snorted as if he didn't believe her. "So all the other guys are going to look like firefighters, but I'll be lounging in a pink Cadillac. Are you trying to get me laughed out of the county?"

She couldn't help but chuckle at his words. "Now that you mention it, maybe that's not the best idea." She drummed her fingertips on the tabletop. "But I want Celeste in the calendar."

"I wish I wasn't going to say this, but I could be washing your Caddy wearing—"

"Jeans, boots, and a firefighter helmet."

"No shirt?"

"Never. And wet jeans ought to do it."

He groaned, shaking his head. "If I ever needed drive-in snack food, it's right this moment."

"Big baby." She smiled to take the sting from her words. "Remember, your sacrifice is for a good cause."

"I'd better get a reward, too."

She cocked her head to one side, giving him the once-over. "What kind?"

"The kind named Sydney."

She felt heat swamp her at that statement, wanting to escape his lapis stare but wanting more to dive into its dark depths and find relief from the ache he'd ignited deep in her core.

"What about I take you to dinner?"

"Huh?" She struggled to get her mind back on business.

"Dinner. We've both got to eat, don't we?"

"If it's a reward, then I should be taking you to dinner."

He grinned, revealing his slightly crooked front tooth. "That'd work, too."

"Okay. I do owe you for the engine repair, as well as your help."

"I'm glad to know volunteers get rewards."

"I guess that means I should get a reward, too," she teased with a lilt to her voice.

"You name it, you got it—so long as it's named Dune."

She couldn't keep from laughing at his verbal antics. "Think pretty highly of yourself, don't you?"

"It's a dirty job, but somebody's got to do it."

She laughed harder. "We have so gotten off track."

"My fault." He put a large hand over his heart. "Want me to make amends?"

"Let's not go there."

"My offer's always open."

"If you don't mind, let's stick to figuring out how I'm going to get this calendar completed, printed, collated, and distributed in about a month, or sooner if at all possible. It's got to be available for sale at all the local stores and events during Christmas in the Country and Christmas at Sure-Shot Drive-In, or we might as well forget it."

"Okay, that's what we'll shoot for. You didn't get the guys lined up, right?"

"I keep trying, but as you well know, they've been cagey. Fortunately, a graphic designer has already completed the calendar layout. Nathan at Thingamajigs is waiting for me to slug in photos so he can start production."

"Did the cowboys really bail on you at Thanksgiving?"

She rolled her eyes as she sighed out loud. "I'll never be able to prove it, but a downed fence that let out a herd of cattle onto Wildcat Road from Wildcat Ranch was downright suspicious."

"I guess you're thinking somebody cut the wire and drove out a herd just so the firefighters would have to leave your photo shoot, leap in their trucks, and hightail it to the road to round up the cattle."

"That's the long and short of it. They left me standing in the station's parking lot with nobody to photograph."

"It was the talk of the town."

"Yeah. Maybe most folks laughed their heads off, but I was frustrated as all get-out." She drummed her fingertips on the tabletop. "And it wasn't the first time somebody messed up my photo shoot. You may not have heard this, but Kent's camera disappeared another time when I had them all ready to go."

"I hadn't heard it. I guess they found his camera later."

"Oh yes, but not until everybody had gone every which way but Sunday. I tore the station apart and found it hidden under a pile of towels."

"What makes you think the next photo shoot will work out?"

"It's got to." She smiled at him, feeling renewed hope just in his presence. "You're my ace in the hole."

"I'll give it my best shot."

"If you let those ornery cowboys know you're my new Mr. December, maybe they'll finally stand still long enough for photos."

"I'm not sure how much they'll listen to me, but—"

"I truly believe Jim Bob left the county to get out of

posing for Mr. December. I'm not sure, but I think he may have even put his ranch up for sale."

Dune laughed, shaking his head.

"Not funny. And with that bull-riding body—those broad, muscular shoulders—he'd have been perfect."

"Okay. I'll do my best. Maybe I'd better ask Hedy for help. Nobody wants to get in trouble with her any more than they do with Morning Glory."

"I was trying to leave Hedy out of this since she's so busy with Christmas in the Country, but time is fast running out."

"Kent's onboard to photograph, isn't he?"

"Yes. That is, if he doesn't disappear to Alaska or someplace." She picked up her phone and made a few notes. "You're right about locale. Let's plan to meet at the new fire station."

"Think we can shoot everything in one day?"

"We've got to." She set her cell back down and twirled it around in a circle as she thought about logistics. "Our timeline will depend on their work schedules, but we can't get started too early, because everybody will be taking care of animals."

"We can still get going pretty early."

"True." She picked up her cell again. "Let me see if I can get hold of Hedy and start that ball rolling." When he nodded in agreement, she hit speed dial for her friend.

"Sydney, I've been thinking about you," Hedy said when she answered her phone.

"Good things, right?"

"Always."

"Dune and I are at the drive-in. We've been discussing the best way to handle the photo shoot."

"Dune?" Hedy's voice slid up an octave. "I didn't know the two of you were—"

"He volunteered to help out. That's all."

Dune grinned at her. "That's *not* all."

"What'd he say?" Hedy asked.

"Nothing." Sydney rolled her eyes at him. "Could we set up a schedule for the day after tomorrow at the main station? I'm hoping Kent can get all the photographs we need in one day."

"We can surely try."

"Dune's going to stop by and talk with you about how to light a fire under those cowboys so they'll actually let Kent take their photos."

Hedy gave a bark of laughter. "They've been running you a merry race, haven't they?"

"Tell me about it," Sydney said.

"Dune and I will work out something. We're not going to let this opportunity for a fire station fund-raiser slip through our fingers."

"Thanks."

"By the way, what do you think of the drive-in?"

"It's wonderful. Bert and Bert Two have made it a showplace."

"That's what Bert said when he stopped by the store to buy another Bluebird of Happiness."

Sydney smiled at the news. "Bert sure has a passion for glass bluebirds—or for the lady who sells them."

"Oh, go on now." Hedy gave a husky laugh. "Still, I guess one of these days, I'm just going to have to go to his home and see his bluebird collection. He's been asking forever."

"Like since high school?"

Hedy laughed harder. "I don't think he had any blue-birds back then."

"I bet not." Sydney laughed with her. "I wish you'd take pity on the guy and go see his collection."

"It's Christmastime, so maybe he'll get his wish."

"There you go," Sydney agreed. "But back to the calendar. You'll be there for the shoot, won't you?"

"Wouldn't miss it." Hedy cleared her throat. "Now don't do anything I wouldn't do at the drive-in."

"Nothing but a little jitterbug."

"Glad to hear those lessons are paying off."

"Sure are."

"See you later," Hedy said.

"What was that all about?" Dune asked.

"Hedy said she'll help you get the guys wrangled for the photo shoot." Sydney set down her phone, sighing at the fact that everybody in Wildcat Bluff was always trying to get her interested in a cowboy to heal her broken heart. She had no doubt that by the time they got back to town, word would have spread about Dune's volunteer work, and it would go well beyond a calendar and a holiday event.

"Is Bert really sweet on Hedy?"

"Far as I know, he's been trying to get her to go out with him since high school."

"Now that's persistence."

"That's Bert."

Dune reached out and squeezed Sydney's hand. "I'm hoping persistence pays off."

She smiled as she squeezed his hand in response, noticing the strength, the calluses, the short nails that all spoke of a hard-working cowboy. "I'll tell you what—"

She was interrupted by Slade's ringtone on her phone. She grabbed her cell, feeling a little spurt of concern because he was with Storm at the ranch. Her daughter was nothing if not wild. "Hey, what's up?"

"Storm's riding her four-wheeler like a maniac," Slade said. "She won't listen to me. Mom and Granny are down at the café taking care of business, so they're not here to rein her in. You'd better get home and lay down the law."

"She's not hurt, is she?"

"No. But there's something in her today that reminds me of when I took that tumble off a bad bull. You just got a drive that won't let you quit."

"Please keep her safe. I'll be home as quick as I can."

"Will do," Slade agreed. "Bye."

Sydney looked into Dune's sympathetic gaze. "I need to go."

"What's the trouble? Can I help?"

"No, not really." She stood up, feeling surprised that she wanted to lean—even for just a moment—on Dune's big, broad, strong shoulders. "It's Storm. I suspect she's thinking about her daddy. She's been too quiet ever since his birthday a few days ago."

"She misses him," Dune said flatly as he got to his feet.

"Emery was an Army Ranger." Sydney felt sick at the heartbreak of her child and the fact that she couldn't do a blessed thing about it. "And she thinks she's a chip off the old block. She's been wild— dangerously so—since we got the news that he wouldn't be coming home."

"How are you handling it?"

"I'm keeping her busy. She talks to a counselor. She's

winning at rodeo events. But she appears to feel no fear about anything. That alone scares me."

"I don't blame you, but she's got a strong support system with her family and Wildcat Bluff."

"True. I just hope it's enough."

"Come on. Let's get you home and see what's going on."

She searched Dune's face, seeing concern that touched her grieving heart. "You don't need to go with me."

"I'll follow you." He stepped close to her, invading her space as if to emphasize his point. "There's no way I'll let you drive that distance alone, not with so much worry on your mind."

"But—" She thought to refuse him, until she remembered how Celeste had died on the side of the road. She couldn't go through that again, particularly not when Storm needed her. She pulled the key ring out of her purse and glanced up at him.

"You're not in this alone." He clasped her hand, threaded their fingers together, and led them toward the door.

Chapter 9

FOR SYDNEY, THE DRIVE FROM SURE-SHOT TO WILDCAT
Road seemed to take a million years, even though she'd
opened up the V8 engine with her foot smashed against
the gas pedal. All her mother's instincts screamed at her
to get to her daughter as quickly as possible. And fortunately, Celeste was no slacker when it came to power
under the hood.

When she passed the turnoff for Wildcat Ranch,
where Trey and Misty now lived in happiness, followed
by Cougar Ranch, where Lauren and her daughter,
Hannah, blissfully resided with Kent in his family's old
farmhouse, she breathed a sigh of relief. After her closest neighbors, Steele Trap was next, even if technically
not too close, since they were all thousand-plus-acre
ranches, but that was the way of it in Wildcat Bluff
County—your neighbors were those who lived closest
to you, no matter how far away.

She drummed her fingertips on the big steering wheel
with its glossy pink center, impatient to reach Storm
and Slade before anything untoward happened to them.
She was probably overreacting to the situation, letting
unfounded fears ratchet up her tension, but Slade wasn't
one to overstate anything, particularly since bull riders
were a laid-back lot.

Finally, she saw the black metal cutout that read
"Steele Trap Ranch," with clear blue sky shining

through the open letters and a red-suited, white-bearded Santa Claus perched on one corner, slowly waving at passersby with his battery-operated, animated arm. She smiled at the sight and waved back, still feeling amazed they'd managed to get the contraption up there. But where there was a will, there was a way—particularly at Christmastime.

She cast a quick glance upward to check the weather in case it was going to impact her daughter, but the few fluffy white clouds lazing high above the Red River reassured her that nothing was building over the water.

She turned off Wildcat Road, felt her low-slung car bumpy-bump across the cattle guard, and slowed down, even though she wanted to hit the gas pedal and rocket forward. A little farther down the lane, she put on her brakes again and maneuvered around several potholes, noticing in her rearview mirror that Dune rode high and dry in his big dually with probably little concern for a few bumps.

She followed the rough road upward till she came to the sprawling redbrick ranch house with a red metal roof where her mother and grandmother lived together. She liked the cozy appearance of Granny's house with its brick arches enclosing a shady portico where cedar chairs livened up by bright-yellow cushions were tucked together in conversation groups. For Christmas, they'd outlined the arches with long ropes of red and green lights to match the bright wreaths in every window. They'd also positioned a multi-piece, hand-carved, wooden Nativity scene under the spreading limbs of a green live oak.

She wound her way toward her own home where she'd grown up, roping and riding on the ranch. After her father and grandfather had passed away, her mom had moved in with Granny. Sydney had returned to her family house after she'd lost Emery. For a while, Steele Trap Ranch had been run by women and a little girl.

Once Slade was injured on the rodeo circuit, he'd returned to heal. He might've been bruised in body and spirit, but they were thrilled to have him back, as much for his upbeat, fun-loving company as for his much-needed help with the family businesses. The Chuckwagon Café was always dependable income, particularly important when downturns in the economy or cattle futures affected ranch profits. Thanks to Slade, they'd been able to ease off their workload just a bit. She'd hoped he'd have more time for Storm, since she needed a father figure in her life, but now he was busy creating his own new business, and his injury still restricted his movement, although he was improving over time.

As she came abreast of her house, she paused to look for Storm, but the yard was empty except for the tire swing hanging from a rope on a lower limb of the big oak tree in front that in spring would shade much of the grass and the wide front porch. She'd had fun adding a few touches of cheery aqua to the old farmhouse, which was still painted the original white with a high-peaked, gray-shingled roof. A large crimson-and-gold Christmas wreath added a dash of holiday color to the natural wood entry door.

If not for her worry about Storm, she'd have invited Dune up to her porch to sit side by side with her on the aqua cushions of her hanging swing and drink sweet tea from holiday glasses while they made plans.

She checked her rearview mirror. He was staying

right up with her as she followed the road toward Slade's place at the highest point on the bluff that overlooked the Red River.

When her brother had returned home, he'd been too impatient for regular construction, so he'd opted for modular housing. He'd chosen a contemporary structure with lots of glass windows and doors, wood-looking siding, and all the modern conveniences, plunked down on the edge of an old pecan grove. He'd planted muscadine vines nearby and started a small vineyard. Unable to rodeo, he'd turned his considerable energy into baking pies and making wine in addition to everything else. Now he'd developed a well-deserved reputation among hipsters who enjoyed specialized, small-batch food options.

She stopped on the gravel parking area near Slade's home. Dune pulled up beside her. She cut Celeste's engine, left her purse on the passenger seat, and stepped outside. She smiled at Slade's new Christmas decoration. He'd put up a hand-painted wooden cutout of Santa in his sleigh pulled by five prancing wildcats. Of course, like their family Nativity scene, it was crafted by a Wildcat Bluff artisan with an eye to local culture.

Dune stopped beside her, eyeing the decoration. "Bet he got that from one of the Christmas in the Country vendors."

"No doubt about it."

"We need something similar for Christmas at the Sure-Shot Drive-In, don't you think?"

"Do you mean like souvenirs?"

"T-shirts, ball caps, travel mugs." He pointed at the decoration. "What about local artisans? Are there going to be booths or tents or something?"

"Yes, we've planned for vendors, and we've gotten some takers. Still, lots of folks were already committed to Christmas in the Country."

"Maybe they could split their merchandise between the two events."

"But how would they split their time?"

"Good point." He reached out and stroked the lead wildcat. "Nice work."

"Next year we'll figure out how to do more. For now, I'm just hoping we can get through our events without a major crisis." She didn't want to discuss the drive-in right now. She just wanted to get to Storm. But Dune made good sense. She appreciated the way he was really getting involved with everything.

"If not, we'll deal with whatever comes along. Remember, I'm here to help you."

"Thanks. I do appreciate it." She looked toward Slade's house but didn't see anybody. "For now, let's check on Storm."

"Right. I didn't mean to get us off track."

"Good ideas for the future." When she heard the revving engine of a four-wheeler before the harsh whining as it took off, she felt her heart speed up in alarm. Slade was exactly right. Storm was pushing the limits of the ATV.

"Sounds like she's riding on the other side of the house," he said, taking a step in that direction.

"Makes sense. She uses that empty horse pasture over there." Sydney pointed toward it, then clasped Dune's hand without even thinking about it. "Let's go." She tugged him with her as she hurried toward the pasture.

When they reached the other side of the house, she

immediately saw Storm—long, blond hair flying out-ward—as she raced across the golden stubble of grass inside the silver-metal horse fence. Eight years old going on eighteen, because she'd instantly aged at the loss of her father. Maybe Storm thought if she went fast enough, drove hard enough, grew up soon enough, she'd outdistance the emotional pain that she'd bottled up as if it didn't exist in her world. Perhaps she even thought that if she didn't acknowledge fear, she wouldn't have to admit to the fear that her father was no longer there and never would be again to catch her if she fell into one of life's many unforeseen cracks.

Slade stood by the open gate, one hip cocked to relieve the pressure on his injury—what he jokingly called a catch in his get-along. Her adorable brother was not for the faint of heart. He was six-four of solid muscle with a thick crop of ginger hair, sharp hazel eyes, and a contagious laugh. He ran hot and fast, so that even in winter, he didn't need much in the way of clothes. He wore a gray sweatshirt with the sleeves ripped out, revealing the barbwire tattoo that circled his right bicep and the rope tattoo around the other. Scuffed brown cowboy boots led to soft, faded Wranglers to a scratched rodeo buckle on a natural leather belt.

No doubt about it, with those looks and that attitude, he'd cut a wide swathe through the ladies for years, but not so much since he'd lost his battle with a big bad bull. Sometimes she worried about him being alone, but other times she knew it was the perfect choice for him right now.

As if he'd heard Sydney's thoughts, Slade glanced over at her and then inclined his head toward Storm rocketing up and down the peaks and valleys of the land, not slowing at all when she went up a slight hill to plunge down again.

Sydney caught her breath in dismay. She'd seen Storm ride this fast before but never with this type of intensity, as if she thought she could bust through some sort of invisible barrier and reach her missing father.

She felt a chill run up her spine and shivered at the sight of her daughter's reckless ride. Dune squeezed her hand, as if he understood her worry, and she felt immediate comfort. But nothing could stop her concern till she had Storm off that ATV and out of danger.

She dropped Dune's hand and jogged the rest of the way to her brother. He gave her a slight smile and a big hug.

"See what I mean?" Slade gave a nod of welcome to Dune.

"I thought she was going to help you with Christmas decorations."

"So did I." He put a hand on top of the fence. "She drove up here on her four-wheeler, and we drug out those decoration boxes Mom dropped off yesterday. I got caught up in old memories looking at them, and next thing I knew, I heard the ATV start up."

"Old memories." Sydney felt another chill run through her. "There wasn't by any chance a box of Christmas decorations that I packaged up and set aside after Emery—"

"Oh no." Slade appeared stricken with guilt as he quickly turned from Sydney to look out at Storm. "I didn't think about it till now, but that last box held the ornaments y'all picked out for your Christmas tree."

"Those were used for our *last* family Christmas

together." She felt tears sting her eyes. "Storm and Emery went together—a father-daughter outing—to pick out the perfect tree that year. When they got back, they were laughing and hugging and so pleased with themselves. I'll never forget that moment, or afterward when we trimmed the tree with those Christmas ornaments."

"She hasn't either." Dune leaned against the fence and pointed at Storm racing up and down the pasture. "It's not easy to deal with loss, particularly for a kid."

Slade looked from Sydney to Dune then back again. "You two, uh—"

"Dune volunteered to help me with the calendar and Christmas at the Sure-Shot Drive-In."

"That's good," Slade said, but he sounded skeptical.

"Saw her on the side of Wildcat Road and stopped to help," Dune explained in an overly casual tone as if suddenly treading on thin ice.

"Yeah," Sydney agreed. "Celeste just up and stopped on me."

"Why didn't you call me?" Slade frowned, eyebrows drawing together.

"No time," Sydney said. "Dune happened along and—"

"Nothing to it. Battery cable was loose," Dune interrupted, obviously trying to ease the tension.

"He followed me to Sure-Shot to make sure I didn't have any more trouble. And one thing led to another." Sydney smiled at Slade as she realized her big brother was suddenly on high alert and in protective mode.

"Okay," Slade agreed. "But you know you can always call me if you run into trouble."

"I know." She patted his broad shoulder to settle him down like she would a skittish horse.

Slade gave Dune a narrow-eyed stare. "And I'll be watching you."

Dune tossed him a big grin and a slow shrug. "I'll do my best not to get you on my case. Right now I'm just helping out your sister."

"She can use the help," Slade agreed. "She's always biting off more than she can chew."

"Not so," Sydney protested. "Anyway, if you two are through bumping chests, I want to focus on my daughter." She noticed with satisfaction that both cowboys looked properly chastised—or at least a little bit so—at her words.

"If you can get her off that ATV, I'd do it sooner rather than later." Slade turned to lean against the fence.

Sydney watched in horror as Storm hit another high point and bounced up before she came down and hit the ground hard again.

"She'll run out of gas at some point," Dune said. "Was the tank full?"

"Don't know." Slade glanced down at Sydney.

"I don't either," she agreed. "But it doesn't matter. I'm going to go flag her down. She'll stop for me. And now that I know old Christmas memories are upsetting her, I'll help her make new happy ones."

"We'll all help," Slade agreed.

"I'm in," Dune added.

"Thanks." Sydney gave each of them a brief smile, and then she stepped past the open gate. If her daughter was hurting, so was she, and she'd do anything to heal the wound in both their hearts.

She took a step into the pasture and felt her ankle wobble. She glanced down at her retro heels and gave a big sigh. She couldn't have been dressed more inappropriately, but that wasn't going to stop her. She plunged ahead, feeling her heels sink into the soft dirt with each step.

She waved her arm to get Storm's attention, but her daughter either didn't see her or ignored her. Either case wasn't good, so she tromped farther across the short dry grass, trying to decide if she should just take off her shoes and go barefoot. Still, she didn't want to take a chance on dangerous rocks, broken limbs, prickly pear cactus, or anything else that might lurk in the thick grass that could injure her feet.

She stopped at a high point where Storm would have to see her when she made her turn on the far end of the pasture and headed back. She listened to the four-wheeler's loud drone as she watched Storm's blond hair blow back from her face, feeling more agitated the longer she had to wait for her daughter to make that last turn at the end of the fence.

Suddenly a gray-and-white rabbit leaped out of hiding and ran straight toward the ATV. Storm made a quick, hard turn to the right to avoid the rabbit and hit an incline at high speed. As she came down on the other side, she lost control and tumbled out right in front of the four-wheeler.

Sydney gasped, feeling her heart leap into her throat as she kicked off her heels and started running toward her daughter. She heard Slade and Dune right behind her. But there was nothing she—any of them—could do as Storm hit dirt and the airborne ATV followed her downward toward the ground.

Sydney jerked her narrow skirt up high to give her

room to run faster. As she ran with her heart almost beating out of her chest, she didn't know how to save her wonderful little girl.

And so she prayed for a Christmas miracle.

Chapter 10

As Sydney pounded one foot after the other against the hard-packed ground, she knew she was hurting her feet, hitting rocks with her toes, stumbling across broken branches, stepping on cactus, but she barely noticed the pain. Nothing mattered except getting to her daughter.

She heard her ragged breath and felt her racing heart as she crossed the pasture that appeared to stretch out for miles when she knew for a fact it wasn't actually that far away. She kept her total focus on the ATV that poised over Storm—as if defying gravity—for what felt like a long, terrifying, agonizing moment before the heavy vehicle crashed back to Earth, sending a tsunami of straw-colored dust into the air.

She didn't hear Storm make a single sound of pain, of fear, of complaint as the dry dirt of winter fell across her daughter like a sorely used, tattered blanket. That lack of sound worried Sydney almost more than anything that had come before it—particularly because she couldn't see if the four-wheeler had struck Storm, possibly unconscious or even unimaginably worse as she lay so very still on the ground.

Sydney prayed harder as she put on a final burst of speed.

When she reached the ATV, she dropped to her hands and knees, gasping in the dust-laden air as she tried to catch her breath. She heard Dune and Slade come to a stop behind her, but they were of no matter to her right now. She crawled closer to her daughter so she could get a better view, terrified to see and terrified not to see. And then all became clear.

Against all odds, she'd gotten her miracle. Storm's head—with long, blond hair covering her face—lay just an inch or so from the tail end of the four-wheeler. She hadn't been hit. Yet her daughter remained too pale, too quiet, too motionless. She appeared to be a rag doll tossed aside, landing with her limbs spread out at odd angles.

"Storm, I'm here. Mommy'll take care of you now." She reached forward to pull her daughter into her arms but felt a hand grasp her arm and stop her.

"Wait," Dune said. "We don't know the extent of her injuries."

"She's strong." Slade leaned over and turned off the ATV's sputtering engine. "Maybe she just had the breath knocked out of her."

Sydney gently pushed Storm's hair back from her face and saw freckles standing out in stark contrast against her too-pale skin covered by a light coating of fine dust. She felt her stomach churn in alarm as she put two fingers on the pulse point of Storm's slender neck. When she found a strong heartbeat, she breathed a sigh of relief.

At Sydney's touch, Storm blinked her eyes, appeared confused, and tried to inhale. She gasped, opening her hazel eyes wide in alarm as she struggled to recover her breath.

Sydney stroked her daughter's forehead to calm her. "I know it feels weird, but you'll get your breath back in a minute. You're okay. I'm here. Slade's here. Dune, too."

"You're safe," Slade added in his deep, comforting voice. "We're taking good care of you. You've got your own personal EMTs right here."

Sydney continued to stroke Storm's face gently while she watched anxiously as her daughter struggled to catch her breath.

Finally Storm inhaled, loudly rasping air into her lungs. She coughed several times as color returned to her face. She shuddered as she sat up, glanced wildly around, saw the ATV, and threw herself into her mother's arms, shivering and shaking all over.

"It's okay." Sydney cradled her close, rocking back and forth to comfort her just as she'd done when she was a baby. "You're safe now. All is well. You're safe."

Storm started crying, and soon tears cut a wet path through the dust on her cheeks. She twisted around and pointed toward the four-wheeler with a shaky finger. "I almost—like Daddy, gone—and never coming back and never trimming our Christmas tree and never putting up holiday lights and never surprising Granny with presents and never eating Uncle Slade's pecan pie." She hugged Sydney tighter and cried harder.

"At least she put my pie on a level with Christmas," Slade said in an attempt to ease the tension with humor, but his words fell flat as he shook his head in dismay. "Storm, I'll make you your own special pecan pie for Christmas."

She raised her head and looked at him with tear-swollen eyes. "For sure?"

"You know I'd do anything for my favorite niece, don't you?"

"I'm your *only* niece." Storm gave her usual reply

to their long-standing joke, lending a normal air to the abnormal situation.

"Now you're talking like my Storm." Slade glanced at Sydney and gave her a relieved smile.

Sydney nodded to let him know she appreciated his humor in helping to bring Storm back to her usual self. She continued to stroke her daughter's long hair, holding her close, murmuring comforting words as much for Storm's sake as for her own. The accident could have been so much worse. They were lucky.

"Good thing we're trained as EMTs," Dune said. "She looks shaken up, but I'd say it's nothing a little tender loving care won't cure. Still, we'd better take her to the clinic and get her checked out."

"Absolutely," Sydney agreed, holding Storm as if she'd never let her go. She simply couldn't bear the thought of anything bad happening to her daughter. Lots of folks took tumbles off ATVs, for one reason or another, but they usually got up, got back on, and went about their business. Right now, she didn't want Storm anywhere near a four-wheeler, but she knew that wasn't the right attitude. If you got bucked off a horse, you got back on, the sooner the better, or fear might paralyze you throughout life. Still, until a doctor pronounced Storm okay, she'd keep her away from ATVs.

Slade pointed toward Wildcat Road. "We'd better get her checked over, but the vet's closer than town."

"What? A vet?" Sydney shot her brother a quelling look before refocusing on Storm.

"It'd be quicker. I mean, I'd trust my body to Sue Ann Bridges," Slade said as he tried to explain his suggestion and faltered to a stop.

Sydney was so surprised at Slade's idea that she gave him a closer look. "Sue Ann's good, yes. But are you going to see her more often than is strictly necessary for our animals?"

Slade shrugged and glanced away. "I'm just saying she's an excellent vet, and she'd probably take a quick look at Storm."

"Why don't we just take Storm to the clinic and not put Sue Ann into an awkward position," Dune intervened in a conciliatory voice.

"Yeah," Slade quickly agreed. "I just didn't want to wait."

"Thanks," Sydney said to ease them past her brother's suggestion. He normally preferred flashy rodeo cowgirls, but maybe he was getting healed enough and past his bull-riding days enough that he was developing an itch to expand his horizons. She hoped that was the case, but she'd just wait and see. For now, she'd put Slade and his love life on a back burner. Storm needed her full attention.

"I don't want to go to the clinic," Storm said in a small voice. "I want to go home and go to bed."

"I'll take you straight home after the clinic."

Storm pointed with one finger of her small hand at the four-wheeler. "I won't ride that thing again. It's mean."

Sydney felt alarm bells go off in her head. This wasn't like her fearless Storm at all. "In time, I'm sure—"

"And no more horses." Storm put her arms protectively around her waist and shuddered, as if in horror. "They're big and dangerous. I could get hurt riding them."

Now Sydney was even more worried about her daughter. Storm was going straight from no fear to overwhelming fear. She didn't know the words to make this right, so she reached out to draw Storm closer to comfort her.

Storm shrugged away and quickly stood up. "You can't make me ride anything."

"Nobody's going to make you do anything that'll hurt you," Dune said in a calm, steady voice.

"That's right," Slade agreed. "Fact of the matter, I'm not much for riding myself these days."

Storm gave him a quick nod as she took a deep breath. "You get it."

"I do, too," Sydney said, standing up and brushing off her sadly stained and wrinkled dress. "We're here to protect you."

Storm tossed her long hair over one shoulder, sending out a cloud of dust. She walked over and kicked the ATV's front tire. "You can take that thing to the garbage dump."

"How about I keep it at my place for the time being?" Slade asked.

Storm cast a narrow-eyed look his way. "Okay. But it's mean. I wouldn't ride it."

Sydney reached out to Storm but dropped her hand to her side. She couldn't push or pull her daughter, not now, not till the fear ratcheted down to a controllable level. She pressed her lips together to keep from crying for Storm, wanting to make everything right but knowing it'd take time.

"It's okay," Dune said in a low tone and grasped her hand, twining their fingers together.

She glanced up at him and squeezed his hand to let him know she appreciated his comfort.

"Storm, how about we go into town and get you checked out," Slade said in his deep, rumbling voice. "Not that you need it, but moms will be moms, so let's give Sydney a break and reassure her."

Storm gave him a long, assessing once-over before she nodded slowly in agreement.

"After that, why don't you come down to the café and help me make pies? Would you like that?" Slade added.

"Or you can come back home," Sydney said, not wanting to let go of her child so quickly. "I'll make soup, and you can go to bed, or we can watch a movie—whatever you want to do."

"I'm not a baby just 'cause I was riding a mean four-wheeler."

"I know you're a big girl now," Sydney agreed, even as she felt as if she was losing ground in keeping her daughter safe.

"She might want to keep busy," Slade said in a gentle tone. "I know I did when I took a plunge off that bull."

"Bet I can make my own pecan pie." Storm thrust her chin out and her shoulders back.

"I don't doubt it a minute," Slade agreed.

Dune gave Sydney's fingers another squeeze, then stepped away from her. "Slade, if you'll get that ATV out of sight, I'll drive Sydney and Storm into town."

Slade gave a snort, sounding like an irritated bull. "She's my niece. I can take her to—"

"I know," Dune quickly agreed even as he inclined his head toward the four-wheeler. "But aren't you going to deal with—"

"That's right." Slade gave Sydney a look that silently asked if the plan was okay with her.

"Good idea," Sydney agreed, feeling shaky enough that she didn't want to chance driving into town. "Dune's got his big dually here."

"I'll lower the back seat so Storm can lie down on the drive to the clinic," Dune said.

Storm gave Dune a little smile. "I like your fancy pickup." She dusted off her jeans with the palms of her hands, sending dirt flying outward. She grimaced as she pulled a twig out of her hair. "Maybe I oughta get a shower first."

"Later." Sydney clasped her daughter's hand, feeling as if they were all getting back on track. "Let's go to the clinic. After that, we'll see how our day goes."

"I can tell you how it's going to go," Storm said, swinging their hands together. "I get a lollipop at the clinic, and then I get pie and ice cream at the café."

Sydney couldn't keep from chuckling in relief that Storm sounded much more normal. When Dune and Slade joined her laughter, she felt even better.

"Not funny." Storm gave them all a quelling look. "Don't you want to make a little girl happy?"

"I can see how it's going to go," Slade said. "She's going to milk this for all it's worth."

"It's worth a try anyway," Sydney added in her best mommy voice.

"You bet," Dune agreed with a wink at Storm.

Storm simply rolled her eyes at them and then took a step toward Slade's house up on the hill.

Sydney held her daughter's hand, feeling as if she never wanted to let her go, as Dune fell into step with them. Slade walked over to the ATV and sat down behind the wheel. She gave him a nod of encouragement, knowing they wouldn't see that vehicle again till Storm was ready for it.

As she passed the four-wheeler with Storm in tow, she felt a shudder pass through her daughter's body as if she were communicating her almost overwhelming fear and anxiety to her mother.

Sydney felt renewed heartbreak. Storm's new-found fear was as worrisome as her lack of fear. She needed to help her daughter develop steady confidence in her ability to handle life. But how was she going to do it? Maybe Slade was right. If Storm developed confidence in other areas — perhaps baking pies — maybe she would come to feel safe riding an ATV or horse again.

It was Christmastime. She had already received a great miracle. She hoped she didn't seem too greedy by praying for another one, but if she did seem greedy, that was okay, because she'd do anything to help her daughter.

For now, she simply needed to take care of Storm. She took another step toward Slade's house and yelped as pain suddenly radiated upward from the bottoms of her feet. She dropped Dune's hand, and then Storm's, so she could bend over and put her hands on her knees for support as she took short breaths, trying to control the discomfort.

She remembered how she'd kicked off her shoes and run across the pasture with no heed to her own safety. She must have blocked out her body's pain receptors until she knew her daughter was safe. Now she was paying the price as her feet screamed in protest at the abuse.

"What is it?" Dune put a hand on her back and leaned over her.

"Mommy?" Storm hunkered down and peered up at Sydney's face with her brows drawn together in worry.

"Are you okay?" Slade hurried over to them.

"Shoes." Sydney took shallow breaths that left little room for words. "Hurt my feet."

"I saw her throw off her shoes in the pasture, so she could run faster." Dune rubbed Sydney's back in comforting circular motions.

"She needs to go to the clinic, too." Slade glanced back up the pasture. "Who knows what she stepped on?"

"Is she bad hurt?" Storm patted Sydney's face.

"I'll be okay." She reassured her daughter as best she could at the moment.

"We'll get you a lollipop, too," Storm said.

"Thanks," she huffed against the pain.

"You're not walking another step." Dune gently lifted her with his strong arms and cradled her against his broad chest. "We're taking you straight to the doctor."

She didn't voice a word of protest at him taking charge. She simply tucked her face against his shoulder and gave a loud sigh of relief that she was no longer standing on her feet. For just a little while, she trusted she could lay her burdens in his capable hands.

"Maybe I ought to drive them to the clinic." Slade put his big hands on Storm's small shoulders.

"It might be better if you told your family and put up the ATV while we went to the clinic," Dune said.

"I'll need my purse. It's in the car," Sydney said. "And please don't forget my shoes. They're up—"

"Don't worry. I'll get them," Slade said. "You're right, Dune. Besides, I need to get into work. Just make sure these two want for nothing. And call if you need anything."

"Will do," Dune agreed.

"When you're done, meet us at the café," Slade added.

"Mommy gets pie and ice cream, too. Right?" Storm said in a no-nonsense voice.

"Right," Slade agreed as he clasped Storm's hand. "Now, let's get on up to the dually. I'll fix the back seat so you two can lie down and get comfortable."

"Thanks." Sydney took a deeper breath as the pain eased up in the comfort of Dune's strong arms. "And don't think about making Christmas plans without me. I'll be back in the saddle in no time at all."

Chapter 11

DUNE HAD WANTED SYDNEY IN HIS ARMS FOREVER, IT felt like, but he hadn't wanted her injured to make it happen. He hoped to hell she wasn't too badly cut or bruised on the soles of her feet. He was anxious to get her, as well as Storm, to the clinic and make sure they were both completely all right. Until then, tension rode him hard, as if he was on the back of a half-tamed horse.

He figured the only upside to their predicament was Sydney cuddled against his chest and dependent on him in a way he could never have imagined in all the time he'd known her. She'd been too strong, too independent, too sassy to let anybody get this close—particularly a cowboy with a yen for her.

Slade and Storm led him out of the pasture, through the open gate, and up to his dually. Fortunately, he'd left his pickup unlocked, and he always carried a couple of fleece blankets on the back seat just in case. Sydney felt a little too cool to the touch. He didn't want her edging into shock, so he'd wrap her in one of the blankets.

Slade opened the back door, pulled out the fleece, set it on the hood, and lowered the leather seat to make a flat, carpet-covered area. He lifted Storm and set her on the makeshift bed. He patted the top of her head, wrapped a blanket around her small body, made sure she lay down, and closed the door. He glanced at Dune, gesturing with his head to go around to the other side of the pickup.

When Dune got there, Slade already had the back seat door open, so the vehicle was ready and waiting for Sydney. Dune didn't want to let her go. He wanted to keep her safe and close forever. But he knew better. Safe was getting her quickly to the clinic. He gently set her down, making sure he didn't jar her feet, and took a quick look at her injuries. As far as he could tell, she wasn't terribly hurt. He felt a vast sense of relief, so he grabbed the other blanket off the hood of the dually, wrapped it around her shoulders, and squeezed her hand in comfort.

"All done." He shut the door, stepped back, and glanced at Slade.

"I'll pick up a pair of thick socks and athletic shoes at her place. I'll drop them off along with her purse at the clinic," Slade said.

"Thanks. She'll need them."

"And take it real easy on the drive out," Slade warned in a low voice. "It's bumpy as all get-out to Wildcat Road."

"Tell me about it."

Slade rolled his eyes. "It's just one more thing on the ranch that needs to get done, but not before Christmas."

"I hear you." Dune opened the driver's side door and looked back. "I'll take good care of them."

"You better, or you'll have the Duval and Steele clans both on your case," Slade said in a half-jesting tone.

"Trust me, that's the last thing I want, but more than anything, I want Sydney and Storm to be okay."

Slade gave a crooked smile. "They will be. I'd call this a minor blip on the road of life."

"Yeah." Dune nodded in agreement, and then he hesitated as he shared an unspoken moment of harmony with Slade that acknowledged they'd both spent way too many

long miles on bad roads that had brought them to this
time and place. Another acknowledgment of silent agreement was that their loved ones—women and children in
particular—were to be protected at all costs. In this day
and age, cowboys didn't usually come right out and say it,
but the instinct and training were as old as the hills.

"Right." Slade cleared his throat and moved back,
breaking the quiet moment of truth. "I trust you to take
care of them."

"I won't let you down." Dune stepped up, buckled in,
started the engine, and backed away from Slade.

He took it easy driving out of the ranch, not wanting
to jostle his passengers, but there was only so much he
could do on the rutted road. They didn't say anything or
complain in any way, so he tilted his rearview mirror so he
could look in the back seat. Sydney cradled Storm's head in
her lap as she gently stroked her daughter's long blond hair.

Oddly enough, the sight hit him in the gut. What
the hell was going on with him? And then he got it. He
wanted that kind of love and family in his life. He'd had
it growing up, but he'd considered it too confining when
he was big enough to compete on his own in rodeos, so
he'd become a rolling stone. After all this time, maybe
he'd rolled to a complete stop at the feet of Sydney
Steele—and her daughter, Storm.

First Slade. Now Sydney. He wouldn't have believed
it just yesterday, but he had to accept the fact that the
entire Steele family was drawing him into their orbit as
if he might be a wayward piece of cosmic debris looking
for a home.

He came to the cattle guard, eased across it, and turned
onto Wildcat Road. Finally, he could make some time.

He was more than ready to get to the clinic—not only for Sydney and Storm, but for himself. He needed to get his mind back on the situation at hand instead of flailing around like a fly caught in an East Texas sludge pit. He was helping out friends, nothing more, nothing less.

By the time he reached Wildcat Bluff Medical Clinic, he had his emotions in control and his priorities in order. He pulled into an empty parking spot away from the entry, so he had plenty of room for his dually. Fortunately, the place didn't look too busy, although it did a brisk business almost any time of the day.

He appreciated the community's hard work through benefits, donations, and grants to fund the clinic, a much-needed addition to the county. The simple red-brick building with a forest-green metal roof outlined by blinking red Christmas lights housed medical, dental, lab, and insurance personnel with more on call for emergencies. He figured Sydney already had her family records in order here, so it'd simply be a matter of getting her inside and in line to get help.

He stepped down from his pickup, opened the back door, and looked inside the cab. "How're we doing in here?"

Sydney smiled at him as Storm sat up with a big yawn. "Much better, thank you."

"Let's get you both inside and let them get to work on you."

"I don't think it'll take much." Sydney swung her feet over the edge of the seat toward him.

"Don't let Mommy walk!" Storm crawled around Sydney and flung her arms around him.

"It's okay. I'll carry her," Dune said. "How about I

lift you down to the ground, and then you walk in on your own two feet?"

Storm looked up at him and grinned mischievously. "If I do it, do I get two lollipops?"

"Storm, stop that," Sydney said with laughter in her voice. "It's one lollipop a visit, and you know it."

"But he didn't know it."

Dune chuckled as he picked up Storm, noticing how small and light she felt, and carefully set her feet on the asphalt. He turned back to Sydney, lifted her in his arms, thinking she wasn't all that much heavier than her daughter, and shut the door with his hip. He quickly covered the distance to the front door, and it slid open automatically to accommodate them.

Inside, Christmas music played softly over a speaker system. A few folks waited in colorful plastic chairs and glanced up at him from magazines and cell phones. He nodded in their direction while they gave him sympathetic and appreciative nods in return. He realized they viewed him as a father and husband taking care of his small family. He felt a sudden warm glow at the idea, but the feeling took him by surprise.

"Over there!" Storm tugged at his belt loop as she pointed at the check-in counter.

He walked over there and started to speak, but the woman sporting big blond hair and tight colorful scrubs jumped up from her chair.

"Sydney, heavens to Betsy, what have you gone and done?" She gave Dune the once-over, grinning as she did it. "And where did you pick up the hunk?"

He didn't say a word, not about to step into the middle of woman-speak.

"Ah, Linda, would you believe it? I found him in a pasture." Sydney patted Dune's shoulder. "Lucky me, huh?"

"Yeah, I'd believe it. You always did have all the luck," Linda said. "Where'd you say that pasture was?"

"I didn't say."

"Lucky—and greedy." Linda chuckled as she shook her head. "Guess you don't have a mind to share."

"Not today."

"In that case, I'll live in hope." Linda winked at Dune. "Cowboy, what can I do for you, or even better, what can you do for me?"

Dune sighed, not in the right frame of mine to flirt or tease, although that's obviously what was expected of him.

"Guess I'd better introduce you," Sydney said. "Linda Malone. Dune Barrett."

"Yum," Linda said. "I've read the books—you know, the *Dune* series."

"Never heard of them," he said through gritted teeth. "But it's good to meet you."

"That's what all the guys say."

"Linda, you're such a firecracker," Sydney said, sounding a little tense. "But give Dune a break. He's already had to rescue two ladies today."

"Want to go for a third?" Linda gave him another wink.

"As lovely as you are," Dune finally said, "I believe a third rescue will have to wait for another day."

"I'm always in need of rescue by a good-looking cowboy," Linda said. "Stop by any time, and I'll be ready."

Sydney patted Dune's shoulder again. "I wouldn't recommend it. There's not a guy alive who's safe once he gets in Linda's crosshairs."

"I've never heard a complaint yet." Linda patted her updo. "But let's reminisce about cowboys another day. Looks as if you need some help."

"And I need a lollipop." Storm held up her hand.

"First, she needs to see a doc," Dune said, trying not to sound impatient but knowing he'd missed the mark. "Storm took a tumble off a four-wheeler."

"Well, bless your heart." Linda looked down at Storm. "How are you feeling?"

"Once I get my lollipop, just fine."

"First, you see the doctor," Sydney said.

"They both need to see a doctor." Dune had had it with all the friendly chitchat. Sydney was in pain. Storm probably, too. "And soon."

"I'll get right on it." Linda looked him over again as she raised an eyebrow. "I just love to take orders from cowboys."

Dune gave up. A pretty, flirty gal like Linda thought she could have any guy she wanted any time she wanted him. And it was probably true. Maybe he'd even have fallen for her well-worn line if he'd wandered in here eight or nine months ago. But now? Linda didn't even warrant a flicker of interest—particularly not with Sydney snuggled in his arms.

"Linda, as much as I appreciate your appreciation of Dune," Sydney said in a voice suddenly gone cold as ice, "I guess I'd better warn you to stay away from him."

"Really?" Linda opened her eyes wide in surprise. "But I thought you were off cowboys ever since…well, for a long time."

"That's over," Dune said, leaving no room for discussion. "And she needs a wheelchair."

Linda's eyes opened even wider as she looked from Dune to Sydney and back again. "Okay. You got it."

Dune hugged Sydney tighter, feeling a burst of male pride. She had taken a strong, defensive position against a woman encroaching on her territory—namely Dune Barrett. Life didn't get any sweeter. His woman was defending her man.

And he was taking care of what he was coming to think of as his own little family.

Chapter 12

DUNE SAT ON A HARD, PLASTIC, UNCOMFORTABLE CHAIR tinted a bright orange as if to remind him that he'd left all the comforts of home…at home. Worse, he'd been left behind due to clinic rules and regs just because he wasn't actual family when Sydney and Storm were taken back to visit the medical team. That'd been a slap in his face, particularly since he'd been feeling like family and protective of them. They'd been reluctant to leave him, too, but there'd been nothing for it except to let them go this time.

Slade had already come and gone, giving Sydney her purse along with comfortable athletic shoes and padded socks. After that, Slade had hightailed it out to start cooking at the Chuckwagon Café. Dune had to admit they served the best country food in town.

Now he sat twiddling his thumbs like a lump on a log and avoiding the gaze of Linda, who made no attempt to control her avid interest in him. At least she wasn't flirting with him anymore, but he could tell she was hot to get the inside story on his relationship with Sydney. No matter. She was getting nothing from him, and he figured she knew it, but she'd surely pounce on Sydney when she came back out.

He checked his phone again, but nobody needed him, since he'd taken time off working on Cougar Ranch to help Sydney. Right now, he'd be happy to hear he was desperately needed to ride out and rope a wild bull that had broken through a fence and gotten out of his pasture. It'd be better than sitting, waiting, and worrying. He'd just have to accept that no news was good news till he heard different.

He fiddled with his phone as he let his mind drift back over the day, which felt longer than a month. He'd never spent so much time around Sydney outside of the intensity of fighting a fire. Now he liked her even better—maybe more than liked would be a truer assessment. They'd been through enough tribulation together to develop a bond that ran deeper than desire. He'd thought all he wanted was a quick roll in the hay, but that idea paled in comparison to what he wanted now. He hadn't ever thought to put down roots and raise a family in a strong community, but Sydney and Storm were fast changing his mind.

Galvanized by that revelation, he hit speed dial. He had business to take care of, and he wasn't letting any more grass grow under his feet.

"Now what?" Kent answered in a grumpy voice.

"About Sydney's calendar," Dune said.

"Not that again. We all figured if we stalled long enough, she'd run out of steam and time."

"Y'all are acting like a bunch of spooked yearlings."

"What? I thought you were on our side and were just going along with Sydney to get in her—"

"If I'm going to be Mr. December, the rest of you are going to fill in the other eleven months."

"Oh hell, you're not going to let this go, are you?"

"You volunteered to be the photographer."

"Yeah. But I didn't actually think we'd go through

with it. I just didn't want her chewing on me for weeks or months or however long it took for her to lose interest in a cowboy firefighter calendar, of all the damn things."

"She's doing it to help the community."

"I know, but there are other ways."

"Not this late in the game." Dune took a deep breath, deciding to put it all on the line for Sydney. "Okay. I'm calling in my marker."

"What!"

"Remember that time at the rodeo in Mesquite—"

"Don't remind me." Kent snorted over the phone. "You've really got it bad, don't you?"

"Might be. But that's not the point. She's put her life on hold to get this benefit up and running for the fire station. All she's asking is for twelve guys to take a few minutes and pose before a camera."

"My camera."

"Yep. You're first on my list to get onboard. Bottom line, she needs our help to set up a photo shoot at the fire station in the next couple of days and get the guys there. Hedy will help us."

Kent sighed long and loud. "I know I'm going to regret it, but okay. I owe you, and I owe Sydney, so I'll help."

"And mean it?"

"You've got my word," Kent said. "But you know we're going to end up owing every volunteer firefighter in the county."

"Let's get the Chuckwagon Café to donate barbeque and fixings to offset the grumbling and owing."

"That'd help."

"Do you think we can set up the shoot for this week?"

"Let me think. There are a few things going on that

can't be rescheduled, but give us four days, and we ought to be able to do it."

"Great. I'll let Hedy know our plans so she can help out." Dune hesitated, glancing around the waiting room, but there was no sign of Sydney or Storm. "Listen, I'm at the clinic right now."

"What's going on?" Kent's voice deepened with concern.

"Storm took a tumble off her four-wheeler, and Sydney hurt her feet rescuing her."

"How bad?"

"Basically, they're okay, but they're seeing the doctor right now to make sure all is in working order. I'm hoping they'll take it easy for a while."

"Good," Kent said with relief in his voice. "That's part of why you're so hell-bent on getting the calendar photos wrapped up."

"Yeah. I don't want Sydney worrying when she needs to be resting."

"Agreed. Guess the joke's over, and we better get down to business. You take care of Sydney and Storm. Let me get hold of Hedy, and we'll wrangle up the cowboys, one way or another."

"Let's plan to get the shots done in one day, okay?"

"You bet. The less time this takes, the better for everybody." Kent groaned out loud. "You know, folks in Wildcat Bluff County are never going to let us hear the end of this calendar."

"I know. It'll go from a joke about Sydney trying to corral us for photographs to us being the laughingstocks."

"Tell me about it," Kent agreed. "Oh well, it's for a good cause. I'll get right on it. Now, take care of those two ornery cowgirls, and I'll talk with you later."

"Will do." Dune punched off and tucked his cell phone back into the front pocket of his jeans, feeling satisfied that Sydney finally would get her photo shoot.

As he glanced around the clinic again, the front doors slid open, and a guy walked inside. He held his left hand wrapped in a green-and-white striped towel tight against his stomach, and he grimaced in pain.

Dune caught a whiff—faint, he had to admit, but still, he'd had enough experience to recognize the scent—of accelerant and burned flesh. He went on alert as the man walked up to Linda and spoke in a low voice. He strained to overhear the stranger but couldn't make out any words.

He well knew that lots of accidents involving fire happened all the time that didn't need firefighter intervention. This guy could've been grilling a steak and added too much fuel to the charcoal, or he could've been burning leaves and brush and got too close, or he could've been doing any number of other things that involved fire at a house or ranch.

But the man wasn't dressed for those types of accidents, at least not in Wildcat Bluff County. He wore a brown golf shirt with tan chinos and brown loafers. He looked city, not country. And he was about a six in a land of tens. He was medium all the way—hair, face, height, weight. Most folks would see him one minute and forget him the next, but he stuck out like a sore thumb to Dune.

He was no longer bored or disinterested in his surroundings. He wanted to know the name of the man, where he was from, what he was doing in the county, and the extent of his injuries. Normally, Dune wouldn't have any trouble getting that information, but he was at the clinic as a regular person, not an EMT or firefighter. He chafed at the restriction.

As he watched, the guy became more agitated and finally insisted in a loud voice that he had no insurance and was paying cash. Linda had him fill out and sign some forms, then the man turned around, spotted Dune, narrowed his eyes, and selected a seat on the opposite side of the waiting room.

Now he was doubly interested in the guy. Nothing about him added up, but on the other hand, maybe boredom and worry were making him cast about for anything to fill his mind. He'd discovered over the years that unexplained fires were frequently puzzles that could be solved if a firefighter looked at the evidence and trusted his instincts. Refinery fires and oil field fires were another matter since they were simpler in some ways and trickier in others, but he wouldn't be dealing with that type of fire around here. Hopefully, he wouldn't be responding to any fires at all, a particularly important gift to folks during the Christmas season.

Suddenly, Johnny Cash's "Ring of Fire" announced an incoming call from the fire station. He stood up and jerked out his cell phone. As he started to check his text message, he felt watched, so he glanced up. The stranger quickly averted his eyes, got to his feet, and headed toward the clinic's inner door where a nurse stood motioning for him.

Dune shrugged, figuring it was none of his business anyway, and instantly forgot the guy when he read Hedy's text, "Fire at drive-in. Booster ready. You available?"

He didn't even hesitate as he quickly typed, "On my way."

Now he was glad of Linda's interest in Sydney, so he could leave a message with her. He pocketed his phone and started toward her. He checked one more time for Sydney and Storm, and he saw them coming into the lobby. Sydney wore shoes and wasn't using the wheelchair. Storm looked more her usual self. He felt a surge of relief at the sight.

When Sydney saw him, she broke into a big smile just as Storm held up a lollipop.

He strode over and gave each a quick hug, then gave them a closer look. "How are you?"

"We're okay." Sydney pointed down at her feet and then at Storm. "A few bruises and scrapes for both of us, but nothing a little time won't heal."

"That's real fine." He couldn't wait any longer. "Are you good to go?"

"Yes. What's up?"

"I'll take you and Storm to the café, then I'm headed to the station." He started toward the outside doors.

"Wait!" Sydney pulled him to a stop in front of the check-in desk. "Is there a problem?"

"I just got a text about a fire at the drive-in. Hedy's got the booster ready, so I'm on my way."

"Not alone, you aren't," Sydney said loudly, tucking her handbag over an elbow as if readying for battle. "I'm riding shotgun, and I don't want to hear another word about it."

"I'll get somebody else to help. You need to take care of your feet."

"I might limp a bit, but I'm good to go."

"Hey, you two," Linda called as she stood up. "If there's a fire, you best get gone. I'll take Storm to the Chuckwagon."

"Thanks." Sydney knelt and hugged her daughter. "Is that okay with you?"

"Mommy, it's a fire! Go. Go. Go."

Sydney gave Storm a quick kiss on the cheek, waved to Linda, and grabbed Dune's hand.

He held on tight as he led her outside. He didn't doubt she'd keep up if they faced a bad fire situation, but he didn't want her to hurt her feet any more. Still, this was Sydney Steele. She'd ride hell-bent for leather to help somebody or save a structure and never mind her personal cost. He'd been there, done that. He understood the drive. It was okay when he put himself on the line, but he didn't want her doing the same thing. She was too precious to risk—yet he knew he could never say that to her, or he might insult her by suggesting she couldn't handle what she was trained to do. So he kept his mouth shut even as he worried about her.

He hit the remote on his dually, making sure the doors were unlocked before they got there. They parted at the tailgate, hit the front seats at the same time, and buckled up. He tore out of the parking lot and headed for Cougar Lane.

He glanced over at her, still hoping he might persuade her to stay home. "I can get somebody else to go with me."

"There's no time. Besides, I might as well get back on the horse now. With so much to do, I can't put my feet up any time soon."

"Did they take out any thorns?"

"A couple."

"Those are dangerous as all get-out."

"Tell me about it." She gave a slight shiver. "No way am I getting an infection in those wounds. I've got antibiotic cream and bandages at home. I'll change the nurse's dressing later."

"Good. But still—"

"It's not like the old days when a cowboy could lose a foot—or worse—if he stepped on prickly pear cactus and didn't get the thorns out fast."

"Bad memories die hard in cowboy country."

"True." She gave a big sigh. "Right now, I'm just worried about the drive-in. Is it the snack shed?"

"Hedy didn't say. I hope not."

She sighed even harder. "No matter how fast you drive, I doubt we can get there in time to rescue the structure."

"If nothing else, we'll contain the fire."

"Maybe we'll get lucky. If somebody saw smoke early on and called in the alarm right away, we might save part of the building. And don't forget the water sprinklers. Surely smoke would've activated them."

"Let's hope." He wanted her words to be true, but odds weren't in their favor, not with the drive-in isolated and unoccupied. He wished he'd already talked with Bert and Bert Two about security. Should've. Would've. Could've. No point in even going there. They'd simply make the best of whatever situation confronted them when they got to the fire.

"I guess there's no point in worrying ahead of time."

"True." He wheeled into the parking lot of the Wildcat Bluff Fire-Rescue Station. "You know where we go from here."

"Focus." She pretended to zip her lips shut with her fingertips. "I'm done with needless worry."

"We just changed hats. We're firefighters first and foremost now."

"Right."

Dune parked beside Hedy's van, then piled out of his dually on one side with Sydney following suit on the other. He jogged with her up to the open bay door and went inside.

Ash, the fire station cat, meowed from atop the hood of a booster with *Wildcat Bluff Fire-Rescue* emblazoned on the outside front doors. Ash appeared all decked out for Christmas with a big crimson bow tied around his neck that contrasted perfectly with his sleek silver fur.

"Hey, Ash," Sydney said. "As much as we'd enjoy you going with us, you'd better stay and take care of the station."

"Is that where he got to?" Hedy zoomed up in her power wheelchair, her silver hair worn in a single long plait dangling over one shoulder and sporting a crimson bow to match Ash's. "Come here!"

Ash immediately leaped down, sauntered over to Hedy, and jumped into her lap.

"Glad you two were nearby," Hedy said as she gave Sydney a closer look. "Land's sake, what are you wearing?"

Sydney rolled her eyes. "I didn't plan on fighting a fire today, so it seemed like a good idea at the time."

Hedy nodded in understanding, then pointed at the rig. "Gear's ready to go. As far as I know, that booster will get the job done. If not, let me know, and I'll send in the engine."

"Okay." Dune opened the driver's door of the booster that was basically a four-wheel-drive pickup with a flat-bed that carried a two-hundred-gallon water tank with a three-hundred-GPM pump and an automatic coiled hose.

"Hang on." Hedy wheeled around, disappeared in an open doorway, then returned with a gray sweat suit in one hand. "Sydney, you'd better change on the way."

"Thanks." Sydney grabbed the clothes and then opened the passenger door. "Is the snack shed on fire?"

"Don't know," Hedy said. "Moore Chatham discovered the fire and was wetting stuff down with a hose while he called me, so he didn't stay to chitchat."

"No wonder," Sydney said as she climbed into the rig.

"Does Bert know?" Dune asked.

"Yeah. Bless his heart. I called him with the bad news." Hedy shook her head in dismay. "They'll probably be there by the time you get there."

"Good. They'll have keys to everything." Dune stepped up into the booster.

"I let Billye Jo know, so you'll have whatever help you can use," Hedy called out. "And y'all, I got a call from Kent. We're getting that photo shoot all set for four days from now."

"Perfect," Sydney said.

"Thanks!" He slammed the door shut, started the engine, and glanced over to make sure Sydney was ready to rock and roll.

"Let's do it." She snapped her seat belt in place and gave him a decisive nod.

He backed out, hit the siren, and headed for Sure-Shot.

Chapter 13

As Dune barreled out of Wildcat Bluff, Sydney took deep breaths to try to slow her racing heart. It didn't help much. She felt trapped in a day without end—one that kept piling crisis upon crisis.

She'd started off the morning happy, feeling smart and chic in her vintage dress and driving Celeste, but life had quickly taken unexpected detours. Still, she was grateful for the day's blessings, because things could have been much worse. Storm was okay. She was okay. And Dune had turned out to be not only okay, but her champion as well. Now if they could only find a way to save the drive-in, she'd be as happy as when she'd begun the day.

She glanced down at her sadly wrinkled dress. She tried to brush off the dirt and stains but gave it up as an act in futility. Maybe the dress could be saved by the cleaners, but she wouldn't count on it any more than she would count on saving the pretty heels. Fortunately, when she'd shopped in Dallas, she'd found other vintage clothes, shoes, and accessories, so she was still set for Christmas.

At the moment, all she needed to do was focus on fighting a fire, but she couldn't be an effective firefighter in her tight dress. She'd taken off her panty hose and thrown the shredded nylons away at the clinic, so that wasn't a bother now. Hedy had come up with a solution for that issue, thinking way ahead of her.

She reached down and picked up the soft cotton

sweat suit from the floorboard and checked to make sure it was the right size. They kept an assortment of new T-shirts and sweats imprinted with the Wildcat Bluff Fire-Rescue logo at the station. She was doubly grateful for that foresight right now.

Still, it brought her face-to-face with a new problem. She wasn't overly modest, but she hadn't stripped down to her skivvies with a guy in a long time—particularly in a less-than-romantic setting such as a firefighter rig. And what if a pickup passed close by? She didn't much care for that thought at all.

"If it helps, I won't look," Dune said in a low, husky voice.

She glanced over at him, realized he knew exactly what she was thinking as if he had the code to her mind, and saw his lips twitch in amusement. "What if somebody passes us or—"

"They'll get a good show."

"It's not funny." She tried to sound stern, but she could almost see the humor in her situation.

"You might as well laugh, because you're not fighting a fire dressed in that getup."

She sighed, putting an extra oomph in it.

"It's not that I don't appreciate your clothes today, but maybe you didn't pick the best day to wear them."

"That's an understatement if ever I heard one," she muttered more to herself than to him.

He pointed down the road. "We're coming up to the turnoff for Sure-Shot pretty soon. If you don't want to moon the entire town as we drive down Main Street, you might want to get busy."

"I guess I better." She didn't know why she was so

reluctant to change clothes. Maybe it simply felt too intimate, too sexy to share with a guy who already had her
on edge. She wasn't usually a procrastinator, but right
now she needed a sharp push, so she gave it to herself.

She reached down and quickly untied her shoes. She
eased one sneaker off after the other, but she left on her
comfy socks covering her abused feet.

"You're starting with your shoes?" Dune sounded
disappointed as he drummed his fingertips on the steering wheel.

She tossed him what she hoped was a suitably quelling look, then shook out the gray sweatpants, probably
men's, because the length looked about right to handle
her long limbs. She eased her feet into the legs, grasped
the elastic waist, and quickly pulled the pants up under
her dress, shimmying to get them firmly in place so they
wouldn't later fall down around her ankles.

"What happened to my show?"

"You weren't supposed to watch."

"Guess I stretched the truth, didn't I?"

She rolled her eyes, then raised her arms and reached
behind her neck. She clasped the hook and eye with both
hands, fumbled the metal pieces before unhooking them,
and then slid the zipper down as far as she could make
it go from that angle.

Now came the tricky part. She leaned forward,
reached behind to the middle of her back, and unzipped
all the way. She quickly slipped down the bodice, pulled
out her arms, tugged off the dress, and tossed it on the
floor. She felt the air chill her bare arms and upper torso.
Hopefully, there'd be no passing pickups until she got
into her sweatshirt.

"What are you wearing?" He glanced over at her, appearing puzzled, then looked back at the highway.

"Slip." She'd been proud of finding pale green underwear, particularly pretty with delicate lace around the bodice and hem, to match her dress. Now she wished she'd waited to wear the entire outfit.

"A what?"

"These retro dresses require a full-length nylon or silk slip underneath if the dress doesn't have a lining. It covers my bra and panties clear to the bottom of the skirt." She felt as if she should be in a museum giving a tour instead of discussing her most personal clothing with a too-interested cowboy. At least it distracted them from the worry of not knowing what they'd find at the drive-in when they got there, so she went with the discussion.

"Why?"

"Without a slip, light might shine through the skirt and reveal...well, legs."

"And that'd be bad?"

"For the era, yes."

He chuckled as he gave her another quick look. "Are you sure that's the real reason? It's slinky and sexy as all get-out."

"You may have a point about there being several reasons for wearing a pretty slip."

"Don't doubt that I do."

"But I won't need it under sweats."

"You don't need it at all."

She rolled her eyes at his logic. Maybe once she had her body covered with a comfy sweat suit, he'd forget all about her slip. She raised her hips, grasped the slip's hem, and quickly pulled it upward, but the fabric tangled in her hair and trapped her arms above her head.

"Need help?" he asked in a voice gone deep and rough.

"Just drive," she mumbled against the soft silkiness of the slip, then gave a hard tug and jerked it free. She took a deep breath as she tossed her slip toward her dress on the floorboard.

"I'll take that." He quickly grabbed her slip in midair with one hand and tucked it by his side near the door—all while keeping the other hand steady on the steering wheel.

"Dune!"

He tossed a smile her way. "You said you didn't need it anymore. I could use some sweet memories. At night. In bed. With the lights out."

She felt the heat all this lingerie discussion with him was building in her ratchet up a notch, but she didn't want to admit it or she'd have to accept how he was truly affecting her, even on a firefighting mission. "You're just doing this to distract me from the drive-in, aren't you?"

"If you say so."

"I do."

He glanced back and forth between the road and her bra. "Now there's a sight for sore eyes."

She glanced down and realized that she wore nothing but a pair of gray sweatpants and a lacy vintage bra. Talk about getting distracted by him. She quickly shook out the sweatshirt, looking for the front.

"I've always wondered how they got that particular shape of women in the old movies. Now all is explained—stiletto bras go with stiletto heels."

She couldn't help but chuckle. She knew exactly

what he meant about those impressive double points under pinup girl sweaters, because she now sported a couple herself. "Like I said, I'm going vintage all the way, except for the panties, of course."

"That's not all the way," he said with a touch of humor in his voice. "You don't need panties, now do you?"

"I can't believe we're talking about my underwear." She did her best to sound huffy, but actually, if she wanted to admit it, he was upping her heat level with every single word. She lifted the sweatshirt, thrust her arms into it, pulled it down over her head, and slipped it into place. That ought to take care of any more lingerie discussion.

"You're teasing me, aren't you?" he said quietly.

She didn't look at his face, not wanting to see what he might be feeling about her that could turn her smolder into an outright blaze. Even so, she noticed that he gripped the steering wheel with both hands hard enough to turn his knuckles white. If truth be told, those fifties ladies knew quite a bit about more being less, or wearing provocative clothes while fully dressed to the nines.

"If you keep this up, you may need to hose me down before we start putting out the fire," he said in a tight voice.

"You started it. Not me." She turned partly in her seat to look at him, but that was a bad idea. He looked big and strong and oh-so-kissable. Plus, he'd been flirting with all this talk till she hardly knew which end was up. She needed to push back, so they didn't get into deeper water. "You're acting as if you've never seen a lady in her unmentionables."

"Unmentionables?" He gave a dry chuckle. "Not

hardly. I'm going to be mentioning them—for sure seeing them—the rest of my life."

She sighed, realizing she wasn't going to win this one and that she didn't even want to win it. If he'd been doing a striptease, maybe she'd need a douse of cold water, too. Whatever spark had ignited between them wasn't getting any cooler. It was getting stronger by the moment despite everything they were dealing with on so many fronts.

"Good thing you're dressed in sweats." He turned off Wildcat Road. "I'm not sure if Sure-Shot could handle you in primo retro."

"I'm not sure Sure-Shot can handle you either."

He slowed down on Main Street as a cowboy jogged across the street to the Bluebonnet Café. "You got anything in vintage for a man?"

She grinned, chuckling as she followed his thoughts. "I've got a fedora—and nothing else."

"That might do it."

"I suspect it just might." She caught his gaze and felt as if she'd somersaulted into the deep blue water of a hot spring that spiked her own internal temperature to a rolling boil.

He nodded, as if acknowledging their mutual heat, then stiffened and pointed down the road. Dark gray smoke spiraled high into the blue sky over the drive-in's location.

She inhaled sharply. All the banter and humor they'd been using to keep their worry—and much more—in check went right out the window. Now they were professional firefighters, and they'd allow nothing to get between them and containing or extinguishing the blaze.

Chapter 14

SYDNEY LEANED FORWARD, GRIPPING THE DASHBOARD, as Dune stepped on the gas at the far edge of Sure-Shot and rocketed down the street. She could only hope against hope that the snack shed was safe.

When they reached the drive-in, the front gates gaped open, and smoke billowed upward from somewhere deep inside the white fence. He slowed only long enough to get the booster safely through the open area, then drove around the side of the big screen, and the drive-in spread out before them.

"It's not the snack shed!" she gasped in relief.

He hit the steering wheel with the flat of his palm to emphasize her point. "So what's on fire?"

"Down there!" She pointed at several pickups that were parked haphazardly at the end of the horizontal parking rows on the far left.

"It's the trailer." He upped his speed as he headed down the outside lane toward the fire.

She reached behind the seat where Hedy had stashed firefighter gear and grabbed a pair of rubber boots that would protect her feet. As she slipped them on over her socks, she watched Dune turn onto the outer lane in back and drive across to a group fighting the fire.

She recognized them. Billye Jo and her daughter, Serena—blond-haired, blue-eyed cowgirls—held fire extinguishers. Moore sprayed water from a long hose, appearing tall and lanky in sweatshirt, jeans, and boots. Bert and Bert Two looked dressed for boot-scootin' instead of firefightin' in their rancher suits with fancy cowboy boots, but they both gripped the handles of shovels. At the sound of the booster, they looked around, and their faces split into big grins of welcome.

Dune stopped the rig on a dime and then backed into an optimal position to fight the fire. He switched off the engine, and then he folded Sydney's slip and set it on the dashboard.

She started to say something or try to take back her slip, but she decided they had bigger fish to fry right now. She opened her door, stepped down, and hurried over to the trailer. "How are y'all doing?"

"We're doing our best to control the fire," Billye Jo said, raising an arm and rubbing sweat from her forehead with her long shirt sleeve. "If Moore hadn't decided to check on the place, this building would be gone, and the fire might've spread to engulf the entire drive-in."

"Lucky break," Moore agreed, continuing to spray water from the hose.

"Moore, you've been our lucky charm since we decided to revamp the drive-in," Bert said.

"That's the truth of it," Bert Two agreed.

Dune walked over. "It looks as if the fire started in these old tires."

"We thought first to move them," Serena explained, "but we decided to wait for the experts in case we made matters worse."

"So we opted for containment," Billye Jo added.

"If I'm not mistaken, I smell accelerant. And those tires look like they've been piled against the front of the trailer." Sydney leaned over to get a closer view but stayed well back from the gagging smoke.

"I hate to say it, but you're right on both counts," Bert quickly agreed.

"And the smell was stronger when I got here," Moore said. "This fire was no accident."

"Here we go again," Bert groaned, banging the edge of his shovel against the asphalt with a clang. "I'm telling you, somebody's got it in for us."

"Too true," Bert Two agreed. "We called Sheriff Calhoun, but I bet it'll be just the way it always is when there's a fire on our property."

"Yeah," Bert said. "No evidence. No nothing. Except—"

"A ruined reputation," Bert Two finished for him. "Until we catch the culprit, folks are going to think we're setting fires to our own buildings for the insurance money or some other reason."

"I'm right sorry about your troubles," Billye Jo said. "But not everybody thinks that way."

"Thanks." Bert gave her a quick smile.

"I sure don't think that way." Moore nodded his head in emphasis.

"Most folks don't," Sydney reassured them, although she couldn't help but be aware that Moore, Bert, and Bert Two would all be under suspicion until concrete evidence pointed in a different direction.

"Let's let the sheriff deal with it," Dune said. "Right now we need to get these tires away from the trailer. Best thing to do is let them burn out on their own. We can clean up the mess that's left before Christmas."

"Maybe you'll end up with nothing more than smoke and water damage," Sydney added.

"That'd be good," Bert said, "but it wouldn't be much loss one way or the other."

"Trailer's mostly empty," Bert Two explained. "We used it to store building supplies, so there's probably not much left in there except a few two-by-fours."

"Glad to hear it." Sydney walked back to the rig and pulled out two shovels. She handed one to Dune.

"Thanks." He motioned toward Bert and Bert Two. "Let's use our shovels to move the tires back." He glanced around the group. "Everybody else, will you please step away from the trailer and give us some room?"

"Safety precaution," Sydney explained as she hefted her shovel. "Sparks might fly, or worse." As she took a step toward a burning tire, she felt a sudden sharp pain in her right foot. She grimaced and took a deep breath, but she wasn't about to let a little discomfort stop her.

"Sydney," Moore said in a gentle voice, "if you'll trade me the shovel for my hose, you'd be doing me a favor."

She glanced at him in surprise, cocking her head in question.

"I've put my life's blood into returning this drive-in to its glory days. I'm mad as a wet hen thinking somebody tried to destroy all my hard work. I want—I need to fight back with that shovel."

Sydney's estimation of Moore went up another notch. He was helping her save face while helping himself save the drive-in. She quickly traded the hose for the shovel, then walked over and turned the water off at the spigot. With the booster here, they didn't need a small hose anymore. She moved to the back of the rig, hit the automatic switch on the coiled hose line, and let it reel out enough to be effective but not get in the way.

As the guys cautiously shoved the tires away from the trailer, she held the rig's water nozzle. She'd spray if anything got out of hand. She felt blazing heat, took shallow breaths to hold back the horrible stench, and blinked hard to clear her eyes from the toxic smoke. She didn't like to see Dune or the others so close to such a nasty fire, particularly without much protection, but she knew without Dune telling her that he wouldn't put on protective gear while Bert and Bert Two worked in nothing more than tough cowboy boots and their regular clothes. But that should be okay, because the fire was already contained in the tires.

When they finally had the tires safely away from the trailer, Sydney assessed the damage. Black streaks rose up the side of the structure where the metal had buckled from the heat, but she didn't see evidence of a smoldering fire just waiting to ignite the entire building. Still, she wouldn't take a chance, so she glanced over at Dune, who was doing his own assessment.

"I'll spray the undercarriage and wet it down good, so there's no potential problem later," she said.

"Good. I'll pump and roll." Dune walked over to the booster, slid his shovel inside, and hit the switches to roll out more hose and pump water.

She pulled the fire hose around the burning tires, got down on her knees, and aimed the nozzle under the trailer. She sprayed water until it dripped down from the underside of the trailer and drenched the asphalt beneath it.

"Looks fine to me," Dune called.

She nodded in agreement, then stood up and sprayed

across the trailer's front, flat roof, and both ends. When she was satisfied with the containment, she glanced back at Dune and held up a thumb.

"I'll unlock, so you can check inside." Bert quickly stepped around a burning tire and up to the trailer. He pulled a set of keys out of his pocket, unlocked the double doors, and slid them open.

"You got electricity in there?" Dune asked.

"No," Bert Two said. "It's strictly storage."

"Let me grab a flashlight." Dune pulled a long metal light out of the rig and hurried over to the trailer.

Sydney stepped back, making room for him, and then looked around his shoulder as he lit the interior. "Bert, you're right. There's not much here."

"But we ought to douse it with water to be on the safe side," Dune said as he cast light all around the inside of the building.

"Do it. We've got nothing to lose." Bert glanced at Moore. "Do we?"

"Nope. Equipment's up in the snack shed storeroom."

"Okay," Bert Two agreed. "Shoot the water."

"Dune, if you'll keep holding the light steady, I'll spray." Sydney leaned inside the open door and positioned the nozzle.

"You got it," he agreed.

Sydney quickly sprayed from ceiling to floor, from wall to wall, and back again to make sure she left no spot untouched by water. Finally, she turned off the flow, then stepped back.

Dune switched off the flashlight. "I can stay and keep an eye on the place till these tires burn out, but I'd like to get Sydney back to town."

"That's okay." She shook her head to let him know that he didn't need to baby her because of her feet.

"I'll stay," Moore said as he set his shovel inside the rig.

"And you'll get paid for doing it." Bert turned to Dune and Sydney. "No point keeping the booster here. Somebody else might need help."

"Thank you," Bert Two said. "I know I've said it before, but Wildcat Bluff Fire-Rescue has been our savior over and over."

"Somebody'll be out later to take samples," Dune added. "Maybe we'll get lucky for a change and get enough evidence to lead to a conviction."

"I've got my fingers crossed, but I'm not counting on it," Bert said.

"Tell Hedy there'll be a donation check in the mail for fire-rescue," Bert Two added. "We sure do appreciate your fine work."

"Thank you," Sydney said. "The station can always use the help."

Bert looked down at his dusty boots, then back up at her. "You're friends with Hedy, aren't you?"

"Longtime friends."

"It being Christmas and all," he said in a low voice, "maybe you could persuade her to come and see my bluebird collection. I've got them all duded up for the season."

"It's quite a sight," Bert Two agreed, shaking his head as if in amazement. "Not to be missed."

Bert glanced around the group. "For that matter, you're all welcome. Billye Jo, Serena, Moore."

Moore stepped up close to Serena, looked down at his

scuffed cowboy boots, then up at her with a shy smile. "Anytime you want, I'll be happy to take you. I've got the new—well, new to me—pickup."

Serena gave Moore a considering look and then smiled at him. "I just might take you up on that offer."

He grinned from ear to ear. "I'll stop by the beauty station."

"There's an electrical switch that needs looking at anyway."

"I'll bring my toolkit."

"Thanks." Serena tucked a strand of blond hair behind her ear as she gave him a sidelong look.

"Any of you, just give me a heads-up," Bert said, smiling at the young couple with a knowing gleam in his eyes.

"Guess we'd all better get back to work," Billye Jo said. "All's well that ends well."

"Y'all go ahead," Bert said. "We'll stay here and wait for the sheriff."

"We'll head back to Wildcat Bluff and write up a report." Dune glanced around the area. "But so far there's not much to report."

"That's the way of these fires," Bert Two agreed. "Just do what you can do."

"One thing before we go." Dune gestured around the drive-in. "I noticed you installed a sprinkler system in the snack shed. Do you have other security features?"

"That's on our to-do list," Bert replied with a sigh. "We thought we'd put up surveillance cameras after Christmas at the Sure-Shot Drive-In. But now—"

"We'd better do it sooner rather than later," Bert Two finished for him. "We don't like the intrusiveness of it, but we'd be better off now if we had an image of the culprit who started this fire."

"We'll talk with Sheriff Calhoun about it when he gets here," Bert said. "And we'll follow his advice."

"Glad to hear it," Dune agreed.

"If you get any more trouble, don't hesitate to call the station." Sydney gave everybody a smile, then walked over to the booster, stepped up, and sat down inside.

Dune climbed up and sat beside her. "Are you doing okay?"

She took off her rubber boots and rubbed the soles of her feet through the thick socks. "I won't lie to you, I'm really glad to be sitting down again."

"Let's get you home where you can put your feet up."

"But there's so much to do."

"Remember, you've got help now." He squeezed her hand, then started the rig and put it into gear.

"Thanks." She gave a quick wave to the group, then reached down and pulled her cell phone out of her purse. "I'd better send a quick text to Hedy so she'll know everything is okay here."

"Good idea."

She let her fingers fly over the keys, reading as she wrote, "Drive-in fire under control. Not much damage. Headed back."

A moment later, Hedy texted back, "Good. See you soon."

Dune chuckled as he glanced over at Sydney. "That Bert never gives up, does he?"

She laughed at the thought. "It's Christmas, and the best present anybody could give Bert is a visit from Hedy."

"Let's put it on our to-do list."

"Okay. Let's do it."

As he drove by the snack shed, he pointed toward it. "There's something else I want to put on our to-do list."

"What?"

"Another dance with you."

She smiled, feeling warmth unfurl deep within her as she imagined slow-dancing in his arms again. "Only one?"

Chapter 15

As Dune drove toward Wildcat Bluff, he kept noticing Sydney's silk-and-lace green slip on the booster's dashboard. Neither of them had touched it. He kept expecting her to try to take it back, but she hadn't—at least not yet. She might as well not go there, because he planned to keep that little bit of her. It'd smell like her, remind him of her, and he could relive the way it had caressed all the naked curves of her body just the way he wanted to do with his hands.

He abruptly stopped those thoughts. He didn't need to go down that road right now. He hadn't acted like a professional firefighter about the slip, but that striptease she'd done in the rig had set him on fire. It was a wonder with his distraction that he'd been able to safely drive. A little more and he'd have had to pull over to the side of the road and stop the rig till she was completely covered up.

Truth of the matter, he'd thought it was her body that had pushed him into overdrive, but now he was beginning to believe it was every little thing about her. She was funny, brave, strong, and flat-out irresistible to him in so many different ways.

He thought about her earlier actions. Most folks would have gone home, put up their feet, and cradled their daughter to comfort them both after the four-wheeler accident. But not Sydney. And not Storm.

Instead, Sydney had gone off to fight a fire, and Storm's family had rallied around her. They were both chips off the old Steele block, and their family was nothing if not tenacious. No way around it, the more time he spent in Wildcat Bluff County, the more he admired and liked the down-home residents. What had been a pit stop was fast becoming a way of life.

He glanced over at her, wondering about her quietness. She'd laid her head back against the seat, as if too tired to hold the weight of it upright. He understood. It'd been a long, hard day. He wanted nothing more than to go home with her, take a hot shower with her, and get into bed with her. He'd even settle for a comforting snuggle, since it'd be with her. But that wasn't within the realm of possibility, so he set the thought aside for a later time.

"Do you want me to take you straight to your house?" he asked as he refocused his thoughts. "Hedy'll have the station's bay door open since we let her know we're on our way, but we could swing by your place first."

"I doubt that'll work for me. I need to pick up Storm at the café before I go home."

"Tell you what, I can leave the rig at the station, then I'll drive you wherever you want to go in my pickup."

"Thanks." She raised her right hand and covered a yawn. "But I don't want to put you out any more than I already have today."

"It's no trouble."

"Sure it is, but I'm tempted to take you up on your offer."

"Do it then."

"Slade can get away from the café to help me."

"No point in taking up his time when I'm ready, willing, and able to transport you." He glanced over at her again to see her response as well as hear it.

She rolled her head to one side, looking at him as she smiled slightly. "You've been a rock today."

"You'd do the same for me."

"You name it. I owe you."

"You don't owe me a thing. I'm glad I could help out."

"Let me check in with Slade and see how Storm is doing." She reached down and pulled her phone out of her purse. "Oh, look, Slade sent a text."

"What does he say?"

She swiped her cell screen and then read aloud, "Storm and I are at your place. You okay?"

"Bet that means Storm is fine."

"I won't know for sure till I see her, but it sounds as if everything is under control." Sydney hesitated a moment, staring at her phone. "It'd be easier for them if I take you up on your offer."

"Let's make it easy on them."

"All right. I don't think there's a big rush to get there. Let's go back to the station first. Somebody else might need the booster."

"Okay."

"I'll text Slade we're on our way and the drive-in is all clear."

"Sounds good to me."

Dune felt a sense of relief to know Storm was stable enough to go home and wait for her mom. He was also glad Sydney had accepted his offer. Slade didn't have any business getting out and bringing his niece with him to pick up Sydney, since it'd only cause unnecessary stress and trouble. It'd also be easier on Sydney for him to take her straight home.

Out of the corner of his eye, he noticed that she finished her text, put her phone in her purse, and started putting on her shoes. For the moment, all was right in the world, so he pushed down the accelerator to hurry them home.

A little later, he turned onto Cougar Lane and pulled into the parking lot of the Wildcat Bluff Fire-Rescue Station. The last of the dying sun bounced golden rays off the windshield of his pickup parked beside Hedy's van with its transparent, colorful Santa Claus stencils on the back windows. As he'd anticipated, the bay door was open, so he drove inside and killed the engine.

Hedy gave him a wave from her wheelchair before she pushed the button to lower the bay door.

As he turned to look at Sydney, he picked up her slip and folded it into a smaller shape.

"You aren't giving that back, are you?"

He grinned, knowing she knew he was teasing her. "You said you owed me something. Why don't I take this as payment?" He tucked her slip into his front pocket.

"Okay," she said, drawing out the word as if in thought. "But you owe me something in return."

"What?"

"I'll let you know."

He chuckled as he opened his door. "I'm happy to owe you. Maybe I'll come up with an idea on my own."

She laughed as she shook her head. "I'd better not leave it up to you. No telling what you might want to give me."

He stopped, looked back, and clasped her hand. "There's a lot I want to give you if you'd let me."

She smiled, hazel eyes twinkling with special warmth as she squeezed his hand. "First things first."

"Right."

"Hey, you two," Hedy hollered. "Time's a wastin'."

"We'll pick this up later," he said, letting go of her hand.

She gave him a quick grin, picked up her purse, tucked her dress inside, and stepped down from the booster.

He took a deep breath as he felt her slip like banked fire in his pocket, threatening to ignite at any moment. He forced that thought from his mind as he jumped down from the rig and shut the door behind him.

He walked around the front of the booster and saw Sydney reach down to give Hedy a hug.

"I've got good news for you," Hedy said. "Kent and I have been on the phone, corralling our cowboy firefighters."

"Did you actually get them all to agree to a date—again?" Sydney asked, sounding hopeful.

"Did you ever doubt me? Thursday at nine. We gave them time to finish ranch chores before showing up here, all spiffy." Hedy gave a sharp nod of her head, chuckling. "I told them to 'be here or be square.'"

"I bet that lit a fire under them," Dune said with a laugh.

"Nope," Hedy disagreed, chuckling. "I don't think that retro phrase meant a thing to them, but who cares? They'll be here."

"Thanks." Sydney gestured toward Dune. "He'll be here to help us, too."

"Even better." Hedy raised an eyebrow at Dune, cocking her head to one side as if considering the implications of his actions in helping Sydney.

He grinned, letting Hedy know he knew exactly what she was thinking about his volunteer work. "I'm Mr. December."

"Hot dog," Hedy teased, fanning her face with one hand as if he was too hot to handle.

"And I'm taking some time off work to make sure these Christmas events come off without a hitch," he explained.

"That's right generous of you," Hedy said. "I hope you get a little something for all your trouble."

He grinned even bigger. "I suspect I will."

"Anyhow," Sydney added, "now that the drive-in fire is taken care of, we can move forward on the calendar."

"Glad all's well that ends well," Hedy said, "but I'd feel a whole lot better if Sheriff Calhoun caught that arsonist before somebody gets hurt."

"Me too," Sydney agreed. "I bet Bert and Bert Two wish it even more than us."

"They've had their share of trouble. That's for sure," Hedy said.

"Bert invited you over to see his Bluebird of Happiness collection. *Again*." Sydney gave Hedy a sassy grin. "After all, he bought them all from you at Adelia's Delights, so you just might finally go over and see them."

"He invited us all," Dune added. "Bert Two said at Christmastime, the collection is well worth seeing."

Hedy shrugged her shoulders. "I'd think summer with bright sunlight would be the time to see all that pretty blue glass sparkle."

"Oh no," Sydney disagreed. "It seems Bert dresses up the bluebirds or puts tinsel around them or some such thing for Christmas."

"Dresses up the bluebirds?" Hedy appeared shocked as she looked from Sydney to Dune and back again. "I can't imagine such a thing, or where he'd get the time to do it."

"Maybe it's not dresses." Dune tried to make the blue-birds all dressed up for Christmas sound more reasonable, even though he definitely agreed with Hedy's opinion.

"I hope not," Hedy said in a clipped tone. "Anyway, where would he get dresses or ties or aprons or whatever to fit the bluebirds?"

"It's probably just regular Christmas decorations like we all wear." Sydney pointed toward Ash as he walked out of the back room, still wearing a big red bow around his neck. "But you've got to admit, we're curious now, aren't we?"

"Yeah, I'm getting there." Hedy glanced at Ash and held out her hand. She wiggled her fingers, and he quickly leaped onto her lap. She stroked his sleek silver fur for a moment. "I may finally have to go over to Bert's place and see all those bluebirds, or I'll never hear the end of it."

"You'll make Bert's Christmas if you do go." Sydney leaned over and ran the palm of her hand down Ash's back. "You could take a pie or cookies when you go, so you two could share a snack."

"Just listen to you." Hedy gave her a mock frown. "I'm about to get enough of your matchmaking ways."

Sydney laughed, throwing back her head in delight. "Go ahead and admit it. You're kind of sweet on Bert, now aren't you?"

"Not a bit of it." Hedy zipped her motorized wheel-chair back. "Why don't you two get out of here and let me take care of business?"

"Okay," Sydney agreed. "I want to get home to Storm. But please say you'll at least think about making Bert a happy man this Christmas."

Hedy gave her a wink. "I'll think about it. There, I've said it, so be off with you. And give Storm a kiss for me."

Sydney gave a little wave, then turned to Dune with a smile.

"I haven't got any bluebirds—" he started to say.

"Don't even go there," she interrupted as she slipped her bulging purse up over the crook of her arm.

Hedy chortled behind them. "Hey, Dune, I can fix you up real quick with a bluebird collection."

"Thanks. I may need it." He gave Hedy a knowing look before turning back to Sydney.

"Maybe you ought to go see Dune's bluebird collection after he gets one," Hedy said. "I bet once he gets done, they'll be dressed up like cowboys and cowgirls."

"I doubt he'll ever have a bluebird collection," Sydney insisted, chuckling.

"I bet he can come up with some kind of collection real fast if he puts his mind to it," Hedy added. "And there are always bluebirds in my store."

Sydney grabbed Dune's hand and tugged him toward the door that led outside. "You win. No more collection talk. And, Hedy, I'm done trying to get you to see Bert's bluebirds, but why don't you at least take pity on him?"

Hedy grinned as she waved goodbye. "Why don't you do the same thing?"

Dune turned back and gave Hedy a conspiratorial look before he followed Sydney out of the station where night was quickly falling and a few stars were twinkling in the sky overhead.

She released his hand and whirled around to look at him. "Hedy knows just how to get everybody's goat, doesn't she?"

"You did push her a little hard about Bert, so naturally, she came back at you."

"Yeah, maybe so. But it's for her own good. And his."

"She's pretty observant about folks—like us." He gave Sydney a long, slow, up-and-down perusal. "How about you show me your vintage lingerie collection? It'd be for my own good."

"And mine?" She grinned as she put her hand in his pocket and fingered the soft fabric of her slip. "I guess I'd better invite you over some time, hadn't I?"

He groaned, feeling heat surge through him. If she went any lower or tugged any harder, she'd know exactly how much she affected him, and in exactly what way. Maybe that'd be good. Maybe not. For now, he caught her hand, lifted it, and placed it over his heart. "Let's go home."

"I'd like that. I'd like it a lot."

When she glanced up at him with a soft, searching look in her big hazel eyes, he couldn't resist the temptation of setting his mouth to her soft pink lips. She tasted of honey and tangerine—sweet and tart and totally delectable. As he nibbled teasingly across her mouth, he felt a surprisingly warm breeze kick up. He heard the scatter of crisp, dry winter leaves as the sudden whirlwind danced around them, cocooning them in their own private little world.

He deepened the kiss, surging into her mouth, drawing her closer, driving their emotions higher and higher. He could almost hear the crackling of fire as their combined heat combusted into flames, but it was surely the leaves whipping around them. When she moaned and trembled against him, he felt his own body shudder in response. He wanted more, so much more, but now was not the time.

He raised his head to look at her. "As much as I want to continue this," he said in a deep, rough voice, "I'd better get you home."

She nodded in agreement, rubbing her arms with both hands as if suddenly cold now that she was no longer close to him.

"But I want a rain check on seeing your lingerie collection."

"Is that what you want for Christmas?"

"That's what I want to see you *wear* for Christmas."

"Nothing else?"

He reached out and rubbed his thumb across her lower lip, now plump from their heated kisses. "That'd just be the appetizer."

Chapter 16

A few days later, Dune pulled up in front of Sydney's house after another long day of getting things ready for Christmas at the Sure-Shot Drive-In. He'd been quiet on the drive back from Sure-Shot, letting her catch a few winks of sleep.

He had no idea how she'd have managed all the coordination for the promotion, parade, and vendors on her own. Fortunately, they'd been able to make their headquarters in the snack shed and pick up food at the Bluebonnet Café while they pulled much of it together. Slade had been a big help taking care of Storm while they worked long hours. For the moment, they'd caught up enough that they could catch their breath.

He glanced at two tall, black wrought-iron vintage gas lamps that cast light across the front lawn. He parked beside Celeste and a shiny red four-seater ATV, a style that, fortunately, didn't appear too similar to the one that'd thrown Storm for a loop. He figured the four-wheeler belonged to Slade, since it had *Steele Trap Ranch* written in Western curlicue lettering across the hood.

Sydney's home looked ready for Christmas. Red-and-green light ropes twinkled from the tire swing, the oak tree's broad trunk, the top of the porch railing, and along the peaked roofline of the old farmhouse. A soft yellow porch light emphasized the large crimson-and-gold wreath on the front door.

He turned off his dually and glanced over at Sydney. She'd leaned her head back against the seat and closed her eyes, obviously feeling the effects of another busy day. He wanted to kiss her and make it all better, for her as well as himself. Even more so, he'd like to take her to his place. Still, she belonged here on her family spread with her loved ones. Storm was doing well but still feeling the effects of her ATV spill. Sydney had stayed off her feet the last few days, so she was doing better, too. All in all, they were on course to make the holidays special for lots of folks.

Sydney took a deep breath, yawned behind her hand, and glanced over at him, looking a little sleepy, a little relaxed, a little vulnerable. When she gave him a small smile, he felt the heat he'd experienced before surge through him. Suddenly, he wanted nothing more than to throw out his best of intentions, take her back to Cougar Ranch, and join her on the narrow bed in his cowboy cabin.

"Here already?" She sat up, loosened her shoulders with a shrug, and stared outside the truck. "It's pretty on the ranch at night, isn't it?"

"Sure is. And it looks like your fireplace chimney is ready for Santa."

"I'd just as soon he comes in through the front door, so he doesn't make a sooty mess all over my floor."

"Guess that could be a problem." Dune reached over and squeezed her hand. "Let me walk you to your door, then I'll get out of your hair."

"You're not in my hair, but I do need to go inside. I'm anxious to check on Storm, although I'm sure Slade has been taking good care of her."

"I don't doubt it for a minute."

She pushed loose strands of blond hair back from her face. "It's been quite a few days, hasn't it?"

"That's an understatement if ever I heard one."

She nodded in agreement. "Thanks again for all you've done."

"I'm glad to be of help." He leaned toward her, wanting at least a goodbye kiss, but he abruptly stopped when the front door squeaked open and Christmas music flowed out into the night.

"Hey, you two, get on up here," Slade called out in a deep, loud voice as he loudly thudded across the porch's wooden floor.

Dune abruptly felt like a teenager caught bringing his girlfriend home too late. "I didn't know you had a curfew."

She chuckled, shaking her head. "That's what having a big brother gets you. I can't tell you the number of times he's driven off guys who might've come back a second time."

"Nobody's driving me off." He gave her a hot—if short—kiss that Slade couldn't help but see from his stance on the porch.

"You do like to live dangerously, don't you?" She caressed Dune's cheek with the palm of her hand.

"If that's what it takes to keep you in my life, then yes, I do."

She leaned over and kissed him, making it long and steamy. "That'll give Slade something to think about."

"And me, too." He cocked his head to one side, contemplating how leaving her was going to affect him. "Guess I won't get much sleep tonight."

She gave him a sensual smile before she leaned down and picked up her handbag. "And why not?"

"After that kiss? You know why not."

"But what about—" she started to say, but she was interrupted by a loud knock on her window.

"Keep it up, you two, and you'll steam the windows," Slade said as he pulled on the door handle.

Dune quickly unlocked the doors, then watched as Sydney got out and joined her brother. He didn't know what to expect from Slade, but he was prepared for anything—even trouble. He opened his door, stepped outside, and walked around the front of his truck.

Slade drew his eyebrows together in a frown as he gazed at Dune. "Do I have to give you the talk about respecting my sister?"

"Oh, Slade!" She slapped her brother's broad chest with the flat of her hand. "We are way past you trying to intimidate guys."

He grinned, white teeth gleaming in the lamp light. "It's about time." He thrust out his big hand to Slade. "Give me a shake. I'd pay you to take her off my hands, but here you are doing it for free."

Dune shook Slade's hand, chuckling at the cowboy's teasing words and feeling a surge of relief that they weren't going to end up in a fight.

"Slade, stop it." Sydney snagged Dune's arm and tugged him toward her. "Nobody's up for your jokes. We're tired. And my feet hurt."

"Well, come on inside," Slade said. "I've got hot cider and gingerbread that'll fix you up."

"Thanks." Dune meant the word in several ways, because he caught the look in Slade's eyes that said he wanted his sister to be happy, even if it meant a drifter of a cowboy making that dream come true. Dune knew Slade would be watching out for his sister's welfare, and he didn't plan to give any room for complaint, because he respected Slade, and he was committed to giving Sydney the best he had to offer.

For a long time now, he hadn't given anything to anybody. But maybe—just maybe—the path to his personal happiness and well-being was to make life a little better for others. In any case, he was well down the path of happiness with Sydney, and he had no intention of turning back.

"By the way, Kent and Hedy double-teamed me on the photo shoot," Slade said in his deep voice. "Guess we'll all have to show up now."

"It's about time." Sydney gave him a light punch on his shoulder.

"And I talked with Granny. The Chuckwagon is donating a big barbeque feed to ease the pain of us getting caught on camera with our pants down."

"You cowboys better keep your pants on!" Sydney put her hands on her hips as she frowned at her brother. "There'll be no mooning the camera at my photo shoot."

Dune and Slade both broke into laughter at her reaction.

Slade raised his hands in surrender. "Okay. We'll be good—or we'll try to be."

"You better be, or I'll sic Hedy on you."

"Oh no, please not that," Slade said in mock horror, even as he continued to chuckle.

"Okay," Sydney agreed. "But you've been warned." She gave each guy a quelling look, then started for the house.

By the time they all tromped up to the floor of the porch, Storm stood in the open doorway, hopping from foot to foot in obvious impatience.

"Mommy!" Storm flung her small body—dressed in a bright red onesie with a green elf embroidered on the front—into Sydney's arms.

Dune watched the incredibly strong connection between mother and daughter, and he felt warmth blossom and expand in his chest. *Love*. He'd been pondering one type of love between a man and a woman, but here was another kind just as powerful or maybe more powerful between a parent and a child. He understood, because he felt as protective and concerned about Storm as he did about Sydney.

He glanced over at Slade, who was watching him, understanding of the situation dawning in his hazel eyes.

Slade quickly glanced away, as if he'd glimpsed an emotion too intimate, too vulnerable to be shared with another person, particularly a cowboy. "Hey, folks, let's get this train chugging into the station. Cider and gingerbread await us cowpokes."

Storm giggled, then pushed away from Sydney to look up at Slade, putting her small hands on her narrow hips. "I get to be the caboose!"

"Okay. I'll be the engine." Slade pointed at Sydney and Dune. "They're dining and sleeping cars."

Sydney grinned at Dune, holding out her hand. "I take dining, so that makes you sleeping."

"Suits me." He clasped her fingers, enjoying the fantasy of one big, happy family. He'd never have thought it before, but now he realized just how easily he could want this type of fun on a permanent basis.

Slade stepped close to the door and held out his hand. Sydney grasped it, still holding Dune's hand. He looked behind and saw Storm already in place as the caboose. She gave him a shy smile and held up her hand with total trust. He felt warmth expand in his chest again. He silently vowed never to do anything that would break this little girl's trust in him. He gently grasped her small, soft hand, and she gave him a wide, happy grin.

"Choo! Choo!" Slade called out in front. "All aboard the Steele Express, bound for the best Christmas treats in the whole wide world."

"Choo! Choo!" Storm responded in a high, sweet voice.

"All aboard!" Sydney chimed in with the others.

"Choo! Choo!" Dune added, not feeling like as big a fool to say it as he'd thought he would now that he was drawn into their family fantasy.

He stayed right up with the others as they choo-chooed their way across the living room floor of glossy oak to the sound of Gene Autry singing "Here Comes Santa Claus" softly in the background.

Dune got a quick impression of decorations that included flowery chintz, camel-back sofa with aqua wingback chairs in front of a redbrick fireplace where five decorative stockings hung on the mantel. For a moment, he wished there was a sixth stocking for him, but he wasn't part of this family, so that wasn't even in the realm of possibility.

He happily followed the enticing scent of fresh-baked goodies into the updated country kitchen with white appliances, glass-fronted upper cabinets, and wallpaper filled with sunflowers.

Slade stopped their train beside a battle-scarred

golden oak table with eight spindle-back chairs nestled around it. A red silk poinsettia floral arrangement with three red candles took up the center. On one end, some-one had placed poinsettia paper plates, napkins, and plasticware, along with a large crystal plate holding big chunks of dark-brown gingerbread stacked high in the shape of a pyramid.

"Steele Station," Slade boomed out. "Exit now or forever hold your peace."

"That's not how it goes, Uncle Slade," Storm com-plained, sticking out her tongue at him.

"I'm the conductor, so I say how it goes." Slade glanced back with a big grin at the caboose. "If you want goodies, you better exit now."

Storm dropped Dune's hand and rushed over to the table. "I'm starved for something yummy."

"Guess you don't include broccoli in your assessment of yummy?" Slade asked with a laugh.

"Broccoli isn't even food." Storm reached for a piece of gingerbread.

"Mind your manners." Sydney gave Dune's hand a squeeze before she stepped toward her daughter. "Tonight we're going to sit down at the table and eat like ladies and gentlemen."

Storm screwed up her face, frowning. "Do we have to?"

Slade chuckled as he walked over to the cooktop where fragrant steam rose from a big stainless steel pot. "I wouldn't argue with the dining car, she might close the kitchen."

"Right." Storm quickly sat down and smiled sweetly up at her mother. "Please, may I eat?"

Slade laughed harder as he picked up a ladle and

started filling big red mugs with apple cider. "Acorn didn't fall far from the tree, did it?"

Sydney joined his laughter as she rolled her eyes at Dune. "Would you care to sit, Mr. Barrett?"

"Thank you," Dune said, joining the game. "I'd be delighted to share a light repast with all of you."

"Repast?" Storm squinted at Dune, as if trying to bring him into focus. "How about sharing some food?"

"That's what he said," Sydney explained with a chuckle. "Repast means food."

"Oh." Storm glanced mischievously around at them. "One word for one thing is good enough for me. I don't know why grown-ups have to make life harder with broccoli and too many words."

Dune couldn't keep from chuckling along with Sydney and Slade. "I've got to admit, Storm, you make a really good point."

"I do?" She looked taken back by surprise—as well as pleased as punch.

"Yep." He glanced at Sydney, who was staring at him. "Sometimes we make life way more complicated than it needs to be."

She nodded, as if understanding that he was talking about them.

"Out of the mouths of babes." Slade set four mugs of cider on a red tray embellished with a big Santa Claus face. He carried the tray over to the table and set it down beside the gingerbread plate.

"Thanks," Sydney said. "Everything looks wonderful."

Slade sat down beside Storm and gave her a wink. "Do you think your tummy can handle more after that pecan pie?"

"Bring it on," Storm said, chuckling. "My tummy can handle anything you can make in a kitchen."

"Big words from a little girl." Slade set a mug in front of her and then set two mugs on the table in front of the chairs opposite him.

Dune pulled out those two chairs, then stepped back so Sydney could sit down first, letting her know that he could play the cowboy gentleman in her home just fine and dandy.

"Before long, she'll be a big girl." Sydney sounded wistful as she gave Dune a thank you smile for pulling out her chair. She quickly sat down, picked up her mug, and cradled it between two hands.

"Yay!" Storm grinned from ear to ear. "Big girl means I get to eat twice as much."

"She's got a good point," Dune agreed as he sat down, enjoying the sassy little girl who was fast finding a way into his heart.

Slade set pieces of gingerbread on four plates, then passed them around with forks and napkins. "Eat up, folks. There's always more in the Steele kitchens."

Dune took a bite and then nodded his head in appreciation. "Slade, you sure know how to cook."

"I helped make it," Storm said, stuffing a big piece into her mouth.

"She was a great help." Slade gave Sydney and Dune a considering look, and then he nodded at them as if reaching a decision. "Storm, your mom's going to be busy tomorrow working on the benefit calendar. I'm thinking we might saddle up a couple of horses and ride the range. How about it?"

Storm dropped her fork and stood up fast, screeching

her chair across the floor as she backed away from the table. "Not me! I told you, no more horses or four-wheelers."

Slade raised his eyebrows in surprise, quickly setting down his fork while he looked questioningly at Sydney as to how to go forward with Storm.

Dune glanced from one to the other, realizing they didn't know how to reach Storm at this point. An idea popped into his mind. He hoped he wouldn't be stepping out of line if he suggested it, but he couldn't stand to see a little girl frozen in fear. "Storm, how are you at roping and tying?"

She twisted her hands together in an agitated motion. "Not so good yet."

"I've done some roping and tying in my day."

"You have?" She edged toward him, rubbing her palms against her onesie as if to still her worry. "Are you any good?"

"I won a few buckles and some other stuff." He glanced at Sydney, and she gave him a subtle nod to go ahead with his line of thought.

"Me too." Storm suddenly smiled at him, but then frowned as worry returned to her hazel eyes. "But not now. It's no good without my pony."

"No need for a horse," Dune said with conviction. "If we had a goat-tying dummy and goat rope, I could show you a few tricks. Maybe we could practice together."

Storm brightened, giving him a bigger smile. "I got a goat-tying dummy last Christmas. And I got pink goat rope, too!"

"She hasn't used it much yet," Sydney explained with

a nod toward her daughter. "She's just now getting big enough for the dummy."

"I'm plenty big now." Storm puffed out her small chest.

"Dune and I can surely make time to practice goat tying," Sydney said.

"Yay!" Storm ran around the table, gave Dune a big hug, then plopped back down in her chair.

"Thanks." Sydney squeezed Dune's hand under the table. "You came up with just the right thing at the right time."

"You said it," Slade agreed. "We all need to pull together for family at Christmas."

"I'm glad to help spread a little cheer." Dune finished off his gingerbread, then took a sip of cider.

Slade looked from one to the other, cocked his head as if in thought, and abruptly stood up. "Tell you what. I bet you two need to make more plans for the calendar and Sure-Shot tonight. Why don't I take Storm home with me? I'll take her down to the café early tomorrow, and that will leave us free for the photo shoot."

"That's thoughtful," Sydney said, "but Storm might want to stay here with me."

"Storm," Slade said, "do you want to go home with me and cook popcorn in the fireplace?"

"Yay! I'm getting my stuff right now." Storm jumped up and ran out of the room.

"Not fair," Sydney said. "You know that's one of her favorite winter things to do."

Slade simply grinned at her. "You two finish the snacks while I walk Storm over to my house." He headed toward the living room, then stopped in the open doorway and looked back.

"Brother dear, you get your way too much." Sydney threw her balled-up napkin at him in mock annoyance, but it landed short.

"That's not what that last bull I rode had to say." Slade chuckled, even as he appeared pained at the memory.

"I hear you," Dune agreed, knowing what all cowboys knew—at a rodeo or on a ranch, the luck was with you or it wasn't.

Storm raced into the living room wearing red satin slippers and carrying a backpack. "Bye, Mommy! And Mr. Barrett!" She gave a quick wave, opened the front door, and rushed into the night.

"Don't do anything I wouldn't do." Slade gave Sydney and Dune a mischievous grin, stepped outside, and shut the door firmly behind him.

Sydney leaned her elbows on the table and put her face in her hands. "I'm trying not to be embarrassed by my family."

"No need. They're terrific."

"Do you really think so?" She raised her head and looked at him with worry in her big hazel eyes.

"Yes. They're great—just like you."

"Thanks." She smiled at him, revealing relief and pleasure at his complimentary words.

"I'm the one who owes you thanks for inviting me into your beautiful home." He glanced around the cozy kitchen. Nothing had felt more right to him in a long, long time.

Chapter 17

SYDNEY TIGHTENED HER GRIP ON THE RED MUG OF cider as the last strains of Willie—and his sister Bobbie—Nelson's "Joy to the World" faded away, leaving the farmhouse silent except for the crackling flames in the living room fireplace. She was so used to Storm's laughter and chatter, as well as Slade's comings and goings, that the house seemed much too quiet. And yet it also felt right with Dune by her side.

Slade had practically thrown Dune into her lap as an early Christmas gift, revealing just how concerned her family must be about her living as a single parent, seeing no one special, and taking no interest in forming her own family again. What would Dune think about being practically thrown at her? She hoped he wasn't trying to figure out how to get out the front door as fast as possible without leaving hard feelings behind him.

And yet she didn't think that was the case. They'd spent long hours together, flirting and working and kissing, jump-starting their relationship. She hadn't planned on it, but Dune simply brought her alive. She finally felt as if she could move on with her life. Maybe it was his gentle caring, his strong support, and his sensitivity to Storm's fear. Maybe it was that she'd been too long without a man. Maybe it was that she'd shouldered so much responsibility for too long alone. She didn't know, and she didn't want to try to figure it out.

If Dune could get past Slade's clumsy matchmaking and if he wanted to be with her as much as she wanted to be with him, then maybe he'd stay—at least for a little bit—and she could bask in the warmth of his presence. She took a deep breath to steady her nerves, because she was setting off down an unknown path.

"Do you want a refill?" She set down her almost empty mug of cider and turned to look at him.

"Let me get it." He quickly rose from his chair, holding his mug with one hand and picking hers up with the other.

"You don't have to get our refills." She took another deep breath before she plunged ahead. "And you don't need to stay if you have other things to do at home."

"Not stay?" He set the mugs on the countertop and then looked over at her with an intense stare. "Do you want me to go?"

She wasn't sure, but she thought she heard pain in his voice that matched what she felt at the thought of him leaving her. "No. *Never.* I just didn't want you to feel obligated to stay after Slade so obviously left with Storm in a rush to leave us here alone together."

"Oh, that." A smile spread across Dune's face and lit up his dark-blue eyes with an inner fire. "I guess subtlety isn't his strong suit."

"Not hardly. He's a bull rider, not a poet." She stood up, unable to sit still a moment longer as energy came bubbling up in her.

"I want to stay awhile, if you want me."

"Oh yes." She returned his smile, feeling completely happy. "Let's take our drinks in by the fire. It'll be more comfortable there."

"And more like Christmas." He ladled cider into both their mugs, then turned off the flame beneath the steaming pot. "I was thinking about going home to the Hill Country for Christmas, but after the last several days—"

"Oh, I didn't think—please, don't let me stop you from being with your own family." She accepted the full mug he handed to her. "Now I feel guilty for drawing you into my plans when you're bound to have your own."

He picked up his mug and walked over to her. "Don't feel guilty. I'd been putting off making a decision about going down to the ranch. I guess I really don't want to go this year."

"Why not?" She led the way into the living room, realizing she didn't know too much about his background, but of course he'd have family and other commitments. She stopped in front of the two wingback chairs in front of the fireplace.

"My parents are on a Christmas cruise in the Bahamas."

"Really?" She felt shocked at the idea, because never in a million years would her family even consider being separated at Christmas.

He gave a slight chuckle. "My brother Dan's got a new girlfriend, and they're spending the holidays with her family. I'm up here. Maybe my parents felt rejected by their two sons. Maybe they figured we were all grown up and didn't need or want a traditional Christmas anymore. Maybe they just wanted to get away from their family and ranch responsibilities. I don't know."

"Maybe they simply wanted to be alone together."

She set her mug on the redbrick hearth, thinking that's what she wanted this very night.

He nodded, appearing thoughtful. "I hadn't considered that idea."

"Could it be a second honeymoon for them?"

"Now that you mention it, Mom said something on the phone about renewing their marriage vows."

"It sounds romantic." She gestured toward a chair and watched as he eased his big frame down onto it.

He looked up at her. "I come from a big family that's been in Texas since the first settlers. That's a lot of land, a lot of cattle, and a lot of people to ride herd on from dusk to dawn, seven days a week."

She sat down and gestured around her with one hand as if to encompass Steele Trap Ranch. "I understand that lifestyle. It's not easy to get away."

"Yeah. I can see that now."

"Good for them."

"I hope they're having a fine ole time." He looked down into his mug, then back at her. "Thanks."

"For what?"

"You saved me from being at loose ends here and having to explain why I'm still a rolling stone to my relatives there."

"Glad I could be of help." She felt warmed by his words.

"Families." He took a swallow of cider. "Can't live with them."

"Can't live without them," she finished the old adage. "Now that you've brought it up, a cruise isn't a bad idea. Mom and Granny deserve a getaway. Tickets would make a great Christmas gift for them, don't you think?"

He nodded in agreement as he set his mug on the hearth.

"I'll talk to Slade about it. We never know what to get them. I think he'll jump at the chance."

"They can catch a ship out of Houston or Galveston, so it's not that far away."

She clapped her hands together. "I'm excited. This is so perfect for after the holidays when they're worn out and need complete relaxation."

He gave her a slow smile, looking a little bit mischievous. "You know, Valentine's Day is coming up in a couple of months."

"I don't think that's quite right for them."

"Not them. I was thinking about us."

"You and me? A cruise?" She felt surprise then heat rush through her at the realization that he was thinking long term—intimately long term. Suddenly, she wasn't sure she was ready for such a big change in her life. She grabbed her mug and took a slug, swallowed wrong, and coughed to ease the tickle.

"Are you okay?" he asked in concern.

She nodded, trying to get past the lump in her throat.

"Now tell me, are you really surprised at my suggestion after our time together?" he asked in a voice gone deep and husky.

"I—yes, I suppose so."

"What do you think about it?" He leaned toward her, reducing the space between them.

"The cruise?"

"That. *And us*."

"I think…" she started to say, then abruptly set down her mug and stood up. "I think Slade forgot to turn on the Christmas tree lights." She walked away from Dune as quickly as possible, needing distance to help her think straight.

She knelt beside the tree, reached behind it, and plugged in the lights. She smiled in pleasure at the vintage ornaments. She'd managed to snag delicate glass balls in all shapes, sizes, and colors. Storm and Slade had helped her string red and green tinsel round and round the tall cedar tree and drape it with long, silver icicles. Colorful packages already nestled around the base with names for everyone in her family.

Now she wished she had a present for Dune since he was staying in Wildcat Bluff this Christmas. He'd probably been invited by the Duval family to be with them, but now she wanted him here. She felt a sinking sensation in the pit of her stomach. Had she been living in fear? After Emery, had she been afraid to open her heart, or her life, to a man again? If she'd been bucked off a horse, she'd have gathered her courage and gotten back on again.

She stood up and whirled around to look at Dune. He was watching the dwindling fire and turning his mug round and round in his hands. Had she offended him or made him feel rejected? She hadn't meant any of those emotions. She'd simply been caught in her own stuck emotions, afraid—like Storm—to get back on an ATV, a horse, or even life.

"Would you care to spend Christmas here with us?" She sounded a little unsure at the suggestion, heard it in her voice, and cleared her throat. "I mean, now that I know you're here alone, I wouldn't want—"

"You don't need to take pity on me." He set down his

mug with a sharp click and stood up in one motion. He took several steps toward the front door, jerked it open, and looked at her. "Kent and I are old friends. I'll enjoy being with his family for Christmas, or I can go down to the Hill Country."

She felt flooded with shame. She'd hurt him and rejected him all in one fell swoop. He deserved better. And he obviously had enough self-respect to leave where he thought he wasn't wanted anymore. She reached out to him, wanting to say something but unable to articulate words in her embarrassment.

He glanced at her open hand, shook his head in reply, and walked out into the night.

She couldn't believe he was leaving just like that. And he wouldn't be back, not a cowboy with pride. He was taking with him the memory of a slow, sultry dance to "Unchained Melody," and he was also taking with him the possibility of a future that included slow dances, hot kisses, and Valentine cruises.

How could she let him go? Would she actually let fear get in her way of reaching out and grasping happiness when it was offered to her? He'd made it clear from the first—so many months ago—that he was interested in her. She'd repeatedly rejected him, unable to imagine moving emotionally onward in life. Now he'd left no doubt that he wasn't just interested in her, but he could come to love her, along with her daughter, who desperately needed a father figure, particularly now that she was afraid of life.

Sydney had thought she'd been strong and brave after losing Emery, but now she relooked at her actions and realized she'd simply been afraid of life. To keep herself safe, she'd walled off her heart behind a smart mouth and busy life. She had her daughter, her family, her friends to fill her days with love. What more could she want? She gave a sharp, hard laugh with no humor in the sound. It'd taken a strong, determined man like Dune to help her see the light of day.

Only now it was too late. And yet, was it? She hurried to the open door and felt the chill of night envelop her, or was it fear of what she was about to do? She stepped onto the porch and stopped in the soft lighting as she looked toward his pickup.

He opened the driver door, paused, and glanced up—as if for one last glimpse—with no expression on his rugged features except stoic acceptance of his fate.

She raced down the stairs, feeling completely vulnerable in the face of his withdrawal. She stopped a few feet from him and held out her hand again.

"Dune, I need you."

Chapter 18

DUNE DIDN'T MOVE, NO MATTER THAT SYDNEY WAS standing there and reaching out to him. She might think she wanted him this time, but did she really mean it? Did she even know? A guy gets bucked off the same horse one too many times, and he either wises up or ends up with busted bones. About now, he felt decidedly busted up.

Still, it was Christmas, and miracles did happen now and again. But he shouldn't count on a magical blessing with Sydney Steele. She was nothing if not true to her name of steel. Only one question remained—when push came to shove, did she break or did she bend? He didn't want her broken, and he sure as hell didn't want to be the cause of breakage. And yet, could he walk away from her?

"I apologize," Sydney said in a tight voice. "I'm not usually so insensitive. It's just that you keep catching me by surprise."

He continued to stand still and quiet, having learned long ago to be patient with skittish critters. He'd let her say her piece, then he'd either stay or he'd go. He wasn't sure which would be best for both of them, or if best was even an option anymore. He didn't want to leave, never that—not with his blood running hot. But sometimes the best part of valor was to leave the field to fight another day.

And say what you will, he now realized he'd been in a battle with Sydney from day one. Bottom line, she might never be willing or able to leave the memory of her husband behind to start a new life. She didn't know it, but she was helping him come to terms with the loss of Vonda. He'd mourned and beaten himself up over his inability to save his girlfriend long enough. He wanted to move on with life, and he hoped he might be able to do it with Sydney.

But was he a fool to care? Was he simply asking for heartache? Was he one ride away from another broken bone—only this time, it'd be a broken heart that might never heal?

"I wish you'd say something." She took another step toward him, but his big dually squatted between them like a giant boulder blocking their path.

"Is there anything left to say?" He finally broke his silence as he grasped the side of his door, knowing he should throw himself inside and drive away if he wanted to come out of this confrontation unscathed.

"Will you spend Christmas with us?"

"No more commitments," he said, feeling as if he had to drag the words out of his depths. "I won't go back on my word. I volunteered to help you and Storm, and I will." He didn't say it, but he wondered how he could be with Sydney so much and not spontaneously combust. He'd thought they were finally on the same page, but now he couldn't count on it.

She put her hands on her hips. "I won't hold you to your word. *There*. You can drive right out of here and run all the way back to the Hill Country."

"If I did, it wouldn't be running." He felt anger

override every other feeling at the idea that she'd think he'd run from anything.

She raised her arms, clenched her fists, and let her hands drop back to her sides. "I'll admit something if you will."

"What?"

"Agree first."

"I'm not agreeing to something I don't know anything about."

"Then I'm not telling you."

He sighed, feeling exasperation join his anger. "Are you trying to drive me away?"

"I'm afraid." She ducked her head, looked down, and then back up at him, tears shining in her eyes. "I think you are, too."

"I've never been—" He stopped his words, knowing if he continued, he'd be lying to her and to himself. Truth of the matter, he'd been afraid many times—on the back of a horse, in the blazing inferno of a fire, at an emergency room waiting to learn if a victim lived or died.

"Storm is afraid now, too," she said in an even smaller voice, as if she were shrinking to escape her terror.

That did it. Somehow, she knew how to rip through all his carefully constructed barriers and grasp his beating heart to hold in the palm of her hand. He took a deep breath to win back some semblance of control.

"I think I've been afraid," she continued in the same small voice, "since I learned about Emery. Now I can see that the news ripped open my world, and everything spilled out to get blown away by the wind."

He gripped his pickup's doorframe with both hands,

not wanting to hear her words, because they were echoing what he'd thrust so deep down inside.

"I couldn't stop. I couldn't mourn. I couldn't admit fear. I didn't do any of those things, because I had a daughter to raise and keep safe."

"You're lucky. Storm needs you night and day."

"Yes, it's true," she said, sounding sad and wistful and lonely.

"Nobody's needed me, wanted me, or called my name in the middle of the night since—" He hesitated, wanting to stuff the words back into the dark depths of his soul.

"Since?" She cocked her head to one side as if trying to see him in a different light.

"You're right." He swallowed hard, knowing he was going to open up, knowing he was going to allow himself to be vulnerable, knowing he couldn't resist what had been building between them for so long. He closed his door, moved to the side, and put the palms of his hands on the cold metal of his truck's hood. He didn't walk around his pickup, because he needed that last semblance of barrier between them.

"I am?" On the other side of the truck, she stood tall, slim, and achingly vulnerable.

"I'm afraid, too."

She clasped her arms around her waist, hugging herself the way she wanted to hug him.

"I lost someone I cared about, just like you."

"You have my deepest sympathy. I know words don't help a lot, but—"

"Yes, they do." He leaned toward her, still keeping the truck between them as a wedge against his crumbling barriers. "*Vonda*. She was smart, talented, and full of life. And she was a damn good firefighter."

"What happened?"

"I'll never know. She ran back into a fire when we were all pulling out. I went back and tried to save her." He looked down at his hands, thinking how worthless they'd been at the time. "Couldn't. Too late."

"Do you blame yourself?"

"I try not to." He leaned farther across the hood, suddenly wanting to get closer to Sydney but still feeling too vulnerable to touch her.

"It's hard, isn't it? Survivor's guilt, they say. We're alive, and they're gone forever." She hesitated, hugging herself harder. "Are we—do you think?—afraid to let them go and move on with our lives?"

At her words, he felt a click in his mind, as if she'd had the right key to insert and twist to unlock his deepest emotions. He felt flooded with despair, regret, loss, envy, and pain, so much so that he staggered against the truck. He leaned against it, so that his pickup took all of his weight as the negative feelings he'd thought long gone weighed him down like cast iron.

"And yet we can't stay in one place forever, can we?"

Again, he felt her words click in his mind, flinging open a window so that crisp, fresh, fragrant air drove out the stale, dank, and fetid. Suddenly, he felt light as a feather—almost carefree—and full of hope, happiness, and love.

Maybe Sydney *was* his Christmas miracle. He straightened up, no longer requiring a barrier between them. She'd said she needed him. Well, he needed her, too.

"Can we?" she asked, flinging wide her arms.

"It's time to move on." He walked around his truck, one foot in front of the other, with a determination he hadn't felt in a long time.

"I don't mean necessarily together." She stepped back, as if feeling the power of his intent. "But maybe we can help each other find a new way to live."

"I don't want to go on without you." He stopped in front of her, watching as red and green Christmas lights—symbolizing hope and joy and renewal—splashed across her face, but he kept his hands at his sides. He didn't want to spook her with a touch, not when their trust was so raw and fragile. "If you tell me to go, I'll go. If you tell me to spend Christmas with you, I'll spend it with you."

"Oh." She put her hand over her mouth, as if to hold back a riot of emotion-filled words.

He slowly reached out, gently pulled her fingers away from her lips, and placed the softest kiss possible in the palm of her hand. "Go? Stay?"

She flung her arms around his neck. "Stay, of course."

He wrapped her tightly in his arms, molding her to the long length of his body as he gave thanks for second chances. And then he noticed she was leaning against him as if to take the weight off her feet. He should've noticed before now. She was probably in pain. Still, she hadn't complained or gone back to the house. She'd remained for him. He quickly lifted her into his arms.

"Dune?"

"You've been on your feet way too long. Let's go inside."

She didn't say anything. Maybe they'd both said too

much already. Instead, she laid her head against his chest and nestled against him. He needed no other answer. Somehow, they were going to muddle through their individual hurts and come out stronger together or stronger apart—like the old adage said, if you survived your wounds, you came out stronger at the broken places.

He took long strides to the house, up the stairs, through the open entry, and kicked the door shut behind him. Finally, they were alone together without the specter of past loves haunting them. Everything in the house felt different, as if welcoming him instead of excluding him. He looked past the decorations to feel the heart of a home that had been lived in and loved in for generations. He recognized and welcomed the feeling, because he'd grown up in something very similar with his own family.

He gently set her down on the sofa with her feet on the floor. He knelt before her, unlaced her shoes, and slipped them off her feet. He was glad to see she wore protective thick, padded cotton socks that reached up past her ankles. He started to remove one, but she stayed his hand. He glanced up at her face in question.

She gave him a soft look so different than her usual expression—a look filled with exquisite tenderness. "Let me." She slipped off both socks, tossed one to the floor, then stood up and carried the other one to the fireplace.

He couldn't see what she was doing, since her back was to him, so he simply sat down on the sofa to watch and wait, feeling endless patience now that they had reached this point.

After a bit, she turned back, gave him a mischievous glance, then stepped aside and gestured upward with one hand in the way of a model demonstrating a favorite product.

He looked up where her fingers led his eyes to the fireplace mantel. At the end of the row of colorful, fancy stockings hung a single white sock.

"We can do better later," she said, smiling, "but for now, that's your Christmas stocking. Welcome to the Steele family holidays."

Touched beyond all reason, he simply nodded in acknowledgment of her great gift to him. "Thanks. You couldn't do better."

She chortled out loud, shaking her head in denial. "I do believe I can do way better than a dirty, smelly old athletic sock."

He stood up, experiencing an emotion so strong that his chest felt too full to expand. He walked over to her, where she stood like a beautiful Christmas ornament in front of the row of embroidered stockings and the red and orange flames crackling in the fireplace with the scent of cinnamon and cedar in the air. "You leave me breathless."

She reached up, placed her palms on his broad chest, and curled her fingertips into his shirt. "*Please*, take my breath away."

Chapter 19

SYDNEY WAITED FOR DUNE'S RESPONSE, BUT INSTEAD of the kiss she expected, he gave her a slow, thoughtful smile that lit up his blue eyes like the golden glimmer of sunshine on a deep blue lake. She vibrated with expectancy as she waited for him to follow his words with action.

"I'd be remiss as an EMT," he said, glancing downward, "if I didn't see to your feet."

"My *feet*?" She clutched his shirt harder, wanting to complain that her feet were the last thing she wanted him to see to, and yet there was such tender concern written across his face that she bit her tongue to keep her silence.

"You've been on them all day." He covered her hands with his own big, strong ones. "I'm going to be responsible here."

"*Why?* I mean, it couldn't be helped, so—"

"Will you humor me and go get antiseptic wipes, antibiotic cream, bandages, and fresh socks?"

"*Now?*" She was having a little trouble—actually, a lot of trouble—getting her mind to twist from the direction she wanted to go to the direction he wanted to go. "I'm not an emergency."

"And that's the way we want to keep it. With everything going on at Christmastime, the last thing you need is an infection."

And that was that. She could see he wasn't going to back off, no matter their potentially intimate time together right this minute. For some reason she couldn't fathom, he'd gone into cowboy firefighter protective mode. She sighed, giving in to him for the moment, but not for the entire evening.

He squeezed her hands before he let them go, and then he backed up a step to give her space.

She felt the air between them cascade over her like a cold winter draft, demanding to be warmed by a fleece throw or better yet, Dune's hot body. She resisted another sigh as she resolutely turned and trudged on bare feet from the living room, across her bedroom, and into the large bathroom that had been converted from a small bedroom. She glanced into the gilt-framed mirror festooned with purple tinsel around the edges. She stopped and looked closer. She hardly recognized herself. She appeared pale with a splotch of rose color standing out on each high cheekbone. Her eyes were so dark that their normal hazel color was almost a deep, velvety brown.

Now she understood Dune's concern. She appeared on the edge of shock, and she still felt way too cold for normal. Maybe she'd pushed herself too long and hard the past few days. Suddenly, she wasn't in the least adverse to a little tender loving care.

She glanced around the luxurious room that she'd designed just for her own pleasure. Purple and lavender towels. Claw-footed tub with gold trim. Shower curtain in a flowery design to match the towels. Golden oak cabinets with lavender porcelain knobs. Original oak wood floors with thick cotton throw rugs in deep purple.

She shivered, feeling colder than ever. She picked up a soft lavender throw, wrapped it around her shoulders, and sat down on the purple cushion of a hand-painted vanity stool. She took several deep breaths, inhaling the fragrant scent of lavender soap, bath salts, and candle. Everything in her bathroom was familiar and comfortable, just as she'd designed it to be. When she glanced up at the mirror again, she was pleased to see that the color in her face looked a little more normal. She relaxed a bit, letting the peace and harmony of her home seep deeply into her.

When she heard Willie begin singing "Silent Night," she knew Dune had restarted the music. She let that familiar song flow over her, and she relaxed even more. Dune was right. She needed a little time alone to catch her breath and stabilize from all the stress.

When she felt warmer, she stood up, still keeping the throw around her, and selected the medical items that she always kept available. With both hands full, she walked into her bedroom to the corner where her reading chair—plump, overstuffed, in a velvety floral pattern—nestled beside her antique torchiere floor lamp. She used her toes to push the brass button on the sculpted metal base with its faux marble Bakelite cover over purple bulbs to turn on her soft night light.

She set the supplies on top of her distressed oak dresser beside the ivory celluloid hairbrush, hand mirror, and powder box set. She opened a drawer and picked out her most comfortable pair of padded white socks and tossed the pair beside the supplies.

Everything in her room comforted her, because she'd selected it over time with an eye to beauty and function.

She slid her palm along the cast-iron footboard of the Victorian bed she'd found rusted and neglected in a junk store. It'd only needed a little TLC to be perfect, so she'd cleaned the rusty headboard and footboard before she'd painted all the flowery curlicues a lustrous ivory color. Finally, she'd completed the bed with a silk ivory bedspread accented with a multicolor quilt across the bottom and purple and lavender throw pillows across the top, all of which sat on a large, hand-hooked rug with a faded floral pattern.

Few people ever saw her most intimate living area, so they'd probably be surprised at her choices because of the contrast to her normal get-it-done cowgirl firefighter lifestyle. Yet here she could enjoy the beautiful setting in complete privacy.

Of course, Emery wouldn't have cared for her decorations. After losing him, she'd eventually had to completely change their bedroom, because everything had reminded her of their lost love and renewed her heartbreak daily. And so she'd gone from farmhouse utilitarian to resplendent Victorian.

She glanced from her bedroom to the living room, realizing there was a final piece to the puzzle of her life. She hadn't moved on, despite all the change in trappings. She'd simply been in limbo—waiting, watching, wanting—from the sidelines of life. She felt a chill invade her from top to bottom, and she quickly pulled the soft throw tighter around her shoulders. She had a choice. Dune had given her that choice. She could continue to hide in the luxury of her bedroom…or she could choose to share it.

Was she strong enough to get back in the saddle and

risk her heart to a cowboy who could so easily break it? Was she willing to take the chance? Was she even brave enough anymore?

"Sydney?" Dune called from the living room. "Are you okay?"

She took a deep breath as she heard his footsteps head in her direction. Now was the time to make a decision. She could easily head him off at the pass in the living room so that he never reached her bedroom, or she could wait for him to find her here, where he could see what lay in the depths of her heart.

She shivered again, but she didn't reply. Instead, she walked over to her torchiere and twisted the brass knob underneath the alabaster glass shade on top of the long, slender, white lamp pole. Light flooded upward to illuminate the room.

She'd wait for him here, knowing what it meant to let him find her in her bedroom. Now that she'd made her decision, she felt a little like a sheltered Victorian lady must have felt waiting for her gentleman to leave his calling card with the hope of being invited to see her.

Dune appeared in the open doorway, a large, dark silhouette with broad shoulders, narrow hips, and long legs.

She stepped forward and put a hand on the cool metal of her bed's footboard for support, because the sight of him—and all he represented in life—still left her breathless.

"Are you all right? I'm concerned, since you took so long to come back." He glanced around the room, hesitated, and then looked again. A slow smile spread across his lips. "So this is you at home?"

She nodded in reply, feeling a small frisson of anxiety

as she wondered if he liked what he saw and if she had exposed too much of herself.

"It's beautiful. Cozy and comfortable. I wouldn't have expected this of you, but I like it."

"Thanks. I'm glad." She pointed at the supplies on top of her dresser. "Will those do?"

"Looks good." He picked them up. "If you'll sit in that chair, I'll get to work."

"I don't think there's much to do. My feet are a little sore, but nothing too bad."

"Let me check."

"Don't you trust me to know my own feet?"

"My concern is that you gloss over the wounds and keep going, no matter what. Didn't you do that all day?"

She shrugged, knowing he was right but not wanting to admit it. She quickly got in the chair and did her best to look innocent.

"I'm not trying to give you trouble."

"I know, but—"

"I just want to make sure you're okay." He sat down in front of her, selected an antiseptic wipe, and tore open the package.

She crossed her right ankle over her left knee and angled her foot so he could get a closer look.

He gently rubbed her ankle, as if to distract her, while he carefully removed the old bandages, and then he used long strokes to clean the bottom of her foot.

She felt his tender touch reassure her, but he also caused a slow burn to spread from her deepest core outward that had nothing to do with rest or relaxation or the healing arts. Suddenly, she was way too hot. She jerked the throw from her shoulders and tossed it on the floor.

"Did I hurt you?"

"No. I just—"

"You're returning to a normal temperature. That's good."

"How does my foot look?" She didn't want to discuss how hot he was making her, since he was focused on helping her heal, but she couldn't help but think about how his hard body would look sprawled across her soft bed.

"Looks better than I expected. How does it feel?"

"The antiseptic stung a little, but not bad."

"Good. What I see is mostly bruising with a few shallow cuts."

"No cactus thorns that we missed earlier?" She'd been concerned about that possibility for days.

"No. You'll heal fine, although you may be tender for a week or so."

"I can live with it."

"How about your other foot?"

She placed her left foot on her right knee. She was feeling better about carrying on through the holidays, although she'd have gone on no matter the condition of her feet.

As he examined her foot, he gently massaged her ankle while he stroked with a fresh antiseptic wipe. "No cuts on this foot. I see only a few bruises that will cause slight discomfort."

"That makes me really happy. By Christmas, I might be able to wear my vintage shoes again."

He shook his head, glancing up at her. "I could ask you not to rush it, but I know it won't make any difference."

"Christmas calls and fashion answers." She laughed

at her own words, feeling a little giddy because she was on the precipice of changing her world.

"Let's finish this up before you decide to get out the spike heels and prove you can wear them."

"Not for a little longer—I promise."

He just shook his head again. "Let me see your right foot again."

She put her foot in position on her knee and waited for him to doctor her, feeling self-indulgent since she could have done it herself. And yet she wouldn't have passed up his tender touch for the world.

He selected a sheer bandage strip, opened the package, applied antibiotic cream, and gently covered a cut on her foot. He followed the same procedure three more times and then looked over the result. He nodded in satisfaction before he slipped a sock over each of her feet. He leaned back and glanced up at her face.

"Thank you."

"You're good to go." He gave her a warm smile.

"Great. Where do you want to go?" She felt all warm and cozy in the glow of his smile.

"Maybe it's time for me to go home."

She felt dismayed at his words. "Cougar Ranch?"

"Yes."

"Do you mean to say you prefer your cowboy cabin to this luxurious room?" She gestured around to encompass all of her favorite things.

"I prefer to be where you are, but you've had a long day, and I don't want to impose on you."

"Perhaps I'd like a little imposition about now." She leaned down, pressed her palms to each side of his face, and placed a gentle yet firm kiss on his full lips.

He gave her another smile in response, white-hot heat dancing in his dark-blue eyes. "I wouldn't want to do anything to impede your healing progress."

"I do believe you're just what the EMT ordered." She couldn't resist a little chuckle, feeling much more naughty than nice.

He glanced over at the bed, then back at her. "Are we talking early Christmas presents?"

She stood up and held out her hands to him. "I'll unwrap you if you'll unwrap me."

Chapter 20

DUNE COULD HARDLY BELIEVE HIS LUCK, OR MAYBE IT was sheer persistence, or maybe it was Christmas when dreams sometimes did come true with a little help from this magical time of the year. And yet beyond all the warmth of Sydney and the specialness of the holiday, he felt a persistent cold deep inside because he wondered if he truly deserved happiness.

He took a breath, grasped her outstretched hands, and rose to his feet. He looked down at her expectant face. He suspected it'd been a long time since she'd taken a man to her bed. She honored him with her trust and desire, so he didn't want to disappoint her. He'd been a rolling stone, meaning he'd been no saint with women, and he'd failed Vonda when she'd needed him most. Above all else, he wanted to get it right this time.

Yet he wasn't sure he knew how to please anybody anymore, particularly himself. But right now, *he* didn't matter. Sydney mattered. Christmas mattered. Happiness mattered. If he could make even one person—Sydney Steele—happy this season, then maybe he'd have set foot on his personal path to redemption.

He leaned down and kissed the tip of her nose, noting the splatter of small freckles across her sun-kissed cheeks. She looked vulnerable and adorable and so ready to be loved by him. He hesitated, wondering if he was up to fulfilling all her desires, or even a few of

them. He'd never had a problem in a bedroom
but now he was feeling an intense pressure to perf...
well. Still, if he let his mind keep up the worry, he'd
disappoint them both.

Truth of the matter, all he really needed to do was
let the passion that'd driven him for so long take over.
She wanted him. He wanted her. All they had to do was
unwrap each other to make Christmas perfect.

"Dune," she said, squeezing his hands. "I'm feeling
a little anxious. It's so not me, but you—you're almost
overwhelming here in my bedroom."

"If we think too much, this isn't going to work, is it?"

"I don't know, but—"

"It's been a long time for me, too."

"That's a relief. I'm glad I'm not the only one."

He turned to look at the bed, squatting like a big,
black bull in front of the only gate that led out of the
pasture. He might as well go ahead and admit they were
never escaping out the gate into the wildflower meadow
if they had to get past the bull, or in this case, the former
marriage bed.

He raised Sydney's hands, placed a soft kiss on
each palm, and let them go. He quickly turned, grabbed
the colorful quilt off the bed, put a hand around her
waist, and ushered her into the shadowy living room
where the only light came from the glowing embers in
the fireplace.

"What's going on?" she asked as she walked ahead
of him.

He tossed the quilt on top of the carpet in front of
the fireplace, and then turned to smile at her. "It's cozy
here."

"Yes, I love this room."

"Join me?" He sat down on the quilt and patted the open area before him as he listened to the soothing sound of music and the crackle of burning wood. He realized that he felt more at peace here than he had in a long, long time.

She cocked her head to the side and gave him a thoughtful look. "You're a good cowboy firefighter, but you may be better at understanding people."

"I just like the fireplace." He wasn't about to admit anything else, although he'd been so alert to her for so long that he recognized her subtle feelings and body language.

"So do I." She sat down and gave him a mischievous look before she reached out, grabbed the front of his pearl-snap shirt, and jerked it open.

Surprised, he grinned at her, liking that she was taking the bull by the horns now that they were out of the pasture and into the meadow.

"I want to see firelight dance across your skin."

"Like what you see?"

"Oh yes."

He quickly unsnapped his cuffs and pulled his shirt out from his jean's waistband, letting it hang loose. "Seems to me this is the way we started off at the drive-in."

She chuckled, rolling her eyes. "You're right. I'd almost forgotten."

"How could you forget?"

She simply shook her head as she placed her palms against the bare flesh in the center of his chest, then softly stroked from side to side before she pushed his shirt off his shoulders so it fell down to the quilt.

He growled low in his throat, a sound torn from him

as his entire body came alive with her touch. He tugged his shirt off his wrists and tossed it aside. Now he felt amused by his earlier performance concern, because he was getting harder by the second, and they'd only begun to unwrap their living, breathing gift to each other.

She leaned forward and pressed a hot kiss to his lips, then trailed kisses down his throat, across his chest, then teased each nipple with her tongue before she ran long fingers through the golden blond hair that angled downward until it disappeared behind his big gold rodeo buckle.

"You keep it up and—"

"Hold that thought." She raised her head and grinned at him. "We're unwrapping presents, and there'll be no rush."

He groaned again, wondering how long he was going to be able to resist pulling her into his arms and burying himself deep inside her.

"Let's get back to my gift." She lifted his leg, tugged on his boot, then pulled harder till she slipped it off his foot. She quickly removed his sock before she did the same to his other foot. She set his boots and socks aside, and then trailed fingertips up the top of his feet to his ankles.

"That tickles." He quickly jerked back his feet, biting his lower lip so as to control his need to push her over backward and be done with the torment she was inflicting on him. If he'd thought she was sensual before, now he knew there was a damn good reason he'd waited for her—*and only her*.

She simply chuckled at his response, giving him a coy look from under her long eyelashes.

"How about I take a better gander at that vintage underwear under your fire-rescue sweats?"

"Think it's time to unwrap me?"

"It's way past time." He rose up on his knees, grasped the bottom of her sweater, and pulled it up and over her head. He quickly tossed it on top of his shirt, sat back down, and let his eyes feast on the blue satin that was all that kept him from seeing what he really wanted to see—and had imagined—for months of long nights in his lonely cabin.

"I think you're in a rush."

"Now why would you think that?" He tackled her around the waist, tipping her over backward as he took hold of her waistband and tugged downward, quickly revealing hips, legs, and finally feet. One last tug, and he freed her pants. He tossed them across the room—far enough that she wouldn't be tempted to put them back on any time soon. And then he feasted on the banquet of her nearly nude image.

She gave him a hesitant smile that made her appear naughty and nice at the same time.

"You're so beautiful." He realized his voice held awe as if he was seeing a work of art or the birth of a calf or a goddess rising up from the Earth.

"I'm not a spring chicken anymore." She rubbed her hands up and down her legs as if to reassure or to warm herself.

"I'm not either." He reached out and clasped her hands to still them as he reassured her. "Age works for us both."

She gave him a rueful smile. "As in Slade's fine muscadine wine?"

"Better than that."

"Why don't we prove it?" She pushed his hands aside and tugged on the hems of his jeans. "Got anything on under your Wranglers?"

He chuckled at her words, knowing she was toying with him and enjoying the hell out of it. "Why don't you unwrap me and find out?" He spread his legs so she'd have to come in between them to reach his belt buckle. He leaned back on his elbows to give her complete access to him.

She tossed him a narrow-eyed look that let him know she knew exactly what he was doing in that position, and then she crawled up to him and wrapped her fingertips around the edge of his tooled-leather belt.

With that small touch near the heart of his desire, he was hit with a need so great, it almost took his breath away. Yet he'd agreed to this unwrapping game, and he wouldn't back out now. He simply had to call on all his willpower to stay still and not grab her, toss her to the quilt, and finally be done with it.

When she ran the pads of her thumbs over the engraved front of his rodeo buckle, he was reminded of his favorite win against all odds ten years back. That was a fleeting thing. With Sydney, he realized that he wanted their win to last a lifetime.

She glanced at his face, gave a mischievous smile, and then looked down again. She unhooked his big buckle, undid the button of his jeans, and stopped as if considering what to do next.

He waited impatiently, wondering if he was going to have to help her out. Maybe she'd forgotten how to get a man out of his jeans. Pretty quick, he was going to be in uncomfortable territory—as if he hadn't already been there for months.

Still, she gave him no relief. She lingered a little longer before she leaned in close and kissed his lips—nibbling, licking, sucking—while she slowly swept her hand lower and lower till she clasped the hard bulge in his Wranglers.

He groaned aloud as he instinctively pushed up with his hips and against her hand, feeling her clasp and stroke till he was completely at her mercy. "You'd better stop," he whispered hoarsely against her mouth, "or this won't take long."

She lightly bit his lower lip in reply, then quickly unzipped his Wranglers, jerked them down, pulled them off his feet, and tossed them aside. She sat back on her heels and perused him—slowly but surely—from head to toe. "You're beautiful, too."

"I can't hold a candle to you." He was glad he'd decided to wear navy briefs that morning. If not, he wouldn't have stood a chance of getting through their agonizingly long unwrap.

She reached for the shoulder straps of her blue bra, cocking her head to one side. "Do you want me to go next, or do you want—"

"I want to watch." Now he wished he could see her in bright sunlight instead of shadowy firelight. She almost didn't appear real in the glow of the flickering flames, because he'd imagined this moment so often in his mind. Now that it was finally here, reality put imagination to shame.

She slowly stripped for him, lowering one bra strap then the other till she finally unclasped the back and let that little bit of soft fabric fall away.

He took a gulp of air to remind himself to breathe, because she took his breath away. She was all peaches and cream with tiny freckles scattered like glitter across her full breasts tipped with rosy pink. Maybe he was getting poetic about her, but she still ranked right up there with a tangerine-tinted sunrise, a silver-gray mare, a yellow rose covered in morning dew—all of nature that spoke volumes to a cowboy's heart of hearts.

And then she went further, putting her fingertips under the waistband of her panties and slipping them slowly, tantalizingly down her long legs to leave her completed unwrapped and bathed in a rosy glow.

He swallowed over the lump in his throat. He hadn't expected to be so affected by her. He was suddenly reminded of the time long ago when guys woke up one day to the fact that the gals in their school halls suddenly had fascinating curves. They'd become goddesses overnight, and how do you get the nerve to approach a goddess?

"Your turn," she said in a husky voice as she leaned toward him with a seductive smile.

Maybe a cowboy simply had to give a goddess the best night of her life. He went with that thought. He tossed her a naughty grin as he jerked down his briefs and threw them away.

"Oh my," Sydney said, staring at him with awe in her expression. "It's been a long time. I'm not sure if—"

"We'll make it work." He didn't want any more words between them. He wrapped her in his arms and pulled her close, so that the heat of their bodies touched, merged, ignited.

And then he was kissing her and sliding his hands all

over her—unable to get enough fast enough—just as she did the same to him. They made the blaze in the fireplace feel cool in comparison to their combined combustion.

He leaned her back over his arm and trailed kisses down her neck to her breasts where he teased and tormented her sensitive flesh till he couldn't resist the lure of moving lower. He toyed with her belly button with the tip of his tongue while she gripped his shoulders and moaned at his touch. He delved lower still, cupping her mound with his hand, feeling her heat and moisture. He used his fingers to explore, thrusting inside with a sensual rhythm until she writhed up against him, shuddering as she succumbed to ecstasy.

He couldn't wait any longer, not when she raised her head to look at him with such passion and a softness that might be love, or at the very least tenderness. He felt all of that for her, and so much more.

She held out her arms, lay back against the quilt, raised her knees, and spread her legs for him. He wanted to give back to her as much as she was giving him. As he knelt over her—so close to bliss—he remembered protection. He didn't have any with him. He groaned and sat back on his heels.

"What is it?"

"I hate to bring it up now, but I just realized that I don't have any condoms."

She struggled up, half sitting and leaning on one elbow. "I didn't think—"

"It's okay." He ran a hand through his hair in frustration. "Tonight we can do other things."

"No. I want this now." She glanced toward her bedroom, frowning in thought. "If you'll look in the back of my nightstand's top drawer, there might be a package left over from—before."

He hated that idea. He'd been trying to get them away from the specter of her husband all night long.

"Dune," she said, grasping his hand and squeezing it, "we're moving forward with our lives."

"Yes, we are, but—"

"You know they loved us. They'd want us to be happy again and share all the good things in life."

"True." Now both specters of their past had risen to stand between them.

"Please check my nightstand. It's okay either way."

"No, it's not." He made a decision. One way or another, this night belonged to them. "I'll look, but if I come up empty, I'll drive into town." He gave her a quick kiss and got to his feet. "It's Christmastime, and we're not going to do without, not after all this unwrapping."

She nodded as her eyes lit up like a vibrant green prairie after a spring rainstorm. "That's my cowboy."

He stalked into the bedroom and up to the nightstand. He grabbed the knob, jerked hard, and the drawer came completely out, causing everything inside to tumble to the rug. Sometimes he didn't know his own strength. He thrust the empty drawer back into the nightstand and looked down at the scattered contents. He passed over cough drops and antacids before he saw the one thing he hadn't actually expected to be there. He grabbed the single condom, walked back into the living room, and held it out to show her.

"You triumphed!" She grinned up at him as she patted the quilt for him to join her.

He knelt beside her, feeling their blaze rekindle as

if nothing had interrupted the flow of their passion. He tore open the package, slipped on the condom, and then hesitated between her legs.

"Please, Dune. I need you. I want you." She clasped him in her arms and drew him to her body. "I'm on fire."

When he thrust into her, she moaned softly in his ear and pulled him even tighter. She felt hot as a raging wildfire. For once, he didn't want to put out a fire. He wanted to stoke this one higher—and burn right along with it as he moved within her, pushing faster and harder as their blaze burned hotter and brighter.

She cried out as she dug her nails into his back and wrapped her legs around his waist so he could plunge deeper into her molten core. He'd never felt this way before, as if their flames were cleansing their sad past and melding their bright future together as one. When they reached a fever pitch of passion, they spiraled higher and higher until they came apart in each other's arms.

"Stay here," she said on a ragged breath. "Don't leave me."

He put his weight on one arm and gently pushed sweat-damp hair back from her face with his free hand. "If you want, I'll stay here all night long."

She nodded in agreement as she gazed up at him with hazel eyes that sparkled in the firelight. "I'm so happy."

He pressed a soft kiss to her rosy lips, realizing that he no longer felt the icy grip of winter deep inside. She'd driven it out with her fiery heat of summer.

And she'd made him happy, too.

Chapter 21

SYDNEY DROVE A LITTLE TOO FAST ONTO THE WILDCAT Bluff Fire-Rescue Station parking lot, still feeling giddy a day after Dune had spent the night—a long night filled with erotic pleasures.

She slipped Celeste into a space under a tree, as if it were summertime when everybody searched for shade so their vehicles didn't turn into ovens from the sun's intense heat, or maybe she just still felt the heat of Dune's touch.

She checked the parking lot for vehicles. Hedy's van was already there, as well as Kent's truck. She was really glad to see Kent in place, since he was their photographer. She cut Celeste's engine and sat still a moment, gathering her thoughts. She hoped this time everything would go off without a hitch, but after so many false starts, she simply couldn't be sure of success until she saw cowboy firefighter photographs on Kent's camera.

Storm was safely with Slade, so she knew her daughter was in good hands. She'd put everything on hold yesterday while Dune caught up at Cougar Ranch, so she could spend quality time with her daughter. They'd sat in front of the fireplace together, drinking hot chocolate and catching up. That'd also given her feet a chance to heal even as her mind had whirled with possibilities, particularly because of all Dune had awakened in her.

She knew that she and Dune had both loved and lost, but she believed they could love again.

For now, romance shouldn't be foremost in her mind. She had cowboys to get in line. She opened her door and stepped out, wearing her vintage style with special consideration for her feet. As luck would have it, she had a pair of retro red moccasins with beaded trim across the toes that were soft, comfortable, and appropriate. She'd paired them with crimson cigarette pants that had a fitted waist. She'd completed the outfit with a forest-green button-down long-sleeved cardigan that sported red-beaded Christmas ornaments.

Dune's special attention and a little rest seemed to have pretty well healed her feet, because she hardly felt any pain at all. He must have that experienced EMT touch, or maybe she was still so happy from their night together that everything felt better. In any case, she wasn't planning any wild cowgirl stunts to cause a setback, because she was grateful for the current relief. It also meant she'd probably be able to wear her vintage shoes for upcoming events.

All in all, she felt good about the day and her future. She glanced up at the clear blue sky overhead with a few puffy white clouds lazing about as if they had nothing better to do than look pretty for the folks restricted to the ground below. And pretty was plenty good enough, because they didn't need rain. So far, the winter was turning out to be fairly normal, meaning not too hot, not too cold, not too wet, and not too dry. If the weather held steady, they looked to have a perfect day for their photo shoot.

Kent had never taken shots like these before, but

he'd been playing around with cameras since high school. Hedy had even framed some of his extraordinary firefighting photos and hung them in the station. They were lucky he was good at capturing events and images, so they didn't have to find a professional willing to donate services.

She made a quick survey of the parking lot again, but she didn't see Dune's truck. Where was he? She'd expected him to be right on time, if not early. Maybe he was still taking care of ranch chores. She hated to admit it, but she already missed him, since life no longer seemed right without him.

When her phone vibrated in her pocket, she quickly grabbed it, thinking it'd be Dune calling to let her know when he'd get there.

"Hey, Sis," Slade said with a chuckle in his voice, as if he was the cat who'd eaten the cream.

"Hey back at you." She hoped he wasn't calling with bad news.

He laughed out loud in his big, booming voice. "You sound a little relaxed and happy today."

"I'm at the station, ready to rock and roll."

"Didn't you already rock and roll the other night?"

"Don't even go there."

"My lips are sealed. I never saw anybody leave your place about dawn." He chuckled again.

She finally joined his laughter, because her happiness felt too good to keep inside. "Okay. I like him."

"I do, too. And he's been bird-dogging you a long time. I like that kind of commitment."

"I don't know if there's any commitment, but we'll be working together for a bit."

"Good enough." He hesitated a moment. "Listen, I know you'll be busy all day. I'll keep Storm with me till I need to get down there and strut my stuff."

"Oh, cowboy, you've got plenty to strut," she said, teasing him.

"Maybe some lovelorn lady will see my photo and bird-dog me till I give up my wild and wanton ways for her."

"As if." She laughed, continuing her tease, because they both knew he was about as committed to his freedom and independence as they got in Wildcat Bluff County.

"You never know," he said in a thoughtful voice. "Look at Trey and Kent. They were the two wildest cowboy firefighters around here."

"You ought to add yourself to that list."

"That ornery bull put a crimp in my style." He gave a big, dramatic sigh for effect that ended on a deep chuckle. "Now Trey's been roped by Misty, and Kent's all starry-eyed over Lauren. It's hard to believe, if you hadn't met the gals in question, but those guys are looking to get leg-shackled for life."

"Guess you're going to have to carry the bachelor banner all by yourself from now on."

"You're not planning to desert me, are you? Hedy's even talking about going over to see Bert's bluebird collection. That banner might get kind of heavy all on its lonesome."

"Never fear. You're up to carrying on alone."

"Yeah, sure, but—"

"No doubt, you're up to it." She saw the bay door open in the station, so she knew it was time to focus on the photo shoot. "All right, Mr. DeMille, you're ready

for your close-up," she said, unable to resist a little para-
phrasing from a famous movie.

"Norma Desmond. *Sunset Boulevard*. 1950," Slade
said. "If you're comparing my upcoming stint before the
camera to classic film noir, you'll be sadly disappointed."

"I just thought I'd take your mind off lonely hearts."

"How? By quoting Norma Desmond, the loneliest
heart of all? You're just trying to distract me by mentioning my favorite movie genre."

"I was hoping to impress you with my sudden
knowledge of fifties flicks, too. I've been watching a
lot to get in the mood for Christmas at the Sure-Shot
Drive-In."

"You could've just asked me about them. But I'm
impressed. Okay?"

"Good." Mainly, she'd wanted to get him away from
the subject of loneliness, because she couldn't help him
with that, and it made her hurt for her big brother. He'd
been happy as a rodeo star, but when the music stopped
and he was left twisting in midair, there was no way
back to recapture the melody.

"I'll leave Storm with Granny at the café later," he
said, filling up the silence. "I swear our little tike is
taking to cooking like a duck to water."

"You're a good uncle."

"I do my best."

"Thanks."

"Better go. No rest for the weary around here. I just
wanted to put your mind at ease about Storm."

"You did. See you soon." She put her phone back
in her pocket, feeling thoughtful and a little concerned
about him. But for now, there was nothing she could do

except keep moving forward one step at a time. Maybe the old adage was right—time healed all wounds.

As she shut her car door, she glanced at the station. Kent waved to her from where he stood in back of the booster with Hedy to one side. He was a tall cowboy with sable-brown hair and a muscled-up body strong from ranch work. A moment later, Hedy joined him, motioning for her to hurry up.

Sydney started across the parking lot, then glanced toward Cougar Lane, hoping Dune was finally getting there, but the road was empty. If he didn't arrive soon, she'd text him, although she'd prefer for him to contact her first after their day apart. Maybe she just needed reassurance that he still wanted her, needed her, and what they'd shared was as special to him as it was to her. She'd know it by the look in his eyes—just one look was all it'd take, so she really wanted him to get there.

And then she had another thought. She knew it was silly, but she felt a little worried about him. What if something had happened out on the ranch? Nobody would even think to let her know if he'd had an accident and was with a doctor. He'd been such a comfort to her when she'd taken Storm to the clinic, but she wasn't family or girlfriend or anybody who'd be notified if he needed her. She disliked the fact that she might be the last to know.

She picked up her steps as she quickly crossed the parking lot. She'd just ask Kent. He'd know if anything had happened on the ranch, since Dune worked for him. But she couldn't be too obvious about her concern, not unless she wanted a whole lot of gossip to hit the local grapevine. She didn't even want to think how news about her one night with Dune could get turned into a wild night in Dallas with a rodeo team. It'd be better than TV drama for local entertainment. She shuddered at the thought. No, she'd just act cool and casual.

As soon as she reached Kent, she put her hands on her hips and leaned toward him. "Dune's supposed to be here to help with the photo shoot. Where is he?"

Kent stepped back, glanced at Hedy, and then gave her a big grin. "Lose your boy toy?"

She felt her face turn pink with embarrassment. She'd just done the opposite of what she'd intended to do. Somehow, Dune had already gotten under her skin.

"Now, Kent, why are you teasing Sydney about Dune? Everybody knows he's been after her for months, not the other way around," Hedy said, obviously coming to Sydney's rescue.

"Yeah," Kent agreed. "I thought maybe she'd finally come to her senses and given him a break now that she's letting him be her gopher on her projects."

"Guess he's not much of a gopher." Sydney felt a vast sense of relief as her face cooled down with the knowledge that her night of passion hadn't spread around town.

"He'll be here," Kent said. "I bought a bull a while back that thinks the whole county is his pasture."

"Is that the new Brahman?" Hedy asked.

"Yep," Kent agreed.

"I don't know why you bought him. Brahmans are nothing but trouble," Sydney said, remembering how she'd never liked the breed after a run-in with one when she was a kid.

"Favor for a friend. Only now I'm having second thoughts." Kent gave a big sigh of frustration.

"So he broke out again?" Hedy asked, zipping a little closer to them in her automated wheelchair.

"Yeah. He's probably on Steele Trap Ranch."

"Had I better go saddle up and get him?" Sydney asked. "Slade and Storm are down at the café."

"Dune'll get him," Kent said with a chuckle. "I told him I'd come on down here, since I'm the photographer and more important than he'll ever be."

"I'm sure he'll pay you back for that remark." Sydney laughed with him.

"And when you least expect it," Hedy added with a chuckle.

Sydney let their laughter die down. "Guess we ought to go ahead and get started on the calendar. Who's first on our list?"

"That'd be me." Kent shrugged his broad shoulders as he gave Hedy a narrow-eyed look.

She grinned, tossing her long, silver braid over one shoulder. "Just so you know, Sydney, you owe me one. I had to go to all the trouble of getting out my big black leather whip to get the cowboy firefighters in this county in line."

"Thanks. I thought that might have to be my job." Sydney winked at Hedy. "I can see that must've been some hard work on your part."

"Don't you ever doubt it." Hedy threw back her head and filled the parking lot with laughter.

"All I've got to say is we're all going to have a miserable time," Kent added, giving Hedy a big smile, "but it's for a good cause."

"True enough," Hedy agreed.

Sydney gave the booster a pat on its shiny red paint, feeling relieved that Dune was okay. He'd get that troublemaker of a bull under control soon and join them. "So, folks, let's get this show on the road. We're burning daylight."

Chapter 22

DUNE FELT SWEAT TRICKLE DOWN HIS BACK AS THE SUN made its way higher into the sky, burning off the coolness of the night. He hadn't needed to wear anything more than a long-sleeve shirt, Wranglers, and boots on such a pretty day.

December. It was a good month, not too hot and not too cold, but it could've been better if the days were longer. They were about three weeks away from the winter solstice, the shortest day of the year on the twenty-first. After that, they'd head into longer day territory, but it'd be spring till the days really got rolling again. For now, he just had to put up with not enough daylight hours. He supposed that was better than the reindeer herders up near the Arctic Circle in Scandinavia, seesawing between mostly light and mostly dark during the year. That situation didn't bear thinking about, so he shoved it from his mind to get back to the matter at hand.

And that'd be the wily, quick, and cantankerous Brahman that was leading him a merry chase. The big bull was typical of his breed with a pale coat and dark neck and hump. Dune realized now that he should've gotten another guy to help him bring in the animal, since it was actually a job best handled by two cowboys. But he'd been feeling so full of himself after his night with Sydney that he'd thought he could tackle anything and come out a winner. Famous last words, or thoughts.

He'd put himself between a rock and a hard place, because after a bit, he'd gotten as stubborn as the bull. He wasn't going to back down. The bull wasn't going to back down. His horse had had about enough of the whole mess. And Sydney wasn't going to be impressed with a no-show at the station. He could only hope she wasn't mad as a wet hen, particularly after he'd done his best to impress her. Some days it just didn't pay to get out of bed.

Still, he hated to think what might be on Sydney's mind with him not at the photo shoot when he'd promised to help her. He'd chased the damn bull all over a good part of her ranch, so she wouldn't thank him for scaring her herds either. At least the bull appeared to be tiring, but so was Dune's buckskin, bless her stout heart, and he wasn't fresh as a daisy anymore.

He held a rope—lime green for high visibility—in his left hand, coiled around his palm and clasped between his thumb and first finger with his reins tucked underneath his fourth and little fingers to leave his right hand free. He didn't actually need the hi-vis team rope, but he liked the bright color on short days when he worked part of the time in low light. He also liked the stiff but pliable four smooth strands of nylon that made a cowboy's life easier.

Not that he was roping the bull. He didn't figure he stood much chance of leading or towing two thousand pounds of horn, muscle, and mad back to Cougar Ranch. Instead, he was using the rope to guide the animal in the right direction by slapping the coil against his thigh for sound and waving it like a red flag for visual. At least, that'd been the original plan, although the idea was getting a tad threadbare by now.

He pushed back his cowboy hat to get a better look at the sky, so he could figure the time of day by the position of the sun overhead. Pretty quick, it'd be mid-morning, and that was not going to do, not with Sydney on a tight schedule. Besides, he'd had enough of the Brahman's mangy ways. Maybe if he hadn't been so distracted with thoughts of Sydney, he'd already have the animal back in his pasture.

Dune tugged his cowboy hat down on his head as he brought his mind into a tight, determined focus on the bull. Now or never. He gigged his horse into a lope, tossed the rope over to his right hand, and raised it high over his head. He hollered as he bore down on the Brahman, leaving a trail of dust in his wake. A cottontail rabbit leaped out of hiding and raced out of the way.

Maybe the bull was ready for brunch in his own pasture, or maybe he was tired of being on the lam, or maybe he finally figured out that Dune was never going to give up. In any case, the Brahman turned and trotted back toward Cougar Ranch with the loose skin under his neck swaying back and forth as his dark hooves kicked up prairie dust.

Dune stayed right on the bull's long, swinging tail with its tuft of black hair on the end. He guided the Brahman ahead of him with his horse and rope toward the break in the fence line. When the bull finally leaped over the downed fence and into his own pasture, Dune gave him a sharp rap on the butt with his rope to make sure he kept going in that direction.

He leaped down from his buckskin, led her over the fence, then ground-tied her. He examined the fence. It had to be fixed without delay, or it'd be too big of a lure to the bull. He quickly rooted his leather gloves, hammer, and galvanized steel staples out of his saddle-bag. He jerked on his gloves and pulled two posts into straight alignment before he nailed the barbwire back into place. He jiggled the fence to make sure it was sturdy and then put away his equipment.

He glanced up at the sun again. He wouldn't be too late getting to the station, but he still had to get back to his cabin and get cleaned up. No point in crying over spilt milk. He'd done his job, and now he was free to join Sydney.

He mounted his horse and headed for the barn, feeling good about a job—finally—well done. As he rode across the pasture, he felt crisp air that heralded frost on the ground in the morning, but for now, the day was perfect enough for Sydney's photo shoot.

When he'd almost reached Cougar Ranch's big barn where they had cell coverage, he pulled out his phone and called Kent.

"Hey, Dune," Kent answered. "Did you get that bull sorted out?"

"He's back in his pasture, and the fence is fixed."

"Thanks. Listen, I should've had somebody else do that job, because I've got a gal here getting in a tizzy 'cause you aren't around."

Dune growled into the phone. "Tell her I'll be there as soon as I get done here."

"I'll do it. In the meantime, I called B.J. He's waiting in the barn to curry your horse. Drop him the reins and get out of there."

"Thanks. That'll save time."

"And don't bother to get gussied up. You can shower here."

"I'm not going to—"

"Trust me. You want to go straight to your truck and get over here."

"She's that mad?"

"She needs your help. We all do."

"Okay. I'm on my way." Dune tucked his phone back in his pocket, shaking his head. He could think of a lot of good ways to see Sydney after what they'd shared in her home. This one was so low down, it didn't even make the list. But there was nothing he could do about it now.

He rode up to the large red barn with a silver metal roof that had all the modern conveniences that a ranch the size of the Cougar needed to compete in the cattle market. A dozen or so saddle horses waited patiently in a corral while six ATVs were lined up nearby.

B.J. stood outside with a big lump of chewing tobacco stuffed in one cheek of his leathery skin. He had grizzled hair worn shoulder-length with white stubble on his craggy face. He wore a faded red plaid shirt under striped overalls and scuffed work boots. He spit to one side, then walked over and held out his hand for the reins.

Dune dismounted and tossed the reins to him. "Thanks. Kent's waiting for me."

"So he said." B.J. eyed him up and down. "Trouble with a fox, huh?"

"Sydney's in charge of the calendar."

B.J. nodded with a sage look as he squinted his brown eyes. "Not a lady to cross, you want my two cents."

"No disagreement there."

"You going like that?" B.J. took off his stained cowboy hat, looked inside it, and put it back on, as if that action explained everything.

"I hear you." Dune resisted a loud sigh. "But Kent said to get right over to the station."

"Better get."

Dune raised his hat in goodbye and jogged over to his pickup parked beside his cabin. He quickly stepped up, tossed his hat onto the passenger seat, pulled his keys from a front pocket, started the engine, and tore out of the ranch. He hit several bumps and dips getting to the gravel road, but he hardly noticed them. By the time he drove over the cattle guard and under the Cougar Ranch sign, he knew he was in trouble—not so much with Sydney, hopefully, but with himself for wanting to do everything in his power to keep her happy. He was getting in deep, and he didn't even want to pull out.

He turned on the Wildcat Den, their local ranch radio station, as he hit Wildcat Road, wanting a distraction to keep him from putting his boot too heavy on the pedal. Last thing he needed was to be pulled over by a trooper and lose even more time.

He expected to hear Christmas music, but instead, Reba came on singing "Buying Her Roses." Yeah, he could go for roses. Sydney was bound to like them. Cowgirls liked flowers. If he had time, he'd pick up some and take them to her. But then he thought about how that'd look to the other firefighters. And Hedy. They'd tease him mercilessly. No flowers. No candy. No greeting card.

On second thought, he'd enjoy buying Sydney underwear. Something sheer and soft in red or black or the color she wore in front of the fireplace, a kind of ocean blue that put him in mind of islands with swaying palm trees, drinks with pink umbrellas, and hammocks with room for two. Maybe they could go to the Bahamas after Christmas. He could surprise her with New Year's Eve tickets to paradise. It'd be a romantic getaway just for the two of them.

And then he thought of Storm. It wouldn't be fair to leave her behind, but it wouldn't be a romantic getaway with her along. Disney World or a Disney cruise would be more the thing for Storm. He bet she'd want to escape the recent memories of her ATV spill. Maybe it'd help her regain confidence in her ability to take on anything that life could throw at her.

He reached to turn off the radio, not willing to let Reba take him down any other fantasy lanes. He heard Wildcat Jack's deep Texas drawl spin out over the air waves. Nobody ever knew what the legendary DJ was going to say next, but he could spin a yarn with the best, and he had a line of old Texas sayings that'd fill a book. He reminded Dune of the popular DJs on ranch radio in the Hill Country. Up here, Wildcat Jack made the Wildcat Den everybody's favorite home away from home.

Dune realized he was twisting his mind into a pretzel just to keep it off Sydney. He'd spent some special time with her, and here he was plotting out holidays with her and her kid. He didn't know how she even felt today, except she wouldn't be happy that he'd stood her up. It wasn't the best way to gain a cowgirl's confidence, particularly one like Sydney.

He flipped off the radio and then hit his steering wheel with the flat of his palm. She'd either accept him as he was, warts and all, or she wouldn't accept him at all. He could do a few things that might encourage her to like him better, flowers and such, but she either liked him or she didn't. Storm either liked him or she didn't. Trouble was, he liked them both way too much, because he was risking his heart with every step he took in their direction. And yet it'd be worth it—similar to competing in a rodeo—if he could win in the end.

With that goal in mind, he gunned his dually's engine to get to the Wildcat Bluff Fire-Rescue Station sooner. He might be sweaty and smelly when he got there, but he'd be exactly where Sydney wanted him to be even if he arrived a little on the late side.

Chapter 23

ABOUT NOON, SYDNEY DECIDED THAT THE WILDCAT Bluff Fire-Rescue Station had taken on the role of party central. She hadn't expected it, but their photo shoot was now much more than the means to an excellent benefit to help fund the station. Cowboy firefighters were bonding and celebrating and congratulating each other on a job well done for another year of volunteering to support their community.

Things had really taken off once Slade arrived with takeout from the Chuckwagon Café, lowered the tailgate of his truck, and laid out the spread of barbeque, fixings, and sweet tea. Country and western music from inside the open doors of the station filtered outside where everyone had gathered after completing all but one of the photographs for the calendar.

Unfortunately, there was a big downside. Dune wasn't there. If he had been, everything would have been about perfect. As it was, she was alternating between mad, sad, and worried. Kent had tried to call Dune again. She'd even tried to call him. Their calls had gone straight to voicemail, so they couldn't directly reach him. Kent had reassured her that Dune had said he was on his way over two hours ago. How long could it take to get from Cougar Ranch to the fire station? Not long, as she well knew.

She'd finally decided that he either didn't want to face her after their one night together, or he didn't want to do the photo shoot, or he didn't want to help her at all. Maybe all three options were viable.

In any case, he was putting her in a bind, and she didn't appreciate it one bit. She also felt like a fool to have believed his words, his hands, his body. He'd gotten what he wanted from her, and now he was probably headed to the Hill Country, never to be seen or heard again. It was just as well she'd found out now instead of later that he wasn't trustworthy. And yet she couldn't stop the tightness in her chest or the pain in her heart at that realization. At least she wasn't in too deep, or was she? No, it'd simply been a one-night stand that had woken her up to how life could be again. That was a good thing. And if she kept telling herself that often enough, maybe she'd eventually believe it.

For now, she'd simply cross Dune Barrett off her list. She didn't need him to get done what had to be done. So far, everything was going according to plan. They'd photographed firefighters wearing their turnout gear—but not too much gear—in front of the fire station, in the rec room, in, on, and around the engine and the booster. Kent had taken lots of shots, so they'd have plenty to choose from later. She had to admit their cowboy firefighters looked just as hunky as they looked ready to take care of business. And that was great for the calendar.

Unfortunately, Dune left them one month short, so she was trying to decide how to fill that month. She had to get the picture now, because she absolutely had to have all of the photographs that day so she could drop the photos into the calendar layout and get it in production.

She tamped down her concern about Dune, because she knew if he'd had trouble such as a truck wreck or something else disastrous, they'd have been alerted at the fire station, so they'd be almost the first to know. That meant he was okay out there wherever he'd gone. She comforted herself that he wasn't in danger. Still, it was cold comfort because it meant he just didn't want to be with her.

Yet now was not the time to think about Dune. There was simply too much left to do. She took another swig of sweet tea through the red-and-white straw in her cup, determinedly breaking her thoughts. She put a hand on the fender of Slade's pickup as she watched a tall, willowy, blond-haired, green-eyed newcomer, looking good in a forest-green sweater and slacks set, walk over. Trey Duval followed close on her heels, wearing his traditional Santa Claus belt buckle with red shirt, Wranglers, and cowboy boots.

"Thanks for everything you're doing for the county." Misty Reynolds leaned in close, gave Sydney a hug, and stepped back with a big smile.

"That goes for both of us." Trey's hazel eyes gleamed as he put an arm around Misty's waist, looking as pleased and possessive as all get-out.

"I'm just relieved we're about to wrap up the photo shoot," Sydney said.

"About that." Trey glanced around the group, then back at her. "Dune's not one to slack off his responsibilities."

"It's okay." Sydney shrugged, trying to look nonchalant as she flailed about in her mind to come up with a solution to his absence in the calendar. Finally, something struck her as workable. "I have an idea about that last picture."

"What?" Misty asked, taking a step closer.

"Why don't we do a group shot of all our firefighters since they're still here? We could gather around the food like it's a tailgate party for Christmas."

Misty laughed, glancing up at Trey. "Good idea. Everybody knows firefighters are foodies."

"Not true," he said, chuckling. "We just know firefighting requires a lot of fuel, so we make the most of it."

"Sure," Misty and Sydney said as one, and then both burst into laughter.

"Anyway, that'll work." He turned aside and motioned toward his cousin, Kent Duval, to come over.

Kent noticed and tossed a gnawed-to-the-bone rib into the trash. He grabbed the hand of Lauren Sheridan, a honey-blond, brown-eyed cowgirl who'd recently returned and recaptured their high school love.

"What's up?" Kent asked, wearing his usual snapshirt, jeans, and boots, as he glanced toward Cougar Lane before he focused on Sydney. "Any news?"

She shook her head in the negative as she shrugged her shoulders, wishing she at least knew what'd happened to Dune.

"Sydney's got a good idea." Trey glanced at her in encouragement.

"I'm all ears." Lauren leaned closer.

"Okay." Sydney tossed a smile at them. "I'm thinking it'd be good to have a group shot of our firefighters around the barbeque—or what's left of it—like they're celebrating at a Christmas tailgate party. I believe it'd work for December. What do you think?"

"Love it!" Kent clapped his hands together.

"So do I." Lauren glanced toward the road, then back

again. "I mean, if Dune's not going to be here, then that idea works fine."

"We have to assume he's not coming to the shoot," Sydney said in a firm tone, knowing she had to get everybody on the same page.

"Right," Kent agreed. "My camera's already on a tripod. I just need to focus on the group, set the timer, and join it."

"Perfect." Sydney said the word, but she didn't mean it. "Perfect" would be if Dune was there, but he wasn't, so they'd go with the next best thing. And anyway, a group shot was probably a good idea. If Dune had been Mr. December as she'd planned, then she would've used the shot on the calendar's cover. But this would work, too.

"Are you going to be in the group photo?" Lauren raised her eyebrows at Sydney. "You're a volunteer firefighter, too."

"I hadn't planned on it. This is about the guys."

"Wait a minute," Kent said. "I think Lauren's right. Sydney ought to be in the group shot, along with Hedy— and Ash. Lauren, you too, since you're volunteering at the station again."

"I like it," Misty agreed. "And I think Hedy with Ash on her lap ought to be front and center, since they're the backbone of the station."

"I agree about Hedy and Ash," Sydney said, "but I'm not so sure about me."

"Or me," Lauren agreed.

"We're sure about both of you." Trey gave a big grin.

"But I'm not even dressed for it," Sydney said. "My hair. Makeup."

"Stop right there," Misty interrupted. "We'll put you in a firefighter jacket. And a cowgirl hat will take care of your hair. Lauren, too."

"Good." Kent glanced around the group. "It's a done deal."

"I'll get the group assembled while you set up the camera." Trey turned and headed toward the nearby firefighters.

"I'll tell Aunt Hedy," Lauren said. "I'm really excited about this picture."

"I think it'll work." Sydney just wished Dune was there to be in the photo with them.

"You bet it'll work." Kent took a step away, then looked back. "Maybe you and Slade can get the food and containers set up for the photograph."

"Okay." She looked around, caught Slade's eye, and motioned him over to his pickup.

"What's up?" Slade glanced around at all the sudden activity, then focused on her. "No Dune?"

"Nope."

"I'll be hornswoggled. I'd never have thought he'd just take off. Are you sure he's okay?"

"I'm not sure of anything, except we've got to get one more photo for the calendar."

"What do you need me to do?"

"We've decided to do a group shot as if we're celebrating Christmas with a tailgate party featuring the Chuckwagon Café food."

Slade laughed, shaking his head. "I like it."

"We just need to arrange the food so it looks good in the photo."

"Too bad I didn't know ahead of time or I'd have

gotten our café's name emblazoned somewhere in the picture."

"That'd be crass advertising, wouldn't it?"

"Yep. And it's just the type I like," he said with a chuckle.

"They want Hedy, Ash, Lauren, and me to be in the photo, too."

"Great idea. Y'all contribute plenty to the station, so you ought to be included with the group."

"Looks like we're all in agreement. Let's get this food set up."

"I'll make room for Hedy in front of the tailgate. Ash will be sure to stay with her if we lure him with his favorite food."

"I'll stand near her, so we womenfolk are together," Sydney added.

"Suits me." Slade put a big hand on her arm. "I'll take care of the food. You go ahead and get yourself all dolled up. The rest of us are ready to go."

"Are you sure you don't need help?"

"Go!"

She glanced around, saw everybody was getting into place for their final photograph, and jogged over to Celeste. She sat down inside, opened her purse, and pulled out her makeup bag. She added a little extra blusher, eyeliner, and lipstick. She ran her fingertips through her hair, grabbed her cowgirl hat, and put it on her head. She pulled her hi-vis yellow firefighter parka off the back floorboard, slipped it on, and was good to go.

She noticed that Hedy hadn't joined the group. She simply sat with Ash on her lap, as if waiting to make up her mind as to what she wanted to do next. Sydney quickly walked over to her.

"Are you sure about us being in the photo?" Hedy asked. "I thought this was all about the cowboys."

"We might as well throw in a little extra eye candy. That'd be you and Ash." Sydney stroked the cat's sleek silver-gray fur and straightened the big red bow around his neck.

"Ash is definitely eye candy," Hedy said. "Me? I might break the camera."

"Not on your life." Sydney leaned down and kissed her cheek. "You're going to make the photo, so just come along."

When they reached Slade's pickup, everyone and everything looked in position while Kent stood behind the camera, still fiddling with it. Sydney gave everybody a thumbs-up.

Hedy slipped into position, and Sydney maneuvered into the open space slightly behind her next to Lauren. Misty stood just in back of Kent, watching, waiting, and obviously ready to help if anybody needed them.

"Okay, folks, say cheese," Kent called as he quickly stepped away from the camera and headed for his place by the truck.

Sydney put a big grin on her face just as Kent tucked his body in beside her. They both froze in place.

As the camera's shutter clicked to capture the group, a pickup tore into the parking lot, careened to a stop beside them, and a cowboy jumped out.

Dune jogged over to them, wearing dirty, sweaty, ripped Wranglers and carrying a crushed cowboy hat. "Am I late?"

Chapter 24

DUNE DIDN'T LOOK AT ANYBODY EXCEPT SYDNEY, trying to gauge just how mad she was about him being so late to the photo shoot, or the former photo shoot from the look of things. His attempt at a joke to ease the situation had fallen flat, so he was left with his backup position—which meant no position at all.

Nobody said a thing as all heads swiveled to see Sydney's reaction to him, because she was in charge of the calendar, and they'd follow her lead. Besides, he wasn't local, so he bet they'd band together if put to the test. So what? By now, he didn't care much one way or the other. He was hot, tired, and out-of-sorts, but he was here, so that ought to count for something. If not, he was plenty ready to load up his truck, head south, and say to hell with Wildcat Bluff County. But then there'd be no Sydney, Storm, Slade, Kent, or the other friends he'd made here. He resisted a big sigh, knowing he was caught between a rock and a hard place.

"You're just in time for our group photo," Sydney said, looking him over from head to toe.

He glanced down and realized he was in no shape for photographs. He hit the crown of his hat against his thigh to knock off the dust, then he punched the felt back into a recognizable shape with his fist. "Guess my clothes have seen better days."

Sydney nodded in agreement as she put a hand

over her mouth, as if stopping the words she wanted to say.

But he saw a little light at the end of the tunnel, because he'd seen one corner of her mouth twitch as if she was resisting the urge to laugh. Well, he'd take a laugh over a cry any day of the week. Maybe funny was the way to play this train wreck of a day. Everybody knew Texas folks liked nothing better than to laugh at themselves when they shared some long, tall tale about their misadventures. He'd sure had his share today.

"Well," he drawled out the word into several syllables just to whet their appetite for a good story. "It all started with a big, bad, Brahman bull." When they all leaned slightly forward, as if anxious to hear more, he knew he had them in the palm of his hand. He needed a win to get his life back on track, so he'd just give them the best story they'd heard in a coon's age.

"I take it you're talking about the Cougar Ranch Brahman," Kent said, helping the story along.

"Yep. That'd be the one."

"Wait." Sydney pointed toward the camera. "We want to hear your story, but first join the group so we can finish the shoot."

He looked down at his clothes again, then back at her—glad she was at least talking to him but not so optimistic about his appearance. "Are you sure you want me to be in the picture?"

"You're one of our fire-rescue volunteers, aren't you?"

"That'd be a yes."

"I rest my case."

"I can get a jacket out of the station." He figured that'd help cover up his clothes.

"No, not now," Sydney said. "We're ready to go, and the group's getting restless. Why don't you get in back of Trey and put on your hat. That way, you'll be mostly covered up."

"Guess that'll work." It looked as if he'd put off that trip down to the Hill Country a little longer.

As he stuck his hat on his head, Trey gave him a big grin and stepped aside so he could muscle into the group. Maybe it'd have been easier to have hightailed it out of here and licked his wounds with several bottles of Shiner under his belt. One thing for sure, he wouldn't have had to see the suppressed laughter at his condition, and that wasn't just his clothes but his letting Sydney tell him what to do because he was obviously so besotted with her that he wouldn't chance any trouble between them. It could be a damn right embarrassing situation, if all the other cowboys hadn't been there before him and understood what he was going through until he got her on a secure lead and she put one on him.

He got into place just back of Trey and tried to put a pleasant look—at least not a grimace—on his face for the photograph. A few snaps of the camera later and the photo shoot was finally put to bed. And he'd at least made it in time for one picture.

Soon everybody was milling around the back of Slade's pickup, shaking Dune's hand or slugging him on his arm, doing the male-bonding thing. It felt pretty good, particularly after the morning he'd had and the concern he'd had about being sent back to the ranch without his supper, or some such. He figured it just went to show if you scratched a cowboy, you'd find they were all the same underneath.

Now if he could just get Sydney not to hold a grudge, they could get on with their day. He glanced around for her. She was over with Kent, talking together as he took his camera off its tripod.

Slade slapped him on his back. "Better grab some grub while you can. Everyone's diving back into it, so it won't last long."

"Thanks. I will." He glanced at the open containers of food. "Is that Chuckwagon barbeque?"

"You're darn tootin'," Slade said from his position by the food. "I made it myself."

"In that case, I sure don't want to miss out." He picked up a chopped beef sandwich and iced tea.

Slade leaned in close. "I doubt if she'll admit it, but she was worried about you."

Dune glanced into the hazel eyes so like Sydney's and gave a quick nod of appreciation that her brother had shared that important piece of information.

"Still, you're gonna have to make up for being late."

Dune nodded again as he took a big bite of the delicious sandwich. "Okay," he mumbled around the wad of food.

Slade glanced over at Sydney. "You better eat quick and get on with your story before everybody gets gone."

Dune swallowed, then swallowed a slug of tea. "It's a good one."

"Remember, she needs to save face." Slade picked up his drink, tossed several empty containers in the trash, and moved what food was left to the edge of the tailgate. "She's got a lot of social capital invested in you doing right."

"I won't let her down." Dune finished off his sandwich and tossed the wrapper in the trash. He drank the last of his tea and threw the cup away, too.

Storytelling was as old as the Hill Country. Comanche warriors and German settlers had kept dangerous nights at bay with myths, legends, and stories told round the comforting flames of campfires. He'd been brought up on stories. You earned your family spurs when you could hold the attention of an audience with a well-told yarn. Now he had even more at stake, but he was ready to put everything on the line to earn a second set of spurs with his Wildcat Bluff family.

"Okay, folks," Slade called out, "Dune's got a tale that's gotta be told."

"It better be good!" Kent hollered from where he stood beside Sydney and Lauren.

"I can't say if it'll be good or bad." Dune glanced around at the group. "That'll be for y'all to decide."

"Go on, get back to my pesky Brahman." Kent handed Sydney his camera, folded his tripod, tucked it under his arm, and grinned at Dune.

Dune pointed at Kent. "He could've warned me I needed to strap on my spurs when he called me at dawn."

"I figured you were a big enough cowboy without them," Kent goaded him right back.

"Yeah, that's what they always say after they send you on an impossible mission."

"Kent, give him a break," Hedy called, laughing. "We know all about the tasks you set cowboys."

Kent joined her laughter. "Okay, I admit that stupid Brahman managed to get off Cougar Ranch and onto Steele Trap *again*."

"Is he in love or what?" Slade asked, chuckling at his own joke.

"He's in love with your pasture, that's for sure," Dune agreed, tossing a look at Sydney to see if she was still with him. "I chased that bull all over Steele Trap, seems like, before I persuaded him to go home."

"That's when Dune let me know he was on his way here," Kent added. "But I admit, I should've handed that job to another cowboy."

"Or two," Dune added with a shake of his head.

All the cowboys laughed, nodding their heads as if they'd been there, done that too many times to count.

"That's right," Sydney spoke up, giving Kent a sideways look. "You knew he was supposed to be here early to help with our photo shoot."

"And I doubt I'll ever hear the last of it," Kent said.

"That's right," Slade agreed. "You're gonna be in hot water till you make it up to her."

"We got the photos," Sydney said. "That'll do."

"Okay," Trey pushed the story. "You got the bull back in his pasture. Then what? You sure weren't here."

"Yeah." Dune sighed, taking off his hat, looking inside it, then putting it back on his head. "I hit Wildcat Road okay, but then—" He paused for dramatic effect before he continued, "I swear if I didn't see another bull loose beside the road near the turnoff for the old Perkins place."

"Angus?" Trey asked, leaning forward.

"Yep. Black. And he was spooked, looking to cross the lane and get hit."

"Owner?" Kent called out.

"Here's the odd part." Dune glanced around the

group, knowing he had them now. "He wore the Holloway brand."

"But their ranch isn't along that patch of road," Sydney said, frowning in puzzlement.

"That's right," Dune agreed. "Well now, it looked to me like Bert and Bert Two had another spot of trouble, and the last thing they needed was a loose bull on top of the fires on their properties. It made me wonder if they'd had another fire that nobody knew about yet."

He walked over and picked up a drink, then he took a sip to wet his whistle. "Anyhow, I tried to call Bert and y'all, but—"

"That's a tricky area for cell phone coverage," Slade added.

"Anyhow, I could've driven back to the ranch, but that'd have left the bull on the road too long. So I figured I'm cowboy enough to find the break in the fence, get the bull back in there, and fix it. I'd done it once already, so it shouldn't take long."

"Famous last words, huh?" Kent said.

Dune just shook his head. "Yeah. Anyway, I found the break in the fence, but it was clean-cut as if it'd recently been snipped. That was odd, but no odder than a bull that didn't belong in that pasture anyway. So I was back to chasing the four-legged, only this time on foot, and he was mad as all get-out, so he butted me, knocked me off my feet, stomped all over my hat, and then had the nerve to trot back into that pasture as if I hadn't just busted my butt getting him there."

Everybody burst out laughing as they nodded their heads in agreement that it was just the way of a cowboy's life.

"I pulled my truck off the side of the road onto that old, overgrown road that leads to the empty Perkins farmhouse, parked, and found enough stuff in my tool chest to fix the fence."

"What was the bull doing?" Hedy asked, stroking Ash as she grinned at the firefighters.

"Chewing his cud and eyeing me like roadkill while I cobbled together the fence," Dune said. "Anyhow, I got back in my pickup, pulled out on the road to come here, and had a flat tire. So I pulled off the side and parked again."

"Oh no!" Hedy shook her head. "And still no cell coverage?"

"No nothing," Dune agreed. "And the road was empty. Of course, nobody was driving by when I needed a lift. Anyway, another odd thing. I shouldn't have had a flat, since my tires are good. I went back and looked at where I'd been parked. Lo and behold, there was broken glass all over the area in front of the cattle guard leading into the farm."

"That is odd," Kent agreed. "That place has been empty for a number of years. Maybe kids?"

"Maybe." Dune shrugged as he continued his tale. "I was in a hurry, so I jerked out my spare tire, jacked up my truck, took off the flat tire, and—"

"It wasn't flat, too, was it?" Sydney asked.

He glanced over at her and saw sympathy in her hazel eyes. "Pretty near. It was leaking air from the stem."

"Are you sure you're not making this up?" Kent challenged with a look of feigned disbelief. "Either that or you used up your bad luck for the year."

"I wish I was making this up, but I guess I finally

used up my bad luck, because about that time, Sheriff Calhoun drove up and—"

"Laughed?" Hedy asked. "Because that's about all that's left to do after this much trouble."

"That's right," Dune agreed. "And I laughed with him, because I was hell-bent to get here and couldn't do it." He looked at Sydney and just shook his head in regret.

She gave him a warm smile. "We're glad you're safely here."

He returned her smile, deciding she'd let him out of the doghouse. "Sheriff Calhoun got to looking around after hearing the oddness of my story. He told me that Bert and Bert Two had bought the Perkins farm some time back to help out Hollis Perkins, who'd got himself in a financial bind."

"Do you suppose," Hedy asked, suddenly looking serious, "somebody added theft and vandalism to arson on Holloway property?"

"That's exactly what Sheriff Calhoun and I couldn't help but wonder."

"I guess he contacted Bert," Hedy said. "Is he okay?"

"Yep," Dune agreed. "But put out."

"I'll call him later, too," Hedy said. "I don't like this business one little bit."

"Nobody does." Dune glanced around at the cowboy firefighters. "I suggest we keep an extra eye out till we get through Christmas."

"Agreed," Hedy added. "We don't want any more property damage, or anybody hurt."

"That's for sure," Dune said.

"And the sheriff was able to blow up your spare?" Sydney asked, giving Dune a warm smile.

"Plus, he gave me an escort into town so I could get here fast."

"I'm glad," Sydney said. "We needed you here."

"That's the best story I've heard in some time, even if it does worry me some," Hedy said. "I suggest we give Dune a big round of applause, then let's all get back to making this the best Christmas ever."

Dune felt as if he'd come home when the other cowboy firefighters put their hands together for him. It'd all just been a day's work on a ranch, but sharing his tale of woe to a sympathetic group who'd been there took the sting out of his troubles. They were all part of the same cowboy tribe, and they were in it come hell or high water. He watched silently as they dispersed to go their separate ways, but they'd come back together when the need arose to help one another and the county through thick and thin.

Sydney walked up to him, holding Kent's camera, and squeezed his hand. "That's a pretty tall tale, cowboy."

"Yeah. I'm surprised anybody believed me."

"Sheriff Calhoun was a nice touch."

"Probably saved my bacon."

"No doubt." She leaned up and pressed a soft kiss to his lips. "I'm so glad you're okay."

"I'm good now." He returned her kiss, well aware that they were letting everybody in Wildcat Bluff know their true feelings for each other. And he was pleased about that fact.

"Are you good enough for another photo shoot?"

"Aren't we done here?"

"You owe me a photo." She gave him a mischievous smile. "Remember my pretty pink Cadillac?"

"How could I forget?"

She held up the camera. "That's where I want to shoot Mr. December."

He groaned, shaking his head. And he'd thought chasing an ornery Brahman bull was bad.

Chapter 25

SYDNEY DROVE CELESTE RIGHT UP TO THE SURE-SHOT Drive-In's entrance. She figured Dune was already inside, since the gate was open. She'd loaned him the keys so she could run by the café and check on Storm. Fortunately—or maybe unfortunately—her daughter appeared to be content helping out when normally she wanted to be outdoors on her ATV or pony. She supposed Storm felt safe there, and that was good for now, but she must find a way to help her daughter past her newfound fear. For the moment, she was simply glad Storm was where she felt safe and loved during the busy holidays.

With Celeste's top down, a breeze cooled Sydney's face as she drove past the big white screen that towered over the parking lanes. She looked around till she spotted Dune's pickup parked near the snack shed, so she headed over there, passing metal speakers on their tall poles.

She was pleased with her clothes today. Misty and Lauren had been appreciative of her vintage look, so she knew she'd achieved her goal in promoting Christmas at the Sure-Shot Drive-In. As far as the guys were concerned, she figured they'd been a lot more interested in Chuckwagon barbeque than 1950s attire. No matter. She was comfortable, ready to finish the photos, and get the calendar into production.

She parked beside Dune's truck and noticed her heart

speed up at the thought of seeing him again—*alone*. She felt a little bad that she'd had such negative thoughts about him while he'd been embroiled in such a horrible morning, but their relationship was still so fresh that she hadn't been able to keep her doubts at bay.

She watched as he stepped out of his truck, one long leg after the other. He looked good. Delicious, in fact. She could hardly wait to photograph him with Kent's camera, looking as if he'd just saved a burning building from destruction. She followed him with her eyes as he walked around Celeste, running his long fingers across the satiny paint, stopped by her door, and leaned down, smiling at her with heat in his gaze.

"Hey, lady," he said, tossing her the drive-in key ring, "are you going my way?"

"Hop in, stranger. I'm going any which way you want to go."

He grinned bigger, nodding in appreciation as he looked her over from top to bottom. "You look real fine."

"So do you." She set the drive-in keys beside Kent's camera on the front seat.

He glanced down at his clothes, shaking his head. "You wouldn't let me shower or change. Surely I can't be what you want for Mr. December."

"You're exactly what I want."

He just shook his head again. "I'm still sweaty, dirty, and my clothes are ripped."

She gave him a big grin, thinking how much cowgirls liked cowboys who didn't mind getting sweaty and dirty while hard at work, roping and riding on a ranch or pumping and rolling at a fire. Dune had it all, but for the first time, she wasn't sure she wanted to share him. Yet a benefit was a benefit, so sharing his photograph—and only his photo—was for a good cause.

"Anyway," he said with his brow creasing in a frown, "all the other firefighters were shot at the station. How come I'm here at the drive-in?"

"You're Mr. December. I want to promote Christmas at the Sure-Shot Drive-In with your photo in the calendar."

He clicked his tongue, glancing up at the big white screen and back again. "Okay. But why am I sweaty and dirty in the photo?"

"You just saved the drive-in from a fire, and I captured you taking a break in my Cadillac."

He clicked his tongue again and scratched his chin where he now had a little beard stubble. "You know that makes no sense. If I was taking a break or the fire was over, I sure wouldn't be sitting around in a vintage Caddy."

She couldn't resist the laugh that bubbled up. "We're not talking logic here. We're talking fantasy."

"That makes even less sense." He straightened up, looked toward the south, and then leaned down again. "My mom would have my hide if she caught me messing up a pristine vehicle like this one."

"She likes vintage Caddies?"

He grinned as he nodded his head. "Yeah. Retro anything. If she saw your closet, you'd probably never get her out of it, or it'd be a lot lighter when she got done looking through it."

"She sounds like somebody after my own heart."

"I think you'll like each other."

Sydney glanced away, drumming her fingertips on the big steering wheel. Was he already talking about her meeting his parents? He knew her family. Everything was moving so quickly—maybe too quickly—for her to get a firm grasp on the situation.

"Don't you want to meet her?"

"Yes, of course. It's just that—"

"I'm going too fast, aren't I?"

"Pretty fast."

He sighed, rubbing his chin again. "Truth of the matter, it doesn't seem so fast to me. It seems as if it's taken a coon's age to get here."

"Our night together was wonderful."

"But?"

"That was then. Today is today."

"And I messed up not getting to the photo shoot on time."

"It was out of your control."

"Yeah."

She reached up and stroked his face, feeling the rough stubble up the heat she now always felt in his presence. "Do you want to make it up to me?"

"Do I need to?" He turned his head and kissed the palm of her hand.

"No." She felt his kiss go straight to the heart of her and set her on fire. "But I want to get that photo of you while the sunlight's still strong."

He grasped her hand and placed a gentle kiss on the tip of each finger. "You know I can't say no to you. If you want the photo, you'll have the photo."

"Thanks." She hesitated, then went with what she knew she should keep to herself but couldn't resist saying to him. "I just wish you were a little more enthusiastic."

"You can't have everything." And then he cocked his head to one side as he gave her a slow, considering gaze.

"I take that back. You *can* have everything—any little thing your heart desires, if—"

"What?" She rolled her eyes, not quite knowing what to expect but figuring it'd have something to do with the hot look in his eyes, but she was only giving him mock exasperation. Whatever he wanted, she figured she'd enjoy it, too.

"If you want me to show enthusiasm in the photo, you need to give me a reason for it."

She sighed out loud as she gave him a firm look. "Benefit for our fire-rescue isn't enough?"

He shook his head in the negative.

"Support for the other firefighters who posed for our calendar isn't enough?"

He shook his head again.

"Staying on Hedy's good side isn't enough?"

He grinned, cocking his head to one side. "Now you're getting warm."

"How about staying on my good side?"

"Every side of you is good."

She chuckled at his words. "You're just looking for trouble, aren't you?"

"Sydney," he said as his gaze turned from mischievous to serious. "From the first moment I saw you, I knew you were trouble. *For me.*"

"Oh, Dune." She felt such a strong emotion cascade through her that tears stung her eyes, so she quickly blinked them away. She couldn't understand how he could affect her so much, but even so, she wouldn't let her feelings interfere with everything she needed to get done for Christmas. "You big lug, step back so I can position Celeste to get the best sunlight for our photo, or you're sincerely going to be in bigger trouble than you can imagine."

"Is that a promise?"

"It's a threat." She gave him a hard stare with a big frown, hoping he'd think she was serious and finally follow her instructions and let her get the last photograph.

He simply chuckled as his eyes crinkled at the corners in merriment, but he did step away from the Cadillac. "Okay. I'll take trouble as my payment."

"Fine." She couldn't resist a slight smile, knowing she might as well give up trying to get him to take his pose as Mr. December serious.

She restarted Celeste and then turned the big, beautiful Cadillac toward the west so bright sunlight gleamed on the chrome grill and the tinsel-decorated longhorns while highlighting the back seat. She cut the engine, tossed a yellow firefighter jacket on the back seat, picked up Kent's camera, and stepped outside onto black asphalt.

Dune raised his arms up and outward, then dropped them to his sides. "Where do you want me?"

"Well now," she said, unable to resist teasing him, "you did say you wanted trouble."

He looked down at the ground, then back at her with a mischievous grin. "Okay. Let's get this shoot done, so I can get my trouble."

"Would you take off your boots, then unsnap your shirt and pull it out so it hangs loose?"

He gave a big sigh, but he went ahead and toed off one boot before the other. He leaned down, tugged off his socks, and stuffed them into his boots. He straightened up and then gave her a slight smile as he popped open his shirt and jerked it loose. "Will this do?"

"Oh yes." At the sight of his tanned, muscular chest, she felt as if summer had suddenly come back and bathed her in moist heat, but she knew that was simply her own personal over-the-top reaction to him.

"Now what?"

She shook her head to get her mind back on track and away from thoughts of tangled, sweaty sheets. "Please get in Celeste's back, then sit on top of the back seat."

"On top?" He opened the car door, pushed the front seat forward, and stepped onto the back floorboard. He glanced at her with a questioning look in his deep blue eyes.

"Yes, please. If you'll sit in the center, put your legs over the back of the seat and your feet on the bottom of the seat, then drape that jacket next to you, and you're good to go."

She watched as he positioned his body and the fire-fighter jacket, obviously uncomfortable with the entire layout, and glanced at her again. She felt her breath hitch in her throat. If there was a money shot, this was it. "Will you spread your arms wide like your legs, then put one hand on the jacket and the other on the back of the seat?"

"Sydney, are you sure?" he asked, even as he got into the perfect position.

"Yes. Trust me."

"As far as this calendar goes, I don't trust you at all."

"It'll be great. People will love this cowboy fire-fighter calendar."

She raised her camera, not telling him that he might not be completely comfortable with how hot and sexy he looked combined with the hot and sexy Cadillac convertible. He appeared to be ready, willing, and able to tumble a willing woman down onto the back seat and show her just what these classic cars were really made for back in their heyday. She'd be happy to be the cowgirl in that back seat with him, but she had to keep her mind on business, at least for right now.

And yet there was skepticism growing in his gaze, and it wasn't the look she wanted and needed to sell calendars. She had to do something to get him in the right frame of mind. She lowered the camera to one side with her right hand. With her left hand, she slowly undid the top button of her sweater, followed by the second button, the third, and by the time she'd exposed a little cleavage, she had his undivided attention—and exactly the look she wanted from him.

She quickly raised the camera and took several shots, moving closer and closer until she rested the base of the camera on the frame of the car to get a steady, up-close-and-personal photograph. He truly looked as if he'd just come from fighting a fire, with the slight beard stubble along his strong jawline, the smear of what appeared to be soot across his chest, and the dampness of his tanned skin stretched across rock-hard muscles.

"Not fair," he said, shaking his head and causing a lock of thick tawny hair to fall across his forehead.

She quickly snapped that shot for posterity, knowing she wouldn't mind one bit having it enlarged, framed, and perched on her nightstand. She took several more pictures, making sure she had plenty for choice, and then checked to see if any of the shots she'd taken would do. She flicked forward, smiling as she saw that she'd outdone even her own high expectations. Oh yes, Dune definitely would heat up chilly winter rooms with his pose as Mr. December.

"Are you done?" He leaned toward her, resting his elbows on his knees, as he gazed at the gap in her sweater.

She flicked him a knowing look, but she was well aware she'd been the one to entice him with a little revealed skin to match his own. "Yes, we're all done here. Now I can finish the calendar and get it into production."

"Not just yet." He wiggled his fingers at her, indicating for her to come to him.

"Dune, we don't have time for games."

"What did you promise me if I cooperated with your photo shoot?"

She never went back on her word, so he sort of had her there if she couldn't get out of it. "Trouble?"

"If ever there was a gal whose name was trouble, it's you."

"Now, Dune—"

"Come here, Trouble."

Chapter 26

SYDNEY HAD BEEN CALLED A LOT OF THINGS IN HER life, such as cowgirl, barrel racer, mother, daughter, and firefighter, but never had she been called "trouble." She was known as the practical, responsible one who got stuff done in a timely manner. In fact, folks came to her to get a project off the ground, just as they had with Christmas at the Sure-Shot Drive-In. She'd come up with the benefit calendar all on her own, and she was driving hard to complete it. But "trouble"?

The single word made her sound like something she'd never been, but something she might want to try just to see if it actually fit her. On the other hand, maybe Dune was simply attempting to maneuver her where he wanted her to go as he would a recalcitrant cow or horse. Either way, she'd gotten all her photos, so she had leeway for a bit of fun before she went home and put the calendar to bed. She deserved a reward for being so good, now didn't she?

If ever a reward was staring her right in the face, it was Dune Barrett. He looked deliciously bad, as if he'd invaded her pink Cadillac with only one thing on his mind. If somebody was trouble, it definitely was him. She'd known that from the first, so she'd resisted him until she had no resistance left. Now all she craved was the soft look in his eyes, the warm touch of his hands, and the driving force of his body. Did she have the strength of will to throw caution to the wind and take what she wanted, no matter the consequences? Could she actually meet "trouble" with "trouble"?

She cocked a hip and put one hand on her waist as she looked him over where he sat spread-legged in her Caddy. "If you want trouble, you're gonna have to come get it."

He grinned, giving her back as good as she gave with a gaze that took her in from head to toe and back again. "Trouble, do you think you've got something worth my time?"

She simply shrugged, raising an eyebrow as she imagined a smart gal back in the day would do. If she was truly trouble, she wouldn't go to him—he'd come to her. "That's for me to know and you to find out."

He grinned even bigger, with sunlight glinting on his white teeth, while he leaned toward her, as if caught in the gossamer threads of a spiderweb that had captured both of them in its iridescent threads.

Satisfied by his response, she opened the door to Celeste, set Kent's camera on the passenger seat, and picked up the Sure-Shot Drive-In key ring. She held up the ring and jingled the keys at him. "If you want trouble, you might look for it in the snack shed."

And with those words, she simply turned on her heel and walked away without looking back. He'd follow her or he wouldn't, but she was pretty sure he couldn't resist her any more than she could resist him. At the very least, she needed to check out the snack shed again to make sure all was still in order for the upcoming event.

She walked up to the patio and noticed that the color-ful metal chairs that faced the screen were still outside.

She wondered if it might not be a good idea to keep them inside when not in use to avoid inclement weather or other problems, but that was a decision for Bert and Bert Two. She was just glad to see the patio was ready for Christmas at the Sure-Shot Drive-In.

After she inserted the key in the lock, she resisted the urge to look over her shoulder to see if Dune was following her, although she wanted nothing more than for him to be here with her. She opened the door, flicked on the lights, stepped inside, and shut the door firmly behind her. Once more, she delighted in the snack shed's fun interior. Somebody had already turned on the heat, so warm air knocked out the chill in the air.

She walked over to the candy counter and was pleased to see that it'd been stocked with all sorts of yummy candy, granola bars, and trail mix. A big glass jar of green pickles stood on one side of the glass countertop. She even saw a display of Sure-Shot Drive-In promotional items with the drive-in's logo on baseball caps, magnets, travel mugs, ballpoint pens, and such stuff.

Now what would a troublesome gal do? She grabbed a cap and put it on her head, figuring she'd pay later, since there was nobody to take her payment now. She felt quite sassy as she glided across the floor in her cigarette pants while setting her cap at a jaunty angle. She ended up at the jukebox. She felt warm tenderness envelop her as she remembered the slow dance with Dune that had turned her life around and started her on a new path—one filled with glorious passion.

She checked to make sure the jukebox was plugged into the wall before she pushed the buttons for

"Unchained Melody." Soon the snack shed filled with soaring music, and then came the heartrending words:

"Oh, my love, my darling… I've hungered for your touch…"

She swayed to the rhythm, hugging her arms around her waist as she imagined Dune holding her in his strong embrace. She heard the outer door open and shut, so she stopped and looked in that direction. She felt her breath catch in her throat at the sight of the tall cowboy with his shirttail loose and shirt front gaping open to reveal the washboard abs of his chest and the dark indentation of his belly button above his big gold rodeo buckle.

Dune flipped off the overhead lights so that only sunlight from two windows illuminated the snack shed, turning the dance floor into a cozy, shadowy, intimate area—except for the bright, bold, luminous colors of the jukebox. He strode toward her, wearing his cowboy boots again, with that special balance riders develop after spending long hours in the saddle.

When he set foot on the parquet dance floor, he gave her a lopsided, mischievous smile as he pointedly looked down at her exposed cleavage and then back up at her face.

She realized she'd forgotten to redo the buttons. She started to automatically button her sweater, then stopped her hand in midmotion. If she was trouble, she'd better act like it. She straightened her back and thrust out her chest, watching him closely for his reaction. She was amply rewarded for a few undone buttons when his blue eyes turned dark with desire.

He nodded as if accepting her challenge or invitation,

and then he held out his strong, long-fingered hand with palm turned upward in invitation. "Dance with me."

Oh yes, she wanted to dance with him, and he knew it, too. Still, she couldn't resist the playfulness that came over her, perhaps in response to her sheer joy in his presence or his desire for—or expectation of—*trouble*. She whipped the baseball cap off her head and plunked it down on top of his wind-blown hair.

He caught her playfulness with a twinkle in his eyes, lifted the cap, smoothed back his hair, and adjusted the cap for a perfect fit. "Thanks."

"Looks as if you're all ready for Christmas at the Sure-Shot Drive-In," she said mischievously, suddenly realizing that she was drawing out this moment, building this moment, upping the intensity of this moment, because it was a special time and place to remember for a lifetime.

"It's a start."

"What do you mean?"

"I'll be more than ready for our Christmas event once we initiate the snack shed."

"Initiate?"

"Yeah," he agreed, a smile tugging up one corner of his full lips. "Remember, this drive-in is also called the Passion Pit."

"I hardly think Christmas at the Passion Pit will bring in the type of folks we have in mind for family-oriented films and events."

He grinned, blue eyes dancing with laughter. "After midnight, that's when the cool cats came out to prowl, right?"

"I think you've got the wrong county for fifties' cool cats."

"It's never too late. Want to be a cool cat?"

"I thought I was *trouble*."

"All cool cats are trouble with a capital T, didn't you know?"

"I just found out about trouble, so how would I know about cool cats?"

He chuckled, a deep sound that rumbled in his broad chest. "You're dressed like a cool cat in your cigarette pants, aren't you?"

"Maybe." She realized he had a point. "But how do you know about fifties stuff?"

"My mom."

"Oh, that's right. I guess she'd know."

"And that means I'd know. Now come here. Let's dance, and I'll show you all about trouble and cool cats."

"But the music's over."

He shook his head in denial. "The music will never be over for us." And he held wide his arms.

She'd bantered long enough. She didn't care about trouble or cool cats. She didn't care about prolonging the moment. Now she wanted nothing more than to be wrapped in his strong arms, so she could feel the beat of his heart in time with her own. She'd missed him. She'd worried about him. And she'd pined for his touch after all they'd shared one night together. Now he was back, and she didn't want to ever let him go.

She put her hands flat against his chest—feeling his muscles harden, feeling his nipples tighten—and then she slowly, so very slowly, slid her fingers upward across his bare flesh, creating goose bumps in her wake as he reacted to her touch. She trembled in response to him, knowing how much more they could draw from each other. She curled her fingers into the hair he wore a little long at the back of his muscular neck, tightening her grip as her entire body tightened with growing desire.

As if he couldn't wait another moment, he crushed her against his chest, molding their bodies together as if they were one instead of two. She caught his scent—sunshine and prairie grass—and that alone almost sent her over the edge, because it was so symbolic of him. And just like the song, she hungered for his touch, wanting him, needing him, maybe even loving him.

When he hummed "Unchained Melody," she put her head on his shoulder, holding him fiercely with both hands. She felt his need for her grow hot and hard as he slowly guided them across the dance floor, teasing and tormenting with every brush of body to body.

At the jukebox, he stopped their dance, squeezed her tight, and let her go. He quickly leaned over and punched several buttons. When a 45 dropped into place, the room filled with "Unchained Melody" again.

She caught her breath, for she knew she'd never hear this song anywhere at any time without thinking of Dune.

As he turned back to her, he didn't say a word, but he didn't need to utter a single sound, because everything he felt was there in his eyes that now blazed blue fire.

She went to him, as if on angel's wings, and put her arms around him. She could feel her hot skin against his hot flesh. Nothing that had gone before, nothing that she had experienced before, nothing that had been in her life before had prepared her for Dune and his overwhelming effect on her.

He kissed her, a light, feathery touch at first that

quickly turned fiery as he nipped her lower lip, traced her mouth with his tongue, and then plunged deep inside. She trembled all over as she returned his kiss, feeling their heat ignite into an out-of-control wildfire that threatened to burn down everything in their vicinity as it completely consumed them.

Finally, he tore his mouth from hers as he gasped for air, lifted her in his arms, and walked to the nearest wall. "I can't wait." He unbuckled his belt and the button on his jeans.

She glanced toward the unlocked front door and the windows without drapes, realizing that anybody could walk in on them or look in on them at any moment. "But what about the door and—"

"Are you saying no?" He pulled a condom out of his back pocket and held it out in the palm of his hand. "See, I'm prepared now."

She couldn't help but smile, feeling her blaze grow hotter because he'd thought about them while they were apart and prepared for this very moment. "Fortunately, we're pretty isolated here."

"Right now, I don't care if the whole town of Sure-Shot walks in on us. I'm burning up." He reached for her pants, frowned in confusion, and looked up at her face. "How do you get these down?"

"Side zipper. Let me."

"Oh no. It'll be my pleasure to undress you."

"But Dune—" As she felt his hands on her zipper, she glanced toward the outside door, deciding they'd hear somebody drive up in time for her to get dressed or get inside the ladies' room.

When he tugged her cigarette pants down to her

ankles, she kicked them off, along with her moccasins. If not for the dimness in the room, she'd have felt much too exposed, and yet she felt even more excited now, particularly with the look in his eyes that was getting hotter by the moment. He put both hands on her hips, tucked his thumbs under the waistband of her red panties, and slowly slid them down her long legs.

"I want these," he muttered in a voice gone deep and hoarse.

"To add to your collection?"

"Only until I have the real thing—that'd be you—permanently in my bed."

She shivered with his words, with his touch, with his determination as she stepped out of her underwear and watched him push them deep into a front pocket of his Wranglers.

"Now we can get somewhere." He unzipped his jeans and tore open the condom container.

When he lifted her again, she wrapped her arms around his shoulders and her legs around his waist. She felt him slide inside her hot, moist depths, and she moaned with so much relief and desire that she thought she would instantly combust. He gave her a quick, hot kiss, then he moved hard and fast, thrust deep and strong as they both panted and groaned and clutched at each other while they rode their spiral of passion higher and higher until they burned white-hot in a blazing inferno of ecstasy.

She felt shaky and weak-kneed when he finally set her feet on the floor. She leaned back against the wall for support as she took deep breaths to still her racing heart.

He braced his body with one hand on the wall behind

her, breathing hard as he looked down at her with adoration in his blue eyes.

She smiled at him, knowing she had the same look in her eyes, for he completed her in a way she'd never known before—not even with her beloved Emery.

"Do you need the ladies' room?"

"Go ahead. Take care of yourself. Let me catch my breath."

"You're okay, aren't you?" He pressed a tender kiss to her lips.

She nodded, feeling as if all words had failed her. She desperately needed a moment alone to come to terms with what she'd just realized about her former husband and herself. She'd never believed there could be anyone else for her except Emery. Now she knew different, but how did she deal with it?

"Guess we initiated the Passion Pit after all." He gave her a mischievous smile, then he quickly walked away.

She took a deep breath, pushed back her hair, and looked down at her cigarette pants. She felt stunned, as much from the power of her reaction to Dune as from her revelation about Emery. Could she actually be in love? She felt such softness when she thought of Dune, as if she were unfolding one petal at a time for him like a flower responding to the irresistible, vibrant rays of the sun.

She had to ask herself—had Dune become her sun and moon and stars? She felt breathless at the idea. Yet excited, too. And even a little scared. What if he didn't feel the same? What if he was gone tomorrow? What if she was just a passing fancy? That'd be almost unbearable, because how would she deal with another broken heart?

And yet she realized that she couldn't think on it now, not when Dune would be back soon, not when somebody could drive up at any moment, not when she felt so vulnerable. She needed her clothes and the slight protection they afforded her. She needed to turn her mind away from her exhilaration and her anxiety. She needed to focus on the mundane, and that meant thinking about the calendar and the festival. She could handle those two items when she wasn't sure she could handle anything else.

She quickly leaned down and picked up her pants. She jerked them on and zipped up the side. She tugged down her sweater and started tucking the buttons back through their holes. And all the while, she looked around the snack shed, trying to settle her mind on anything except Dune. And yet he was all she could think about—even when she looked at the red vinyl booths, suddenly the soft, deep cushions looked perfect for an activity that went way beyond drinking malts and eating fries. Dune would know exactly how to put that red vinyl to good use.

She ripped her mind away from that thought and strode over to the candy counter, but it was no help. She quickly averted her eyes from the pickle jar and walked over to the outside door. Maybe she needed to sit on the patio and let a cool wind freeze the heat in her brain.

She glanced back toward the restrooms, but Dune was still out of sight. That was probably a good thing. She'd just wait for him outside where she'd be away from emotional jukebox music and tantalizing vinyl booths. She put her hand on the doorknob, turned it, and just as she started to open the door, she heard a vehicle pull up outside.

Shocked, she simply stood there, knowing she wasn't

ready—no how, no way—to see anybody right now. She felt too vulnerable, too emotional, too on edge. And even worst of the worst, she had to look as if she'd been thoroughly kissed, what with her swollen lips and too-pink cheeks. Yet that sultry bedroom look was much better than the blatant truth of how she'd just initiated the Sure-Shot Drive-In into the Passion Pit.

When vehicle doors slammed outside, she rolled her eyes and took a deep breath. Ready or not, they had company.

Chapter 27

SYDNEY WANTED TO FLIP THE LOCK CLOSED ON THE snack shed door and keep everybody out. She didn't want to share the place, not after what she'd just experienced with Dune on the dance floor. And yet she now realized that life had to move onward, never stalling, never turning back, no matter how much she wanted to make time stand still.

She'd never refused to face a challenge, and she wouldn't do it now. No matter how many ways she might look at her situation, she was facing a major life challenge, and not just in this particular moment but as she strode into the future. Revelations were revelations, but life was life. She couldn't simply go to bed, pull the covers over her head, and think…not about all she'd lost but about all she could gain. She had to keep going forward right this very moment, because so many people depended on her.

Still, she hesitated with her hand on the doorknob. She wanted to holler for Dune to hurry and join her. But if she did, the folks on the other side of the door would hear and draw conclusions that she didn't want known yet. She lusted after this last moment with Dune before she let the world inside, shattering their time together.

As she started to open the door, she heard the opening strains of "Unchained Melody" swirl across the room, filling her with such emotion that she knew, *absolutely knew*, that Dune would always register on her personal compass as true north.

She glanced back. He stood beside the jukebox, smiling at her and obviously trying for all the world to appear completely innocent. He'd snapped shut his shirt and tucked the tail into his jeans, but nothing could remove the self-satisfied gleam in his blue eyes. She just shook her head. They made a fine pair, both looking as guilty as sin in the Passion Pit.

He nodded toward the door, letting her know that he realized the gig was up and they had company. But at the same time, he put a hand on the jukebox and stroked it, sending a message that he'd always treasure their time here alone together.

She returned his nod, letting him know that she understood and that she'd always remember, too.

And with that vision of Dune—her forever cowboy firefighter—standing beside the jukebox burned into her memory, she turned back to face the future. She quickly flipped on the bright, inside lights, twisted the doorknob, and jerked open the door to let late afternoon sunlight spill inside, dispelling the intimacy she'd shared with Dune.

Bert and Bert Two stepped back in unison, appearing surprised at the sudden opening of the door. They both raised their cowboy hats to her, then set them back on their heads with ready smiles.

"Welcome to the Sure-Shot Drive-In snack shed." She grinned at them as if she was there to give them a tour and stepped back as she gestured toward the interior. "We're almost ready for Christmas."

"Good timing," Bert said as he stepped past her.

"I like what you've done with the place," Bert Two teased as he followed his dad into the building.

"Thanks," she responded, going along with their game. "I do hope you appreciate all the hard work I've put into the drive-in."

"Yep," Bert agreed, smiling at her joke. "We like every little bit of it."

"Seriously, I'm really impressed with your attention to detail and integrity in restoring the drive-in."

"I agree." Dune walked forward from the jukebox to join them. "I bet you get tons of business from here on out. Folks will surely drive out here from Dallas and Fort Worth. They'll come from Sherman, Denison, Bonham, Paris, and other North and East Texas towns."

"That's true," she quickly agreed, then noticed in horror that an edge of red lace peeked out of Dune's front pocket. She couldn't help but worry that the Holloways might notice or that her panties might fall out at their feet. She quickly stepped to the side and turned so she had her back to Bert and Bert Two.

Dune gave her a questioning look before he glanced back at the other guys. "There are so few of these classic drive-in theaters left. I bet it'll be a big family draw, depending on the movies you show here."

She got Dune's attention and then pointed at his pocket before rubbing downward on her pants to let him know what she wanted him to do. She whirled back around, smiling too big and knowing it. "Yes, it's such a good idea."

Bert glanced from Sydney to Dune before he looked over at Bert Two with a raised eyebrow. "Yeah. It's what we have in mind to start."

"But these drive-ins weren't known as passion pits around the country for nothing." Bert Two chuckled as he nodded back at Bert as if in agreement with an unspoken statement.

Sydney suspected what they'd just communicated with each other and sighed silently at their correct conclusion, but they were probably simply imagining a few kisses and hopefully hadn't seen the edge of her red panties. "That's what I've heard," she said loudly, drawing their attention to her so Dune had a chance to conceal her underwear. "Still, Christmas at the Sure-Shot Drive-In is strictly family fare."

"Absolutely," Bert said with a twitch of his lips that revealed he was restraining his amusement.

"No doubt about it." Bert Two turned away and rapidly strode over to the candy counter.

Sydney narrowed her eyes at his quick departure, because she caught the shaking of his shoulders as if he was repressing laughter. She glanced at Dune's jeans and gave a big sigh of relief. No more red. "Anyway, thanks again for letting us headquarter here for the festival."

"Glad to do it," Bert said.

"Yeah," Dune agreed. "We stopped by to finish the calendar photo shoot and came on inside."

"What do you think about the place?" Bert asked, turning serious as he looked around the snack shed. "Have we missed anything?"

"As far as I can tell, it all looks terrific." She followed Bert's glance.

"What do you think about our food selections?" Bert Two pointed at the candy counter.

"I like all the choices," Dune said.

"Looks as if you like our cap, too." Bert gestured toward the ball cap on Dune's head.

"Oh, I gave him that," she explained. "I'll pay you back."

"No need. It's good advertisement." Bert Two selected another ball cap and tossed it to her. "Here you go. Enjoy—promote to your heart's content."

"Thanks. I will." She grabbed the cap out of midair and put it on her head, adjusting it at a cocky angle. "Listen, I've got to get going. We completed the photo shoot, so I need to go home, download the pictures I select into my calendar layout, and get it to Nathan at Thingamajigs. He says he can complete the order in about two weeks, since it's nothing fancy this first time out. We're going with plastic spiral bound to cut cost and time."

"I'm sure it'll be great," Bert said. "How's his office supply and print shop doing?"

"So far so good," she said. "I'd never have thought about opening that type of store in Old Town, but he sells a lot of T-shirts and local promotional items, too. What he says is really turning out to be popular with tourists is the setup he's got in back. Folks can choose from vintage hats, scarves, and other stuff to put on before they pose in front of old-time backdrops. He shoots, prints, and sends customers on their way."

"Clever ideas," Bert Two added. "It's not easy starting a new business and making a go of it."

"That's the truth." Dune nodded at the other guys. "We all know ranchers don't have an easy time of it, so lots run an extra business to get through the tough times."

"I hear you," Bert agreed.

"Nathan is volunteering his time." Sydney wanted

them to know how much she appreciated local merchants. "I wouldn't let him pay for supplies, since those are out-of-pocket expenses, so our fire-rescue station is picking up that tab. We'll easily offset the cost with profit. At least I hope so."

"Sounds as if you've got your head and heart in the right place," Bert Two said. "Let me know if we can be of more help."

"I will," she agreed, liking these two better the more she got to know them. She hoped Hedy would stop by and see Bert's bluebird collection soon, since that'd make him happy, and he deserved good cheer this Christmas.

"Another thing." Bert turned to look at Dune. "Thanks for letting us know about the problem out at the Perkins farm."

"Right," Bert Two agreed. "If you hadn't been there, we'd never have known about it, and we might have lost that bull."

"Glad I could help out," Dune said. "Everything okay out there now?"

"Yeah, mostly." Bert Two gave a big sigh. "We took a look at the house, and it appears as if some folks have been messing around there."

"Maybe teenagers looking for a place to get away by themselves," Bert added. "But we still don't much like it, what with the broken glass and the loose bull."

"And all the other arson at our properties," Bert Two added.

"I don't blame you," Dune agreed. "Is Sheriff Calhoun keeping a closer eye on the place?"

"Yep," Bert said. "And we are, too. Still, we can't be in several places at once."

"That reminds me." Bert Two walked over to Dune. "We want to talk with you about security here. We set up cameras so we can access images through our laptops, tablets, and phones."

"Sounds about right," Dune agreed.

"If you have time," Bert said, "would you take a look at our setup and see if we missed anything or if you have other suggestions?"

"Why don't y'all talk security while I go home?" Sydney interrupted them as she edged toward the open door. They didn't need her for this discussion. "Dune, you might stop by the house later. Storm will be there. She hauled her goat-roping dummy into the living room to show you."

"How about tomorrow afternoon?" Dune gave her an apologetic smile. "After that Brahman busted out the fence this morning, I want to check the line along that section. I'd feel bad if any more cattle got loose."

"Okay," she said, trying not to feel disappointed that she wouldn't see him later. "Storm's goat-roping dummy will still be there tomorrow. Anyway, I need to finish the calendar."

"Good." Dune glanced at the Holloways. "I'm going to help Storm practice her tying and roping."

Sydney caught Bert and Bert Two exchange another knowing glance that she couldn't help but realize fit right into the narrative that was building about her and Dune. She had no doubt that particular piece of gossip would spread fast. She just hoped it didn't include red lace in Dune's pocket. But maybe—other than the panties—it was for the best. She was finally moving on with her life, and everybody would be glad for her.

"I'm sure they're most appreciative," Bert said, giving Sydney a wink.

"You know it." She pretended not to get his underlying message and walked over to the open front door. She gave them all a little wave goodbye before she stepped outside.

Fortunately, the weather was glorious with a crisp breeze and scent of cedar in the air as the sun lowered in the western sky. She sauntered past three pickups to Celeste and sat down inside. She stowed Kent's camera in the glove compartment, started the engine, and pulled away from the snack shed.

Now she had to get her thoughts turned back to business, although that wasn't going to be easy when she still carried Dune's scent on her sweater and the touch of his hands on her skin. Still, she'd do her best to relegate him to the back of her mind, so she could take care of urgent matters.

She drove out the drive-in gate to Main Street, where she slowed down and checked to make sure nothing in downtown looked amiss. Every store appeared to be ready for Christmas at the Sure-Shot Drive-In with holiday decorations in their windows and lights strung along their rooflines. If all went as planned, visitors would go through town on their way to the drive-in and be unable to resist stopping for a snack at the Bluebonnet Café or picking up something at one of the stores—hopefully, that would include a *Wildcat Bluff Cowboy Firefighter Calendar* or maybe several for friends.

With everything in place at Sure-Shot, she turned onto Wildcat Road and headed for Steele Trap Ranch. When she passed the place where Celeste had died on her, she simply shook her head in amazement. Dune had turned her life upside down, and she must have been more than willing, even eager, to help him do it.

When she drove past the turnoff for Cougar Ranch, she thought about Dune living there in his cowboy cabin. Suddenly she wanted to see his place, be there with him, try out his bed. Struck by those thoughts, she realized that all her determination to keep him in the back of her mind had just gone out the window. And she didn't even care. She just needed to figure out a way to finagle an invitation to his home.

She turned off Wildcat Road and drove under the Steele Trap Ranch sign, feeling a little burst of happiness. Nothing was quite as enjoyable as being on acreage that had been in her family for generations, where there was a sense of love and continuity and heritage.

She pulled up beside her pickup next to the farmhouse. She cut Celeste's engine and patted the leather seat next to her. She took a deep breath of the cool air scented with dry prairie grass and evergreen trees. Everything appeared to be just the same as when she'd left it early that morning. A lot had happened since that time—not the least of which was a cowboy named Dune.

She retrieved Kent's camera and put it in her handbag. She quickly got out of Celeste and walked up to the house. She stepped onto the porch and was surprised to see a white poinsettia in a red ceramic pot with a large green bow sitting beside the front door. It definitely hadn't been there when she'd left home that morning.

She opened the front door, set her purse on the entry table, and went back outside. She checked the beautiful plant for a note. She couldn't imagine who'd sent it to her. She found a small gift card, slipped it out of its envelope, and caught her breath in surprise as she read aloud the message.

"Merry Christmas to the cowgirl of my dreams. xoxo, Dune."

She clasped the card to her chest with both hands as tears filled her eyes at his touching gesture. He hadn't forgotten her that morning as she'd worried at the photo shoot. He'd thought of her first thing, or he couldn't have gotten the plant delivered that day. And not only had he thought of her, but he'd wanted her to know it.

She picked up the poinsettia and walked into her home. She carried the plant to her office and set it on her desk. As she ran fingertips across the delicate leaves, she realized that this plant alone could help get her through the daunting tasks ahead, and yet the biggest help of all would be Dune himself—*the cowboy of her dreams*.

Chapter 28

LATE THE NEXT DAY, DUNE REALIZED THAT HE'D started to want more than his solitary cowboy cabin on Cougar Ranch. He glanced around the large room with attached bathroom. He liked the pine walls, ceiling, and floor as well as the vintage wagon-wheel maple headboard with matching dresser. He also had a comfortable recliner with table and lamp for easy reading or dozing. Sometimes he felt like a kid in the fifties must have felt in a similar room, with the furnishings, the roping-and-riding cowboys bedspread and matching drapes over the two windows that was so typical of the time period, not that it wasn't still popular on ranches.

Life had been mostly fine here for months, but not now. After spending so much time with Sydney, he'd started thinking that maybe it was time to grow up and settle down instead of living like a boy who was waiting for life to begin outside his cowboy bedroom—or cabin, as the case might be. At least he wasn't wearing cowboy motif pj's to bed. He'd thought he was a fully grown man, but now he recognized that for a long time, he'd been shirking responsibilities that came with sticking to one place.

If he was honest with himself, he could pinpoint the exact moment when he really started to want more in life. That'd been when he'd realized a cowgirl firefighter needed him, because underneath all her busy activities and commitments, taking care of family, ranch, and community, she was just as alone as him. He'd been alone a lot in his life, but he'd never been lonely. Until now. And that loneliness had one name and one name only: *Sydney Steele*.

She was waiting for him at Steele Trap Ranch, because he'd already texted her to make sure she and Storm were home. It hadn't been easy holding off seeing her or her little chip off the old block, but he hadn't wanted to shirk his responsibilities on the ranch. He'd done chores that morning, helped B.J. with the horses, and checked the fence line. All was in order, so he was free to leave now. He was more than ready to get on with life, and he was ready to pass on hard-won knowledge such as roping and riding to a new generation. Storm had so much potential in her young life.

He picked up the Sure-Shot Drive-In ball cap where he'd hung it on a wooden hook by the door, turning it around in his hands as he thought about the Holloways. He'd approved of their drive-in security measures and had said so yesterday. They'd also discussed protection and fire-prevention options for their other properties, since arson appeared to be an ongoing problem for them. He hoped Sheriff Calhoun would catch the arsonist soon, but he wasn't giving it good odds. For now, extra security was their best bet. He set the cap back on the hook as he set that particular problem from his mind.

He hoped Sydney liked the poinsettia he'd ordered over the phone from a local flower and gift shop. He wanted to give her so much more, but a pretty Christmas plant would do as a start in the right direction.

He walked over to the dresser and smiled at the

sight of her underwear. He ran fingertips over her lacy green slip and silky red panties. He'd placed them where he could see them from his bed. Now he wanted her bra, maybe in white lace, but first he wanted to see her wear it.

Like the poinsettia, her lingerie was a step in the right direction, but it wasn't nearly enough—not for him or for her. They both obviously desired and deserved more in life, hopefully their own family and love and companionship. He squeezed the slip in his fist as he realized what he'd just thought. *Love*. Had he fallen in love with her? *Family*. Did he want to join his life with her and her daughter? *Companionship*. Could they find a way to blend their lives together?

Christmas. Maybe he was caught up in the time of year that brought miracles followed by a new year that brought hopes and dreams. He might even be running down a zigzag path when he should be walking a straight line. It didn't matter. He was determined to grasp this special season by the horns and ride it for all it was worth.

He jerked on his jean jacket with red-plaid lining, set his cowboy hat on his head, and turned on the lamp so there'd be light inside when he returned after dark. He picked up his keys on top of the dresser, stepped outside, and shut the door behind him. Crisp air buffeted his face, carrying the scent of oak and mesquite from ranch house fireplaces taking the chill off a fast-approaching night.

As he unlocked his dually, he glanced over at the barn. B.J. stood out of the wind in the shadows with a big chaw of tobacco bulging in his cheek. He touched his fingertips to the edge of his hat in recognition, and Dune nodded in return. No doubt the cowboy had already put stable blankets on the horses to keep them warm during the chilly night.

He got in his pickup and drove out of the ranch. He wasn't far from Sydney as the crow flies, but it took him a little longer to reach Wildcat Road, turn onto Steele Trap Ranch, and drive up the rutted lane to her farmhouse. He parked beside Celeste, wondering if he'd ever get used to Sydney driving her truck again, since the vintage car fit her so well. But he figured he could get used to anything so long as it had to do with Sydney.

She already had the outdoor lights on for him, so illumination gleamed softly in the black wrought-iron lamps that lit the way to the house. The bright red-and-green rope light along the farmhouse roofline couldn't have reminded him more of Christmas cheer. Oddly enough, he felt as if he'd come home right here, right now—and as if the cabin he'd called home for months was already in his past. Sometimes life had a funny way of changing overnight, and this time, he was ready for it.

He set his felt cowboy hat on the passenger seat, because he wouldn't need it indoors. He stepped out of his truck, took a deep breath of the cool, clean ranch air, and walked up to the porch. He was about to knock when the door opened to reveal Sydney, looking good as always in a green shirt, faded jeans, and red moccasins.

"We've been waiting for you." She stepped back and gestured for him to come inside.

"I had extra chores. Plus, I wanted you to have plenty of time to finish the calendar."

"All done and gone."

"That's great."

"And Dune, thanks for the poinsettia. It's beautiful and so perfect for Christmas."

"I wanted you to have something special."

"It is. Every time I look at it, I think of you." She gestured inside again. "Come on in out of the cold."

He walked past her, noting the blaze in the fire-place, the scent of cinnamon in the air, and the fact that his sock was no longer hanging on the mantel with her family's fancy stockings. He felt a stab of disap-pointment that she hadn't really wanted him to have a stocking on her mantel after all. But that was just plain whiney on his part, so he thrust it aside as unworthy of her or him.

"Storm's in the kitchen setting out the gingerbread cookies she made at the Chuckwagon today. She's excited about you coming to see us."

"That's great." He started to say more, but he noticed the goat-tying dummy with a rope looped around its neck near the fireplace. "That's a good-looking dummy."

"Thanks. It's called Tuffy by the manufacturer."

"Fine critter." He walked over and picked up the dummy, which felt as if it weighed about ten pounds. It was made of smooth black rubber and was in the shape of a goat with pink stitching on its head. It even had ears and a tail. The four legs were bolted onto the body and were mobile so they could be moved and tied with rope. He set it back down and slipped off the rope. He nodded in appreciation at the quality of the leather goat rope braided with nylon in bright pink and red, then he looped it around the dummy's neck again.

"We think so."

"I've seen stripped-down models, but this is the most realistic."

"It's the one she wanted for Christmas last year."

"Good rope, too."

"Thanks. I want you to see something else." Sydney stepped over to the fireplace, reached up, and took down one of the stockings. "I hope you don't mind, but Granny had a fit when she saw what I'd put up on the mantel for you."

"I don't blame her. It didn't fit with all this other finery."

She held out the stocking to him. "Granny made this one with your name on it. I hope you like it."

He was shocked—knocked back on his heels kind of shocked. He'd never dreamed anybody in the Steele family would go to this much trouble for him. He turned the red felt stocking over and over in his hands, marveling at the delicate beadwork in bright colors that spelled out his name above Santa in his sleigh pulled by a single red-nosed reindeer. "It's beautiful. I'm deeply touched that she took time to do this for me when I know how busy your family is during the holidays. Please thank her for me."

"I will. But you know Granny. If we're going to do something, we'd better do it right. And that old sock wasn't right, no how, no way." She chuckled as she held out her hand for the stocking. "We'd better put your stocking right back up on the mantel with the others, or we'll be hearing from her."

"Nobody wants trouble with Granny Steele." He smiled, nodding that he understood about the iron-willed, big-hearted leader of the Steele clan.

"That's right."

"You're making this a Christmas for me to remember." When he gave her back the stocking, he held her hand for a long moment.

She squeezed his fingers, blinking back tears, then quickly turned away and returned his stocking to its place on the mantel.

He hoped he hadn't said anything wrong to bring tears to her eyes, but maybe she was just as touched as him by this holiday. He swallowed against a sudden lump in his throat as he felt the warmth of her family surround him.

"Come on." She turned and grabbed his hand. "Let's try out Storm's cookies before we put you to work."

"It won't be work. It'll be a pleasure to show Storm goat-tying tricks."

Sydney led him into the kitchen, where Storm looked up from where she was setting a platter of cookies on the table.

"I made these for you today, Mr. Barrett, seeing as how you're going to help me with goat tying and all," Storm said in a soft, shy voice.

"Please call me Dune. Mr. Barrett would be my dad."

She gave him a big smile, then ducked her head as she rearranged the crimson poinsettia napkins. "You enjoy hot apple cider with cinnamon, don't you?"

"Yes, I do," he agreed while silently thinking this wasn't the vivacious, sassy cowgirl that everybody in Wildcat Bluff had come to know and love. The ATV accident had set her back on her heels more than he'd realized till this very moment. Somehow, she needed to get her self-confidence back, and then she'd surely be right as rain again.

"Do you want me to pour the cider?" Sydney's voice sounded strained as she stepped toward her daughter.

Dune figured Sydney was seeing just what he was seeing in Storm, and it had to worry her plenty.

"Mommy, I'll pour." Storm cast Sydney a sharp look as she flounced over to the stove.

Sydney glanced at Dune with hurt in her eyes, shaking her head in quiet dismay.

He squeezed her fingers in sympathy before he put a hand on her back to guide her to the table. "Storm, is there any place in particular you want us to sit?" He figured the best thing he could do was to give Storm as much control of her environment—and the people in it—as possible to help her regain her confidence.

Storm looked up from where she was ladling cider into colorful red and green mugs. She pointed to the head of the table. "If you wish, you may sit on the end, Mr.—Dune. That way Mommy and I can sit on either side of you. That'd be proper, I think."

"That's just fine," Sydney quickly agreed as she moved toward the table as if she was walking on eggshells.

Dune pulled out a chair and seated her, then he walked around the table and pulled out a chair where Storm would sit later. Finally, he sat down, but he wasn't comfortable. Nobody in the kitchen was at ease. Storm was trying too hard to be a perfect little lady. Sydney was trying even harder to pretend her daughter hadn't morphed into an unknown quantity. He was the buffer between them, but he wasn't sure he was cut out for the role. The situation gave him an opportunity to show he could be good father material, or at least that he was willing to try his hand at it. But most of all, he didn't want either of them to hurt emotionally—he knew too much about that condition—so he'd do whatever he could to ease their pain.

Storm carefully carried over a red mug brimming with hot cider, but when she set it down in front of Dune, liquid sloshed over the side.

"Oh no!" Storm cried out, sounding upset. "I made a mess."

"It's okay." Dune quickly snatched a clump of napkins and sopped up the spilled liquid. "No problem. See, it's all okay."

"Are you sure?" Storm sounded close to tears. "I was careful."

"Accidents happen to all of us," Dune reassured her, realizing she was equating the cider spill with her ATV spill. She probably didn't trust herself anymore to handle things. "I can't tell you the number of times I spilled something or other."

"Really?" Storm turned big hazel eyes on him.

"Yep." He gave her a reassuring smile. "That's part of life. I've taken spills off horses, too."

"And four-wheelers?" she asked in a small voice.

"Been there, done that. I've got a metal pin in my foot to prove it."

"Does it hurt?" Storm cocked her head at him in interest.

"Not anymore." He took a sip of cider to show her that she'd served them just right. "Truth of the matter, taking spills and making messes is all about growing up and learning to get along during the tough times as well as the good times."

"I guess," she said, looking down at his mug, "that this is a tough time for me."

"Tell you what." He stopped what he was going to say and took a deep breath as he glanced at Sydney. Did she want his help? When she gave him an encouraging look, he nodded. "I've always valued the tough times, because they teach me things I wouldn't learn otherwise."

"That's dumb!" Storm said with a frown, then opened her eyes in horror. "I mean, you're not dumb or anything, but—"

"That's okay." He wanted to take her in his arms and hug her till she knew she was completely safe, but he couldn't do that yet. "I know it sounds dumb, but a lot of stuff in life sounds dumb that ends up being smart."

"How?" She cocked her head as she considered him with her full attention.

He was getting in deeper and deeper, realizing for the first time just how important and hard a job parenting could be. Maybe everybody had been talking around her accident when she'd do better if they just got it out in the open. At least he hoped that was the case. "For example, take that flier you took off your ATV."

She hung her head and gave a big sigh.

"Do you realize how well you handled that situation?"

She looked up at him, eyes big in wonder. "I did?"

"Sure did," he said in a firm voice. "You didn't come away with a pin in your foot, did you?"

"I came away with hardly a scratch." She stood straighter as her eyes brightened a bit.

"See. You did better than me."

"I did?"

"Yep. No doubt about it. You were smart. When that four-wheeler took off on its own—and it can happen— you hung on till you could get off safely."

"I did?"

"Absolutely."

"I don't remember what happened. I was okay one minute, and the next, I was hitting the ground."

"Accidents happen fast, so the best thing you can do is be smart and survive in one piece."

"I guess I did that, didn't I?" Storm gave him a tentative smile, then glanced at Sydney. "Mommy, I didn't know I was smart about it. I thought I'd made a big mistake, and that made me scared to ride."

Sydney reached out and hugged Storm, then smiled at her. "You're a smart and brave girl. I'm proud of you. And I'd trust you on an ATV or the back of a horse any day."

"I'm glad, Mommy." Storm gave a big heartfelt sigh, then swiveled, put her small arms around Dune, and gave him a hug. She stepped back, no longer looking shy or down-at-heart. "I'd better serve up our cider, or it'll get cold."

"And I'm ready for cookies," Dune added.

"They're good. At least, Uncle Slade thinks so." Storm quickly turned and walked away from the table.

Dune leaned over and squeezed Sydney's hand, encouraging her that all would be well now.

"Thanks," she said quietly. "Storm needed to hear that, and I think you're the only one she'd have listened to about her accident."

"Why me?" he asked, sounding as puzzled as he felt.

"You were there to help her when she fell off her four-wheeler," Sydney said, lowering her voice. "I believe she's come to see you as a strong male figure in her life."

"There's Slade."

"Yes. But he's Storm's uncle and familiar. I suspect you've become bigger than life to her, so your voice carries a lot of weight."

"That's a huge responsibility. I'll try to live up to it and not let either of you down." He gave Sydney's hand a final squeeze, then let it go when he heard Storm head their way.

Storm carefully set a mug in front of Sydney before she set the other mug in front of her chair. After she sat down, she picked up the platter of cookies and held it out to Dune.

He selected a cookie in the shape of a reindeer and took a big bite. "Delicious!"

"Thank you." Storm gave him a relieved look before she held out the plate to Sydney. "Mommy, I think you'll like these, too."

Sydney picked up a cookie, sniffed it, and bit into it. "Yummy! You're getting to be an excellent chef."

Storm giggled as she set down the plate and grabbed two cookies. "Uncle Slade says I've got the makings of a good fry cook." She frowned, shaking her head. "I'm not sure what that means, but I think I'd like to tie goats better."

"Good choice," Dune agreed, taking another cookie. "As soon as we get done here, we're going to practice with your dummy and turn you into the best goat-tying girl in North Texas."

Storm cocked her head at him. "I hope you're not funning me, 'cause I've got room for another buckle on my wall."

"You've got room for lots more buckles, and you're going to win them." Sydney looked from her daughter to Dune with a relieved and happy smile on her face. "Thanks. We appreciate your help."

"Don't thank me yet." He gestured toward the living room and the goat-roping dummy. "Tuffy out there will put us through our paces."

Storm's tinkling laughter filled the kitchen. "Tuffy, here we come!"

Dune glanced from daughter to mother, glad he'd been able to help them through this crisis, probably only one of many more to come as Storm grew into the strong, smart cowgirl she was destined to be.

And he suddenly knew that he wanted to be there for every single day of their future.

Chapter 29

TWO WEEKS LATER, SYDNEY STOOD NEAR CELESTE ON the boardwalk in front of Thingamajigs & More. She held a beautiful, colorful copy of the *Wildcat Bluff Cowboy Firefighters Calendar*. She couldn't have been more proud of so much volunteer work. Nathan had pulled out all the stops to get it produced a week before their Christmas events. Now she could only hope that everyone—locals and visitors alike—would love the calendar and support the fire station by buying it.

She smiled in pleasure at the fun-looking group of firefighters on the cover, then flipped through the glossy pages to the last month. *Mr. December.* She traced a fingertip across the hot photograph of Dune. She'd spent much of the last two weeks with him, organizing and finishing up details for Christmas at the Sure-Shot Drive-In. They'd managed to carve out time to be alone, sharing heartaches and triumphs, hopes and dreams, hugs and kisses. They'd discovered they were more alike than unalike. She was even learning to be spontaneous again. Together, they'd helped Storm, working on her goat-tying abilities and increasing her self-confidence, and she was much better.

Sydney glanced up and saw Nathan standing inside the front window of his store, watching her. She gave a little wave of appreciation—as well as goodbye—for his excellent work and then looked down the row of Old Town's businesses. Gene's Boot Hospital, Lone Star Saloon, Morning's Glory, Adelia's Delights, Chuckwagon Café, and other prime location stores were all now stocked with the calendar. She'd just personally delivered a stack to each and every one of them, and they'd happily put the calendar on their checkout counters.

She'd wanted Dune to be along to distribute calendars, but she just couldn't wait for him once she got her hands on the merchandise. Later, she'd go with him to Sure-Shot and other stores, so they could share the experience.

She glanced at the red-and-white checked curtains in the café's front windows, thinking how proud Storm had been to announce to her family that Dune was training her in goat tying. She'd also announced that she was baking him more cookies because he'd liked her gingerbread so much. Sydney had received a little ribbing from her family about Dune, but they were also happy for her. Granny had not only made a Christmas stocking for him, but she'd gone out of her way to make him feel welcome in their family.

She glanced back down at the calendar. Mr. December looked way too hot to handle on the back seat of Celeste, but she figured she was cowgirl enough to meet fire with fire. And come out a winner.

Love. She hadn't expected to feel such a strong emotion for a man again. And yet here she was, teetering on the brink of a new beginning. She wanted to share life's ups and downs with Dune. In the middle of the night, she wanted to turn to him, knowing he would be there for her just as she would be there for him. She wanted him to help raise her daughter, particularly since Storm had come to care for him. Yes, she'd freely admit it—if only to herself—she wanted Dune Barrett in every way imaginable. But for now, she'd settle on them making Christmas at the Sure-Shot Drive-In a celebration to remember.

She looked from the calendar to Celeste and couldn't help but smile. Not only were their cowboy firefighters going to be famous locally, but her beautiful Cadillac would be as well. And they all deserved it.

She opened the door and sat down inside. She tucked the calendar under her seat so it wouldn't get blown out of the convertible and set her purse on the passenger seat. She'd stowed the boxes of calendars in the roomy trunk so they wouldn't get hurt when she drove around the county.

All in all, she was ready to move on with her day. She'd dressed simply and comfortably in a retro green cashmere cardigan with a matching pencil skirt. She still wasn't wearing heels, so she'd selected her crimson beaded moccasins with a matching red leather handbag.

She pulled her cell phone out of her purse and pushed what had come to be her number one speed dial.

"Hey there," Dune answered in his deep drawl. "I was beginning to think you'd forgotten about me."

"Never. What are you doing right now?"

"Waiting for you."

"I mean really."

"Really."

She simply shook her head in amazement. Dune had an uncanny ability to up her temperature with just one word. "I've got the calendars."

"How do they look?"

"Great—particularly Mr. December."

"I don't want to hear about it."

She chuckled, imagining how all the cowboy firefighters were going to feel about being ogled by lusty cowgirls. Maybe they'd start to enjoy their sudden fan base.

"After that laugh, now I really don't want to hear about it."

"Do you want to help me distribute the calendars to stores in Sure-Shot?"

"I'm yours to command."

"Just so you remember who's holding your reins when those calendars get snapped up and you're being chased through the streets by adoring cowgirls."

He laughed at her words. "Sure. That calendar is going to set off a stampede for cowboy firefighters."

"It'll be like the Oklahoma land rush."

"As long as they're in covered wagons and I'm on horseback, I figure I can outrun them."

"Just so you run my way."

"Always."

Again, Dune only had to say one word to make her happy. There ought to be a law against such ability, but she was glad there wasn't. She wanted him all to herself and just the way he was.

"Sydney?"

"My mind wandered there for a moment."

"Do you want me to meet you at the house or in Old Town?"

"Stay right where you are, cowboy. I'm coming to get you in my pretty pink Caddy."

"I don't know if you should or not. You're liable to give B.J. a heart attack when he gets a gander."

She couldn't keep the laughter inside. "B.J. is tougher

than he looks. I bet he's even driven a vintage Cadillac or two when they were new."

Dune joined her laughter. "I wouldn't tell him that he's vintage to his face."

"Never. But he is a classic."

"You know it."

"So I'm in front of Nathan's store right now. Why don't I pick you up in a bit, then we'll tool around in Celeste."

"Do you know where my cabin is on Cougar Ranch?"

"I'll look for your truck."

"Okay. I'll pull on my boots and meet you outside."

"See you soon." She hung up with a strong sense of satisfaction.

She backed out of her parking space and turned off Main Street onto Wildcat Road. As she picked up speed, a cool breeze whipped through her hair, reminding her that they were deep into December.

When she reached the turnoff to Cougar Ranch, she slowed down, not only for the turn but to catch her breath. She was barreling into her future as if she was on the back of a fast horse. Was she letting her heart lead her head? Maybe. If so, was it smart? She had Storm to think about, not just herself. And yet everything within her was telling her that Dune was the one.

Up ahead she saw the big red barn and Dune's dually in front of a small cowboy cabin. She caught the scent of hay, oats, and horse as she stopped beside his pickup. He was leaning against the truck with a piece of straw sticking out of his mouth.

At the sight of her, he pulled the straw from between his lips, tossed it on the ground, and raised his cowboy hat in hello.

No two ways about it, he was a sight for sore eyes. She instantly went back into barrel-racing mode. She didn't want to slow down with him. She wanted to ride with the wind, knowing he was right by her side.

As Dune headed toward her, she heard someone call her name. She glanced toward the sound coming from the barn. B.J. sauntered in her direction wearing his trademark plaid shirt, striped overalls, and scuffed boots—surely vintage by the look of them.

When B.J. got close, he doffed his beaten-up brown cowboy hat and grinned from ear to ear, revealing stained teeth. He spat tobacco to one side, then walked up and down beside Celeste, nodding his head and murmuring under his breath.

"What's that?" she asked, watching him enjoy the Caddy like it was Christmas morning.

"It's pure pleasure to see this fine a vehicle right here beside the barn. Nineteen fifty-nine, right?"

"That's right," Dune agreed as he walked up to the passenger door.

"Moss Werner's Celeste, right?"

"Right," Sydney agreed. "I was really surprised when he gave her to me."

"I'm not," B.J. said. "Moss thought you had the right heart to take care of his beautiful Celeste."

"I'm doing my best."

"Sydney's taking me for a spin." Dune gestured toward the Cadillac.

"You lucky dog," B.J. said with a touch of awe in his voice.

"If you play your cards right, she might take you for a turn later, too."

B.J. turned a hopeful gaze on Sydney.

"I surely will," she agreed. "We've got to distribute calendars right now, but later sometime."

"Thanks." B.J. cocked his head at her. "Calendars, huh?"

Sydney reached under her seat, pulled out a calendar, and held it out to him.

B.J. took it, nodding in appreciation. "Celeste and calendars reminds me of those pretty gals I used to see in car calendars in garages back when I took my Mirage in to get a tune-up."

"You had a Cadillac pickup?" Dune stared at B.J. in obvious envy and amazement. "They didn't make many of those models."

"No wonder." B.J. spat to the side in disgust. "Looked good, but the crazy coots put mules under those engines instead of horses."

"What do you mean?" Sydney asked.

"You heard of horsepower?" B.J. moved his chaw from one side of his mouth to the other.

"Yes," Sydney agreed.

"That's what you want under a hood. Think 1976. Fuel prices skyrocketed. Gas lines at stations. Folks who thought they were smarter than the average bear decided to put a little engine in a big truck. I couldn't pull squat with that Caddy."

"That's a shame," Dune said.

"Bet it looked good." Sydney tried for something positive to overcome the disappointment lingering in the air.

"Yeah." B.J. croaked out a laugh. "Cowgirls loved that vehicle, so I squired quite a few around in it." He walked to the front of Celeste and stroked a tanned, weathered hand down a longhorn. "Now this baby is perfect. Big everything. Cadillac earned its chops on this one."

"It is a beauty," Dune agreed.

"Yep." B.J. walked back and glanced down at the calendar in his hand. "Pinups?"

"Well, in a way, yes," Sydney agreed.

B.J. cocked his head and turned narrowed eyes on her, obviously waiting for an explanation.

"That's the new *Wildcat Bluff Cowboy Firefighters Calendar.*"

B.J. glanced at Dune, and then he guffawed loud and long. "Don't that beat all. Bet you're in it."

"He's Mr. December," Sydney said with a touch of pride in her voice.

B.J. bent over double in laughter. "I'm gonna have to get me one of these calendars and put it in the barn for the horses."

"Thanks," Dune said as he opened the door and sat down shotgun. "It's for a good cause."

"We're raising money for our fire-rescue station," Sydney explained, hoping for a sale.

"That's a right fine cause. I'll take this one." B.J. pulled a worn leather billfold out of his back pocket, selected a twenty, and handed it to Sydney. "Keep the change."

"Thank you! You're our first sale."

"Good luck." B.J. looked closer at the cover. "That's a mighty fine-looking bunch of cowboys and cowgirls. That Hedy, she's something."

"Better not let Bert hear you say that."

B.J. chuckled in a raspy tone. "One thing you got

to say about Bert, he's like a hound dog. Nothing, and I mean nothing, will keep him from bird-dogging that cowgirl."

"Maybe he's finally making progress," Sydney said.

"You think?" B.J. gave her a closer look as if he could hardly believe his ears.

"Bert invited her to see his bluebird collection."

B.J. took off his cowboy hat and scratched his head, then replaced his hat. "Well now, Christmas does come once a year, but bluebonnets don't bloom in December."

"True enough," Sydney agreed, although she was going to think positively about Bert and Hedy.

"Now don't forget my ride in your pretty Celeste." B.J. waved the calendar, chuckling as he headed for the barn.

"See you later," Sydney called as she handed the crumpled bill to Dune. "Why don't you take charge of the money?"

"What'll I do with it?"

"I guess the glove compartment for now."

"You know." He jerked open the glove compartment and tossed the greenback inside. "I'm going to hear that laughter all over the county. *Mr. December*. I knew I shouldn't have let you talk me into that photo."

"You haven't even seen it."

"And I don't want to either."

"Are you getting grumpy?" She backed out, waved at B.J., and hit the lane out of the ranch.

"I'm way past grumpy."

"Remember, it's for a good cause."

"Yeah, just keep reminding me of that."

"Would a kiss help?"

He snorted as he glanced over at her. "Do you think I'm that easy?"

She grinned as she nodded in reply. "Maybe."

"Oh, hell yes. A kiss from you would help about anything."

She stopped right in front of the cattle guard under the Cougar Ranch sign, figuring they were about to put on another show for the entire county. Only this time, she didn't care one bit. "Come here, cowboy. I'll kiss it and make it better."

He tossed his hat onto the floorboard, gave her a big grin, and pulled her into his arms.

When he pressed his lips to hers, she didn't figure hot even began to describe the inferno that blazed between them.

Chapter 30

Dune stood in the midst of a calamity. At first, everything had gone fine when he'd delivered calendars with Sydney to the Sure-Shot downtown businesses such as the Bluebonnet Café. The retailers had immediately set the benefit calendars on their checkout counters for the best point-of-purchase display.

Who'd have thought their cowboy firefighter calendars would cause a near-riot in the Sure-Shot Beauty Station? All he'd wanted to do was deliver the calendars and get the hell out of Dodge. It'd been the last stop. But no, it couldn't be easy. Now he felt as if he'd been roped, branded, and was about to be ridden hard and put up wet.

"Please sign my calendar, Mr. December. 'To Lila with love' will do nicely." A freshly permed-and-coiffed, blue-haired lady batted her eyelashes at him from behind rhinestone, cat-eye eyeglasses. From her diminutive height, she held up a cowboy firefighter calendar and a ballpoint pen.

One thing every cowboy knew for sure, you didn't mess with a strong-willed lady who looked like your toughest teacher and who'd pushed her way to the front of the line like a bulldozer. No, you gave them what they wanted and hoped they'd go away happy. "Lila, you say?"

"Oh yes, Mr. December." She held up her right hand

with freshly painted bloodred fingernails sharpened to lethal points. "Please let me feel your bicep so I'll know for sure you're strong enough to autograph my calendar."

That stopped him in his tracks. He glanced over at Sydney where she stood beside Serena Simmons, the Station's owner, watching and listening to the ongoing debacle. He'd get no help there. She simply grinned and smirked, letting him know—once more—that it was all for a good cause. He leaned down and presented his arm. Nails dug into the cotton fabric of his blue plaid snap-shirt stretched over his muscular bicep.

"Oh yes, Mr. December, I do believe you're strong enough to handle anything a gal might need." Lila wiggled her eyebrows at him.

He grabbed the calendar out of her hands, accepting the pen and managing not to get caught by her strong fingers again. He jerked the calendar open to the last month and stopped in shock. He hadn't seen his photograph till now. If steam hadn't been coming out of his ears already, it would be now. No wonder women were lining up for his signature. He looked as if he was ready to take any one of them, or all of them, for a spin in the pretty pink Cadillac without ever leaving the back seat. It was flat-out embarrassing, particularly because this photo would be seen all over Wildcat Bluff County and probably several nearby counties and clear up into Oklahoma.

He glanced over at Sydney and gave her the hardest glare he could manage. He quickly scrawled what Lila wanted across his chest in the picture and thrust the calendar back into her small hands. He kept the pen, figuring he was going to need it—not only for signing calendars but as a possible defensive weapon.

"Oh, thank you, Mr. December." She batted her eyelashes at him again. "I do believe it's going to be December all year long for me."

"Next." He tried to smile since it was for a good cause, but he was afraid his face was frozen in a look of sheer horror as he contemplated just how far his picture might extend across Texas. He could only hope it didn't reach the Hill Country, or he'd never hear the last of it from his family and friends there.

"You're very photogenic, Mr. December, but I suppose you already know that bit of news." A tall gal with big red hair, professionally made-up face, and pointy-toe boots gave him a wide, white grin.

"Nope. Just found out." He accepted her calendar, being careful not to touch her strong-looking, short-nailed hand. She appeared as if she might still be competing in barrel racing, so he didn't want to get on her bad side either. Those rhinestone-flashy cowgirls were tough and strong with long memories for cowboys who might've done them wrong.

"If you'll sign it to 'Charlene,' I'll be ever so grateful." She leaned in close, reeking of floral hair product. "By the way, Mr. December, I'm having a Christmas party out at the ranch come next weekend. I'd be even more grateful if you could find it in your big, manly heart to be there for little ole me."

He almost stabbed through the paper at that remark, but he remembered his manners and the long memories of barrel racers, so he cracked his face with a smile, finished signing his name, and thrust the calendar back into her hands. He inclined his head toward Sydney. "See that cowgirl over there?"

Charlene turned to look in that direction, then she sniffed in disdain. "Yes. That's Sydney Steele off Steele Trap Ranch, isn't it?"

"Yep. I'd better tell you right up front. She'd skin the hide off me if I so much as glanced at a good-looking cowgirl like you."

Charlene tossed her head much in the way of an irritated horse and clutched the calendar to her ample bosom. "That Sydney Steele did have all the luck, drat her." She leaned in close again. "But I've won a few races in my time, too. Tell you what, Mr. December. If you ever break out of her pasture, give me a call. Running C Ranch. Charlene."

"I'll keep it in mind." As the cowgirl sashayed away, he glanced over at Sydney again. This time she didn't look quite so pleased with herself. Fact of the matter, she looked a little on the put-out side. And that gave him an idea as to how to turn this whole mess around and get the hell out of Dodge. "Step right up, ladies. I'm ready, willing, and able to sign your calendars."

As the group surged toward him, he clicked his pen and got ready to write "xoxo" a lot of times.

Pretty quick, he noted that his ruse had worked like a charm. Sydney said her goodbyes to Serena and sidled up beside him, obviously staking her claim and making sure everybody understood that Mr. December was already taken by a cowgirl strong enough to hold him.

He plowed through those calendars—and all those eager ladies—much like a hot knife through butter. He wanted out of a place that sported too many frilly things, too many torture-looking devices, and way too many sweet, smelly products. And that didn't begin to mention the predatory ladies all in a row.

When he'd signed the last calendar, he tossed the ballpoint pen to Serena, grabbed Sydney's hand, and made a beeline for the front door.

"Now, don't be a stranger," Serena called out. "We style men's hair as well as women's."

He shuddered at the idea of ever returning to the Sure-Shot Beauty Station, but he turned back and gave a slight wave to all the women clutching their calendars before he hustled Sydney out the door.

He didn't breathe a sigh of relief till they were seated in Celeste and headed down Main Street.

"If you ever—and I mean ever—suggest I go back in that place, I'll—"

"Don't you want to be a sex symbol in Wildcat Bluff County?" Sydney glanced over at him, opening her eyes wide in an attempt to look innocent.

"No! I'm a cowboy firefighter, not a—"

"Sex symbol?" she teased.

"As it is, I may have to leave town, the county, maybe the whole state." He still could hardly believe the response to Mr. December.

"Are you afraid of all the cowgirls who'll be after you?"

"We're talking respect here, or lack of it."

"Oh, I think you'll be getting a lot of respect."

"Not the kind I want," he growled, throwing an irritated look her way.

"I think you're overreacting to the situation."

"What? I could've lost my shirt—or more. Those were hungry ladies."

"But nicely put together. Serena does a good job."

"You're not taking this seriously."

"Maybe not." She winked at him. "You're a hunk. You might as well go ahead and admit it."

"I'm a cowboy."

"Do you need a kiss again?"

"A kiss won't even come close to repairing my loss of dignity." Even if he was still grumpy, he was beginning to see the humor in the situation, so he might as well turn it to his advantage.

"Do you need more than a kiss?"

"Yes, I surely do." He glanced over at her, feeling mischievous. "I bet that Charlene could make me feel a whole lot better."

Sydney took a fast, hard turn onto Wildcat Road. "I've outrun her a time or two."

"No doubt."

"I suspect she's made a lot of cowboys feel a whole lot better."

"A cowgirl with experience, huh?"

"Maybe too much experience."

"Is there such a thing?"

Sydney stepped hard on the accelerator, and the Cadillac leaped forward. "If you're trying to get my goat, you'd better think again. I'm in no mood for a Charlene or a Rhonda or a Linda Lou trying to make time with my guy."

He smiled in satisfaction at her response. "You're jealous."

"Am not. It's just—"

"I'm your guy?"

She gave a big sigh as she focused on the road. "I'm

not having this discussion." She clenched her hands on the steering wheel. "If a kiss isn't enough to make up for your loss of dignity, how about I get you a pretty plant for your cabin? A red poinsettia for Christmas might be just the thing."

He decided to let her get away with the change in subject. After all, she'd just let him know that she was well on her way to falling in love with him. Nothing could have pleased him more. He'd even let her tease him about Mr. December, particularly since that photo had made her jealous. "I don't need a plant. If B.J. saw a flower in my room, he'd laugh even harder at me."

"I take it that's a 'no' regarding a pretty flower."

"Yep."

"Let me see." She tapped her chin with the tip of one finger. "What do you do for a sex symbol who has everything?"

"I don't have everything." He gave her a hot look from her head to her toes, letting her know that she was the only cowgirl he wanted in his life.

"Oh." She appeared as if a lightbulb had gone off in her head. "I'm wearing this lacy white bra. Would that interest you?"

"Only because you're wearing it."

"Do you want it for your collection?"

"Only if I can take it off you in bed."

"Would that be the bed in your cowboy cabin?"

"That's the one." He was getting hotter by the moment, knowing she was leading him exactly where he wanted to go.

"If I was in your bed, you wouldn't be all growly anymore?"

"I'd be growly, all right, but in a totally different way."

"In that case, I can handle growly—from Mr. December."

"If there're any more calendars to deliver, let's dump them by the side of the road and head for Cougar Ranch."

"Dump them?" She sounded outraged even as she gave him a quick sideways look that spoke of hot, sweaty sheets.

"Yeah. I'm in need of some tender loving care right this minute."

"Can you wait till we reach your cabin?"

"Not unless you raise your shirt so I can see what kind of vintage you're wearing underneath." He didn't really think she'd do it, but he was in the mood to flirt with her.

"Dune! I've driving, and we're on the road."

"But I'm needy."

"It's a good thing that was our last stop, or you'd be even needier by the time we reached your cabin."

"Think I wouldn't toss them?"

"It doesn't matter. There are only a couple of bundles left that we'll make available during Christmas at the Sure-Shot Drive-In."

"So let me get this straight. We're on our way to my cabin?"

She gave him a quick glance with a smile quirking up the corners of her full lips. "That's the plan."

"Good." He leaned back in his seat, finally fully relaxing after his harrowing visit to the Sure-Shot Beauty Station.

"But don't think Mr. December gets to rest on his laurels. I expect him to show me just how hot he can make a very cold month of the year."

Dune didn't even raise his head or reply. She could tease and torment to her heart's content. He was about to get her where he'd wanted her since the first moment he'd seen her.

As Sydney reached the turnoff to Cougar Ranch, her cell phone came alive, letting her know she had a text message.

"Don't read it or answer it." He wasn't about to let them get distracted by anything other than a fire-rescue emergency, and that wasn't the station's special ringtone.

"Dune, please get my phone out of my purse."

"If I do, you know what'll happen."

"I'm a mother, and I always answer my cell, because you just never know."

"Storm." He felt like a jerk. Still, he wasn't used to being available for a child, but he was willing to step up to this new learning curve. He pulled her phone out of her purse and checked the messages.

"What does it say?"

"It's from Hedy."

"Anything wrong?"

"Nope." He couldn't help but chuckle at the news. "Looks as if she's finally going to see Bert's bluebirds, and she wants us to meet her there."

"I doubt if she'll go alone," Sydney said. "I bet everybody else is too busy to go with her. Will you text her that we'll see her at Bert's place?"

"Yeah. I guess so." He gave a big, loud sigh. Life was easier when he was just a lowly, lonely cowboy living at the ranch. But would he trade that life for this one? No way. He'd found the chili with jalapeños, and he would never be satisfied with mild chili again.

"Thanks, Dune. I'll make it up to you later."

He sent the text and replaced her phone in her purse. "If you think giving me a bluebird will do it, don't bother."

"No bluebirds." She tossed him a mischievous glance. "But if Mr. December is clever enough, I just might sing for him."

Chapter 31

As Sydney turned her car around in front of the Cougar Ranch sign, she suddenly realized that she and Dune had come to a place where they were comfortable teasing each other and sharing private jokes. She hadn't done that with a guy since—well, since Emery. And it made her happy.

She wanted that type of happiness for Hedy. She'd do about anything to help her friend, who had given so much to their community. Bert deserved love, too. After everything she'd seen and heard about the fires, she was fast coming to the conclusion that Bert and Bert Two were not behind the arson on their properties. And yet she couldn't imagine who could be so destructive and vindictive to them. She hoped Sheriff Calhoun would soon bring the guilty party to justice.

She slowed down when she saw the silver double gates with "HF&R" in their centers. They were wide open for Hedy. On either side of the cattle guard rose a four-sided column with "Holloway Farm & Ranch" engraved into the pale sandstone. Blue-and-silver rope lights wound around each column with a large, blue bow on each flat top, obviously representing holiday packages waiting to be unwrapped on Christmas.

She turned off Wildcat Road, crossed the cattle guard, and headed up the well-maintained black asphalt road. Red Angus cattle stood in clusters under the spreading limbs of green-leafed live oaks or grazed on what was left of summer grass now turned golden in the winter. Sunlight glinted on a large pond with green lily pads floating across its blue surface while a weeping willow cast a dark shadow across one corner of the water. In the distance, a large red barn and numerous outbuildings rose above the gently rolling prairie land. A breeze kicked up and brought the scent of dust, hay, and feed.

"Nice place," Dune said. "I've never been here before."

"The Holloways haven't been much for parties or visitors, not since Bert lost his wife to cancer. Bert Two was close to his mom, so it hit him hard, too."

"That's tough. I hope they're doing better now."

"Yes, they are. I know it helped when Bert Two moved back home to support his dad. They've built a number of businesses together now."

"Good for them."

"And it says a lot that they're reaching out to Hedy."

"What do you mean?"

"Maybe they're ready to move on with life."

"Sometimes it takes a while to heal."

"Yes, it does." She glanced over at him and caught the intense expression in his blue eyes. She nodded, figuring they were both thinking about themselves—and each other.

As the lane wound upward, higher and higher, they passed a pasture that contained white-faced Herefords with deep red bodies. They weren't as popular as they'd once been on ranches, although she still preferred the breed for looks and temperament. Black or red Angus was the current favorite among North American ranchers due to economics, because Angus cattle matured quickly and put on weight easily.

She wondered if Hedy was ahead of them or behind them. She hoped they were arriving about the same time, but she wouldn't know until she reached the house.

"Big spread, isn't?"

"Thousands of acres. It's been in their family for generations in the way of most big ranches around here."

"It's that way in the Hill Country, too, but some of the ranches are being broken up and sold for ranchettes nowadays—if you can imagine."

"I can. City folk want a low-maintenance country getaway."

"That translates to not much land or too many critters."

"Right. Ranches are hungry masters at the best of times." She looked out over the vast and beautiful plain that extended as far as the eye could see. "Still, I wouldn't change my life for the world."

He reached over and squeezed her hand on the steering wheel, then sat back against the bench seat. "We both love what we love, don't we?"

She gave him a quick glance, caught the look in his eyes that meant he was thinking about more than ranches, and refocused on the road. "Love can sometimes catch us unaware, can't it?"

"If we're lucky, it sure can." He turned to her with a big grin. "Mr. December is still planning to get lucky later."

She laughed, feeling relieved that he'd broken up the seriousness of the moment, since they were almost at the house. "If the beauty shop is any indication, I'd say Mr. December is the definition of lucky."

"But only if lucky's name is Sydney."

She felt his words wash over her as if she'd taken a quick dip in a hot tub, refreshing and stimulating at the same time. Somehow, he always knew the right thing to say to draw her into the world they were creating between them. She started to respond when she saw Hedy's van stopped on the lane in front of them.

"She's waiting for us," Dune said. "Do you suppose she feels uneasy without friends nearby?"

"Oh no. Still, she's well aware that Bert's hell-bent on catching her. If he comes on too strong, she wants us there so the situation doesn't become socially awkward."

"That's smart."

"That's Hedy. She's always thinking ahead."

As Sydney drew near the van, Hedy pulled ahead, drove to the house that dominated a rise on the ranch, and stopped her vehicle.

"Wow," Dune said. "I hadn't expected to see a mansion."

"The Holloways were originally from the South like a lot of folks who settled in Texas. I know their house looks unusual here on a ranch instead of perched on a cliff overlooking the Mississippi River or on a rise above the Gulf Coast. It's such a beautiful sight. I think the style is called Colonial Revival from the antebellum period."

"Sounds about right."

She pulled up beside Hedy's van and stopped Celeste. She sat still for a moment, admiring the large white two-story house with black shutters on the floor-to-ceiling windows that were overshadowed by the covered portico that ran the length of the front with tall columns holding up the roof. Redbrick chimneys rose majestically on each end of the house from ground to high above the roofline. A redbrick path meandered from the lane up to the house through a golden manicured lawn with neatly trimmed bushes and ancient, leafless oak trees.

Hedy lowered her motorized wheelchair out the side door of her van just as Bert and Bert Two walked out the double front doors of their house. They quickly moved down the wide path in unison, wearing their usual rancher suits, cowboy boots, and Stetsons.

"Guess it's time to see the bluebirds." Dune opened his door and stepped out of the car.

Sydney hooked the handle of her retro purse over her arm, got out of her car, and quickly walked over to Hedy. She gave her friend a big hug before she turned to greet the Holloways.

"Welcome to our humble abode." Bert threw wide his arms with a big, white grin on his face. "Hedy, you look lovely as always. You too, Sydney."

"Thanks," Hedy said, smiling around the group. "But we all know not to trust a smooth-talking, sharp-dressing man."

Bert Two laughed and gave his dad a playful punch on his arm. "She's got you there."

"I'll take that as a compliment, Hedy dear." Bert gestured to one side of his expansive home. "If you'll follow the redbrick path, you'll come to my bluebird house."

"You've got an entire house for your collection?" Hedy asked, giving him an amazed look. "I didn't know I'd sold you that many bluebirds."

"If you'll think back, it's been a while," Bert said. "Years, in fact."

"Well, I guess I should thank you for your business."

Hedy appeared a little flustered at how often he'd
shopped in her store.

"No need." Bert gave her a gentle smile. "You thank
me every time I buy a bluebird."

"Anyway," Bert Two interrupted in an obvious
attempt to get everyone past the awkward moment. "It's
more of a gazebo than a house, but you still must see it
to believe it."

"I'm more than ready to see the home of my pretty
bluebirds," Hedy said, recovering her aplomb.

"Good." Bert Two started walking along the redbrick path. "If everyone will follow me, you can all
see for yourselves just how devoted Dad has been to
his bluebirds."

Sydney shrugged at Dune, not knowing what to
expect now. She got in line behind Hedy, and she was
followed by Dune and Bert as they all headed down the
walkway. She shaded her eyes with one hand against the
bright sunlight that swept across them as the sun dipped
toward the western horizon.

Soon they came to an extensive back garden with
stone benches, gurgling fountains, trimmed hedges
and rosebushes, manicured lawn, flagstone patio with
colorful, plush cushions on redwood furniture, and an
infinity swimming pool and hot tub. Blue-and-silver
rope lights outlined the house's roofline while clusters
of pale-pink amaryllis in large green ceramic containers
adorned the patio.

And yet all of that beautiful luxury paled in comparison to Bert's bluebird house. For in the center of the
garden, a glass-walled gazebo in a hexagonal shape rose
as a delicate work of art into the sky, glowing blue fire

where the brilliant rays of the sun struck the multitude of bluebirds inside.

"Oh, Bert," Hedy said with a touch of awe in her voice as she held out her hand to him.

"Do you like my tribute to your radiant beauty, my dear?" Bert asked as he grasped her hand and knelt beside her.

"It's absolutely stunning." Hedy glanced up at Sydney. "Can you imagine such a thing?"

"No." She couldn't begin to describe how she felt, because it was almost as if Christmas had come early to Wildcat Bluff on the wings of bluebirds.

"Come inside." Bert stood up, walked over, and opened the glass door to the gazebo.

Hedy went first, followed by Sydney, Dune, Bert Two, and finally Bert, who closed the door behind them.

Sydney simply looked around in amazement, turning in a complete circle as she gazed at the clear sky-blue glass bluebirds in a variety of sizes from small to large but all in the same smooth bird shape. Bert had placed them on clear glass shelves around the walls to better catch the rays of the sun. And for Christmas, he'd added decorations in the form of silver tinsel scarves around necks or gold foil hats on heads or red-and-white candy canes at beaks.

"Oh Bert, you've simply outdone yourself." Hedy glanced around the group with tears in her eyes. "It's just so beautiful—and it's absolutely inspirational for Christmas."

Bert knelt beside her again. "Hedy, I did it all for you."

"Thank you so much." Hedy reached out and clasped Bert's hand in both her own hands.

In that instant, Sydney knew it was time to leave the two lovebirds alone so they could enjoy their newfound happiness. It was obviously a tender moment that they could treasure for a lifetime. She caught Bert Two's gaze and nodded toward the door before she put her fingers around Dune's arm. They all walked out of the gazebo together.

Bert Two quietly shut the door behind them. He cleared his throat and gestured toward the fountain with a rearing horse in its center. "Let me show you more of the garden."

"Thank you. It's lovely here," Sydney said in appreciation.

As she walked into the beautiful garden, she hesitated and glanced back. Bert leaned forward and gave Hedy a gentle kiss on her lips inside the blue-fire gazebo. Sydney felt a powerful rush of happiness, because Hedy deserved a man's devoted love just as much as she deserved being able to ride a horse again. She was one lucky lady, but then again, Hedy had worked hard all her life and given more than she'd gotten, so now it was time for her to receive.

Sydney turned away from the touching sight, granting Hedy and Bert privacy as they reached out to each other. She walked over to the horse fountain where Dune and Bert watched cascading water sparkle in the sunlight. She clasped Dune's large hand, feeling contentment and hope for the future that she hadn't felt in many a long year.

Dune squeezed her hand and gave her a smile that tugged up one corner of his full lips.

"Finally." Bert Two gestured with his head toward the gazebo. "I don't know how much longer Dad could've held out."

"If that wonderful gazebo is any indication," Sydney said, "I don't think much longer."

"I don't either," Bert Two agreed. "If Hedy'll give him a chance, she'll make him the happiest man in the world."

"From the look of things, I think he'll make her the happiest woman in the world." Sydney leaned into Dune's strong, warm body.

"Appears to me," Bert Two said, "that Hedy's not the only one giving a guy a chance."

"It's Christmas." Dune draped an arm around Sydney's shoulders and tugged her closer. "Miracles do happen."

Bert Two nodded in agreement as he gave them a big grin. He leaned down and plucked several dry leaves out of the fountain's swirling water. As he straightened up, his cell phone chimed to announce a text message.

Dune's phone alerted him a millisecond later, and Sydney's cell in her purse wasn't far behind with another jarring ringtone.

They looked at each other in alarm as they grabbed their phones to check on what was happening in the county.

"This can't help but be bad," Bert Two said.

"You know it," Sydney agreed as she started to read her message.

"Firefighters!" Hedy called as she zipped out of the gazebo, followed closely by Bert. "The old Perkins farmhouse is ablaze."

Chapter 32

THE LAST THING DUNE WOULD'VE EVER THOUGHT TO do in relation to fighting a fire was to arrive on the scene in a 1959 pink Cadillac convertible. Still, some days that was just the way the cookie crumbled, so he bit his tongue and stayed quiet as a mouse at a cat convention while Sydney barreled down Wildcat Road toward the Perkins farmhouse.

Sundown—that slash of time between day and night when prey hopefully found safe havens and played hide while predators came out of cozy nooks and played seek—gave firefighters a window of opportunity to get the lay of the land before darkness masked potentially dangerous problems. He hoped no critters were caught in the conflagration. Barn owls in the attic or feral cats and possums in or under the house were all vulnerable. They would use an empty structure for shelter in winter. He figured people wouldn't be caught there, but nothing was ever sure in a fire situation.

From his perch in Celeste, he could see red-orange flames lick upward into the rapidly darkening sky and white-gray smoke buffeted one direction then another by erratic south winds. This late in the game, he figured they'd lose the house, but what they couldn't do was allow the wind to whip out and spread the blaze across pastures to endanger livestock and other homes. Out of control was their enemy. Control was their friend.

"You know," he finally said, "you really shouldn't get this car anywhere near a fire."

"I know," Sydney agreed, "but it's just the way it worked out. We're near the Perkins farm, and to go into Wildcat Bluff would take too much time."

"We could've ridden with the Holloways. They aren't firefighters, but it's their property, and they're right behind us."

"I don't blame them for wanting to see what's going on, but they need to stay out of our way."

"Hedy's in her van, taking up the rear of our little caravan, so she'll keep an eye on them."

Sydney drummed her fingertips on the steering wheel. "I wish we didn't have all these vehicles descending on the place, but if something unexpected happens, we might need them to send for help or go ourselves."

"I doubt if we'll need them. Kent and Morning Glory are on their way in one booster. Trey and Slade are in the other. Plus, we're here to help, too. That ought to be enough to stop this fire in its tracks."

"Hope so."

"One thing you'd better not do is drive these pricey whitewalls over that broken glass we found in the entry to the Perkins place."

"Bert Two said he'd had a load of gravel spread over it."

"That's good. I'd hate to see anything happen to Celeste."

"You and me both." She pointed down the road. "Look, there's Sheriff Calhoun. I'll park right behind his vehicle on the side of the road. Bert and Hedy can pull in behind us. We should all be safe enough out here."

"Good idea. I'm glad the sheriff's been checking on the farmhouse more often since the break-in or we'd be in worse trouble, what with this wind whipping around like a wild mustang."

"Maybe it'll settle down pretty quick."

"I wouldn't count on it, but I hope so."

As Sydney slowed down, she raised her arm and pointed toward the shoulder of the road, indicating parking spaces to those behind her. She carefully edged in behind Sheriff Calhoun while Bert stopped near Celeste's bumper and Hedy eased in back of his pickup.

"Go ahead," Sydney said. "I'll leave the keys in the ignition just in case somebody needs to move this car fast and I'm at the fire."

"Sounds good." Dune got out and took long strides over to where the sheriff had just exited his vehicle.

They met on the near side of the wide gravel entry into the farm and stopped to watch the conflagration that was quickly engulfing the entire house. Soon the wind whipped around and sent smoke billowing in their direction.

"Do you smell accelerant?" Sheriff Calhoun asked, sniffing the air. He wore his usual tan police uniform with holstered revolver on one hip, black cowboy boots, and beige Stetson. He carried a large metal flashlight that could be used for illumination or confrontation.

"I hate to say till I get nearer the house, but it smells as if it might be gasoline." Dune made note of the layout of the house and the land around it. He glanced upward, glad to see a utility pole with a security light on top that would come on to illuminate the area as soon as night fell or the smoke got thicker.

"Yeah," Sheriff Calhoun agreed. "It's best not to jump to conclusions simply because the arsonist has used the same technique every time we've responded to one of these fires."

"But it pays to be alert to old patterns," Dune said.

"Right."

Sydney walked over to them, stepping carefully across gravel on the side of the road in her soft-soled moccasins. "Do I smell gasoline?"

"That's exactly what's on our minds," Sheriff Calhoun agreed, slapping the flashlight against his leg.

Bert Two jogged up to them. "Dad's going to try to talk Hedy into staying back here with him. It's rough down there for a wheelchair."

"I agree. I've checked out the place," Sheriff Calhoun said. "It's overgrown and rocky with plenty of creepy crawlers."

"I wouldn't let Hedy hear you suggest she might not go down there because of a few creepy crawlers," Sydney warned with a touch of humor in her voice.

Sheriff Calhoun gave a low chuckle. "True enough. I don't want to get on Hedy's bad side."

"That's for sure," Dune agreed with a smile at the joke, because everybody knew it'd be hard to find a bad side to Hedy.

"What can I do to help?" Bert Two asked. "From here, it looks as if the place will be a total loss."

"I regret to say it, but you're probably right," Sydney agreed. "There's not much you can do at this point except to let firefighters contain it."

"It's a shame." Bert Two sighed as he looked at the blaze. "That was a classic 1930s farmhouse with a big attic and a porch with a swing. We were about to restore it, then rent or sell it."

"You've got insurance on the house, don't you?" Sheriff Calhoun asked.

"Yes," Bert Two agreed. "But you can't replace an original vintage structure like that. It's a crying shame."

"It's that, all right," Sheriff Calhoun said, "but I'm more concerned that this will turn out to be arson again."

"There's one good thing about the fire," Hedy called as she motored up to them in her wheelchair with Bert walking by her side.

"What's that?" Sheriff Calhoun asked.

"Sydney, Dune, and I were with Bert and Bert Two at their house when this fire started, accidental or intentional," Hedy stated in a no-nonsense voice.

Sheriff Calhoun thoughtfully rubbed his clean-shaven chin. "Good point, except it doesn't hold water. Bert, Bert Two, I hate to say it, but even if you were with somebody at the time of the fire—"

"I know," Bert interrupted him. "We could've hired an arsonist so we'd appear innocent."

"They'd never do it." Hedy sounded incensed as she glared at the sheriff.

"Thanks, dear." Bert put a hand on her shoulder. "I appreciate the support, but the sheriff has to look at facts, not theories."

"There's nothing I want more than to clear your names and stop these fires in my county," Sheriff Calhoun said. "I'm frustrated as all get-out."

"We all are," Dune agreed. "But right now we need to focus on containing this blaze as soon as the rigs get here."

Hedy patted Bert's hand on her shoulder. "We'll catch that arsonist, never you fear."

"Thanks." Bert glanced around the group. "I still can't imagine who'd want to do this to us."

"Or why," Bert Two added.

"No telling," Sheriff Calhoun said. "Folks have a way of letting their minds get twisted into pretzels over something as little as an anthill or as big as a mountain. There's no telling what'll trigger them or what they'll think benefits them. Best thing we can do is stay on alert."

"We sure do appreciate the fact that you saw this fire early," Bert said. "You're always a true professional."

"Wish I'd been here soon enough to catch the culprit, but at least the blaze won't spread too far."

"It sure won't now." Sydney pointed down the road. "Here comes our rescue team."

Dune heard sirens blaring as he saw the two red boosters, one behind the other, race toward them from the direction of Wildcat Bluff. Finally, they could get started on the flames, although it'd felt like it'd been forever since he'd gotten the message from the fire-rescue station. But it always felt that way—seconds stretched into minutes while minutes stretched into hours—because adrenaline was flowing and distorting everything as they put their lives on the line and fought against time to extinguish or contain a fire.

When the first rig pulled into the open entryway, Slade lowered the window and stuck his head outside. "We're ready to pump and roll, so we'll get this fire knocked back in no time. And Sydney, Storm is with Mom and Granny, so she's just fine."

"Thanks. That's good to know," Sydney said.

"What do you want us to do?" Dune asked, putting an arm around Sydney's shoulders.

"If y'all are willing, it'd help most if you stayed up here out of the way with the civilians. Kent and Morning Glory are right behind me. Two boosters ought to do the trick," Slade said.

Dune nodded in agreement, although he itched to get into the thick of things, but he wasn't wearing gear, and he didn't want Sydney reinjuring her feet, particularly before the Christmas events.

Trey leaned over from the driver's seat and lifted a hand in greeting. "We'll let you know if we need something." And he took off toward the house.

Kent pulled up next, and Morning Glory stuck her head out the open window. "Mr. December! You surely do know how to inspire the ladies."

Dune didn't say a word, knowing it was useless.

"I don't have time to chat now, but that calendar is pure inspiration," Morning Glory gushed in an excited voice. "I'm already at work on Mr. December's favorite scent to sell in my store. The ladies are going to love it!"

"Later!" Kent called from the driver's side and tore off down to the burning house.

"Mr. December now has a favorite scent? I bet it's yummy." Sydney couldn't keep the laughter from her voice.

Dune gave a big sigh, realizing he might never hear the last of Mr. December. At least he could do something useful, if he couldn't pump water and roll hose to put out the blaze.

"What's this about Mr. December?" Sheriff Calhoun asked.

"Trust me, you don't want to know," Dune said.

"Please let me borrow your flashlight. I can at least go down and walk the perimeter. Maybe the arsonist finally got sloppy."

"I better go with you." Sheriff Calhoun tapped his flashlight against his leg.

"What about crowd control?" Dune asked, gesturing toward the vehicles that were arriving and parking across the road.

"We were bound to get a lookie-loo or two or more," Sheriff Calhoun said, frowning. "I can call in a deputy, but I'm holding off this close to Christmas if it's not absolutely necessary. They'll all be working overtime during Christmas in the Country and Christmas at the Sure-Shot Drive-In."

"I doubt I'll find anything." Dune held out his hand for the flashlight. "I'll call you if I see something suspicious."

"Okay." Sheriff Calhoun slapped his flashlight onto Dune's open palm. "If you find evidence, don't touch it. Call me." He tapped his front pocket with the outline of a cell phone.

"Will do." Dune turned to Sydney. "I won't be long."

"I'm going with you."

"Please don't take a chance with your feet, because too many people are depending on you for the drive-in."

"He's right," Hedy agreed. "Stay here and out of the action for once in your life. Anyway, if I'm doing it, you can do it."

"Okay, Hedy," Sydney agreed. "We can help the sheriff with traffic control, if and when he needs it."

Dune set off down the gravel drive before anybody else tried to stop him or come with him. When he got as close as was prudent, he stopped and watched his

friends pump and roll. They were trained profession-
als, and they didn't need help, because they'd already
almost completed a containment area with water despite
the erratic wind gusts.

There wouldn't be much left in the way of evidence
inside the house, not once it was reduced to charcoal, so
he decided to look in the surrounding yard. He turned on
the flashlight and was rewarded with a powerful beam
that he focused on the ground in front of him.

As he walked forward, he crisscrossed the beam
back and forth in front of him. He rousted a cottontail
rabbit from its hidey-hole, walked into a clingy spiderweb that he hoped was empty, stubbed his boot on a
set of rocks that he realized had been carefully arranged
long ago to form a flower bed. He checked here and
there, but no matter how hard he looked, nothing
appeared out of the ordinary for what had once been the
abode of family farmers.

He also stayed well aware of the fire, looking and
listening and ready for action. He heard the hiss and
sizzle of water fighting fire while weakened wood
beams crackled and fell to the ground, sending out hiss-
ing sparks. Firefighters moved in and out, back and forth
around the burning structure as if they were part of a
choreographed dance in which he was excluded from
action. Smoke swirled in waves around him, stinging his
nose and mouth with an acrid scent as the wind whipped
one way and then another.

As darkness fell, the security light came on and turned
everything into an eerie flat gray with little depth or
color. But that very oddness made him notice an object
that stood out as unnatural against a natural background.

He turned his flashlight on a clump of bushes near the barbwire fence at the far edge of the front yard. He saw red metal that definitely didn't belong there.

He hurried over, knelt down, turned his light on the object, and saw a gasoline can. It was old, maybe as old as the house, because it had greasy stains streaked across red flaked paint. He leaned closer and sniffed. He caught the pungent scent of fresh gasoline. The can had recently been used, maybe to start the house fire. He felt a huge upwelling of relief. Maybe they'd finally caught a break. And then he saw something else. A crumpled, dirty green-and-white striped towel had been wedged in beside the gas can. Something about the towel nudged at his memory, as if it was familiar, but he dismissed it, because a towel was simply a towel.

He stood up, pulled his phone out of his pocket, and called the sheriff.

"You got something for me?" Sheriff Calhoun answered his cell.

"Maybe. Maybe not. I think you'd better come take a look. And I'd bring a couple of big evidence bags."

"I'm on my way."

While he waited, Dune looked at the burning house that appeared to be crumpling in on itself with the roof down in the basement, the windows busted or blown out, and the walls simply gone. No doubt about it, fire was fast, so firefighters had to be faster. A containment perimeter had been established now around the structure, so no flames had escaped to nearby pastures. For the moment, all was safe thanks to his friends and colleagues.

As Sheriff Calhoun approached, the firefighters glanced up and saw Dune with his flashlight trained on something in the bushes. He gave them a thumbs-up, and they responded in kind before they turned back to the fire. He was glad to be part of their team. He suddenly realized that Wildcat Bluff had gotten under his skin in more ways than one. For him, it'd simply started to be home.

When the sheriff reached him, Dune pointed with the flashlight down at the bushes.

"Is that a gas can?" Sheriff Calhoun asked as he knelt down to get a closer look.

"Yes. And it recently had fresh gasoline inside."

"Can we be that lucky?"

"I hope so. After all this time, it's hard to believe, but maybe so. There's a towel, too."

"A towel makes sense. It was probably used to dry spilled gas on hands or clothes or whatever."

"Yeah," Dune agreed.

"Hold the light steady." Sheriff Calhoun put on rubber gloves, reached under the bushes, and gently pulled out the gas can. "It looks old, but serviceable—no cracks or holes or rust."

"Why would the arsonist leave it?"

Sheriff Calhoun carefully put the can in an evidence bag and sealed it. "No idea, unless this was his last stop and he figured the fire would spread and burn any evidence on the can and destroy the towel."

"The good news would be that this was the last fire," Dune said thoughtfully.

"The better news would be if there's useable evidence on this can and the towel." Sheriff Calhoun picked up the towel and bagged it, too.

"Both would be good," Dune agreed.

"Let's go," Sheriff Calhoun said, standing up. "I called in a deputy. He'll take over here while I get these items to the lab."

"Sounds good." Dune glanced up at Sydney where she stood near the Cadillac.

"Fire's under control," Sheriff Calhoun added. "I sent Hedy, Bert, and Bert Two home to get some rest. Lookie-loos are gone. I suggest you persuade Sydney to go home and get some sleep. We've got those Christmas events coming up on us fast."

"Are you sure you don't need any more help here?" Dune walked with the sheriff back up to the gravel entryway.

"Not a bit of it. Trey and Slade will stay to watch what's left of the fire. Kent and Morning Glory will be on their way home soon, too."

"If you're sure, then I'm going to get Sydney and go home."

"Sydney, huh?" Sheriff Calhoun said with a chuckle. "You're some lucky guy."

"Tell me about it."

As Dune headed for Sydney's Cadillac, he did feel lucky—as if he was the luckiest guy in Wildcat Bluff County or, better yet, the luckiest guy in Texas.

Chapter 33

SYDNEY HAD A LOT ON HER MIND, NOT THE LEAST OF which was Dune Barrett, as she drove toward Cougar Ranch. She could feel his presence riding shotgun like banked embers ready to ignite. And that was the way she wanted him, all hot and growly and ready for trouble.

She hadn't felt like trouble in a long time, but maybe he was right about her. She'd banked her trouble in the way he'd banked his fire. Once the two of them came together, they'd nurtured each other's flames till they caught fire. Now they were at a place where they fished or cut bait. Truth be told, she didn't even know how long he'd be in Wildcat Bluff. Could she pin her hopes on somebody who might be here today and gone tomorrow? And yet—no matter what—she wanted to continue building their combined fire till it reached a rip-roaring blaze.

She exhaled sharply, pushing down her thoughts. Now wasn't the time for trouble. Now was the time for congratulations all the way around. Firefighters had controlled another fire for the Holloways and obtained evidence this time. The calendar was published and distributed to local merchants. Storm was better and working on her goat-tying skills. Hedy and Bert had finally committed to each other. So much was going so well that she didn't dare push her luck, although she had high hopes for Christmas.

And that brought her up to their holiday festivals. In about a week, visitors would start checking into the hotel and motels across Wildcat Bluff. Twin Oaks, the most popular bed-and-breakfast in the county, had a standing waiting list for Christmas. She still needed to drop off calendars to her friend Ruby Jobson, since she'd be hosting local holiday parties, as well as guests, at her estate.

Sydney didn't need to be concerned about Christmas in Old Town, since it was a popular event. Christmas at the Sure-Shot Drive-In was still a question mark in everyone's mind. She'd coordinated with Wildcat Bluff to schedule nonconflicting events such as a morning Christmas parade in Sure-Shot with vintage automobiles and equestrians, all-day vendors inside the drive-in with the auto show, and dusk-till-dawn classic holiday films.

In addition, she'd set up promotion with online sites, newspapers, rodeos, radio stations, and other targeted platforms. Even so, she felt as if she'd forgotten something, but she'd felt like that for months. Maybe she'd feel that way till it was all said and done. She simply had to accept the fact that once the events got under way, almost everything was out of her control. At that point in time, she'd simply count on individuals and groups knowing and doing their part in the Christmas pageantry.

Still, was she really down to a single week? She'd been so distracted by so much for so long that only now did reality hit her. She still had more to do, but she was almost out of time.

"Penny for your thoughts," Dune said, reaching over and squeezing her hand. "You're way too quiet."

"My mind's running ninety to nothing."

"I'm not surprised. It's been busy."

"But everything happens in a week!"

"I told you I'd help, and I will."

She clenched the steering wheel with both hands.

"We've done a good job. Everything will work out fine." He turned toward her in his seat. "Look at the calendar. That came off without a hitch, didn't it?"

"It did turn out well." She couldn't keep from chuckling as she remembered Mr. December fending off the ladies.

He joined her laughter. "For you, yes. For me, not so much."

"You can't complain about being a hit at the beauty station."

"Oh, yes I can."

"For a moment there, I thought you might wield that ballpoint pen like a sword."

"Truth of the matter, I thought about it."

She laughed harder.

"Go ahead and laugh at me if it'll ease your tension." He scooted closer to her across the bench seat.

She glanced at him, then back at the road, feeling her laughter die away to be replaced by sudden heat. "Laughter's good, but I know something you do that's even better."

"To ease tension?"

"That and—"

"I never did get lucky today, did I?"

"It seems as if we talked about it a long time ago."

"I didn't forget."

"We're almost at your place." She came to Cougar Ranch, turned off Wildcat Road, and drove over the cattle guard.

"You could come inside."

"It's late."

"I could show you my Sydney lingerie collection."

She smiled at his words as she followed the lane toward the cowboy cabins, feeling torn between going straight home to get a good night's sleep and following him inside where they could start their own personal fire.

"I could relax you."

"A hot bath would do the trick, too." She came to a stop beside his dually, trying to set trouble aside to be the practical cowgirl.

"You owe me a bra." He leaned over, clasped her thigh, and slowly massaged upward.

"I do pay my debts, don't I?" She shivered at his touch, feeling hot and cold all over.

"Far as I know, that's always been the case." He pushed back her hair and pressed a hot kiss below her ear. "I need you tonight."

She sighed, knowing she couldn't resist him—didn't want to resist him. "I need you, too."

"Let's go inside."

She nodded, not needing to say anything else, and turned off Celeste's engine. As she picked up her purse, Dune got out of the car, walked around to her side, and opened the door with a gentlemanly flourish.

"Right this way." He gestured toward his cabin.

She stood up, pressed a soft kiss to his lips, and walked up to the front door.

"Not locked," he said behind her.

She turned the knob, stepped across the threshold, and felt the tension of the long day melt from her shoulders.

"Welcome to my humble abode."

"It's so cozy," she said as she glanced around the room bathed only in soft, white light from a single lamp.

"Small, you mean?"

"Cozy and comfortable and just right."

"I liked it fine till you made me want more." He shrugged out of his jacket and tossed it on the easy chair.

"What do you mean?" She walked over to his dresser, only a few steps in the enclosed space, and turned back to him.

"I mean," he said, stalking over to her, "I want to be with you."

"We've been together almost every day."

"Good, but not good enough." He reached out to her, then dropped his hand. "I'm trying not to go too fast with you, but I can't help it."

"Fast?"

He picked up her green slip from the dresser and held it in his hands. "I don't want just a slip." He tossed it down and picked up her red panties. "I don't even want the bra you're wearing right now."

"I don't understand." She didn't know what he wanted from her, but he was making her feel uneasy.

"None of it's enough, not anymore." He tossed her panties back on the dresser. "I want the place where you keep *all* your underwear. And I want my stuff beside your stuff in the dresser, in the closet, in the nightstand."

"Oh." She caught her breath at the impact of what he was telling her. "That is serious."

He reached down, clasped her hands, and lifted them to his mouth. He gently kissed one palm and then the other as he looked into her eyes. "Sydney, I'm serious about you."

"I'm getting a little on the serious side myself."

"Good. I'm not pressuring you. I just want you to know I'm here for the long haul. I'm looking at Wildcat Bluff as my home."

"You're staying here?" She could hardly believe his words. He wanted to be here. He wanted to be with her. He wanted to get serious. She felt her heart speed up with excitement.

"If you're here, I'm here."

She swallowed hard, feeling words escape her in the intensity of the moment.

"If I'm completely off base, tell me, but—"

"Shhh." She put a fingertip to his lips. "I think we're way past words."

He gave her a slow smile, revealing his crooked front tooth, as his blue eyes turned dark with desire. "In that case, I changed my mind."

"About what?"

"I want your bra."

She smiled as she put a hand to her top button and slowly unbuttoned all the way down her sweater till her white retro bra was exposed to his view. "Is this what you wanted to see?"

He groaned as he quickly pulled the soft material apart, down her arms, and tossed her sweater aside. And then he simply stood there and looked at her for a long moment. "You're so beautiful."

She didn't need any more words. She simply wanted to show him how she felt about him, so that there'd be no misunderstandings between them. She longed to share her pillow with him, put his stuff beside her stuff, park Celeste beside his dually, and share the remote controls. But most of all, she wanted to share their heat.

With that thought in mind, she smiled mischievously— maybe even a bit coquettishly—as she put her hands behind her back, unhooked her white lace bra, slid the straps down her arms, and tossed it across her slip on the dresser to make a complete, if mismatched, set.

That simple act caused him to growl deep in his throat as he crushed her against his chest, pressing hot kisses across her face, down her throat, back to her ears, and finally settled on her mouth where he teased and tormented, nibbled and nipped until he thrust deep inside, kissing her so passionately that he left no doubt that he desperately needed her.

She returned his kiss with fervor of her own, feeling their combined heat merge, blaze, and burn to new heights. She couldn't get enough of him fast enough, deep enough, hard enough as she roamed his body with her hands, thrusting into his hair, digging into his shoulders, clutching the fabric of his shirt. She kissed him with a desperation that grew stronger by the moment, wanting more, needing more, and still more as her heart accelerated in time with his heartbeat.

Finally, he tore his mouth away, gave her a hard look, and set her back from him, hands trembling with repressed passion. He swiveled toward the bed, jerked the cowboy bedspread and top sheet back, and then turned to her with a question in his dark-blue eyes.

She nodded in agreement, wanting to see him, know him, experience him in every possible way. She watched as he unsnapped his shirt, jerked it out of his Wranglers, and threw it on top of her sweater.

She shivered at the sight of his naked, muscular chest with blond hair and hard nipples. She couldn't wait any longer—not for anything.

She quickly sat on the bed and reached down to take off her moccasins, but he knelt before her, slipping off one shoe and then the other. As if that simple act unleashed the last thread that bound her, she reached up and pulled him on top of her, feeling his weight, his strength, his desire crush her into the soft mattress.

He covered her breasts with hot, hard hands and hot, hard kisses until she writhed up against him, struggling for breath, for thought, for his deepest touch. She couldn't wait another moment. He understood, for he didn't make her wait. He unzipped her skirt, pulled it down, slipped off her panties, and tossed them both aside. She lay still, completely exposed to him.

As he watched her with a smoldering gaze, he slowly, gently, deliberately slid his long fingers up the inside of her thighs until he gained the apex of her hot, moist center. He deepened his touch, sending her into a crimson haze of unfulfilled desire. She reached up for him, sliding her hands across his broad chest and tearing a growl from deep in his throat again.

He abruptly pulled away, then quickly undid his belt buckle, unzipped his jeans, and jerked his Wranglers with his belt still in the loops down. He started to toss his jeans to the floor, then stopped and pulled a foil packet out of his pocket. He glanced back at her with a predatory gleam in his eyes, ripped open the package, and slipped a condom on his hard length.

"Love me." And she beckoned him back to her.

"Always."

No more needed to be said because—once more—he understood her need as if it were his own need. She shivered as he knelt before her, raised her hips, and swiftly entered her, joining them completely as one. He thrust deep, stroking harder and faster as he drove them both closer to the edge of fulfillment. She clutched his shoulders as she rode him, twining higher and higher until she cried out, and they reached their blazing peak of ecstasy together.

He gently kissed her lips, then lay down and tucked her close to him, as if he would never let her go. She sighed in contentment as she cuddled against his shoulder and placed her hand on his chest over his heart.

Now she knew that life would never be the same, not after this moment. She'd always thought her family, as well as the ranch, the café, the fire station, even Wildcat Bluff, were home. But she was wrong.

Home was Dune Barrett.

Chapter 34

SYDNEY TOOK A DEEP BREATH AS SHE LOOKED OUT HER front door at the clear blue sky with no hint of rain. It was the Saturday before Christmas, so she'd been up since well before dawn. As far as she could tell, everything was in order for Christmas at the Sure-Shot Drive-In.

She'd worked with Dune yesterday to take care of last-minute details, coordinating with Mom, Granny, and Slade for the festivities. They'd usually go to Christmas in the Country together, but not this year, since there were so many more things to do. Storm was already with Granny, excited but not as much as usual. Once this day was over, Sydney would help her daughter overcome her fears and get on her pony again.

Fortunately, the day was cool but not too cold. She'd selected a pale pink silk blouse the same color as Celeste to go with a white leather pencil skirt that had a long, matching leather coat with cuffed sleeves and a shawl collar. She wore tinted hose with crocodile kitten heel pumps and carried a white leather handbag with gold trim to complete her outfit. Together, she and Celeste made a fine team.

She wouldn't be with Dune for the Sure-Shot parade, because she'd be with the vintage automobiles, and he'd be with the equestrians. All of the local ranches would be represented in the parade, as much to enjoy riding together as to promote the local businesses. Area antique car clubs were always happy to show off their pristine vehicles, so they'd quickly signed up for the event.

She tucked her cell phone in her purse and glanced around her office to make sure she hadn't forgotten anything. As far as she knew, all was in order, and it was time to go. For good luck, she touched one of the poinsettia leaves on the beautiful plant Dune had sent her. She felt a sudden burst of excitement. She'd planned long and hard for this event. Now it was make-or-break time.

Outside, the day was beautiful with a few fluffy clouds in the sky and a slight breeze that brought the scent of evergreen. She walked over to Celeste, appreciating the high gloss that came from Dune's fine washing and detailing. She'd already attached a sign that read "Sure-Shot Christmas Queen" in red letters on a white background in front of the longhorns. It'd stand out well in the parade.

She opened the driver's door, tossed her handbag across the seat, and took a deep breath. She gave Celeste a quick pat for more luck, then sat down inside. A moment later, the big V8 engine purred to life, and she took off down the lane. Once she reached Wildcat Road, she passed more vehicles than usual, which was a good sign that lots of extra people were in the county.

When she arrived in Sure-Shot, she drove to the staging area on the north side of town where vehicles were already lining up for the parade. In a nearby but separate area, equestrians were also getting in line after Sue Ann Bridges, their local large and small animal veterinarian, checked Coggins Test papers for each horse to make sure the deadly virus wouldn't be transmitted between animals. All in all, everything appeared to be running on schedule.

She drove to the head of the antique cars, because Celeste would be leading the parade. She wished Mr. Werner could be there to see his beloved Cadillac admired and appreciated by all. In fact, she'd have asked him to ride with her, knowing he'd have enjoyed dressing in fine retro clothing with a fedora set at a jaunty angle on his head. She gave a quick, silent thanks to Mr. Werner's generosity.

For now, she needed to focus on the day, not the past. She glanced around for Melinda Bright, who'd sold enough tickets to garner the queen title. The hardworking teenager would keep fifty percent of all she'd earned, and the rest would be used to help defray event expenses.

She caught sight of Melinda as she stepped out of a blue pickup and quickly walked over. She looked perfect. She wore her queen's crystal tiara in place of the hat band on her bright red cowgirl hat. She'd added a dramatic red leather vest with fringe and matching gloves to a traditional blue pearl-snap shirt and Wranglers with red pointy-toe boots.

"You look wonderful," Sydney said. "I could almost mistake you for Annie Oakley in one of her sharpshooting costumes."

Melinda gave her a big grin. "Thanks. I'm paying tribute to Little Miss Sure-Shot, even if I missed seeing her perform by a hundred years or more."

"You make a good stand-in."

"Thanks. I appreciate the honor."

"You worked hard to sell that many tickets."

"I wanted to be the first Sure-Shot Christmas Queen." Melinda walked over and ran a hand along the side of the Cadillac. "And I really wanted to ride in this power convertible."

"I don't blame you," Sydney agreed. "Let me introduce you to Celeste. She's quite a treat."

"You named your car?"

"Mr. Werner named Celeste way back in 1959 when he bought her new."

"Really? Is he going to be here?"

"He almost made it to a hundred, but he's gone now."

Melinda nodded her head thoughtfully. "Maybe Celeste will make it to a hundred."

"If I have anything to say about it, she sure will."

"I hope every future Sure-Shot Christmas Queen gets to ride in her." Melinda cocked her head at Sydney. "You look good, too. I heard you'd gone vintage all the way. That's an amazing outfit."

"Thanks," Sydney said. "But between the two of us, I'm about ready to get back into my regular cowgirl clothes."

"I can see it'd be a little hard to ride a horse."

"You know it." Sydney checked her watch. "It's close to time to start. Why don't you go ahead and get in the back seat. You can sit above with your feet on the seat."

"I won't hurt the leather, will I?"

"Not a chance." Sydney opened the passenger door.

Melinda quickly stepped into the car and settled into place above the back seat, adjusting her hat so sunlight glinted off the crystals in her tiara.

Sydney picked up two large baggies of colorful wrapped candy from the floorboard. She handed one to Melinda and set the other on the seat within easy reach. "I thought it'd be fun for you to toss candy to kids along the route."

"That's great." Melinda opened the baggie and selected a handful to throw out of the car. "I'm all set."

"You look terrific. Just wait a here a bit, and I'll be right back."

Sydney quickly walked over to check on the vintage vehicles behind her convertible. She'd requested the car clubs include mostly fifties models, and it appeared they'd done just that for her.

She saw a Chevy Impala with a white roof and aqua body, a yellow Ford Thunderbird with round portholes for back windows, a red and white Chevy Bel Air convertible with red and white leather seats, a red Corvette convertible with red leather seats, and other pristine vehicles.

She stopped beside Duke Daniels, the driver of the first car club in line. He wore typical cowboy clothes in green plaid shirt, jeans, boots, and hat, but he'd added a beautiful retro horsehead-and-horseshoe-design cardigan against the morning's chill.

"All the vehicles are gorgeous. Thanks for joining us today," she said with a warm smile.

"Any time." Duke gestured toward her convertible. "Your Cadillac isn't to be sneezed at either."

"Thanks. Mr. Werner gave Celeste to me so she'd be in good hands."

"You lucky dog! We wondered what had happened to her. I'll let folks know." Duke leaned closer. "Listen, if you ever decide to give Celeste another home, please give me a call. I'd be happy to baby her just like Mr. Werner."

"That's good to know. I'll keep you in mind. For now, Celeste and I are a team."

"I can see it." Duke cocked his head to one side.

"Listen, why don't you join us for some of the car shows? Celeste would be a huge hit."

"Thanks. I'll think about it." She liked the idea of sharing Celeste with the world, but that was for another time. "Right now, I guess we'd better get this show on the road."

"Let's do it!"

Sydney walked back to Celeste, gave a thumbs-up to Melinda, and sat down inside. She started the engine, wrapped her fingers around the big steering wheel, and pulled onto Main Street. She was thrilled to see folks lined up all along the boardwalk, waiting for the parade. They looked happy and excited to be celebrating Christmas in Sure-Shot. She breathed a great sigh of relief. So far, everything was going to plan.

She waited for the color guard from the Sure-Shot American Legion to get into place in front of her. Four veterans wearing white shirts, black pants, and black combat boots with Legion dark-blue caps and vests walked into the center of the street and stood in a row. One veteran carried the United States flag on a long pole while another veteran carried the Sure-Shot, Texas, American Legion flag. They were flanked on each side by a veteran carrying a rifle.

At the designated time, all four men started their forward march to the center of town where they stopped at attention and turned to face the reviewing stand, a small dais in front of the Bluebonnet Café. The Legion flag was lowered to an angle while the United States flag remained high. A cowgirl in a flowery long skirt and matching blouse stood alone on the dais. She nodded to the Legionnaires, then raised her voice to sing the national anthem, letting the strong, pure notes soar up, over, and beyond Sure-Shot, as people put their hands over their hearts and military veterans saluted in respect. When the last strains of the anthem fell away, the color guard executed a sharp right turn and marched off the street.

Sydney moved her hand from her heart to her steering wheel, pressed down on the gas pedal, and slowly started the parade down Main Street. She heard Christmas music piped from a speaker system that had been recently installed for the event. She heard a soaring rendition of "Joy to the World" that couldn't help but ignite the spirit of the season in everyone. Red-and-green, silver-and-gold, blue-and-purple twinkling lights accented store windows while the scent of fresh green cedar boughs filled the air. A rope of shining white light outlined the roof over the busy, bustling boardwalk.

Sydney smiled and waved at folks while they cheered for their Sure-Shot Christmas Queen. Melinda tossed handfuls of candy from the back seat, and kids scrambled to catch it or pick it up off the pavement while their parents put their sweet treats into plastic bags for later.

Everyone appeared so happy to be there that Sydney knew all her hard work was well worth every bit of effort. She glanced back where the parade spread out behind her. Sunlight glinted off the glossy paint of colorful classic cars and warmed the rich earth tones of horses sedately walking or taking a few prancing steps while the crowd cheered in appreciation.

As she drew near the end of downtown, she felt happy and sad at the same time. For something that had taken so long to plan, prepare, and execute, it was going to be swiftly over—at least until another year. And there would be another Christmas at the Sure-Shot Drive-In, because attendance at the parade already made it a success. She took heart in knowing there would always be Christmas to celebrate in Wildcat Bluff County.

Fortunately, folks still lined the road, waving and cheering and picking up candy as she headed out of downtown toward the drive-in, because the next phase of the day was already on her mind.

She wasn't exactly sure what to expect, because Bert and Bert Two were in charge at the drive-in. They'd relieved her of that job, but left her feeling a little uneasy, since she didn't know the details of their plans. Still, she trusted them, since they always did more than strictly necessary when they elevated houses or events to the next level.

When she arrived at the large, wide, circular entry area in front of the drive-in open gate, she was thrilled at what she saw there. Vendors of handmade creative crafts such as hand-cast pottery, tie-dyed T-shirts, goat soap products, knit scarves, and jars of pickled fruits and vegetables were set up around the perimeter of the drive-in fence on white portable tables under large white umbrellas imprinted with the turquoise Sure-Shot Drive-In retro logo.

As she drove into the area, leading the line of vehicles, Bert Two walked out from behind a vendor table and pointed toward a place near the road where he wanted her to park. She pulled in there with Celeste's nose pointed outward so she had a good view of the parade.

Bert Two jogged over, grinning from ear to ear. "So far, so good."

"Everything here looks wonderful," she said, stepping out of her Caddy. "And the parade is going great."

He glanced at Melinda. "If you'll join us, we have a special seat for you at our booth, so you can meet and greet folks as they look at cars and shop at vendor tables."

"I'd love to do it." Melinda picked up a nearly full bag of candy and shook it. "I can also hand out more goodies."

"Perfect," Bert Two agreed. "We have Sure-Shot Drive-In magnets you can give out for free, and we might sell a few caps and T-shirts. Hopefully, we'll sell a lot of cowboy firefighter calendars, too."

"Sounds perfect. And it looks as if you've got everything under control," Sydney said. "Thanks so much for your help and the generous use of the drive-in."

"It works both ways," Bert Two added. "We'll get a lot of promotional value from this event, as well as helping out the town."

"Still, it's a boon to the county," Sydney said with a smile.

"It's great for everybody." Melinda got out of the convertible and gave Sydney a big hug. "Thanks. This is the absolute best day of my life."

"I'm sure you'll enjoy many more best days." Sydney felt warmth blossom in her heart at Melinda's obvious happiness.

"I'll just go over to the drive-in table and see what I can do to help." Melinda smiled at them, then walked away.

"It's worth all the effort to make even one person that happy, isn't it?" Bert Two said.

"You're absolutely right."

"Hey, I'd better show these cars where to park. We'll

see you in the snack shed later." Bert Two quickly left, beginning to direct vehicles to their assigned positions.

"I'd better get back to our booth to help Melinda," Bert said before he sauntered away.

Sydney moved to the front of Celeste to watch the parade, marveling at the unique beauty of the classic cars as they drove into the entryway. Soon the horses came into view and began their turn at the end of the road for their journey back to the starting point and their trailers there.

She wished Storm had felt like braving horseback again, but she hoped Granny had at least brought her to the parade. She watched for friends, eager to see the clothes they wore and the horses they rode.

Billye Jo, Serena, and Moore showed up first, turned out in the Lazy S colors of green and purple with the brand stitched onto classic dark-brown rancher jackets with leather collars worn over pearl-snap shirts and Wranglers. They rode quarter horses, born, bred, and trained on the Lazy S that had a fine reputation in the state and well beyond. Sydney waved at them, and they waved back, looking happy and proud on their mounts.

She laughed out loud when she saw a fancy goat cart with big wooden wheels and a sign on its side that read "Morning's Glory & Adelia's Delights: Gifts to Inspire." From her seat inside the cart, Hedy waved with one hand while she held the reins of a brown-and-white pony in the other. Morning Glory sat beside her, as usual dressed in her flower child splendor of long, multicolor flowing skirt, aqua peasant blouse with a nubby orange sweater, and several of her handmade macramé horse-harness necklaces dangling around her neck. She waved, too.

Fortunately, Sydney had remembered to ask Morning Glory to smudge the snack shed earlier in the week. After burning sage and sweetgrass inside, her friend had pronounced the drive-in all set for new customers. Sydney chuckled at the thought of Morning Glory's new Mr. December cologne. She bet it'd be a big seller at the Sure-Shot Beauty Station.

She watched Kent ride by on a sorrel gelding with Lauren riding a chestnut by his side. They wore jean jackets with the Cougar Ranch brand emblazoned on the front and back. Sydney waved at them, expecting to see Dune riding with their brand, but he wasn't with that group of cowboys.

Trey and Misty rode up next, waving and grinning from the backs of their frisky palominos with silver-studded bridles and saddles gleaming in the bright sunlight. They represented Wildcat Ranch with snarling wildcats emblazoned on their crimson jackets.

She'd thought Dune might be riding with the Wildcat brand since he wasn't with Cougar Ranch, but maybe he'd decided to stay out of the parade altogether. No, that didn't make sense. He'd told her he'd see her at the parade, so he had to be here somewhere.

Finally, she saw the Chuckwagon Café's entry. She waved to Granny and Mom, who rode in a small chuck-wagon replica driven by Slade with his big hands on the reins of a sleek bay gelding. They waved back, and Granny tossed her a Chuckwagon Café key chain with the café's logo printed on it.

She didn't see Storm in the wagon, so she grew a little concerned at her absence. If Storm hadn't wanted to leave the café, maybe they'd left her there with Dune to watch over her. Still, she didn't like not seeing Storm with her family, so she'd find out about her daughter as soon as the parade was over.

A few more riders passed by, but she didn't know them. They must have come from out of the county. She waved anyway, and they waved back, appearing happy and proud to be part of the special event.

She glanced down at the Chuckwagon Café key chain, then tucked it into her pocket, wondering again about Storm. And Dune.

"Mommy!"

She looked up at the sound of her name. And there—shockingly—rode Storm on her white-and-brown pony as if there'd never been an ATV accident or fright or anything. Dune rode right beside her on a buckskin gelding with dark-brown leather tack trimmed in silver. He raised a hand in greeting and smiled at her. Storm and Dune looked pleased at having surprised her, so she simply grinned and waved back, thinking how perfect they appeared together—just as if they were father and daughter.

They obviously weren't representing Steele Trap Ranch, because Storm wore a long pale-pink gown with a dark-pink bodice and net overskirt. A bow had been tied around her forehead with pink net extending behind to flow down her shoulders. Her pony wore a large pink bow on his head with more net wrapped around his neck, and his tail was braided with pink cord.

Sydney felt tears sting her eyes, because Storm looked totally adorable. She suddenly realized that she should've included a princess, along with a queen, in the Sure-Shot parade. Storm had obviously thought about it but said nothing to her. Fortunately, their family had helped make her princess dream come true. Next year Sydney would make sure little girls could enter the contest so they had a chance to be the Sure-Shot Christmas Princess and ride in Celeste.

As Sydney waved at her daughter, Dune rode over, leaned down, and whispered, "I'll be back in a bit. Wait for me."

She nodded in reply, even as she wanted to reach up and tug him down to her. "Thanks. Storm looks so happy."

"She's perfect as a princess, isn't she?" He gave her a warm smile before he turned and rejoined the parade.

Storm threw her mother a kiss, waved her small hand, and then rode off with Dune by her side.

Sydney watched them until they disappeared from sight. She sighed in contentment, knowing nothing could be much better in life than a cowgirl princess and a cowboy firefighter.

Chapter 35

BY THE TIME DUSK SETTLED ACROSS THE NORTH TEXAS plains, Sydney was ready for some TLC, but at the same time, she couldn't have been more satisfied with the extraordinary day.

Turnout for Christmas at the Sure-Shot Drive-In had been phenomenal, particularly for its first year. The Bluebonnet Café had made lots of folks happy with great food. Downtown merchants had garnered new, enthusiastic customers. The car clubs had been well appreciated and left midafternoon so members could drive back to their homes before dark. Vendors had connected with people who loved handmade products, and they'd packed up their belongings and left, too. Bert and Bert Two had overseen breaking down and storing the tables and umbrellas for use at other events.

Best of all—on a strictly personal level—was the fact that vendors and stores had sold out of every single cowboy firefighter calendar. Now everybody was clamoring to make it a yearly tradition. She chuckled at the thought of rounding up their local cowboy firefighters for a photo shoot again. But that was a year away, so she simply put it on a back burner. For now, the calendars had boosted the fire station's bottom line, so they went forward with a much-needed financial cushion.

No doubt about it, the new year was shaping up to be great in so many different ways.

For the moment, she could relax in comfort. She sat in an aqua metal chair on the snack shed's patio, watching a stream of vehicles enter the gate and turn down one row after another as they slowly filled the drive-in. She wondered how many years it had been since people had gathered in this venue to watch movies. Right here, right now, they were together, not separate as they would have been if they'd been sitting in homes watching big screens or little screens. She enjoyed the idea of a like-minded group of folks leaving televisions and computers behind to celebrate Christmas with classic films.

She'd invited her grandmother, mother, and daughter to join them for the dusk-to-dawn movie marathon, but they'd opted to take the traditional Lollypop Lane ride during Christmas in Old Town at Wildcat Bluff. After that, they planned to go home and get some rest. In particular, they wanted Storm not to get too tired or excited by her busy day. Sydney had agreed with their assessment, so she was here by herself except for Dune.

He'd gone to park Celeste at the far end of the drive-in near where the trailer and tires had burned, because he wanted to leave the best spots for customers. It was a little farther to walk later, but she didn't mind—once she rested her feet—because her leather coat kept her warm even with the growing chill in the air.

Farther north in the old days, drive-ins had only been open in summer due to inclement weather, but in Texas, folks had a much longer season, so December was cozy, perfect for snuggling together.

She wasn't needed anywhere, so she could catch her breath. Inside the snack shed, Serena and Moore handled the food while Bert Two tended the cash register.

Bert prowled the place, making sure any last-minute problems were taken care of in an efficient manner.

She'd seen a list of the films, and she was anxious to watch *White Christmas* with Bing Crosby and Rosemary Clooney. They'd also show *Holiday Inn*, *Miracle on 34th Street*, *A Christmas Carol*, *It's a Wonderful Life*, and others. Dune had jokingly—at least, she'd thought jokingly—suggested *Die Hard* since it was set at Christmastime, but she'd nixed that idea right away.

After folks parked vehicles, they exited their cars and descended on the snack shed. She had no doubt Serena, Moore, and Bert Two were going to be kept busy till the first movie came on the screen. She'd offered to help if they needed her, but they'd told her to get some rest and enjoy the films.

For now, she simply sat still in the crisp, clean air as night enveloped the drive-in and vehicles took the remaining slots.

Suddenly the big white screen filled with color and animation to begin the dusk-to-dawn entertainment. She laughed out loud at the sight, because they'd found old snack shed commercials with bright-red hot dogs slathered with too-bright yellow mustard and plastic-looking yellow cheese drizzled over tortilla chips. Oh yes, these retro ads and movies were going to be fun.

But she was thirsty and hungry, no matter how bad the food looked up on the screen, because she could smell the tantalizing aroma of fresh-popped popcorn. Dune was supposed to stop by and pick up lemonade and popcorn for them on his way back, but she didn't know if he'd be able to get close to the counter. Maybe she should get up and go stand in line, but she wasn't sure she wanted to put her feet through it, not in her kitten heel pumps.

About the time she'd decided to pick up her purse and get on her feet, Dune came out the snack shed door, carrying two huge drinks in his hands with two popcorn boxes crushed in the nooks of his elbows. She jumped up to help him before something spilled or dropped to the cement.

She eased one drink out of his hand, set it on the small orange metal table between their two chairs, then retrieved the other drink and set it down, too.

He placed the boxes of popcorn on the table, and then flopped down in a chair.

"Rough inside?" She glanced over at him as she sat back down.

"You know it." He shuddered, as if in horror. "If Serena hadn't already had these ready to go for us, I'd be empty-handed now."

"Good for her." Sydney sucked lemonade through a red-and-white striped straw and moaned in delight. "I needed that."

He took a big drink and let out a sigh. "It feels good to sit down a minute."

"I'm not hiking back to Celeste yet."

"No need. This is fine right here—for now."

"Anyway, they might need us inside."

"Or we might need another slow dance." He gave her a suggestive look out of the corner of his eyes.

"Oh no. I don't trust you on a dance floor."

He laughed, rolling his shoulders in relaxation. "I bet it's not me you don't trust."

She joined his laughter, remembering their steamy time in the snack shed. "I guess I might've had a little something to do with our, uh, dance."

"Anytime you want to dance again, just let me know."

"For the moment, I'm giving my feet a break."

"I was thinking horizontal."

She chuckled, simply shaking her head as she slurped more lemonade and enjoyed their banter.

"It's about time for the first movie to start," he said. "What do you think it'll be? You vetoed *Die Hard*, but there's always *Santa Claus Conquers the Martians* or *The Nightmare before Christmas* to get us started out right."

"You and your old flicks. You never did tell me how you've seen so many and know so much about them."

"Didn't I? It's simple. In certain situations as a firefighter, you can spend a lot of time waiting and watching for fires. It's boring and stressful at the same time. Movies can fill the void—and sometimes, the worst films are the best, because you never want to get too deep into a story line."

"I want to hear more about it."

"I'll tell you but not now." He glanced over at her. "We've got plenty of time to share stories about our lives later. Tonight, let's just be together."

"I like that idea. I like it a lot."

"Look, the snack shed is emptying out, and folks are hurrying back to their vehicles, carrying their goodies."

"I hope *White Christmas* is first."

Suddenly Dune set his drink on the table with a snap and leaned forward, looking toward the far corner of the snack shed. "Do you smell that?"

On alert, she sat up straight, sniffing the air. "Gasoline?"

"Yes."

"No wonder. The drive-in is filled with cars."

"That's not all of it. I'm catching a whiff of smoke, too." He stood up. "You better get Bert and Bert Two out here. Tell them to bring fire extinguishers."

"But Dune—"

He took off running and disappeared around the corner of the snack shed.

She smelled it then—*definitely smoke*. She jerked her cell phone out of her purse and texted Bert and Bert Two with Dune's instructions. If they weren't out in seconds, she'd go get them. In the meantime, she slung her phone back in her handbag, jerked the lids off the lemonades, and picked up the full containers.

As she headed around the building, she heard the door open behind her. But she didn't stop or look back, because she saw fire licking up the side of the snack shed. She noticed several wadded-up towels on the ground next to the wall that were probably the source of the blaze, so she ran over and tossed both lemonades on top of the fire. It shrank back for a second, but then surged upward again.

"Sydney!" Bert called, striding up to her with Bert Two on his heels. "Step back. We've got this now."

She moved out of the way and watched them turn their fire extinguishers on the fire, cover the towels and wall with foam, and quickly extinguish the blaze. She felt a vast sense of relief that they'd stopped the fire before it had a chance to do more damage or hurt people.

"Good thing you were sitting outside, or we'd have been in big trouble," Bert Two said, turning toward her.

"We owe you one," Bert added as he glanced around the area, as if looking for any more trouble.

"You don't owe me a thing. I'm just grateful we stopped this fire in its tracks."

"Where's Dune?" Bert asked.

She looked over her shoulder, but she couldn't see far beyond the perimeter of the outside lights on the snack shed. "He noticed the fire first and took off that way." She pointed in the direction she'd last seen him.

"I'd better go take a look," Bert Two said.

"No," Bert objected. "I'd better call Sheriff Calhoun. He won't be far away, since he's keeping an eye out here till we close down in the morning."

"But if he's in trouble..." Sydney suddenly realized that Dune might be trying to catch the arsonist.

"Wait a minute," Bert insisted as he quickly sent a text and received one in reply. "Okay, Sheriff Calhoun is on his way. He'll turn off his lights and drive up to the snack shed so he doesn't bother any of our patrons."

"I hadn't even thought about causing panic here." Sydney suddenly felt worried about that idea.

"Let's just keep it quiet till we find out the situation here," Bert insisted in a tense voice.

"But we'll find Dune." Bert Two gave Sydney a reassuring glance.

"No need to look for me." Dune walked out of the darkness, pushing forward a guy with his hands tied behind his back with a black hoodie.

"What's going on?" Bert asked, stepping toward Dune.

"We've got our arsonist." Dune shoved the guy to his knees in front of Bert and Bert Two. "Recognize him?"

"No," Bert and Bert Two said in unison.

"Who is he?" Bert peered closer at the stranger.

"That's right." The man spat at Bert's boots. "You wouldn't know me, but you sure knew my dad."

"Your dad?" Bert Two asked.

About that time, Sheriff Calhoun pulled up beside the patio and got out of his vehicle. He walked over, looked at everybody, and put his hands on his hips. "I thought we had another fire."

"We did," Bert said, "but Sydney and Dune caught it in time, and we put it out with our cans."

"Okay," Sheriff Calhoun said. "That's good. But who's the guy? And who tied him up?"

"That'd be Dune," Sydney said.

"I rounded the building just in time to see him set those towels on fire, so I ran after him. He wasn't anxious to come back, so I had to overpower him. I took his hoodie off him, tied him with it, and brought him back for justice," Dune explained in a matter-of-fact way.

"Good work," Sheriff Calhoun said.

"Another thing," Dune added. "Now that we've got this guy in better light, I recognize him. He came into the clinic with his injured hand wrapped in a green-and-white towel while I was waiting for Sydney."

"A green-and-white towel like we found at the Perkins house?" Sheriff Calhoun asked.

"Yes," Dune agreed. "Plus, he was a nondescript guy wearing nondescript clothes, and he didn't fit into Wildcat Bluff then or now."

"Circumstantial, at best," Sheriff Calhoun said. "But helpful."

"Shut up, all of you," the guy ordered. "You don't know a thing, but I'm happy to tell you everything."

"If you want to unload your conscience, we can go right down to the station where you can make and sign a statement," Sheriff Calhoun said in a clipped, official tone.

"Stuff it. I'm talking now." He glanced around the group. "My name is Edgar Perkins. Ring a bell?"

"Perkins," Bert said. "Any relation to Hollis Perkins?"

"Son."

"And you burned down your family's farmhouse?" Bert Two asked, sounding puzzled as well as outraged.

"Revenge," Edgar said. "I got plenty of it, so I don't care what you do to me now."

"But we helped your dad," Bert explained. "He was going to lose his farm to back taxes, so we bought the place from him. We made the deal big enough so he could invest and live on the income."

"Lies!" Edgar shouted. "You paid him peanuts, or I'd have gotten my inheritance and I'd be living like a king in Austin instead of skulking around this deadbeat county setting fires. I'm sick of the whole lot of you!"

"I hate to be the one to tell you, if you don't know," Bert said in a gentle voice, "but your dad had a drinking and gambling problem. That's where the money went, and that's why he crashed his car and died."

"More lies!"

"I realize the truth hurts," Bert continued, "but when there's nothing else but the truth, sometimes you have to accept it."

"Never!"

"Mr. Perkins, let's just take it easy," Sheriff Calhoun said in a calm voice. "You've done a lot of damage to Holloway property, and now you've had your say. It's time to go on down to the station."

Edgar glared around the group, then spit toward Bert's boots again. "Yeah, I did what I wanted to do. And I've had a gut full of cowboys. Get me out of here."

"If you'll leave your hands behind your back, I'll put on handcuffs," Sheriff Calhoun said.

"Whatever," Edgar growled. "I'll get a lawyer on my case and be out of this county in no time."

"Good luck," Bert said. "We don't cotton to breaking the law around here."

"That's right," Bert Two agreed. "We're a law-and-order county."

"And we still live by the Code of the West." Sheriff Calhoun tugged handcuffs off his belt, removed the hoodie, and restrained Edgar's hands behind his back. He held the hoodie in one hand while he glanced around the group. "Thanks for the help. I'm glad to finally catch our arsonist. I'll take him down to the station and book him."

"Just a minute." Dune walked over, grabbed Edgar by his collar, jerked him up on his tiptoes, and leaned down in his face. "You've been playing by your rules. If you ever cause trouble in Wildcat Bluff County again, you'll be playing by our rules. And we play for keeps." He set Edgar down, dusted off the front of his shirt, and stepped back. "Sheriff, get him out of here. He's stinking up the place."

Edgar didn't say a word, but he backed up close to the sheriff, as if for protection.

Sheriff Calhoun took hold of Edgar's arm and led him around the side of the snack shed.

Nobody moved or said a word until they heard the sheriff slam doors, start his vehicle, and drive away.

"All I've got to say," Bert filled the silence, "is that you two have free movie tickets here for the rest of your lives."

"Dad, that's not near enough," Bert Two insisted. "They get free snacks, too."

"Thanks. I won't argue with you—at least not tonight," Sydney said. "I never did get much of my lemonade."

"Coming right up." Bert Two headed for the door, then looked back. "Sit down. Enjoy the movies."

"That's right," Bert agreed as he followed his son. "You two deserve all that and more. I can hardly wait to tell Hedy the good news. She'll be so relieved to know the arsonist is finally behind bars."

"Why don't you go over and tell her in person?" Sydney suggested with a smile. "I think we're all pretty much on autopilot from now till dawn."

"Good idea," Bert Two said. "I can handle things from here."

"Are you sure?" Bert asked, appearing hesitant but eager to be gone.

"You bet." Bert Two motioned toward Bert's pickup. "Get out of here."

Bert pulled his key ring out of his pocket, gave them all a big grin, and headed for his truck.

"Don't move a muscle. I'll have those lemonades out to you in two shakes of a lamb's tail." Bert Two pulled open the snack shed door and disappeared inside.

"If you don't mind," Sydney said, stifling a yawn, "I want to go sit in Celeste. Somehow, the snack shed has lost some of its charm."

"No wonder." Dune reached over and pulled her close. "But it'll get its mojo back."

"I'm just glad it's all over."

"It is for us. But Edgar Perkins has to live with himself, and no amount of revenge can ever fix a life built on a lie."

"I hope he never darkens our door again." Sydney leaned into Dune's strength and warmth, feeling safe and secure and happy.

"He won't," Dune said with conviction.

"Here you go." Bert Two stepped out the door and handed Dune a box holding two big lemonades. "Enjoy."

"Thanks," Sydney said. "We're going to take our popcorn and drinks to Celeste and enjoy movies the old-fashioned way."

"Sounds great. See you later." And Bert Two quickly disappeared back into the snack shed.

Sydney picked up her purse, tucked the handle over the crook of her arm, and grabbed two boxes of popcorn with one hand. She was more than ready to get away and finally relax with Dune.

She held his hand, just as if they were teenagers, as they walked across the patio and over to the side lane. They passed row after row of vehicles and finally came to the back corner where he'd parked Celeste at the end of the aisle in a dark and secluded spot.

He opened the passenger door, and she sat down on the bench seat. As he walked around to the driver's side, she set the popcorn and her purse on the floorboard out of the way but still within easy reach.

After he slid in behind the steering wheel, he handed her the lemonade container. She set it on the floorboard, too. One thing for sure, she missed the convenience of center cup holders. On the other hand, there was nothing separating her from Dune on a long bench seat.

"This isn't the night I'd planned for us," he said quietly as he turned to face her.

She looked at him in the light of the flickering movie screen. "What do you mean?"

"It hasn't been exactly romantic, has it?"

"I don't know. You saved the snack shed. You caught the arsonist. You earned us free movies and treats. In my book, that's about as romantic as it gets."

"It's still not what I had in mind."

"Did you have this in mind?" She slid across the leather seat, put a hand on his broad chest, and placed a soft kiss on his lips.

"That's getting warm."

"More?"

"Wait." He reached into his front pocket, pulled out a small white box, and snapped it open. A ring glittered in the light coming from *White Christmas* on the big screen. "It's vintage. Nineteen fifty-five. I think it looks like a rose with the big center diamond, three smaller ones, and a bunch of little diamonds looping around it."

"Dune?" She felt her heart beat fast as she looked from the ring to his face and back again. Could he mean what she thought he meant with this ring?

"Anyway, I thought you'd like it, retro and all." He took the ring out of the box and tossed the container onto the back seat. "I love you. And I love Storm."

"But it's so soon, barely a month together."

"Time doesn't matter. It's right or it isn't. Nothing could be more right than you and me." He held out the ring to her. "Will you marry me?"

"My home has always been in Wildcat Bluff."

"I know, and I'm not asking you to move."

"Yet now, *you are my home*. I love you, too."

"And you'll marry me?"

"Yes." She felt happiness cascade through her. He was right that time didn't matter. For them, it was all about love.

He took a deep breath, as if he'd just run a race, and slipped the ring onto the third finger of her left hand.

"Thank you. It's beautiful. Absolutely perfect."

"And Sydney, I want to live in Wildcat Bluff. It's *our home* now." He lifted her left hand with the engagement ring on her finger and placed it over his heart.

"My dear Mr. December, I want you to know that you've made me a very happy cowgirl."

"I'm going to make you even happier," he said with a big grin, "when I show you—in your own pink Cadillac's back seat—exactly how this drive-in came to be called the Passion Pit."

Can't get enough Christmas cowboys?
Keep reading for an excerpt from Kim Redford's

a COWBOY FIREFIGHTER for Christmas

ON WILDCAT ROAD, A HALF-NAKED MAN BURST OUT of a pasture and ran onto the two-lane highway. He stopped on the white centerline and waved a bright red shirt back and forth high over his head.

Misty Reynolds slammed on the brakes of her SUV, caught searching for a radio station that wasn't playing Christmas music.

She gripped the steering wheel with both hands as she screeched to a stop, managing to narrowly avoid hitting the guy. She felt her heart thump hard with the burst of adrenaline and slumped against her seat in relief, grateful she'd been able to stop in time. She forced her breath to a slower, calmer pace.

As the adrenaline rush drained away, and she was able to focus, she got a better look at the stranger and licked her lower lip. This guy was all ripped jeans, cowboy boots, and big belt buckle over buff, bronze, sweaty body. His broad, muscular shoulders tapered to a narrow waist, and his long legs looked as if they belonged straddling a horse. He reminded her of her all-time favorite candy, Texas Millionaires.

It'd been a long time since a man had set her senses on spin cycle. And she'd nearly run him over. She wasn't sure whether to be annoyed or frightened. She felt a little shaky. Here and now was not a good time or place. Life was shaking her up enough already. She didn't need this problem.

She was headed toward a wide place in the road called Wildcat Bluff. The Dallas and Fort Worth Metroplex—as in big-city civilization—sprawled a couple of hours south. She had gladly left it and all the Christmas hubbub behind her. She was far away from everything now, except cattle, grass, trees. And the tantalizing stranger. But what was going on here?

Everything about the guy looked like trouble. In the 1880s, Wildcat Bluff had been notorious as a Wild West town that catered to cowboys and outlaws. Cowboys drove cattle herds north with dust in their eyes and returned with gold in their pockets. Desperadoes crossed the Red River from Indian Territory to get liquor by the drink and love by the night. Could this be the modern equivalent of a Texas horse thief? A carjacker? She glanced around as the hair on the backs of her arms prickled in alarm. Fortunately, the stranger appeared to be alone.

Still, she wouldn't take a chance. She hit the buttons on her door and heard the satisfying click of engaged locks and closed windows. She picked up her phone from the center console and checked for coverage. No bars. She couldn't call for help. She flipped open her glove box and looked for something big enough to use as a weapon. Nothing but a small flashlight. She wasn't completely without defense. She unclipped the small pepper spray canister off the metal link on her oversized aqua purse. She'd never used the spray before, but how hard could it be? She hoped that, if necessary, all she'd have to do was point and shoot. Still, it looked small and inadequate.

She mostly worked in the city and hadn't thought she needed to carry anything more than pepper spray. Now she wasn't so sure. Her BFF Cindi Lou had completed the training and paperwork for a carry permit and toted around at least a small .22 handgun, if not something with more stopping power. Cindi Lou, with her big hair and perfect makeup, was fond of reminding Misty that folks in Texas had a proud heritage of relying on personal self-defense in case of trouble since the days of the Republic of Texas when there was no other option. She'd been alarmed to hear that Misty was going into the countryside without a sidearm. Misty shook her head and felt herself tensing up. If worse came to worst, she would simply put her SUV in reverse or outmaneuver the stranger.

He ran the last few steps to her car, pulled on the door handle, and then hit the window with the flat of his hand.

She jerked back, gripping the pepper spray, as she kept him in sight. His belt was embossed with prancing reindeer, and the big buckle sported a Santa Claus face. If she included the holiday-happy red shirt in his hand, she'd assume Christmas, not carjacking, was on his mind. But he could also mean to disarm her with his fashion statement.

This close, he appeared wild. Hazel eyes flicked back and forth, resting on nothing or on everything. Dust peppered his tousled dark brown hair. His broad bare chest was coated with dirt and sweat. He looked good in the rough and rugged kind of way that set a gal's thermostat on "too hot to handle." She quickly flicked her AC to a higher setting and relished the burst of cold air.

"Help me!" he said in a deep voice muted by the closed windows.

"Do you have a medical emergency?" She held up her phone. "No coverage."

"Look over there!" He pointed toward the pasture.

All she saw was a little dust in the air. No telling what was going on. She'd play it safe. Once she put distance between them and could use her cell, she'd call to get him help.

"Do you have a blanket? Water?"

She felt his voice weave a spell around her like the finest of Texas male singers, an unmistakable quality of deep and sultry with a hot chili back-burn that left you wanting more. Classic singers like Willie Nelson, Roy Orbison, and George Strait came to mind.

She shook her head, breaking his spell. "Are you hungry?" Maybe he was homeless. "I have energy bars."

He frowned, drawing his dark, straight eyebrows together, as he shook his shirt at her. "There's a grass fire!"

Too late, she realized his red shirt was blackened and burned in spots. If she hadn't been so busy ogling his glistening sooty body and comparing him to outlaws, she might have noticed sooner. He'd obviously been using his shirt to beat out a fire.

"Only minutes to stop it." He glanced at her back seat, and his face lit up with happiness. "You've got towels!" He dropped his tattered shirt.

"Always. Just in case." Even as the words left her mouth, panic started to seize control. Breath caught in her throat. Chills turned her cold. And she felt pressure on her chest as if from a great weight.

She was terrified of fires.

They ranked as even more nightmarish than Christmas, ever since that early morning when she was twelve. She stopped that thought in its tracks. No good ever came from reliving the past. Right now, she had to get out of there before a panic attack overwhelmed her.

She threw her car in reverse.

"Stop! I'm Fire-Rescue." He hit her window with the flat of his hand again.

She was startled out of backing up and transfixed by his intense gaze, pinning her in place.

"I'm deputizing you as a Wildcat Bluff volunteer firefighter. Open your doors and help me."

Although his voice was muffled coming through the glass, she heard every word he said in that crystal clarity that precedes a full-on, foot-stomping, heart-stopping crisis.

She tried to focus on the fact that he was one of the good guys. Unfortunately, the knowledge didn't help her. She didn't have panic attacks often, but when she did, they were as scary as whatever had set them off. She took a deep breath and worked to stay focused. Breathe and focus, breathe and focus. It wasn't going

to do anybody—least of all herself, and certainly not
the stranger banging on her car window—any good for
her to lose it now. She could get a grip. She had to get
a grip.

She carefully set the pepper spray down beside her
phone and wrapped her fingers around the solid surface
of the steering wheel to ground her body while she
fought her fear with a reassuring repetition of words in
her mind. "Be here now. Safe and sound. Be here now."

"If that fire gets loose, it'll burn across these pastures
and kill cattle, horses, and wild animals. Timber will go
up fast and furious. Wildcat Bluff won't stand a chance,"
the stranger shouted, pounding his fist on the roof of her
car. Obviously he was close to losing it, too.

She felt his words start to override her panic. She
gripped the steering wheel harder. She needed to help
him. She wanted to help him. She couldn't let her weak-
ness stop her from saving others. She was safe in the
here and now. She swallowed down her response, took
a deep breath, then released the locks and opened her
door. The scent of burning grass hit her and she reeled
back against the seat. She put one hand across her nose
to reduce the smell of smoke and another across her
chest as if in protection.

"Thank you!" He jerked open the back door. He
grabbed three towels and slammed the door shut.
"Name's Trey."

"Misty," she mumbled, prepared to do—well, whatever this hot, strong guy thought she could do. He tossed
a blue towel onto her lap, and flashed a quick but genu-
ine smile that filled her with tingly energy from the tips
of her hair right down to her toes. It was a good kind of

warmth, like sunbathing in the summer without a care in the world.

"Well, come on then, Misty!" he called over his shoulder. He took off toward the smoke and a break in the fence line.

She immediately felt the loss of his radiant energy. The sight of him in all his muscular glory running like all get-out didn't hurt her illogical desire to follow him, either. That thought made her smile and set back her panic a bit. If she wasn't careful, she was going to start writing poetry to honor him. She felt her breath come a little easier. Something about this guy made her feel braver.

Yet, did he actually expect her to fight the fire with him? Did he think she would run toward that horrible smell of burning grass instead of fleeing it? Did he imagine she would fight the flames with nothing more than a single, solitary towel in her very vulnerable hands? He must see something in her that she was pretty sure simply wasn't there.

Fear and safety aside, she wasn't dressed to fight a fire. North Texas was experiencing a December heat wave, and she was wearing capris and flip-flops. She could get hurt. She lowered her hands to her lap and gripped the towel. But if she didn't help, how many more might be hurt? People. Animals. Property. Timber.

She had to help. She glanced down and noticed stains on the towel from some long-ago picnic. She couldn't ever have imagined using her towels to put out a fire. But if ratty towels and her shaky courage were all that stood between death and destruction, they would have to do.

Mindful of possible traffic, she put her SUV in drive, pulled to the side of the road, and turned off the engine. She stepped outside. Ninety degrees wasn't a miserable one hundred, but still plenty hot, particularly for the holiday season. Christmas was bad enough. Christmas and a heat wave together was—well, it was like hell on Earth. Complete with fire. How about some brimstone next?

She slammed the door shut, blocking retreat, and forced one foot in front of the other as she edged around the front fender. The scent of burning grass grew stronger. And just like that, she felt the sharp edge of a flashback threaten to overwhelm her. She clenched her empty fist, driving fingernails into her palm. She used the pain to ground her in the here and now. And in her mind, she employed her safe words. "Be here now. Safe and sound. Be here now."

She looked across the fence and took a deep breath, despite the stench. Not a wall of fire. Instead, a line of red-orange flames ate up the dry grass, leaving black stubble behind as the blaze sent up plumes of smoke. She watched Trey beat at the conflagration with a towel in each hand. He was making progress. She felt hope that her towels could actually make a difference. But he couldn't completely stop the flames. The fire line was too wide. Without her help, he was going to lose the battle.

He glanced over his shoulder at her. She felt his gaze as an almost physical sensation, willing her to help, giving her strength, sharing his courage. She felt a surge of determination. She wouldn't let him fight alone.

When she reached the sagging barbwire fence, she

carefully stepped over it and quickly walked to Trey. "What do you want me to do?"

"Can't let the fire cross the road or it'll be hell and gone." He pointed toward the other side of the fire line. "You take that end. Beat out the flames as fast as you can. We're ahead of the blaze, and we've got to stay that way."

"Okay." With one simple word, she knew she'd turned her world upside down, but she wouldn't back down.

As she moved into position, she saw that fire consumed the dry grass at an unbelievably fast rate. They were in the middle of a bad drought. Add unseasonably warm temperatures to the mix and everything was vulnerable. Up close, intensity ruled. Heat. Smoke. Smell. Fortunately, the fire hadn't spread too far. She raised her towel over her head and whipped down hard, smothering the flames. Brief elation filled her. Maybe she—they— could fight this fire. And win.

Trey was slapping at the flames with everything he had, and she followed suit. Quickly they had a rhythm going—*slap, lift, slap, lift, slap, lift*—and with each slap a little bit of the fire gave way.

"Good thing I brush-hogged around here, so the grass is short," Trey called out, without losing a beat.

"It could be worse?"

"You bet."

"I can't imagine."

"Watch your feet!"

She felt heat sear her toes and jerked back. Black soot streaked her tangerine toenail polish and the crystal stones on her sandals. She suddenly felt dizzy and off balance.

"Are you okay?" Trey quickly stomped out the flames near her feet with his scuffed cowboy boots.

"Yes." And strangely enough, she did feel better with him so close by her side.

"I'm buying you a real pair of shoes."

"You don't have to do that. These are fine," Misty said, although she didn't know why she suddenly felt defensive about her footwear. Maybe it was because she prided herself on being practical—usually—not one of those women who dressed in a way that made them appear absolutely helpless.

"Not out here," Trey said as he looked at her in a way that made her suddenly self-conscious.

"I wouldn't be here if not for your fire."

"It's *our* fire." He moved back to his end of the line and beat fast and hard at the flames.

She simply shook her head as she struck the ground again with her towel while she carefully kept her feet back from the flames.

"You'll need boots next time."

"Next time!" She looked over at him in horror. *Mistake.* She felt her mouth go dry. The sun spotlighted him as he raised blackened towels and struck downward. Powerful muscles in his back, shoulders, and arms gleamed with sweat and rippled with exertion. As if he'd been swimming, his faded jeans were plastered to his taut butt and long legs. She shook her head to dispel his image, but nothing helped put out the fire that now burned inside her.

"There's always a next time." He tossed a slightly crooked smile her way as he lifted towels to extinguish more flames.

"Oh no." She hadn't come all this way to get distracted by the first hot guy who literally crossed her path—even if he did flag her down with his shirt. She particularly didn't need to get involved with one who was into Christmas and dragged her into fighting a grass fire in the middle of nowhere. She didn't want to ever put out another fire. This was a onetime deal to help out a man in an emergency and stop a prairie fire from eating up acres instead of one grassy swath. In the future, she would leave firefighting to the experts.

Besides, she was here on business. Texas Timber had hired her as an independent troubleshooter to find out who had burned down one of the company's Christmas tree farms, and possibly caused other problems. She'd been warned not to trust anybody in Wildcat Bluff County. Now, first thing, she was involved with a local. A really hot local. She couldn't hold back a soulful sigh. At least she might excuse her interest in Trey as simply business since he might be helpful in her investigation.

"You're a deputized firefighter now," he said.

"That can't be legal." She attacked the grass with renewed energy. They were actually making good headway now.

"If there's trouble, everybody pitches in."

"Police? 9-1-1?"

"We're the first responders." He struck hard at the ground with his towels.

"There must be a county sheriff. Highway patrol."

"And the Wildcat Bluff Police Department." He stomped at the blackened grass. "How long do you think it'd take help to get here?"

"Good point."

"We all depend on the Wildcat Bluff County Volunteer Fire-Rescue."

"That's why you deputized me? I'm a total stranger! I could have been—well, big trouble. I actually thought you were, at first."

"But you aren't," he said with another charming grin.

She couldn't resist cracking a smile back, even despite the circumstances. She shrugged, beginning to understand that life out here was different than in the city.

Sweat trickled down her body. Soot tasted bitter in her mouth. Sunlight beat down on her head. If she came out of this with nothing more than sunburn, she'd be lucky. Yet, that didn't matter. She was helping stop a fire. She was saving lives and property. She was taking a step toward recovery.

As the flames dwindled in size and scope, she edged toward him. Soon they worked side by side, putting out the remaining hot spots. He loomed well over six feet and made her feel diminutive, even at her perfectly respectable five seven.

Finally, he stopped and stretched his back.

"Fire's out?" She wanted him to confirm what she saw with her own eyes.

"Yep. Looks good." He scuffed his boots across the crusty grass. "Can't thank you enough. If you hadn't come along when you did—"

"You'd have thought of something." She interrupted to keep him from saying another word. His melodic voice with the deep Texas drawl couldn't help but put her in mind of hot, sweaty bodies sliding across cool, satin sheets.

"I needed a miracle and prayed for one the minute I

saw the fire." He walked over to her. "I heard my answer
in your car coming down the highway. I headed back to
the road, running flat out. And there you were in your
pure white SUV, looking so cool and unafraid of the
wild man pounding on your window. You had a miracle
in your car. Towels. Not many people would have had
them just waiting on a back seat."

She didn't feel so cool and unafraid. Who had this
guy been looking at? Still, his words made her swell
with an unusual type of pride. "Like I said, I always do.
Just in case."

He clasped both towels in one hand, and held out the
other. "Thank you. You're my Christmas angel."

"Just plain Misty Reynolds." She shook his hand,
feeling his strength, his heat, his calluses.

"Pleased to meet you." He rubbed the back of her
hand with his rough thumb, and then slowly released
her. "Like I said, I'm Trey...Trey Duval."

For a moment, she couldn't remember the polite
response required of her. She was caught in the magic
of his touch, the mesmerizing sound of his voice, and
the unusual color of his eyes, circles of gold, green, and
brown. She glanced away to release his spell. "Good to
meet you, too."

"Are you going to be around long?"

"A bit. I'm on vacation." She hoped her cover story
would ring true to everyone she met in Wildcat Bluff.

"Where are you staying?"

Misty hesitated, but Trey really did seem like a good
guy. Besides, he'd learn it soon enough from the locals.
She decided to trust the instinct that was telling her to
trust him.

"Twin Oaks B&B. No website, but I caught a couple of good reviews online."

"Ruby's got more customers than she can shake a stick at. No need to promote. That natural spring draws folks."

"Guess a lot of business is the best promotion."

He nodded. "It's usually pretty quiet in Wildcat Bluff. But we'll get plenty of folks out here for our Christmas in the Country festivities."

"I'm not here for anything Christmas. I've been working hard and need a quiet place to get away." She didn't like the sound of festivities. They could complicate her investigation. Still, she doubted a few candles in windows and plastic lighted displays in front yards would draw much of a crowd.

"I'd imagine fighting a wild fire isn't the best way to start your vacation."

"True. But how do you think it got started?" Now that the blaze was out, her mind kicked into gear. Did this fire connect with her investigation? It'd be quite a coincidence if it did, but she couldn't rule out natural causes from the heat and drought. Still, she'd checked topographical maps before she'd arrived in the county. If she remembered correctly, the flames were burning a path straight toward a Texas Timber Christmas tree farm. On the other hand, the blaze had started on a ranch, so maybe it had nothing to do with Texas Timber. Plenty to ponder here.

"Good question." He squeezed the burned towels between his fists. "I'll be following up on it."

"If I can be of help, let me know."

"Think on it. Maybe you saw something."

"Or somebody?" she prodded, sensing his implication.

He nodded as he glanced with narrowed eyes around the area.

"Arson?"

"Possibility."

"I didn't notice anything unusual, but maybe something will come to me." She pushed sweat-dampened hair back from her forehead, shelving her questions for the moment. "You must be thirsty. I've got bottles of water in the car." She wished she'd had enough water to help fight the fire, but at least she had enough to ease their dry throats.

"Thanks. I owe you a big, thick, sizzling steak."

"I thought it was a pair of boots," she teased before she realized she was flirting with him. She pressed her lips together to stop any other wayward words from escaping her mouth.

He smiled as his eyes crinkled invitingly at the corners. "That too."

"I'm glad I was able to help." She spoke as primly as possible.

He held up the towels. "If you don't mind, I'd like to keep these."

She handed over her scorched towel. "Keep mine, too."

"Guess I owe you three towels."

"Not at all. Like I said—"

"You don't need anything from me." He cocked his head. "But if you'd like dinner, I can grill a mean steak." Another killer grin.

"I bet you can." Misty wondered if he meant a date. She felt excited at the idea. She stepped back. If she didn't get farther away from him, she felt as if she might spontaneously combust.

He took her cue and changed the subject. "Would you mind giving me a ride?"

"A ride?" No excuse for it, but her mind skittered sideways to an image of his big empty bed. So much for changing the subject.

He took a step toward her. "To Wildcat Bluff."

She couldn't help but notice his voice held a huskiness that hadn't been there before. "I see. You need a ride to town."

"I sent off my horse."

"You ride horses?"

"That's what cowboys do."

"You're a cowboy firefighter?"

He tipped an imaginary hat.

Acknowledgments

Lots of folks deserve appreciation and thanks for their contribution to my Smokin' Hot Cowboys series. Dee, Ginger, Larry, Chester, and Chris exemplify the type of generous business owners who are the backbone of small towns. Marilyn, Shanie, and Shiane inspired my creation of the Sure-Shot Beauty Station. Christina gave me an insightful guided tour of her fancy dually. Ivy and I enjoyed a lively chat about horse and cowgirl coordination for wins in barrel racing. Pharra—all dressed up as a cowgirl princess on her painted pony—was my muse for Storm in the Sure-Shot parade. Rodeo stars Cathy, Miranda, and River Grace continue to inspire my smart, sassy, spunky cowgirls on horseback. And last, but not least, I'm indebted to Brandon, Christina, Luke, Lank, Logan, and Laren for sharing their roping and riding expertise.

About the Author

Kim Redford is an acclaimed, bestselling author of Western romance novels. She grew up in Texas with cowboys, cowgirls, horses, cattle, and rodeos for inspiration. She divides her time between homes in Texas and Oklahoma, where she's a rescue cat wrangler and horseback rider—when she takes a break from her keyboard. Visit her at kimredford.com.

Also by Kim Redford

Smokin' Hot Cowboys

A Cowboy Firefighter for Christmas
Blazing Hot Cowboy
A Very Cowboy Christmas